Yorkshire, England - two children and five grandchildren. Her various jobs have included working as a qualified nurse and a civil servant in the Prison Service. When her children were young she successfully completed an Open University B.A. degree studying psychology and sociology. She was a member of the Romantic Novelists' Association for four years and is now a member of ALLi (the Alliance of Independent Authors) and Goodreads.

As well as writing she loves country walks and travelling abroad (she adores bus stations, railway stations, airports and ferry ports – any place where people are on the move).

Contact the author by email at
Julia@JuliaBellRomanticFiction.co.uk

or visit her website at
www.JuliaBellRomanticFiction.co.uk

ACKNOWLEDGEMENTS

I would like to thank:

Amanda Lillywhite for the excellent work she did creating the front cover. Amanda can be contacted via her website at www.AJLIllustration.talktalk.net.

Rob White for all his technical know-how, moral support and encouragement for which I am very grateful.

Hazel Garner. Her wonderful proof reading kept me on track and her sensible advice was invaluable.

Cover re-engineered for paperback by
Beenish Qureshi   www.fiverr.com/bqureshi

First Published as an ebook UK 2012

Published in paperback UK 2018

Copyright © 2012 by Julia Bell Romantic Fiction

No part of this book may be used or reproduced in any manner whatsoever without written permission from the Publisher except in the case of brief quotations embodied in critical articles or reviews

Names and characters except for the historical figures are purely the product of the author's imagination.

JuliaBellRomanticFiction.co.uk

First Edition

In memory of Des Kinsman
A colleague who gave me much needed encouragement

THE WILD POPPY

by

Julia Bell

JULIA BELL ROMANTIC FICTION

To Jeanne
Best Wishes
Julia Bell
22/6/2024

PROLOGUE

1860

If Melody had known the truth, she would never have set foot inside the building. But the truth had eluded her, since she had applied and been recruited for the position, simply by letter. Many times she wished she had never heard of Miss Lawson's educational establishment, but now, standing in the headmistress's study, it seemed her misery was coming to an abrupt end.

"You're dismissing me?" Melody stared at the headmistress in disbelief. "For what reason?"

Miss Lawson stood in the centre of the room, her bulky frame made more grotesque by the wide skirts that encompassed her.

"Because you're a disgrace to the school, young lady. And I expect my teachers to behave with the same dignity and propriety as my pupils."

Aghast, Melody realised the reason behind her dismissal. "I only smiled, ma'am."

"And what right have you, to smile at young gentlemen you do not know?"

Melody squeezed her fists into a tight ball. "I was just being pleasant," she answered quietly.

"Pleasant, indeed! I won't have the reputation of my establishment tarnished by some trollop who cannot keep her familiarity to herself. You will collect your wages and leave the premises forthwith."

Miss Lawson's Progressive Academy for the Refined Young Ladies of Gentlefolk didn't exactly live up to its name. The moment Melody had set eyes on the austere building and gloomy surroundings, she wondered at the wisdom of her actions. Now that she had been there six months, her opinion had not altered one bit. Even as a teacher and the youngest member of staff, she had found the regime far too strict. But this was her first position and at the age of seventeen she had a tremendous desire to succeed. Teaching French and English had seemed acceptable for the duration. Until her ambition was realised.

The worst day was Sunday's when they went to church. Walking at the rear of the line, a long, black cloak covering a drab, brown dress, since Miss Lawson insisted that teachers wore only simple attire and sombre colours, she would try and keep her head bent in demure complacency, her face anonymous under the plain, straw bonnet. She knew that Miss Lawson expected her staff to behave the same as the girls, but no matter how hard she tried, she couldn't conform. She often felt like resigning, but the sense of failure made her recoil with shame. And then one day, in the middle of October, something turned her feelings round.

He was standing on the library steps when the silent column filed by and he remained there, watching. Melody, again at the end of the line, lifted her head and stared directly at him. Her cornflower-blue eyes sparkled and caught his attention, the oval face and pert nose made him smile. She grimaced and he responded with a soft chuckle. And then she returned his smile and as his hand went to the brim of his hat in polite greeting, she quickly lowered her head in case Miss Brace at the front of the line noticed her indiscretion and informed on her.

She saw him on a Sunday usually, when the crocodile line wended its way across the heath. He seemed to be waiting for her, since he was always in the same position, standing on the steps of the library and although no more than a smile passed between them, it made her days more bearable. And yet she was to lose her position simply for smiling at him.

Melody climbed the stairs to her attic room to start her packing. She gave a sigh although she couldn't decide if it was from sadness, relief or sheer disappointment. Reaching the sparse room that would have made a holy sister wince, she threw the valise onto the bed and collected together her few clothes. A grin spread across her face; her heart just that little lighter. She would leave the school with her head held high; hailing a cab to the railway station. She could catch the public coach from the Golden Goose at three o'clock, but leaving in a hansom cab with Miss Lawson watching would be a final act of defiance. She knew that Miss Lawson looked down her nose at her. Suddenly Melody felt more cheerful. Home to the brigadier and Aunt Olivia. Home to Hucknall Garth. Home in time for her eighteenth birthday.

She pulled open the cupboards and drawers and gathered up her possessions. And then she searched frantically for her French book. She looked on the shelf and under the bed, but then realised that Celia, one of the pupils, had asked to borrow it the previous day.

She made her way down the narrow stairs to the pupils' bedchambers.

"Celia, are you here?" she called. "Have you got my French book?" Shouting was against the rules but she didn't care any more. She had been dismissed.

A young girl with fair hair and pale blue eyes appeared from a doorway along the corridor.

"Sorry, miss. I'll fetch it straight away." Exasperated, Melody waited for her to collect the much-needed item. Celia appeared once more. "Catch!"

Melody opened her mouth to cry a warning, but it was too late. The missile was already hurtling towards her, the hard back acting like wings on some monstrous bird. Her hands reached out, but it was too high. It thudded against the wall and flapped towards the ground, catching the plate hanging on its hook. Book and plate landed together, the noise echoing towards the stairs and Miss Lawson's private rooms.

Melody sank to her knees.

The young girl was beside her in an instant, her eyes wide with fright. "What shall I do, miss?"

"It'll be all right. Perhaps she didn't hear," said Melody, squeezing her hand.

The sitting room door opened and a shadow fell across them.

"What happened here?" Her voice was low and strangely hushed.

They sprang to their feet.

"I threw the book, Miss Lawson," said Melody. She glanced at Celia, giving her a warning look. Celia started with surprise. Melody's voice had been firm and confident and a feeling of gratitude and then guilt swept through the younger girl.

"I should have guessed," said Miss Lawson. "Celia go to your next lesson." Celia kept still, frozen like a statue. Miss Lawson frowned. "I said go to your lesson, girl."

"I mustn't…It wasn't…" stuttered the young girl. "You don't understand, Miss Lawson." Melody willed her to stay silent, noticing her lips quivering. "I threw the book, Miss Lawson. It wasn't Miss Kinsman."

The headmistress's frown deepened. The fact that the teacher had tried to take the blame for the pupil was lost on her. All she saw was that Melody had been lying. Besides, Celia was The Hon. Celia Sinclair, the daughter of a baron, while Melody was the offspring of a mere brigadier. And such a girl had no right to an abundance of stubbornness and impudence.

Miss Lawson chose her words carefully. "Throwing the book was wrong, Celia and your papa will expect me to punish you for it. However, I distinctly heard Miss Kinsman shouting down the corridor. You might be leaving..." A short gasp escaped Celia as she realised that she was losing a popular teacher, "...but until you pass through the door you will still abide by the rules of this establishment. Please finish your packing and go." She turned to Celia. "As for you, young lady. You will spend this evening translating four poems by Alfred de Musset into English."

Celia grimaced.

Alex's lodgings were at the back of the school and he could see directly into the courtyard. He knew the lovely schoolteacher worked in that building and although they had only nodded to each other, he was always on the lookout in case he spied her. Once or twice he had seen her and had smiled at the tall, slender girl with long hair scraped back and tucked in a bun at the nape of her neck. She had beautiful hair, luxuriant and a vibrant auburn colour. Short, tight curls sprang forward framing her face, dissident strands that refused to be controlled. It wasn't often he glimpsed her. It seemed that the teachers were as much prisoners as the pupils.

He carried his glass of wine to the window and studied the view. The buildings of Hampstead were a hotchpotch of all styles and shapes. Thick smoke belched from the chimneys and in the distance he could hear a church clock striking one. Below him stood the school. His eyes roamed over the dilapidated house, which must have been quite impressive as a family residence at the turn of the century.

Leaning against the window frame, he watched the fleeting figures at the many windows. Christian was sprawled in the chair, his chatter drifting into empty air although the conversation had been heated until Alex had wandered to the window and become distracted. Finally, he turned his back on the school and listened intently to his friend's theory on diseases of the human body.

Melody made her way to Miss Lawson's study where she calmed herself before knocking. A monotone 'come in' answered. The weather had been miserable for most of the day and the light was fading fast causing a cold chill to permeate through the old house. In the headmistress's study, a meagre fire burnt in the grate, its red glow struggling to warm the room; a solitary oil lamp on the desk illuminated the portraits on the wall and reflected off the ornaments of brass littering the shelves and tables. From inside a large glass dome, a stuffed owl sitting amongst dried flowers; his eyes large and glassy stared at the young teacher in cold amazement at her audacity. Melody had always thought this a depressing room, full of dead and decaying artefacts.

"What is it?" Miss Lawson had her eyes down concentrating on her paperwork and Melody waited for her attention, refusing to speak to the top of the headmistress's head. Miss Lawson looked up and scowled. "Oh, it's you. Why haven't you left?"

Melody lifted her chin in defiance. "I've come for my wages and reference, ma'am."

"You expect a character too, do you?" Miss Lawson couldn't hide her contemptuous smile. She rose from her chair and stepped round the desk, coming closer to the young girl. Again, Melody noticed her musty smell, like an old couch, but with a hint of stale lavender water. Pulling open a drawer, she took out a purse of coins and put a sovereign into Melody's hand. "There's your wages." She paused as though reflecting on the problem. "I shall write you a character, but I'll be obliged to be honest. Your wilfulness and utter lack of self discipline will be noted."

Melody nodded. "As you wish."

Melody stood to attention before the brigadier, concentrating on the wall behind him.

He sat back in his chair. "Cashiered, eh!"

"Yes, sir."

"For unacceptable behaviour and insubordination."

"Yes, sir."

"You know what this means?"

"Yes, sir. A court martial followed by the firing squad." She looked him squarely in the face. "I'll not require a blindfold, sir. I want to spit in their eye."

Brigadier Kinsman chuckled. "Well, there's plenty to occupy you here, until we decide what to do with you next. Go and help your aunt. About turn and dismiss."

He watched her march from his study and sighed. Fetching his pipe and filling it with the pungent tobacco he had become used to, and to which his sister strongly objected, he contemplated his daughter's future.

The brigadier had not wanted Melody to leave home, but her entreaties, combined with his sister's persuasive arguments had finally broken down his resistance. Convincing himself that Melody had enough sense to make up her own mind, he had sent her on her way with a purse of fifteen shillings and his wholehearted support.

Melody's father had married late in life after twenty years in the army. His wife had died when Melody was only two years old, and his widowed sister, Olivia, had come to look after him and the child. It was the child's mother that had chosen the name 'Melody' and although he found it pretty, not really his cup of tea. But she had become a melody to him, watching her grow through the years. Blowing out a puff of smoke, he smiled to himself. No doubt she would marry very soon, almost all her friends were married, or planning to marry. A loving husband in a steady profession and two or three children would settle her down. And then he would no longer have to worry about her. He decided to wait and let life unfold its mysteries, but in the meantime appreciate her being home.

Melody fell into her aunt's arms with relief. "Well, it looks like cleaning and laundry detail for the duration," she gasped, laughing and crying at the same time.

"I knew he wouldn't be too hard on you," her aunt laughed with her. "He's missed you so much. He didn't say anything, but I knew."

"Oh, Aunt Olivia, I've missed him too...and you." She threw her arms round her aunt's neck and hugged her. "I hated Miss Lawson's. It was a terrible school, even for a teacher." Melody sighed. "I made a friend in Miss Sinclair. She held my hand so tightly as we said farewell. But we've pledged to write and never lose contact. We'll become good friends, I'm sure of it."

"Well, we'll need to find you something to do, something that suits your abilities. A girl like you must have her mind occupied."

"Don't worry, Aunt. I know exactly what I want to do," she laughed.

CHAPTER ONE

1864

Melody made her way home. She felt downhearted and very angry at the day's events; nothing had gone as she had planned. Oh well, she sighed, as she lifted her crinoline skirt and stepped over a puddle, no use worrying about it. There's always tomorrow, she would try something else tomorrow.

"Could we have tea early, *please*," said Melody, flopping onto the couch, exhaustion showing in her face and posture.

Celia smiled and stood to ring for Tilly. "You look so tired. Is it all getting too much for you?"

"I wish I'd never had the idea in the first place. What I was thinking of is beyond me," Melody replied, pressing her hand dramatically against a weary brow.

Aunt Olivia put down her cross-stitch. "You can't fool us, can she Celia? Your nearest and dearest know you far too well. You're enjoying the challenge."

Melody grunted in reply and rested her elbow on the arm of the couch, cupping her cheek in her hand. "Well, yes, I suppose I am. But I'm only teaching three selfish, spoiled brats, because their father is editor of *The Times*. I thought that if I could get under his roof and earn his confidence, he would give me work on his newspaper."

Aunt Olivia sighed. "A reporter for a newspaper, would you believe. Only you would want to go into a profession where women are not permitted."

"But we should be permitted," said Melody. "Women should be able to report the news just as much as men. We're as good as men. But Mr John Delane says he won't entertain the idea, the stubborn old fool."

Olivia smiled and studied her niece. Reporting the news, highlighting injustices and bringing people's attention to misdeeds was all Melody cared about and she had been warned that the undertaking would be difficult if not altogether impossible. But Melody had her plans. She had taken work as a governess at the residence of Mr and Mrs Delane in order, as she said, to get closer to the editor of a prestigious newspaper. But it didn't look as though her plan was working.

"So, what are you going to do?" Olivia asked.

Melody pursed her lips. "As from tomorrow, I shall be looking for new employment."

"Oh, Melody. You've not been dismissed again?"

"No, Aunt. This time I left on my own accord." She smiled mischievously. "Before they could dismiss me."

Olivia shook her head. This was the third position her niece had lost in as many months.

"Well, if you do have time on your hands, you could help me with the Sunday school play," said Celia.

"Thank you for your offer, but I'd rather not," replied Melody. Seeing Celia's crestfallen face she added hurriedly, "Of course, if you need help, then I'd be happy to assist."

Celia sighed. "I don't think I should have taken on such a daunting project. Why I thought I could produce a nativity play I don't understand."

"It'll be lovely though, when the children perform it," encouraged Melody, looking on the bright side. "All those radiant little faces and sweet voices singing carols."

Tilly struggled through the door and Aunt Olivia rose to help her with the tray, setting it down on the occasional table.

"What's going wrong with this play of yours?" Olivia asked, after the maid had set out the cups and left the room.

Celia grimaced. "Everything! Absolutely everything." She began to count up on her fingers. "The wise men are insisting they should have real gold, frankincense and myrrh in their gifts. The shepherds keep stuffing their toy sheep inside the piano. And Mary and Joseph spend the entire time squabbling and hitting each other with the baby Jesus doll."

Olivia and Melody burst into laughter. For all her shyness, Celia could delight them with the stories of her Sunday school class. Celia joined in but the effort brought strained tears rolling down her cheeks and she sniffed into her handkerchief.

Melody squeezed her hand. "If it's too much for you, Celia, then you must tell the vicar you can't do it. He'll understand."

Celia shook her head. "No. I'll persevere. It's just that…" she paused for a moment and when she continued, her voice trembled. "I would be mortified to let him down when he's relying on me."

"Don't ever be worried about failing," said Melody. "Where would I be if I'd been scared of failure? Working at the Delane's wasn't what I thought it would be. Today, I asked Mr Delane if I could work on his paper for a few hours a week and do you know what he did?" Celia put away her handkerchief. "He just laughed at me." Aunt Olivia offered them both a cup of tea and smiled in resigned sadness. Her experience had taught her that her niece would confront that kind of reaction from the professional male population. They sat quietly for a few minutes. "But I'm not giving up," added Melody. "I shall go on writing what I see and I'll visit every newspaper office in London until one of them does take notice of me. I know I can write about things men would never *think* of. The human side of a story."

Celia nodded. Melody could achieve her ambition; she knew that beyond any doubt. Ever since their days at Miss Lawson's school, Celia had admired Melody, but yet hesitated in following her example. She knew she didn't possess such strength of character and her happiness would be found only in marriage and a family. She would concentrate her efforts in a husband and children. That would be her destiny.

"So, you've left the Delane's?" said Celia bringing Melody out of her reverie with a start.

"Yes and thank goodness. It's time for me to look elsewhere."

"You're a splendid teacher and that's something to fall back on if your plans go awry," said Aunt Olivia.

Melody knew she was trying to be helpful but couldn't help grimacing. "Teaching was only meant to be temporary until I took employment with a newspaper." She sighed and sipped her tea. "Anyway, I don't want to be under the nose of someone like Mrs Delane. I'd rather be in absolute control and make my own decisions."

Aunt Olivia had been delighted that the two friends had kept their promise to each other after Melody had been dismissed from Miss Lawson's. Letters had flown backwards and forwards and been followed up with visits to their respective homes. On numerous occasions, Melody, Olivia and even the brigadier had visited Monkswood, the ancestral home of the tenth Baron Sinclair, situated near Guildford in Surrey. In fact, both elderly gentlemen had become firm friends themselves. On warm summer evenings they would sit on the terrace, the baron smoking his cigars, the brigadier his pipe and compare notes on the problems of bringing up motherless girls, while Melody and Celia would walk arm in arm round the garden.

Although a baron, it didn't take Melody long to realise that Celia's father was far from wealthy. Money was definitely scarce and had to be spent wisely. Hence, Miss Lawson's Academy, Melody had reflected ruefully. With his fortune nearly gone, he and Celia had to live on the rents from the estate and from what little revenue the farms generated. Although Monkswood was a large house, there was very little left of the grandeur and wealth since the time of good Queen Bess. Even so, when Celia reached her eighteenth birthday, the baron had sent her to London for the Season, but insisting that Melody and Aunt Olivia accompany her. They had stayed in a hotel for the first three months, but then the baron had rented a small house for them, since Celia and Melody had expressed a wish to remain in London.

Melody tried to attend all the society functions, in case someone interesting happened to be there and she could pick up an intriguing story, concealing a notebook and pencil in her evening bag. It was no secret that she had used her visit to London as a means of breaking into the world of journalism. And on quiet nights she studied Gurney's Brachgraphy, an absolute must for every aspiring reporter wanting to learn shorthand, and, as she insisted on telling Celia and Aunt Olivia, used by Charles Dickens himself in his days as a reporter.

But even so, Melody was often bored when attending these functions, her temper made worse by having to dress for the social scene in corsets, crinolines, many petticoats and fussing with hairpieces and jewellery. And when they returned from some soiree or ball, she would write up any stories in preparation for her numerous visits to the newspapers.

Celia placed her empty cup down on the tray and coughed before saying, "Lady Sommers has asked Olivia and me to luncheon, but she didn't include you, I'm afraid."

Melody burst into laughter. "Why would she ask me? I'm persona non grata when it comes to social events."

"It was very rude of her not to invite you," murmured her aunt. "Nevertheless I do believe she has her son earmarked for dear Celia here."

Celia responded with a giggle. "Imagine me being a bride."

Melody scanned her eyes over the golden hair, parted in the centre and curled into ringlets. Celia attracted many admirers who buzzed around her at every function and the fact that Melody believed society had made marriage into a cage, a way of trapping a woman and holding her captive for life, didn't alter her desire to see her friend happy.

"I think a husband and children would suit you," she said. "Yes, a wonderful man who would give you the comfort and support you need."

Celia's cheeks flushed and she swallowed with difficulty. "What about you? You will have to marry one day. You can't stay a spinster."

"I doubt I'll ever marry." Melody tilted her head and smiled mischievously. "I'd like to run my own newspaper."

"What kind of newspaper?" queried Olivia.

"Oh, a newspaper run by women for women. Giving the news of the day, of course, but peppering it with items of interest such as advances in science and industry. Probably a page dedicated to how a woman can improve her life and advice with medical matters."

"Medical matters!" chimed Olivia and Celia together.

"Yes, medical matters. Why not? Why shouldn't women be given help on how to improve their health, to have less children and the like?" Melody stuck out her chin. "Don't you agree, Aunt?"

Olivia glanced at her niece. "Why are you asking me?"

"Because you have more experience and I value your opinion." Melody kept her gaze fixed on her aunt's face.

Olivia wriggled like a worm at the end of a fishing line. "I don't know, my dear. I really don't know, except I can't see it being accepted by society."

"Neither can I," sniffed Melody.

Olivia opened her eyes wide. "Then why attempt it? Why swim against the tide of social normality? You'll only get yourself a reputation."

"I don't care about my reputation," said Melody. She hesitated before adding, "What I mean is that I won't let my reputation get in the way of my dreams of becoming a reporter."

"You'll be treading on toes, and offending the sensibilities of society," Olivia argued, wagging her finger at her.

Melody persisted with her argument. "But Aunt Olivia, wouldn't you have liked to have known more? Perhaps had a better understanding of how the female body worked? Wouldn't you have liked more opportunities and been able to make decisions about your life?" Suddenly, Melody realised that her aunt had been her rock throughout her growing years, teaching her much and yet not enough.

"Of course not! I married and my husband made the decisions."

A pair of cornflower-blue eyes focused on her. "And you were prevented from leading your own life because of the restrictions placed on you by society. You had to marry to have some kind of life. Only marriage gave you status." Melody jumped to her feet and paced about the room. "You're an intelligent woman, Aunt Olivia, but you were not able to express or develop that intelligence. It was all wasted."

Olivia picked up her cross-stitch and jabbed the needle through the material. "Still, I did marry and was very happy for over twenty years." she said quietly.

Melody suddenly realised she had gone too far. "Oh, Aunt Olivia," she said, sitting on the arm of her aunt's chair. "I'm so sorry. Sometimes I get so frustrated that I forget about the people around me. Please forgive me, I didn't mean to offend you. I love you too much."

Olivia patted her hand. "I'm not offended, dear. I know you far too well. And perhaps you're right, perhaps women should be more educated. But what would girls do with this new education?"

"They'll not be so ignorant for a start. They'll have more say in their lives. In time, perhaps women will be educated enough to become doctors or lawyers," said Melody.

"You're quite mad!" laughed Olivia.

Melody would have none of it. "Certainly not. It's something I believe in and I shall bear it all in mind for the column I shall write in a newspaper."

"Hark to Lady Wisdom! All of twenty-one years old and trying to change the world overnight," said Olivia. "But, Melody, you'll only stir up a hornet's nest if you write such things. Take it slowly at first. Chase your headlines and try and get an editor to print what you've written. If you become an established reporter, then you can start promoting your own ideologies. Slow down, my girl, you must learn to walk before you can run."

"But education is important," Melody insisted. "And one day women will go to Oxford and Cambridge."

Celia grimaced. "At least it will not be like Miss Lawson's."

"Never like Miss Lawson's." nodded Melody in agreement.

"I'm sorry ladies, but you're going too fast for me," said Olivia. "The world is the way it is and it will change slowly and reluctantly if I know anything about it."

Melody stared despondently at the teacups on the table. "They say that from tiny acorns mighty oak trees grow. We have to start somewhere, Aunt. Perhaps it won't happen for fifty years or more. But one day maybe, just maybe, Celia's granddaughter or great-granddaughter will have a medical practice or defend a prisoner in the dock. Who knows?"

Olivia patted her knee. She loved her niece dearly, but often feared that she was jeopardising her future happiness by chasing such hare-brained schemes. After all, what young man would be attracted to a girl who wanted to change the world?

Celia rose from her place on the couch. They had a function to attend and she wanted to be the first to find Tilly to help her get dressed. She paused at the door.

"Are you really going to help with the nativity play?" she asked, glancing at her friend still perched on the arm of the chair and looking as though her thoughts were in another place.

"Yes, of course. What do you want me to do?" said Melody, shaking herself back to the present.

"Well, you have a fairly passable skill as an artist so if you could drum up a few scenery details I would be eternally grateful. Not a lot is needed, just a pretence of a stable and such like."

Melody opened her mouth to say she was far too busy to become that involved, but Celia had already glided gracefully from the room.

"Serves you right for volunteering," laughed Aunt Olivia.

Doctor Alex Courtney waited at the police sergeant's elbow, while the huge man hammered on the door. His eyes swept along the street and he shuddered. The East End of London had always had a reputation for poverty and squalor, but this area was the worst Alex had ever seen. Dung and household rubbish lay strewn by the side of the cobbled way, sending up a stink that made him feel sick. The putrid liquid oozing from this disgusting mess ran down the alleys, mixing with the offal from the butcher's shop. And all this would drain into the Thames, he thought ruefully, and pollute the water.

It was November and the weather was turning quite cold and yet the stench was overpowering. He had visited this area in the height of summer and knew the place became unbearable then. Cholera and typhoid would result from this terrible lack of sanitation. And Alex knew that they all might have to pay for it, for disease crossed all social barriers.

Deprivation seemed to be everywhere, the inhabitants who milled around looked ill and haggard, their clothing a mishmash of old and much-mended garments passed down from hand to hand. People thronged the street, going about their daily business. Many of them stopped to ogle at the large sergeant beating on the cracked and dirty door of the filthy boarding house. It should be razed to the ground, thought Alex with a grimace, it's not fit for pigs to live in.

He watched a child of three or four years old standing by the entrance of an alley, her face and arms hidden under a layer of grime which would have befitted a miner. She was thin and her ragged dress wasn't enough to keep her warm by any stretch of the imagination. He gritted his teeth to stop himself swearing, although the desperate plight of the girl tore at his heart. In all probability she would be dead before her fifth birthday and her mother, assuming she had one, would be immune to the fact another child was gone. Child mortality was high and often greeted with relief. Ten or eleven mouths to feed were a struggle for any parent.

Two drunken men swayed across the road and rounded the corner, colliding with a constable and a young woman who had suddenly appeared. As the drunken men righted themselves, they made advances towards the young woman and were rebuffed by a sharp word from the constable.

The sergeant's men laughed seeing them lurch down the street in an uncoordinated frenzy of wobbling legs and swaying bodies.

"Drunk for a penny, dead drunk for tuppence," quoted one man, watching the pair fall against the wall, pull themselves up and continue on their hazardous way.

Alex tried to smile but failed. The lives of the people in this street were wretched and the gin houses were often their only way of finding solace. However, he was intrigued by the appearance of the young woman. She seemed out of place since her clothes were of good quality. She was swathed in a thick, blue mantle coat, her head covered by a bonnet that almost concealed her face. She certainly shouldn't have been in such an area. It was far too dangerous.

Alex nodded in her direction. "We seem to have an audience."

Sergeant Dallimore followed the direction of his nod. "Oh, our little reporter. She's good at sniffing out a story, she is. Always there when there's something going on."

"A woman reporter," said Alex, raising his eyebrows.

"I don't think she's actually employed by a newspaper. More freelance, I think."

"It's dangerous her being here," said Alex, glancing around at the sundry groups of people standing in the doorways.

"She comes down to Scotland Yard every morning badgering the duty sergeant for information. Often she'll accompany an officer on the beat, so in a way we keep an eye on her. You watch when we come out of here, she'll pester me with questions." He grinned, but then turned his attention again to the door. "Break it down," he ordered his men. Alex stood back and watched as two of the strongest, threw themselves at the worm-eaten wood. Rusty hinges groaned and after two or three mighty heaves of the shoulder, it gave way and was sent crashing to the ground. The smell from outside met the foulness from inside, sending the five men falling back from the dark opening. "In you go, lads. Smart about it. Let's get this job done with," the sergeant barked. There was no sound inside the house; the boarders having fled the scene as soon as they heard the peelers were on their way. They went in, making their way down the murky passage, the sergeant opening the doors as he went and peering inside the rooms. They finally reached the entrance to the cellar. "Must be it," he mumbled, taking in a huge breath. He flung open the door and was met with a blackness that could be sliced with a knife. The company paused, waiting, gathering their energies for the next order. "Bring the light and we'll go down."

The sergeant led the way, followed by the men, followed by Alex, clutching his medical bag close against his chest. They had become immune to the smell, their only thought to follow the yellow beam from the lamp, its glow a beacon of hope against the frightening shadows.

The doctor looked down and tiny pinpoints of light stared up at him. Long snouts and twitching whiskers greeted the strangers' descent, the piercing squeaks of protest causing a shudder to run through every man. The floor moved as the black bodies made good their escape. One didn't make it and flew through the air on the end of the sergeant's boot.

"'Ope you don't mind rats, sir," the man in front of Alex muttered over his shoulder. "Flippin' army of 'em down 'er."

Alex didn't feel the need to answer; his trousers were tucked well inside his boots. The stench seemed to be getting stronger and he tried desperately not to lick his lips. He failed and the taste on his tongue made him retch.

At the bottom of the stairs they stayed close together, watching out for any brave vermin who would dare to spring at them with teeth and claws. The sergeant's head bumped against something and they heard chains rattling. Someone held the lamp in the air.

"God Almighty!" was all he could say.

The young boy had hurtled into the police station early that morning. He hadn't waited long, but long enough to blurt out that a woman drinking in a tavern the night before, had been bragging she had hung her servant in chains, 'to teach her a lesson'. The address given, the ragged boy had run from the premises as if his very life depended on it.

After collecting his men together and calling for the doctor, the group set off. They took weapons concealed under their coats, not wanting to provoke any dispute with a resident of Fetter Lane. Drunkenness and prostitution were the normal way of life and these states created antagonism towards any man showing authority with firearms.

The girl was dangling by her wrists from a heavy chain attached to a huge metal hook screwed into a wooden beam. Alex couldn't see much, but the fact she was so still gave him little hope. How long she had been there was impossible to say, but it was obvious she had been hoisted and whipped. The lashes were so merciless, blood had seeped through her ragged clothing. The men set to work.

One man climbed up and lowered her gently to the ground. Her eyes were closed and while the sergeant held the lamp aloft, Alex quickly examined her. He crouched next to her, noticing how her dark hair spread out in a cascade, framing her face. She was only young, perhaps thirteen or fourteen years old and a lovely child at that. There was a bruise on her left cheek, but otherwise she looked beautiful in death, as she must have done in life. A cursory examination confirmed there was nothing he could do.

Two of the men were sent to fetch a cart and when it arrived they lifted her from the floor, carried her up the cellar steps and outside into the street. Once placed in the cart, the driver urged the horses into a steady walk and she was taken to the hospital. As the cart rumbled over the uneven cobblestones, it passed the young woman, now on the opposite side of the street speaking to neighbours. The sergeant ordered the rest of his men to scour the area to search for the prisoner and bring her in for questioning.

Alex stayed only long enough to shake hands with the sergeant, before he made his way past the doorways of the neighbouring houses, ignoring the calls of the residents asking him what had happened. The young woman in the blue coat had obviously been keeping her eyes on the proceedings for as soon as the cart had left, she and the constable crossed the street and made their way along the dirty cobbled way, towards the sergeant. Alex tried to make out the young woman's features but her bonnet obscured her face. Before he turned the corner, he glanced over his shoulder and smiled. The sergeant had been quite right; the young woman, notebook and pencil in hand, was plying him with questions. Alex noticed that the sergeant seemed very pleased to tell her all, smiling and gesticulating in turn, as he described the events in the cellar. When they both turned and made their way inside the house, Alex was filled with horror. Had she really asked to view the scene? Obviously she had, for a few minutes later, young woman and sergeant reappeared and made their way in the opposite direction.

The hospital was quiet that night. Only the occasional noise impinged on the concentration of the man absorbed in his task at the desk; the sound of someone passing in the corridor, a door banging, a wagon rumbling by outside the window, people calling to each other as they made their way home from the public houses.

Alex worked on his report until everything was completed. He blotted the drying ink and lifting the paper so he could see it more clearly, began to read what he had written.

Christian Jenner entered the room. "All done?" he asked.

Alex nodded. "Yes, just finished. The examination showed she had a defective heart valve. She probably wouldn't have lived more than another couple of years, but the punishment meted out to her did the trick."

Christian drew in a deep breath through his nose and let it out between his teeth. "Well, they've caught her." Alex lifted his head and frowned. "Her mistress. Sergeant Dallimore and his men went to one of the taverns and there she was, merry as you like. Nancy Buckle she's called. Hope she's locked up securely before they hang her."

Alex smiled. "I thought a person is innocent until proved guilty?"

"Oh, they are, they are," Christian grinned back. "Only this woman confessed she'd punished her for being lazy."

Alex looked sadly towards the table on which the young girl lay. "Have we a name for her?"

"Hannah Silcox," said Christian. "They said her employer didn't put up much of a struggle when they arrested her."

"She's still entitled to a fair trial," said Alex.

"Of course. And then she'll hang immediately after," said Christian.

Melody was exhausted by the time she reached her home in Hyde Park Gardens. She had insisted the sergeant take her into the cellar and then she had gone to the hospital to find out if an examination would be made on the victim, only to be told that it wouldn't be done until much later, there being no doctor available until that time. Her visit to the hospital later that night had been eerie, the corridors resounding to her footsteps as she made her way to the mortuary. But the attendant had been helpful and had answered her questions willingly, concluding his narrative by spelling his name, watching curiously as she wrote it in her notebook in a language he didn't understand.

Melody stepped into the kitchen, threw some coal into the stove, filled up a large pan with water and placed it on top to heat. She had to immerse herself in a bath and try and get rid of the macabre taint that seemed to surround her.

"What are you doing, miss?"

The sudden appearance of the maid caused Melody to spin round. "Oh, Tilly, I didn't mean to disturb anyone. I thought I would take a bath, before I retire. Can't go to bed smelling like this."

Tilly ambled across the kitchen floor and looked her in the face. "It's my job to prepare water for the bath, not yours. You sit down and I'll put the kettle on too. Could do with a cuppa myself."

"I didn't want to..."

The maid clicked her tongue and pushed her into a chair. "You're quite right, miss. You whiff something awful. Not at all like a respectable young lady ought to," she said, wrinkling her nose.

Melody sat back and let Tilly take charge.

Wonderful Tilly! Petite and with a rounded figure, she had a motherly nature in spite of her youth. She was the oldest of eight children, three already dead, and was used to life below stairs. But even Tilly had to admit that life with the three ladies was unusual, to say the least. Especially with Miss Melody. Tilly could never understand how a lady of quality would have any desire to go to places she shouldn't, and see scenes she had no right to see. And the endless questions! The times they had sat in the kitchen and Miss Melody had asked about her childhood and Miss Melody wanted to know everything. About her brothers and sisters, how her mother coped with such a large family, what illnesses they had suffered and all manner of things.

"She needs looking after, she does," Tilly had told her mother, on one of her visits to the family home. "And it's up to me to do it or she'll come to some dreadful harm. A big city like London could swallow a girl like that."

Melody sighed and watched the dumpy figure waddle around the kitchen, filling up the kettle and placing the tub in front of the roaring stove. She felt so exhausted she could hardly move and when Tilly finally helped her into the hip bath of warm water and gently washed her back, Melody surrendered to the wonderful feeling of being pampered and enjoyed the comfort of the warm soothing water on her body. Some time later she slipped into bed, but her eyes wouldn't close, the images of the day stinging her memory. It was many hours before sleep finally released her.

CHAPTER TWO

Early the following morning, Melody put on a plain skirt and blouse, brushed her hair back from her face, tied it up with a ribbon and got down to work. Sitting at her dressing table, she carefully transcribed her shorthand notes into longhand, dipping her pen frequently into the ink as she described the events of the previous day. But she kept it concise, stating the facts, dates, times and names of people involved. She used quotes sparingly, realising these were more subjective than factual, but interesting observations from the sergeant could not be ignored, nor the findings from the post-mortem.

Melody finally finished and putting her manuscript into a leather pouch, she ran downstairs into the hallway. "I'm going out, Aunt Olivia," she called, as she pulled on her boots, flung her coat over her shoulders and tied on her bonnet. "Don't worry, I'll get a cab there and back."

Aunt Olivia appeared at the sitting room door. "Will you be long?" she said. She really didn't like her niece going out alone, but she might as well stop a speeding bullet, as stop Melody going where she wanted.

"It all depends on the editor of The Cork Street Journal. I've decided to sit on his doorstep until he sees me!"

"Well, Celia and I are having luncheon with Mrs Ansell. If you can, join us at the vicarage."

Melody nodded, but knew that her quest might take all day.

The hansom cab pulled up outside an impressive row of premises in Cork Street and Melody jumped out. She quickly paid the driver and as he pulled away she turned and stared up at the four-storey building in front of her. It was blackened by the relentless smoke from chimneys and the steam trains that chugged across the bridge nearby. On the ledges, pigeons cooed and fluttered leaving their droppings in messy white streaks on windows and brick. Even the brass plaque reading The Cork Street Journal had a large glob of the stuff across its shiny surface. Melody took a big breath and stepped between the imposing pillars and through the door.

It led into a large entrance hall, surrounded by many doors. One seemed to lead to the printing room, as a young man with ginger hair and a face full of freckles, came hurtling through, allowing the rhythmic sound of the printing press to invade the peace. The pungent smell of ink and machinery wafted about Melody, a smell she had come to know so well from her endless journeys around the numerous newspaper establishments of London.

"Oh, are you the new maid?" he said, stopping in his tracks. His eyes swept over Melody's blue coat and fashionable bonnet and his face flushed with embarrassment causing his complexion to go bright red from neck to the roots of his hair. "Of course you're not. How silly of me."

Melody smiled in amusement. "I've come to see Mr Wyngate, if you please."

"Do you have an appointment?"

"No, do I need one?" she said, feigning ignorance.

"Usually, yes, but I'm sure he'll see a lovely young lady like you. Follow me and I'll show you to his office." Melody pulled a face at his patronising manner, hoping he was just overdoing his politeness after his previous embarrassment.

She followed him up the stairs, noticing that his clothes were just a little too small for him, the sleeves on his jacket not quite reaching his wrist. He was a tall, lanky youth with a long stride and Melody had to walk quickly to keep up with him. He showed her into an office that obviously belonged to the secretary, as a middle-aged man with a profusion of whiskers, rose from his chair as the boy tapped on the door. He allowed Melody to enter first and she glanced around at an untidy office; the shelves and cupboards filled to overflowing with files, old newspapers and paraphernalia of ledgers and assorted paperwork.

"This young lady has come to see Mr Wyngate," the boy explained quickly, before disappearing back into the corridor.

"I don't remember him having an appointment this morning," the secretary said, scanning his eyes over the large diary lying open on his desk.

"I didn't make one. My business will only take a few minutes."

"The editor is a very busy man," he said sharply.

"I only need a few minutes of his time," she insisted.

"Could you tell me your business, then perhaps I can intercede on your behalf."

Melody sucked in her breath. She had never really trusted any secretary of an editor, but she had to accept every offer of help.

"I've written an article on the murder committed in Whitechapel. I would like to offer it to Mr Wyngate for publication in his newspaper."

The secretary peered at her over his horn-rimmed spectacles and pursed his lips at yet another freelance reporter. He had had his bellyful of them, developing a technique to get rid of them quickly, although he had to admit that a woman journalist was unique.

"He's with someone at the moment. Come back tomorrow," he said, turning his attention back to his ledger.

Melody didn't move. "I'm not going until I see Mr Wyngate. I told you my business would only take a few minutes."

"It doesn't matter whether it's a few minutes or a few seconds, Mr Wyngate is too busy to see you," he said acidly.

Melody looked towards the adjoining office where a nameplate on the door read *Mr Guy Edward Wyngate* and underneath was the word *Editor*. She listened carefully.

If the editor was with someone then she should be able to hear voices coming from within, but she heard none. However, she did hear the sound of a chair scraping against the floor, footsteps walking across the room and a drawer opening and closing. Mr Wyngate certainly had no one with him and she decided to take her chance. Gathering up her hooped skirt she slipped past the secretary, opened the inner door and stepped into the office.

Guy Edward Wyngate was standing by a cabinet, a file in his hand. Tall, with dark hair and deep brown eyes, Melody guessed his age at about his early forties. His youth was certainly behind him, as shades of silver were starting to appear at his temples, giving him a distinguished appearance.

"What the...!" He turned sharply towards her.

"Mr Wyngate, I'm sorry for being so rude," Melody said hurriedly. "My name is Melody Kinsman and I've written an account of the murder in Whitechapel, the one where the victim was found hanging in chains. All I ask is if you'll read it and tell me what you think."

She gasped for air, her heart pounding in her ears. She almost tore the manuscript from its leather pouch and pressed it towards him. He reached for it without thinking and once in his hand, Melody breathed a sigh of relief, smiling at him. His eyes swept over her in bewilderment.

The secretary was standing in the doorway, his back stiff with indignation at such impudence.

"I'm sorry, sir. I told her you were too busy to see her, but she wouldn't listen."

"It's all right, Marsh, I get the impression that, sorry, what did you say your name was?" She quickly told him, "Miss Kinsman doesn't take 'no' for an answer." He looked down at the sheaves of paper in his hand. "Tell me, young lady, why should I read your particular report, when I have so many others to choose from?" He gestured towards the pile of papers on his desk.

She bristled with annoyance. "Because it's an excellent account and you'd be a fool not to!"

A hint of a smile flittered across his face, but then quickly disappeared. "Well, since I have it, I might as well look it over."

Melody's heart nearly leapt out of her chest. "You'll read it!" she said, her throat tightening.

"In my own good time," said the editor. He threw the precious manuscript onto the desk and it landed with a thud on the others waiting for his attention. "But at the moment I'm really far too busy. Call back tomorrow and I'll give you my decision then." He turned away and went back to his desk, sitting in the large leather chair and bending his head to the work that she had interrupted.

She stared at the top of his head for a few seconds, a sinking feeling in her stomach. He wouldn't read it, she thought, he was simply being polite to get rid of her. He was just like all the others. Disappointment welled up inside her making her feel nauseated.

"Thank you," she murmured.

He lifted his face once more and his eyes told her that her presence was an intrusion. Tossing her head defiantly, she twirled round, walked with dignity past the secretary and out of the building.

The cab ride to Oxford Street was melancholy. So much for Mr Guy Edward Wyngate, thought Melody, alighting from the vehicle outside Hyde Park. It had all been a waste of time. Aunt Olivia had been right all along.

Melody walked into the park and found a bench. She had failed, she reflected mournfully. She had hoped to elicit some support from the editor of The Cork Street Journal; hoped he would have a more modern outlook to journalism. He was certainly the youngest editor she had talked to. The others had been much older and either patronising or arrogant. But he was simply indifferent.

"Horrible man!" she said aloud, causing a young man hurrying along the path to turn his head sharply in her direction. She smiled at him, spots of pink appearing on her cheeks with embarrassment.

Melody looked towards the houses on the Bayswater Road. The buildings reflected the affluence of the upper classes of London. Each five-storey Georgian house seemed like a mansion, the front doors of varnished oak gleaming with brass knockers. Carriages, coaches, footmen in smart livery and daintily dressed maids thronged the area, going about their business in making the lives of their masters and mistresses as comfortable and easy as possible. A nanny ambled by pushing a perambulator and nodded a greeting at the young woman sitting on the park bench.

It was a beautiful day and although cold, the sun shone brightly in a sparkling blue sky, the breeze feeling fresh on her face. She glanced around and noticed how empty the flowerbeds were although she knew the bulbs and seeds were sleeping below the surface of the soil waiting for the spring. But spring was a long way off yet and winter was still ahead of them. The onset of cold weather would prevent their impatient thrust into the cruel outside world.

Yes, it was a cruel world, Melody thought. This part of London was so different from the one she had witnessed in Whitechapel. But she could write about it and bring it to people's attention. She knew she could. Perhaps in her small way she could make a difference. She couldn't believe she had failed again. He said he would read it and she would keep faith. She would go back the following day and hear what he had to say. She wouldn't give up; she couldn't give up. It wasn't in her nature.

She looked across to where the Crystal Palace once stood and she remembered its hundreds of windows mirroring the blue of the sky and glinting in the sun. It had been an impressive building, built to house the Great Exhibition of 1851. The brigadier and Aunt Olivia had taken her on the first day it opened and even as a little girl she had marvelled at the objects that were not only meant to be useful but also aesthetic. Her papa had called some of the exhibits quite exotic, but at eight years old, Melody hadn't understood what he meant. But at twenty-one she did and she also knew the Exhibition was a tribute to the skill man could accomplish. She was skilful too and she would accomplish her goal. A feeling of hope began to well up inside her, and with a lighter step, she made for Oxford Street and luncheon at the vicarage.

The following morning, Melody climbed out of bed still filled with hope. Where this hope came from she had no idea, but she was pleased that it was still there, making her breathless with anticipation.

As she dressed, she smiled at her insane notion of wanting to become a newspaper reporter. She pulled a face at her reflection in the mirror. Should she settle for a teaching position at a ladies academy? After all, it was a worthy profession. But then she remembered Miss Lawson's and shuddered. No, it wouldn't do. She yearned to work on a newspaper, to bring the news to the people. She didn't wish to work as a seamstress, or as a governess, or a domestic servant, or one of the numerous other mundane, poorly paid occupations that were open to women. She pressed her lips together in determination as she pinned up her hair and tried to tuck the unruly curls into some kind of order. Today she would face the editor of The Cork Street Journal and hear his decision. And if he turned her away then she would just have to start again.

"Happy birthday, my dear." Aunt Olivia kissed the top of her niece's head, as she sat down to breakfast.

The fact it was her twenty-second birthday had completely escaped her and Melody stared in disbelief at the brightly coloured parcel sitting next to her coffee cup.

"She's forgotten," Celia giggled. She too stood up and presented her friend with a gaily-wrapped gift tied up with a shiny, silver ribbon.

"Goodness me," said Melody. "I really did forget. How foolish of me." She surveyed the parcels with delight. "Thank you so much." She unwrapped the first one and revealed a beautiful fan lying inside a velvet box. She caught her breath with surprise as she spread it out, studying the design painted on it, depicting a beautiful pastoral scene painted in watercolours and showing a boat sailing down a river. In the distance was a snow-capped mountain. "Aunt Olivia, it's exquisite," she cried, grasping her hand and giving it a squeeze.

Olivia smiled and said thoughtfully, "I liked the idea of a mountain, since the summit is where you seem to be aiming for." She winked at Celia. "I thought it would come in handy next month."

"Why, what's happening next month?" asked Melody.

"We've organised a birthday dinner for you," her aunt answered and before Melody could query the date, she added, "And before you ask why it's belated, Celia has requested we postpone it until after her nativity play."

"You don't mind, do you?" asked Celia, biting her lip. "It's just that I want to get this blessed play behind me and then I can enjoy your birthday dinner."

"I don't mind at all," Melody laughed.

"Now open my present," said Celia, her eyes sparkling. Melody undid the ribbon and opened the parcel containing a walnut box. She lifted the lid and discovered a set of pens, pencils, inkpot and everything else a writer would need for their art. "Do you like it?"

"It's beautiful, Celia. Thank you so much," breathed Melody.

The journey to Cork Street wasn't all that bad after her delightful breakfast surprises. Melody felt ready to face Guy Wyngate and even felt acceptance at anything he might throw at her. She alighted from the cab and made her way upstairs to the secretary's office.

Marsh jumped up from his chair in surprise. "Oh, Miss Kinsman. Mr Wyngate is ready to see you. Do go straight in." Melody nodded and knocked on the door before entering.

He was standing at the window, looking down at the morning traffic in the street below. He must have seen me alighting from the cab, Melody reflected with interest. The thought pleased her that he might have been waiting for her.

He turned from the window. "So, you decided to come back after all," he said, taking his seat behind the desk. He gestured for her to sit down and she obeyed.

"Of course," she answered dryly. "I've put my money on the horse. I might as well let it run."

Her reference to horse racing seemed to amuse him and he smiled. "I've read your account of the Fetter Lane murder and found it quite…interesting."

"I'm pleased about that. And…" she queried. Her heart started to speed up.

He leaned back in his chair. "Tell me, Miss Kinsman, do you actually read The Cork Street Journal?"

"Well, no," she said honestly. "My aunt reads *The Evening Chronicle* and I usually buy *The Times*."

Raising his eyebrows he let out a sigh and reached for the folded newspaper on his desk, passing it to her. She took it and noticed that most of the front page was taken up with news of the Civil War in America. She became engrossed in reading that Sherman had taken Atlanta on the first day of September, completely forgetting the man patiently sitting opposite her.

"What do you think?" he said, after thirty seconds of silence had passed between them.

"I think General Grant will definitely win this war," she answered casually.

"Bottom right hand column if you please, Miss Kinsman."

Her eyes swept to where he indicated and to her incredulous delight, there was her article in its entirety.

"You printed it!" she said. "You actually printed it in last night's edition."

"And if you'd taken the trouble to buy the paper, you'd have seen it yourself," he said dryly.

She didn't mind his reprimand; she barely heard it. Her eyes sparkled with excitement and she tried to control her breathing that suddenly seemed to be coming in short gasps.

Guy Wyngate watched her and he couldn't prevent the merest hint of a smile at her enthusiasm, her youth.

She continued reading and then came to the bottom, where in small letters was printed the initials M.K. "Oh, you've only put my initials." Her delight faded. "The readers won't know who wrote this."

"I thought you might say that, but I want you to understand my position. I'm not sure how the readers will take to a female journalist and I'd like to tread carefully for the moment."

"You sound like my Aunt Olivia."

"Then your Aunt Olivia is a sensible woman. Even if she does read *The Evening Chronicle*." He reached into his desk drawer and brought out a brown envelope. Handing it to her he added, "This is for your article. It's the standard commission for freelance work."

She placed the newspaper on the desk, reached for the envelope and felt two coins inside. She guessed they were guineas and decided to accept it as a victory.

Rising to her feet she held out her hand. "Thank you, Mr Wyngate, I appreciate all you've done."

The editor also stood and took her hand. "Going already?" He gave a wide grin, his deep brown eyes crinkling with the delicate laughter lines on each side. For the first time Melody noticed how attractive his smile was. "I thought you would have wanted more work, but never mind, if you're in a hurry I'll not keep you any longer."

"More work," she said. "I'm sorry, I don't understand."

"Why don't you sit down and let me continue." She sat down, confused. Was he going to give her an assignment? She could hardly believe it. "Nancy Buckle's trial date has not been set yet, but my guess is that it'll be before Christmas. They'll want to get it over with before closing the court for the festive season. How do you feel about covering the proceedings for The Cork Street Journal?"

Melody felt stunned. "You want me to cover the trial?"

"I do. Have you ever been to a trial?"

"No, but there's always a first time for everything."

"I take it you know shorthand."

"Of course," came back her firm reply.

"Who taught you?"

"No one. I taught myself from Gurney's Brachgraphy."

He raised his eyebrows in surprise. "How fast are you?"

"I really don't know. I've never timed myself."

He pushed a notebook and pencil towards her. "Let's find out, shall we." He took a gold watch from his waistcoat pocket as Melody picked up the notebook and pencil. He retrieved the newspaper and turning to the middle pages, he read aloud, glancing at his watch now and again. She concentrated and began to convert it into shorthand. He finally finished reading. "Now read it back to me." After she had finished he nodded at his watch. "That's about one hundred words a minute. That'll do. You don't have to be too fast to follow the proceedings in a court of law." He smiled at her pensive face. "Don't worry, Miss Kinsman, I'm sure you'll do well. I have every faith in you."

Her confidence returned and she nodded. "I'll enjoy the challenge, I'm sure," she said firmly.

He watched her for a moment or two before saying, "I'm going to send Eric with you. He's our artist and will be drawing the scenes to illustrate your article. He's attended numerous trials so don't be afraid to ask his advice. Come, I'll introduce you to him."

She followed him out of the office, past Marsh who gave her only a cursory glance.

Eric turned out to be the tall, lanky youth with red hair and the profusion of freckles. He shook her hand warmly. "This is a turn up for the books, I must say," he said, blushing from ear to ear.

After agreeing that they would get in touch when the trial date was fixed, Melody left the building walking on air.

"I think you're expecting too much from that slip of a girl, sir," said Marsh, as the editor strode to his office five minutes later.

He turned to his secretary. "Probably, but let's see what she's made of, eh! Send Holbrook to shadow her and if her account is unsuitable, then at least we have a backup." He gave a wicked smile. "Chances are we won't see her again." He stepped into his office closing the door quietly behind him.

Melody travelled home in a daze. Alighting from the cab outside the small house she shared with Aunt Olivia and Celia, the truth suddenly dawned on her. She was to sit in the press gallery in a court of law, amongst other journalists and report on a murder trial. It was the best birthday present of all and she rushed into the house in a whirl of excitement.

CHAPTER THREE

Despite the mayhem behind them, Melody and the vicar had been working hard and managed to achieve their objective. The majestic drawing room at the vicarage had been cleared of any unwanted furniture and a space had been allocated at one end. On either side of this area, screens had been erected to give the effect of a stage, and from behind which, the children could make their entrances and exits.

The vicar, a small, wiry man, had earned Melody's admiration by demonstrating his extraordinary skill at carpentry. The manger and other miscellaneous contents in a stable had been cleverly fashioned by the elderly cleric in such a way they appeared as works of art. To one side he had manufactured the outside of an inn and a real door which would open to Joseph's knock.

Melody had then followed him by painting the wood, to give it the appearance of a stone wall, with a fig tree growing at the end. She had even drawn a lamp hanging by the side of the door, a halo of light shining round it that created an aura of welcome. In the stable she had sketched a life-sized depiction of a cow and a horse, their heads turned in the direction of the manger. Above the stable she had represented a black velvet sky, studded with stars. Pride of place was the Star of Bethlehem, mystical and beautiful and for the children, very real.

"Excellent!" said the vicar, standing back and admiring the heavenly body that would lead the wise men on their quest. "Truly remarkable. It's a shame it's only for Christmas. If I'd had my way I'd let it all remain after the play is finished, but I'd answer to my wife for it."

Melody beamed with satisfaction and wiped her brush on a rag. "I must say I feel rather proud of it myself. Although your work is wonderful." She paused in thought and added, "Don't you think it remarkable that you, a man of God, should also have such a wonderful skill as a carpenter?"

The Reverend Ansell chuckled with delight. "Ah, but I discovered my skill at woodworking after my calling to the church, not the other way round."

"Still, it's a nice thought."

They studied the wonder in front of them, scrutinising every part, checking for any missing detail.

"So, the trial starts tomorrow?" the vicar asked softly.

"Yes, tomorrow," nodded Melody, equally as quiet.

"And what's your thoughts about it?"

"I've been asked to do it and I'll do it to the best of my ability. I don't think my feelings come into it somehow." Melody seated herself on one of the many chairs scattered around the room and watched Celia trying to direct a dozen children in the various characters of the Christmas story. The vicar took a seat next to her. "But, I must admit," she mused. "I feel on trial too."

"How so?"

"Mr Wyngate is testing me, I'm sure of it. If I fail at this, he'll believe he has a perfect right to exclude women from journalism. And the other editors will feel they were justified in turning me away." She gave a wry smile. "In short, I must be better than the best male reporter." They were both lost in thought for a few seconds until Melody added, "The things I've seen these last few months have been unbelievable and I yearn to write about it and bring it to the attention of people."

"It's a cruel world, but a changing one too."

"But it's not changing fast enough," said Melody irritably.

"I know what you mean." He patted her hand. "There is so much poverty and deprivation, it doesn't bear thinking about."

Melody sighed. "If every person, women as well as men were allowed the vote, then we could all have a say in how our country is run. Parliament would speak for all of us. Politicians would have to answer to us, the electorate, and bring about the social changes we want."

"Why, Melody, I do believe you're a political activist as well as a social reformer." His tired, blue eyes twinkled.

Melody gave out a delighted laugh. "Then let's hope I have a long enough life to do some good."

"Nancy Buckle certainly won't," he said sadly.

"Do you think she'll hang?"

"No doubt about it. The evidence points to her guilt." He sighed despondently. "That poor, poor girl."

"Well, it all starts tomorrow," she said.

"Good luck, my dear. Do what you must and let the judge and jury decide the rest."

Melody smiled and nodded.

A mighty crash echoed across the room, followed by a shriek from Celia.

"Luke! James! Stop it!"

Melody and the vicar turned to see Celia struggling with two young boys who were intent on knocking each other senseless with shepherds' crooks. In minutes, Melody was at her side, separating the warring pair by grabbing them by the collar. The Reverend Ansell called the children together and ordered them to sit on the floor and contemplate their sins while the grown-ups had some tea.

When the tea arrived, so did Mrs Ansell who had been upstairs finishing off the costumes for the shepherds and angels. She lay the mound of white, brown and blue cloth on a table and joined the others for a hard-earned rest.

"I've never done so much sewing in my life" she exclaimed, holding up her finger and showing a red mark produced by a thimble. "I'm sewing in my sleep now."

Her husband took her hand and kissed it. "Yes, sewed me to the sheets last night, she did," he chuckled merrily.

"Oh, Wilfred. Don't be so ridiculous. What will our guests think." Melody and Celia exchanged amused glances. "Well, we're nearly organised," added Mrs Ansell, rubbing her hands together with satisfaction. "On Thursday evening, the children will perform the play and then we'll sing carols before we settle down to our mulled wine and mince pies. Oh, it will be wonderful and the children will look sweet in their costumes."

Melody glanced at Celia and saw her gulping her tea down, fighting back tears. As Mrs Ansell collected up the cups and left the room and her husband went to complete some work on the stable, Melody bent her head towards Celia.

"You're doing such a wonderful job. It's going to be a success, I just know it."

Celia sighed. "I appreciate your help, I really do, but I'll be so glad when it's over."

"Well, it's only two more days and then you'll be able to enjoy my birthday dinner," said Melody, smiling.

But even before the play, Melody knew she had her own hurdle to jump and her thoughts drifted elsewhere.

Melody's eyes flew open in fright and she sat up in bed, staring wildly around her room. She had been dreaming she was on trial for her life and had been condemned to death. She could feel the noose round her neck and the low drum roll that preceded the drop. She was awake now, but she could still hear a drumming coming from somewhere. Then she realised it was someone at the door.

"Come in," she said, rubbing the sleep from her eyes.

Tilly stepped into the room, a lamp in her hand. "You told me to wake you at six, miss. Shall I bring in your tea now?" As was her way, the maid didn't wait for an answer but set the lamp down on her lady's dressing table and then went to bring in the tray of tea she had left on a small table just outside the door. Melody lay back against the pillows, blinking at the bright light that suddenly illuminated the room, the cheery glow chasing away the dark shadows. It was bitterly cold and she shivered. Tilly was back in a few seconds and placed the tray beside her. "I'll have a good fire going in just a moment," she said. "And then I'll bring you some hot water."

"What would we do without you," Melody sighed, snuggling down in her warm bed.

Tilly noticed and wagged her finger at her. "Now don't be getting too comfy, miss, you've got a big day ahead."

It was the day of the trial and Melody was meeting Eric outside the Old Bailey at nine. He had suggested going early to get a good place in the press gallery and she was glad of his advice. He might be a gawky youth, but he was full of information and seemed more than pleased to guide her through her first assignment.

She dressed plainly for the trial, deciding not to wear a crinoline since the hoop would only get in her way.

Instead she opted for a full skirt but with the obligatory numerous petticoats. With this skirt she chose a high-necked blouse and smart jacket that she could wear under her coat. Eric had warned her that it wouldn't be very warm in the courtroom. Tying on a velvet bonnet she examined herself in the mirror and felt she looked every inch the businesswoman. Brimming with confidence, she set off to meet Eric.

He was standing by the main door, a large drawing pad tucked under his arm.

"Ready?" he asked.

"I believe so," she said and then looked upwards.

Melody studied the imposing building that had dispensed justice for centuries. The cold was biting and the morning dew had frozen on the stonework making it gleam in the weak morning sun. Eventually the frost would thaw and water would run down, mixing with the grime and causing ugly streaks.

They climbed the steps and entered the large expansive foyer. A statue of Oliver Cromwell dominated one end, while the Duke of Wellington the other and along the walls were portraits of former judges in their gowns and wigs. The marble floor echoed to the many footsteps, making their way to Courtroom Number One. Melody followed Eric into this high vaulted chamber and then up the winding steps to the gallery.

They found their way to the press section and took their seats. Even though it was still early, Melody noticed that every bench seemed to be filling quickly, people coming from far and wide to witness justice being played out. The low hum of voices was punctuated with the occasional cough or burst of laughter. Melody looked around her, observing the high oak panelled walls and long, rectangular windows. The pale winter sun was only just filtering through, illuminating the polished brass fittings and the dust particles dancing in the air.

She jumped with fright when a knuckle tapped her shoulder. She turned her head to see a young man sitting behind her, his cravat loose and pulled to one side.

"Excuse me, miss," he said. "But you're sitting in the wrong place. The public gallery is over there." He gestured to her left.

"Ah, but I'm not a member of the public," she informed him. "I'm part of the press." She gave him a cheeky wink.

The young man sat back in his seat, his mouth falling open in utter surprise. He turned to his neighbour and a heated discussion followed. Eric threw back his head and gave out a guffaw of laughter that echoed round the chamber. Miss Kinsman could certainly hold her own and she would do well. His editor had shown good sense in selecting her. He quickly glanced along the press contingent to see who was there and suddenly spied Holbrook sitting in the corner. His heart sank with dismay, knowing exactly why he was there. Mr Wyngate had not placed any trust in the young girl at all, he thought sadly, he was merely playing lip service. A feeling of disappointment washed over him that his editor could be so underhand.

He turned to the young woman sitting next to him. "They'll be starting soon," he said. "Good luck and I mean that."

Melody smiled.

The jury filed in and took their seats. Twelve good men and true, chosen to listen to and weigh the evidence. Then the prisoner was brought up from the cells below and placed in the dock, her feet and hands chained together. A muscular prison officer sat each side of her. Melody noticed she was clean, her bonnet just revealing greying hair that was combed and parted in the middle. Her clothes were neat and tidy. After a couple of minutes the official cried, "All rise." And there was the judge in voluminous black gown and impressive wig. A hush fell over the courtroom as the public prosecutor opened the proceedings.

In the press gallery, pencils began to scribble and chalk started sketching in a frenzy of activity not to miss one single detail. Melody had no legal knowledge but as soon as the public prosecutor started speaking, she could see almost immediately, the way his argument was going. The prisoner was only guilty of being ignorant of her servant's medical condition. Had she known of her weak heart, she would have treated her more leniently. Melody wrinkled her nose and wondered if this would wash with the jury. She thought not and paid full attention to everything that was said.

It was nearly midday and the judge had just taken his watch from his waistcoat pocket, when there was a disturbance in the dock. The prisoner fell forward and was hurriedly supported by the guards sitting each side of her. They leaned her back in her chair, and Melody could see she was deathly white and shaking like a leaf. The judge told the officers to take her below and she was almost carried from the dock and down the steps to the cells. The court was then informed that there would be a short adjournment while the situation was assessed. The official again cried, "All rise," and the judge and jury left the court.

A babble of voices began as people stood up and stretched themselves after being confined for so long.

"Goodness, she did look unwell," exclaimed Melody, watching the movement going on below her.

"Unwell my Aunt Fanny," said Eric. Realising he had been rather rude added, "Sorry, Miss Kinsman…"

Melody interrupted him. "Why don't we call each other by our first names? After all we are work colleagues."

"I'd be delighted to," he grinned and then continued, "As I was saying she might have looked unwell, and she must have certainly felt unwell, but she isn't unwell in the true sense of the meaning."

Melody pursed her lips. "Is this supposed to be a riddle?"

"Certainly not," he said. "What I'm saying is that she's suffering from a condition commonly know as the 'shakes'." Seeing Melody remained confused, he explained further. "She's been a gin-drinker for many years and her body has got used to it. Whilst in prison, she's not been getting her daily dose of the stuff, so she's having a reaction. Withdrawal symptoms the doctors call it."

"Oh, dear," murmured Melody. "I never realised. I've not come across such a thing."

"And what's more," went on Eric, delighted, "the judge and jury will have realised that and will be none too pleased. It confirms her liking for the demon drink, you see. And the upstanding gentlemen of the jury will be on their moral high ground over it."

"I see," she answered quietly. "I hope it doesn't prejudice their decision."

"Probably will," said Eric, nodding. A booming voice announced that the court would adjourn until the following morning. "And that won't go down very well with the jury either," he said, clicking his tongue. "There's nothing so annoying as a delay in the proceedings. They'll be wanting to get back to their desks. They're losing money being here."

"What happens now?" asked Melody. The press gallery was emptying quickly, the noise of hurrying feet echoing around the chamber. Downstairs people were starting to leave, making their way to the main doors, voices raised in complaint.

"Everyone's rushing back to their offices to get their articles into the evening edition," Eric said. "And we'd better do the same. Come on."

He gathered up his drawing pad and leapt down the staircase to the entrance hall. Melody, not wanting to be left behind, was hot on his heels. They hurried into the hall, past the statue of Oliver Cromwell, trying to stifle their laughter and failing miserably.

Alex was deep in conversation with Sergeant Dallimore when he turned to watch the young couple running past amongst the contingent of press people. And then he felt his heart leap into his throat. He hadn't seen her for four years and yet he knew her on sight. Her oval face and pert nose, her sparkling cornflower-blue eyes and rich auburn hair told him that this was the lovely schoolteacher now grown into a beautiful woman.

"Ah, our little journalist is here I see," said the police sergeant.

Alex couldn't hide his amazement. "You mean that's the young lady who came down to Fetter Lane?"

"The very one. Obviously she's here to cover the trial," said Sergeant Dallimore and then added, "Well, if we're not needed today, I'll say good afternoon to you, sir."

He touched the brim of his hat and quickly left through the main doors and out into the thoroughfare that was now thronged with people going about their daily business.

Alex stood on the steps of the courthouse for a few minutes looking up and down the street. He knew that he had missed his chance to speak with her, but there was always tomorrow. Tomorrow he would take the stand as witness for the prosecution and afterwards he would search her out. He must speak to her again. He had never forgotten her and now that their paths had crossed once more, he was determined that he would not lose her a second time.

CHAPTER FOUR

For the second time, Melody and Eric made their way to the Old Bailey for the resumption of the trial. The previous day, Melody had submitted her article to the editor who had simply swept his eyes over it and told her to take it to the typesetter, without saying another single word. She had obeyed with a heavy heart. Not that she was looking for compliments, but she had hoped that he would have acknowledged her work in some way. However, despondency turned to delight that evening when she read The Cork Street Journal and saw that *M Kinsman* was printed at the conclusion of her article. It was a small concession but meant everything to her.

The court was just as full as it had been the day before. When the prisoner was brought up, she looked subdued but in better health. The trial started and witnesses were called. Eventually Police Sergeant Dallimore took the stand and told the jury of how they had found the girl and the subsequent arrest and interrogation of the prisoner.

Then the court clerk shouted "Doctor Alexander Courtney" and a young man made his way to the stand. His manner caught Melody's attention and she leaned forward in her seat to get a better view; he looked so familiar and she searched her memory desperately trying to place him. She watched him intently as he took the oath and listened with interest as he was questioned by the public prosecutor and asked to recount his part in the case, his examination of the body at the scene and the post mortem he had performed later.

He answered the questions clearly and concisely, but then it was the turn of the prisoner's counsel who knew he was fighting a lost cause but didn't want to give up just yet.

"Doctor Courtney, how was the prisoner to know her servant was in poor health?"

"It only takes a bit of common sense to notice when someone is unwell. The girl's lack of energy and pale colour would have told her so."

"The prisoner is an uneducated woman! She put her lethargy down to laziness. She had no cause to think her servant ailing." The counsel turned and smiled smugly at the jury.

"It's only my opinion, but it was obvious there was something wrong with the girl."

"As you say, that's only your opinion."

Alex looked down at his notes. "Hannah Silcox fainted in the marketplace three months ago. The apothecary took her home and told her mistress that he had concerns about her bluish complexion and that there might be something wrong with the girl's heart." He glanced at the jury of twelve men and spoke firmly. "The prisoner did have an idea that something was wrong, but obviously chose to ignore it."

"The apothecary said 'might be'. It was purely conjecture. An apothecary is not a physician."

"No, he's not. But they can be very astute. I've known them detect quite serious illness and advise patients to see a physician. If the prisoner had listened to him and taken the girl to a physician, then he would have been able to diagnose the problem. And given the appropriate advice on how to make her life more comfortable."

"But, Doctor Courtney, people in abject poverty cannot afford a physician's services…"

"She ran a boarding house," interrupted Alex, "accommodating three or four people to a room and she had the money to employ a servant...and spend time in a public house."

"Even so, a physician's fees can be exorbitant."

Melody smiled to herself. The barrister was obviously trying to discredit the young doctor's testimony by slighting the entire medical profession. She admired the tenacity of the man taking the stand.

"Saint Thomas's, The London and Saint Bartholomew's treat patients free of charge," came back the terse reply.

"That's as may be. But I say again, except for her lethargy which the prisoner took as laziness, there was no reason for concern."

"The condition was diagnosed by the apothecary," said Alex, raising his voice angrily. "The prisoner chose to disregard it. That's not ignorance, that's negligence!"

A loud cheer erupted from the spectators and an official called for 'order'.

The prisoner's barrister turned away to consult his notes, his face dark with defeat. "Doctor Courtney. If the prisoner had taken her servant to see a physician what would he have advised?"

Alex answered without hesitation. "No strenuous labour and taking frequent rests. A mixture of mandrake and foxglove would have made her life more manageable and probably prolonged her life."

"No strenuous labour and frequent rests? Do you think that would have been appropriate for a servant employed to work?"

Alex raised his hands in a gesture of despair. "The girl was not well enough to work. It would have been the prisoner's prerogative to decide what to do with her. Perhaps she should have been sent back to her parents."

"She was taken from an orphanage, Doctor."

"Then her employer could have been considered her guardian and therefore, responsible for her welfare. And this didn't include the severe punishment that was inflicted on her."

"But since the prisoner didn't consider the girl unwell, then chastising her lazy servant would seem quite in order. In effect, Hannah died because of her heart condition not because of her punishment?"

"Yes," the doctor answered. "But her punishment in this case had been extreme and her heart condition would have made her more susceptible."

"Thank you, Doctor Courtney," he said, dismissing him quickly from the stand. He didn't want the doctor to remind the jury of the catalogue of injuries the girl had sustained. The public prosecutor had already done that.

Alex gave a gentle smile as he left the witness box and looked up into the press gallery. Since Melody was the only woman there she was plain to see and their eyes met. Melody started with surprise and suddenly she knew where she had seen him. Watching him take his seat next to Sergeant Dallimore, she found her heart skipping a beat as she remembered those awful Sundays at Miss Lawson's Academy, when they had been on their way to church. He was the young gentleman standing on the steps of the library. The one she had smiled at and the reason behind her dismissal from the academy.

The counsels for the prosecution and defence were now making their closing speeches before the judge summed up the case. Melody kept her pencil moving along the page, but at the same time she also kept casting a glance towards Alex. Her mind raced with the idea of going down and introducing herself, but she felt tormented by the fact he probably wouldn't remember her. Then she realised that Sergeant Dallimore would introduce her. She would search out the sergeant and if Alex happened to be there then she would discover quite naturally, if he remembered her.

The jury started filing out and after the door had closed behind them she turned to Eric.

"I'm going downstairs to talk to the police sergeant," she said casually. "I'll only be a few minutes."

"Don't go too far. I don't think it'll take the jury too long to come to their decision."

Melody made her way down the winding stairs and into the main part of the court. Alex was standing with his back to her, talking to the sergeant and a second young man with blond hair.

"Why if it isn't Miss Kinsman," said Sergeant Dallimore, moving forward slightly to draw her into their little group. "Let me introduce you, gentlemen, to an admirable young lady who's got more pluck than any person I've met."

He introduced her first to the fair-haired young man and then she came face to face with Alex.

Melody felt as though her heart would spring out of her chest as he took her hand and raised it slowly to his lips.

"Ah, but we've met before I believe," he said softly.

"You remember me?" She couldn't hide her delight.

Suddenly someone called the sergeant's name, and giving his apologies, he left to talk to a constable standing at the door.

"I certainly do," Alex continued. "The young teacher at that awful school."

"Do you mean this is the young lady you've not stopped talking about," laughed Christian, his pale blue eyes twinkling.

"Is that true?" Melody asked.

Alex gave his friend a withering look. "I've mentioned you from time to time I must admit, but Doctor Jenner does exaggerate somewhat."

Melody gave him a bright smile. "It's so wonderful to meet you at last."

"Although not in these circumstances," said Alex, looking around the court.

Eric suddenly appeared. "Melody, they're coming back in," he called.

She suddenly had an idea. "I'm having a birthday dinner on Saturday. Please, please come, both of you. Fourteen, Hyde Park Gardens, at eight o'clock. It's just off the Bayswater Road."

She scurried away, hardly waiting for their answer. Soon she was sitting next to Eric, pencil in hand, ready for the verdict on Nancy Buckle for the murder of her servant, Hannah.

Melody had been proved right, for the production of the nativity play by the children of that parish was a resounding success. When Luke took his place at the side of the stage and began his narration in a clear, steady voice, Celia couldn't have been more surprised or delighted. The play continued, the small actors delivering their lines to perfection, their performance faultless.

Melody had arrived at the vicarage minutes before the play started. She slipped into the seat next to Olivia.

"How was it?" her aunt whispered.

"Not very pleasant, but all at an end now," she said and then added, "She was found guilty and sentenced to death."

"She deserves it, Melody. God forgive me for saying it, but she does."

"There was no doubt about the verdict. Still, it jolted me when the judge put on that black cap."

"How did she take it?"

"She screamed the foulest language I've ever heard. She had to be carried below like a madwoman."

Aunt Olivia shook her head sadly. "I thought it would be the death penalty," she said.

"I must admit, I didn't. I really believed she would be transported to Australia."

"It's not usual these days," said Olivia. She gave a chuckle. "Not since they discovered gold out there."

Melody slipped her hand through her aunt's arm and turned her attention to the children in the play. It was always better to think of nicer things at times like this. After the play, they would sing carols and eat mince pies. And on Saturday there was her belated birthday dinner to look forward to. She must remember to tell her aunt that she had invited Doctor Alex Courtney and his friend. What was his name? Melody puzzled for a few seconds trying to remember and then it came to her. Jenner, that was his name, Christian Jenner.

She turned her attention to the play and her thoughts concentrated on that first Christmas of so long ago.

Alex Courtney and Christian Jenner arrived early at Hyde Park Gardens the evening of Melody's birthday dinner, two days after the conclusion of the trial. Melody was overjoyed to see them again, especially Alex as she had feared he might not come at all after such a hasty introduction and invitation. She hadn't even waited to hear if they were free that evening and it was only later that she wondered if she had been rather rude and forward in her manner.

Aunt Olivia and Celia greeted the young men warmly and listened intently to their many views on the trial.

The aunt was disappointed that Christian Jenner wasn't related to the famous Doctor Edward Jenner, the discoverer of smallpox vaccine. However, she and Celia were stunned by the boy's elegant beauty. Tall and slender, blond and blue-eyed, Celia described him later that night, as an Adonis, a perfect model for Michelangelo's *David*, whilst Aunt Olivia called him a ladies' man and added that if he had taken to soldiering he would have had an army of females of his own.

But Melody only had eyes for Alex. For her, Alex was much more attractive, with his light brown hair and that tenderness in his hazel eyes that she remembered from her days with Miss Lawson.

It was to be an informal dinner with just a few chosen guests and these were to include the Reverend Ansell and his wife who had still not arrived. The table was nearly set with the best silver and glasses, lying on a snow-white linen tablecloth. As Aunt Olivia and Tilly were in the kitchen and Celia was engrossed in conversation with Christian, Alex helped Melody finish setting the places.

"I'm glad you came," she said, folding a napkin and placing it near a side plate.

"I wouldn't have missed this for the world," he said.

"After dinner you must tell me all you've done in the last four years." Melody moved a chair and then exclaimed, "Oh, we're going to be an odd number. Seven of us."

"Never mind, as long as I can sit next to you, I'll be oblivious," Alex answered and then smiling added, "I couldn't believe it when I saw you at the trial. I knew you straight away."

"I'm afraid it took me a little while to remember you. I don't think I really looked at you properly those days you were standing on the library steps. I wasn't supposed to be looking round at anything never mind someone."

He chuckled. "I don't think a convent school is run on such strict lines. You must have been so miserable in that God forsaken place."

She gave a half-smile and cast her eyes over the table. "We need another napkin."

Excusing herself she made her way to the cabinet in the hall, but as she searched through the linen, the doorknocker resounded sharply.

Aunt Olivia called out from the kitchen. "Would you get that, dear. We're up to our elbows in flour and gravy salt in here."

Melody flung open the front door revealing the Reverend Ansell and his wife beaming with pleasure on the doorstep.

"Happy belated birthday, Melody. I hope we're not late," said Mrs Ansell.

"Not at all," she answered and then she let out a scream of delight that sent the vicar into robust laughter. "Papa! Papa! You're here too!" A portly man had suddenly stepped forward from out of the shadows where he had been waiting his turn to surprise his daughter. The vicar and his wife stood aside to let father and daughter hug each other and then ushered them indoors out of the cold.

Her arm round her father's rotund waist, Melody led him into the dining room. "Look everyone. It's Papa," she called, hardly able to hold back her tears of joy.

Minute's later Aunt Olivia scurried from the kitchen and greeted her brother with a whispered, "Thank goodness you're here. I've been on tenterhooks all day wondering if you'd make it on time."

Melody had been in the process of introducing the guests to each other, but caught the surreptitious comment from her aunt. "Do you mean this was all planned?" she asked, glancing from aunt to friend and then back to aunt.

"Like a military operation," said the brigadier. "And very well organised if I may say so."

Celia fanned herself vigorously. "We didn't postpone your dinner because of the play," she admitted. "It was because the brigadier couldn't get away until now and we so wanted him to be here for your dinner and Christmas and the New Year."

Melody smiled and hugged her father closer. "You're staying for Christmas and the New Year too. This is wonderful," she said.

Tilly bustled in and out, bringing the tureens of vegetables and the brigadier performed the task of slicing the large piece of beef, even though Alex offered with the boastful quip that he could wield a knife with expertise.

After they had eaten, Brigadier Kinsman suggested forgetting the usual tradition of the ladies retiring and leaving the gentlemen with their port and cigars.

"I don't think Melody agrees with it, anyway," he said, winking at his daughter.

"It's a ridiculous custom," she answered. "Why should women be excluded from interesting conversation and be sent to the drawing room to gossip on their own?"

"Who says it's interesting conversation?" asked the reverend. "Sometimes it's a load of old twaddle and you ladies are not missing anything."

Aunt Olivia grimaced. "Yes, but only my niece would want to change convention. No wonder the editor of The Cork Street Journal gave her work. He was probably afraid she might break his windows."

"Certainly not, Aunt," said Melody pretending offence. "He gave me work because I'm good at what I do. He just couldn't ignore my genius."

"What's this editor's name?" asked the brigadier.

"Wyngate. Guy Edward Wyngate," said Melody.

Brigadier Kinsman thought for a moment. "You don't mean *the* Guy Wyngate, from *The Evening Chronicle*?"

Melody realised she had been caught unprepared. "I'm sorry, Papa. I don't know much about him."

The brigadier turned to his sister. "Olivia, you remember Guy Wyngate, don't you?" When she shook her head, he explained. "One of the first war correspondents during the Crimea. He used to send back comprehensive reports on the battles. They were very informative."

Suddenly Olivia remembered. "Of course, Guy Wyngate. We used to read his column all the time. Didn't he receive a medal from the queen?"

Brigadier Kinsman nodded. "I'm embarrassed to say I don't remember why he won a medal. I know it was for something courageous." He started laughing. "But then when someone wins a medal, it's usually for bravery, isn't it."

Olivia turned to the reverend. "Do you remember why he won the medal?"

"I'm afraid not, dear lady," he said, shaking his head.

"It was probably for fending off female journalists whilst under enemy fire," laughed Celia.

Melody threw a napkin at her.

As laughter echoed round the table, Melody glanced at each guest, her heart soaring with the pleasure, but then she noticed Doctor Jenner. He seemed subdued, staring into his wineglass as though it fascinated him.

"Do young doctors always live at the top of the house?" gasped Celia, hanging onto Melody's arm.

"Probably. The rooms are much cheaper," she laughed.

Olivia followed a few steps behind them. "Well, Alex talked about renting a townhouse. And then we won't have all these stairs to climb."

"Thank goodness," said Celia. "Will Doctor Jenner share this house with him?"

"I have no idea," said Olivia.

It was five days after Melody's birthday dinner and the ladies had been invited to luncheon with Alex and Christian. The cab had dropped them off in front of a four-storey Georgian house, with wrought iron railings encompassing a small garden and large sash windows.

"I can't remember stairs being so steep," said Olivia, holding her side to ease the cramp.

They reached the top landing and waited while Olivia caught her breath. Celia fussed with her hair, curling her finger round thick, blonde ringlets and adjusting her bonnet.

Melody looked around her. "It's not a bad lodging house, really," she admitted, noticing that it was kept clean and in good order by the landlady. "Alex told me that some doctors live in appalling conditions."

"But surely his family would have wanted Alex to be comfortable," said Celia. "While he's making his way in the world."

Melody grinned. "Do you mean until he makes his fortune as physician to the rich and influential citizens of London? Somehow I think Alex will always want to treat the poorer classes."

Celia tossed her head indignantly and refused to answer.

They tapped on the door and it was immediately thrown open by Alex. "Dear, dear ladies, I said one o'clock and it's exactly the hour."

"I like to be punctual," smiled Olivia, stepping into the room.

Although the attic rooms, Alex and Christian had made themselves cosy. The room they entered was obviously the main living area, furnished with a couch and two armchairs, a dresser and bookshelves. At the far side was a small oval table littered with medical books. But a wonderful fire burnt brightly in the grate, since the weather was still very cold and there was a hint of snow in the air. Melody could see a second door that obviously led to the bedroom. Glancing around, she saw the table set for a meal, the flames of the fire reflecting in the cut glass goblets.

"Would you like some wine?" asked Alex.

"Do you have any tea?" Olivia replied.

Alex looked crestfallen. "No, I'm afraid not."

"Wine will do for me," said Celia, wandering over to the table and examining the books. She turned the pages of a large tome.

"Then we'll have wine," nodded Melody.

Alex had been watching Celia's interest in his medical literature and suspended his action of pouring out four glasses. "Those books won't be of any interest to you."

Her eyes suddenly became wider at the diagrams. "Goodness me!" she exclaimed.

Alex walked across to her and smiling politely closed the book and guided her back to where the others were taking off their coats. Melody frowned. Why had Alex prevented Celia from examining the book? Did he think that a woman shouldn't be privy to such things? She hoped not and then dismissed the notion from her mind.

Doctor Courtney was young and his outlook on life must be progressive: he wouldn't have the same attitude as so many of his sex. He probably didn't want Celia to be put off her meal by seeing grisly drawings, she thought, smiling.

"Don't spill it on your clothes," murmured Alex, offering the glasses to Olivia and Celia now seated on the couch.

"This is a lovely room, Alex," said Melody. "You have a glorious view of Kensington Gardens." She walked to the window.

Alex carried two glasses to her and offered her one. "Yes, I often stare out at the trees. It helps me think." He took a sip of his wine. "I'm so pleased you've come. I've been looking forward to seeing you again."

Melody turned and smiled. "And I've been looking forward to seeing you."

"What's this about you wanting to be a reporter? Are you actually employed by a newspaper?"

Melody shook her head sadly. "No, I'm only freelance. But I live in hope that I'll be offered a position sometime in the future."

Alex pulled a face. "Well, I suppose it's better than being a schoolteacher."

"Much better. And a lot more interesting," she smiled.

"Well, I hope you're successful."

"Oh, do you, Alex? It would mean so much to me if you agreed that women should have a profession."

Alex gave a nervous cough. "I'm not saying that exactly. Perhaps a woman is better off in the home bringing up a family." Seeing her shocked expression he added hastily, "What I'm saying is that I hope you do well, since you've worked so hard to achieve it."

Melody felt slightly disappointed with his answer and tried to change the subject. "Where's Doctor Jenner?"

"He should be here soon." He pulled his watch from his waistcoat pocket. "I hope he's not too late. I've employed the landlady to make us luncheon. She's an excellent cook and she and her daughter are bringing it up at one-thirty."

Suddenly the door opened and Christian stuck his head round. "Good afternoon ladies." He gestured to Alex. "May I have a private word with you?"

Alex stepped out onto the landing where a heated discussion took place before Alex came back into the room, his eyes dark with anger. "Jenner can't join us." Melody saw Celia's face crumple at the news. "He has an appointment elsewhere."

"He was in a bit of a hurry," laughed Melody, trying to ease the situation.

"Meeting a lady," whispered Alex, so that only Melody could hear.

"Oh, well. That's natural," she sighed.

"He promised to stay and have luncheon," said Alex bitterly. "Christian is always meeting a lady."

Melody didn't reply, but exchanged glances with her aunt, smiling slightly. It seemed Olivia's observations of Christian Jenner had been absolutely right. Doctor Jenner was a ladies' man and enjoyed the attentions of the fairer sex.

Alex noticed her amused expression. "But he's a good friend. We've been through a lot together. He can offer some sensible advice when asked."

"Your loyalty to your friend is admirable," said Melody. "I only hope he appreciates it."

CHAPTER FIVE

Christmas was fast approaching and the household at Hyde Park Gardens threw themselves into the spirit of the festive season. Alex and Christian set up the tree and then helped decorate it with ribbons and candles. Presents were heaped about its base and then the rooms were trimmed with holly and ivy. On Christmas Eve, Melody and Celia, accompanied by Alex and Christian went carol singing with the Reverend Ansell and a motley assortment of his congregation.

Carrying lamps and dressed warmly in coats, hats and scarves, they set off from door to door, singing with gusto, their breath coming in white mist and their noses and cheeks stinging with the cold. All around them were signs of Christmas; the chestnut seller standing by the brazier; shop windows laden with meats, vegetables and fruit; the stalls covered with toys and yet more, selling ribbons of satin and delicate lace. And all about, shoppers carried home their precious gifts.

On Christmas Day, only Alex came to dinner as Christian was on duty at Saint George's Hospital, much to Celia's disappointment. But her face lit up when she was told he would join them a little later for the musical evening they had planned.

The following day, the news was circulated that Nancy Buckle wouldn't see the New Year. She was to hang on the thirtieth of December, the execution to take place outside Newgate Prison.

"Are you listening, Miss Kinsman?"

Guy Wyngate's voice seemed to be far away, a distant murmur that barely impinged on Melody's conscious mind. She quickly turned her attention to the editor. They were in his office; he seated behind his desk, she sitting opposite him.

She bit her lip. "Yes, Mr Wyngate, I heard you. You want me to cover the execution."

"With Eric, of course."

"Of course."

He watched her closely, as if studying her. "If you can't do it, then say so now and I'll send Holbrook."

Melody tried to keep her temper under control, but she knew her cheeks were flushing. Why did he persist in provoking her? Did he realise he was doing it, or was it just force of habit for him?

"I can do it, Mr Wyngate. After all, it's only an assignment, like all the rest."

"Good, that's what I like to hear."

Seeing that the interview was over, Melody gathered up her gloves and umbrella. "Thank you. I appreciate your consideration." She felt the words stick in her throat and quickly rose from her seat and left the office closing the door quietly behind her.

Marsh was talking to Eric as she entered the outer office. "Are you all right?" said Eric, a frown darkening his face. "He shouldn't have given you that kind of thing, not a young lady like you."

"No, Eric," she answered. "If I want to enter journalism then I must accept whatever comes my way, no matter how unpleasant."

Marsh pursued his lips. "Might not be unpleasant. A drop can be sweet as a nut sometimes."

"But she's never been to an execution," said Eric.

Melody began to feel irritated. "I've been given this to do and I'll do it," she snapped. "Please stop mollycoddling me." Glaring at them, she picked up her skirt and swept out of the office.

"I'll take care of her," said Eric.

"More like she'll take care of you," said Marsh with a chuckle.

It was a desperately cold morning when Melody and Eric set off. The sky was already darkening with snow-filled clouds and as they arrived outside Newgate Prison, a flurry of flakes was already starting to float to the ground.

An execution always attracted a crowd and the execution of Nancy Buckle was no exception. Eric pushed his way through the thickness of the throng that had already gathered and Melody followed him, trying to avoid the hands that tried to grab her and the foul language that assailed her ears. It seemed to be mayhem.

"I'm afraid a hanging seems to bring out the worst in people," said Eric, as he reached the far side and found a space for them.

"Why are they so…."

"Violent?" asked Eric.

"Yes, violent and uncontrolled."

"Fear, I guess. I suppose they're attracted and yet repelled at the same time at watching someone die."

"It's terrible," said Melody, looking to left and right at the people of London who wanted to see a hanging.

"There's talk of reform," said Eric. "Mr Wyngate says that public executions might be a thing of the past soon. They'll be conducted privately inside the prison."

"The sooner the better," agreed Melody.

Nancy Buckle had made her servant's life hell, hanging her from a hook in the roof of the cellar and whipping her until she died through pain and exhaustion. And now she was to hang. Two thousand people screamed for her blood and the soldiers detailed to hold back the crowd, showed a fear usually reserved for battle. Rifles ready, they surrounded the scaffold outside the prison, keeping at bay those that wished to push forward to reach the condemned woman.

When she appeared at the gate, escorted by guards on either side, the roar from the throng was deafening. Then hoots, whistles, cheers and obscenities filled the air, causing the military to raise their bayonets at the ready.

Melody and Eric were already working, she scribbling as fast as she could, he filling his pad with rough charcoal sketches.

"I need to be in a better position," shouted Melody above the roar. She was starting to be shoved back and kept losing her balance.

Eric quickly looked around. "Over there," he said. He pushed his way through the crowd and scrambled up onto a parapet. He pulled Melody up with him.

Now Melody had a much better view, but when she saw the rope suspended from a crossbeam, supported by posts and standing on the wide platform raised above the heads of the people, she began to wish she were elsewhere. But worse than that was the sight and sounds of the crowd. They seemed like animals, fighting and tearing at one another in their eagerness. She turned to Eric to suggest moving, but was halted by the appearance of Nancy Buckle starting to climb the steps on her last journey.

She seemed a great deal thinner and her eyes had a blank stare, but there was a strange calmness about her. She walked up the steps unaided, her hands secured behind her back, and made her way over to the trapdoor, which would send her into oblivion. The chaplain accompanied her, muttering into his prayer book, knowing that his place in all this was purely decorative. Nancy Buckle neither wanted nor needed his presence.

Melody gripped her pencil tighter, feeling the nausea rise in her throat. She wanted to leave. She wanted to find some nice park to walk in, a lake to boat on, or sit and have tea with Aunt Olivia. Anything was better than this, she thought.

"How long will it take," she yelled above the sound of the crowd.

"The hangman knows his job. It'll be done in five minutes."

Melody flicked over a page in her notebook and kept writing, concentrating on the scene in front of her, her eyes on the scaffold. The prayers were finished and the chaplain stood aside while the hangman came forward to place the bag of sackcloth over the head of the waiting prisoner.

Suddenly, he reeled back as Nancy Buckle hit out at him with her foot and caught him a glancing blow on the shin. Another roar went up, only this time it was laughter at the hangman's comical dance on the scaffold.

However, the grim business of the day soon returned. "Keep the bag off, keep it off so we can see 'er face," screeched one woman and the rest of the crowd took this up.

The prison officials standing on the scaffold began to fidget nervously and one elderly gentleman with a profusion of whiskers gestured to the hangman to get on with his duty. Stepping forward once more, he quickly bound Nancy Buckle's legs with a thick leather strap and thrust the bag over her head, following this with the noose round her neck.

The hangman took his place at the lever, waiting for the signal. A deathly hush fell over the crowd causing Melody to look about her in surprise at the sudden and sharp contrast in their manner. Tension filled the air as though everyone had stopped breathing. And when the signal was given the well-oiled lever silently slipped into place and the trapdoor opened. A murmur rose up from the crowd as the unfortunate woman dropped, twisting and spinning in space.

Melody almost stopped writing at the horror of Nancy Buckle's death, her mouth dry, her heart beating furiously. Eric suddenly lost his balance and fell from the parapet on top of the group standing close by, landing on his shoulder with a cry of pain. This simple act of clumsiness released the tension in those surrounding the ledge and a burst of laughter erupted on all sides.

A woman yanked him to his feet. "Good thing you 'adn't a noose round your neck, lad. Or you'd follow 'er example," she said, jabbing her thumb in the direction of the swinging corpse.

Melody climbed down to join him and helped him pick up his drawing pad and charcoal that had been scattered in all directions. Looking about her, she sincerely hoped she would never have to witness an execution again, but with an editor like Guy Wyngate, she knew it was a forlorn hope.

"I think it's disgraceful," said Alex, as he folded the newspaper and placed it on the table.

"Don't you like my account?" Melody couldn't hide her disappointment. She wanted Alex, more than anyone else, to appreciate her work.

"No, not your report. That's excellent. I'm talking about the sheer lunacy of the editor to send you to cover it."

"But he only offered me the assignment, Alex. It was my decision to do it."

"It was no place for a young lady like you."

"I'm a journalist, it's what I like doing," she said.

"Going to an execution?"

"Not necessarily an execution. I mean reporting the news in general. In this case it happened to be an execution, but it could be anything."

"And you follow the news wherever it takes you?"

"Yes, of course."

"Even into dangerous situations?"

"If it's necessary. But I always try to be careful. I don't take any unnecessary risks." She gave a sigh, her despondency evident.

Alex had remained by the table, but when he saw her sadness he came to sit next to her on the couch.

Taking her hand he kissed her fingers. "I'm not chastising you, please don't think that," he said gently. "It's just that I'm afraid for you. A man is used to protecting the woman he…cares for. I don't want you to come to any harm."

Melody began to feel more cheerful. "Why, Doctor Courtney, I didn't know you did care."

"Of course I do, you silly goose. I care for you a great deal."

She glanced at him and saw a look in his hazel eyes that she didn't recognise. "That's nice to know. But I'm a grown woman," she said.

He smiled and briefly caressed her cheek. "I did notice that."

She caught his hand. "I love what I'm doing and I do want you to understand that."

He let out a slow sigh. "I do understand. I only want to see you happy."

"I am happy, Alex. Really I am."

He didn't answer; he wanted to change the subject. "Are you looking forward to tonight?"

Melody nodded. "Oh, yes and it's so strange. I don't usually enjoy social occasions but to celebrate the New Year seems special this time."

"It might be because we're all attending including your father."

"And Christian too?" asked Melody.

"I don't know about Christian," Alex said. "He spoke of coming but he wasn't sure."

"If he isn't there, Celia will be so disappointed."

Alex looked anxiously into the flames leaping in the grate. "I hope Celia isn't losing her heart to Christian."

"Goodness me, why ever not?"

"She could get hurt, that's why."

"By Christian! How?"

"It's hard to explain." Seeing she wouldn't be satisfied with such a vague answer he tried to clarify the situation. "He's a good doctor, Melody. There's no doubt about that. But he has something of a reputation."

"What kind of reputation," she said slowly.

"A reputation for charming rich widows and married ladies out of their money."

Melody threw back her head and started to laugh. "I thought for a minute you were serious."

"I am."

Melody reached over and tapped Alex on the cheek. "Then I think you're being unkind. Christian has a good heart."

"Yes, but he's also ambitious. He saw an easy way of acquiring fame and fortune quicker than any average doctor and that was by using *all* his talents. He wants to reach the top of the tree before he's thirty." Alex began to feel uncomfortable and rubbed his hand over a troubled forehead.

"You really are serious, aren't you," she said, watching his pained expression.

"He's been my friend a long time and I hoped I could turn him into a respectable physician."

She pondered on this for a moment. "Well, Celia has no influence and she certainly isn't wealthy, for all she's the daughter of a baron."

"That's what I'm talking about. Jenner is fond of her, but I don't think he sees any advantage in wooing her."

The clock started to chime twelve and Melody jumped to her feet. "Goodness me, I have an appointment with Mr Wyngate at twelve-thirty."

"Shall I come with you?"

"Certainly not," she said.

Within five minutes they were at the door and hailing a cab that dropped Alex off at the hospital and then took Melody on to Cork Street and her appointment with the editor of The Cork Street Journal.

Marsh was at his usual place in the outer office when she rushed in. "Ah, Miss Kinsman," he took his watch from his pocket. "And with at least two minutes to spare." He was eating his midday meal and small bits of cheese were stuck in his whiskers.

"Is Mr Wyngate in?"

"No, he had to go out unexpectedly, but he's asked me to deal with this business." He indicated the chair opposite him and she sat down feeling bewildered.

"What business?"

He reached into his desk drawer and took out two pieces of paper and passed them over to her. She immediately saw *Contract of Employment* printed in large letters on the top of each sheet.

"Please read it and then sign both copies. You keep one and the newspaper keeps the other. But please take note that the contract is for two years and if you cannot fulfil it then you must not sign." He watched her closely over his spectacles.

"Mr Wyngate is giving me a contract?" she gasped in surprise.

"Yes, although I warned him strongly against it," he said dryly. She pulled a face at him, picked up the document and started to read. It set out, in legal language, the terms and conditions of employing her as a reporter for The Cork Street Journal. As Marsh had said, it covered a period of two years and stated that all assignments, whether instigated by the newspaper or by her own soliciting must be the sole property of the said newspaper, for which she would receive an agreed commission of five guineas for every article submitted. "What's it to be, Miss Kinsman?"

"May I borrow your pen, please?" she answered as calmly as possible.

Her calm manner didn't extend past Marsh's office door, as once she was through it, she was off to the print room to tell Eric her good news. It seemed he already knew and beamed from ear to ear. And then it was out into the cold December day like a whirlwind, colliding with someone just coming through the front door. Melody was almost knocked off her feet by the impact and was steadied by a strong hand catching her arm.

"For goodness sake Miss Kinsman, do you have to rush around as though the end of the world was coming?"

She looked up into deep brown eyes and laughed, "If it was, then I would be hurrying. To be the first journalist to report on it."

His face crinkled into a smile. "And I'm sure you would be the first there." A moment of embarrassed silence followed as her gaze went to his hand still resting on her elbow. He quickly removed it. "I take it you've seen Marsh?"

"Yes, and thank you for the contract. I have my copy here." She pattered the leather purse hanging from her wrist.

"So you agree with the terms and conditions?"

"Absolutely."

"I'll expect you to abide by them."

"But of course, and I shall expect you to do the same," she said. He was watching her in that disarming way of his so she felt compelled to add, "I have a social engagement this evening."

"So I hear. The New Year ball at the Carlton Club."

"How on earth did you know that?" she said.

"A good journalist has his sources. Always remember that, Miss Kinsman."

"I will, Mr Wyngate."

"Off you go, then." He turned to push open the door. "Happy New Year."

"Thank you and a Happy New Year to you too," she answered.

Melody couldn't understand where her self-assured manner disappeared to that evening at the Carlton Club. It seemed as if it had been blown away on the breath of tumultuous joy and hope. To be with Alex was one thing, but to dance with him at a social event seemed the most wonderful thing of all.

Their attention to one another made many a person whisper behind hand or fan and heads to nod in their direction. Aunt Olivia and the brigadier couldn't help smiling, knowing that tender young feelings were starting to grow. Melody and Alex made great efforts to remain together for the entire evening, but were often thwarted when one or the other was dragged away to be introduced to a member of the gathered party. However, the formalities over, they would return to each other and continue the evening side by side.

"They seem so perfectly matched," whispered Aunt Olivia sitting next to the brigadier. "Do you think anything will come of it?"

"Who knows with a girl like Melody," he said.

He had stopped second-guessing his daughter long ago. He knew his daughter was not one for affairs of the heart and yet watching the pair he couldn't help seeing what a lovely couple they made. Melody was certainly the most beautiful woman there. Her becoming turquoise gown of watered silk swished as she moved, emphasising her youth and vitality. The silk flowers that adorned her hair made her seem like a nymph from the woods, a creature of nature, at home among the trees and flora of creation. The brigadier bristled with pride and thought that it was little wonder Alex couldn't take his eyes off her.

"Oh, dear! Look at Celia," said Olivia sadly.

"What's wrong with Celia?" asked the brigadier, turning his attention to the young girl swirling around in the arms of a handsome merchant banker. "From what I've seen, she's not stopped dancing all evening."

"Yes, her dance card is full, but her attention went straight to Doctor Jenner when he arrived."

"I hadn't noticed," he admitted.

"Men never do," she said. "I think she's quite smitten with him, but it's plain to see he's not interested."

"Not interested in Celia? Never!"

"I think he has other interests."

"And what might they be?" The brigadier had always found his sister's theories highly amusing.

"Just watch him and you'll see for yourself," said Olivia, opening her fan and sending cool wafts of air round her neck. For all that it was winter, the room was remarkably warm with the heat from the numerous candles flickering in the crystal chandeliers and the many bodies spinning round the dance floor.

The brigadier watched Doctor Jenner, who was standing on the opposite side of the room and seemed to be surrounded by a bevy of females all vying for his attention. They were fluttering their eyelashes at him and giggling girlishly and yet a great majority of them were at least in their middle years.

"He's being pampered and admired by women who should know better and he's using all his charm and appeal to get what he wants," said Olivia, after a few minutes.

"And what do you believe he wants?" asked the brigadier. He chuckled mischievously, his love of teasing Olivia quite apparent.

"You know exactly what he's after, Liam. And my guess is that poor little Celia will fall short of it."

They turned their eyes on Celia who seemed to be enjoying herself as she skipped around the room with the good-looking banker.

The dance ended and Alex with Melody on his arm came towards them. Melody sank down on the couch next to her aunt.

"Goodness me, the polka is a strenuous dance," she exclaimed. She opened her fan and wafted her face vigorously.

"You need a glass of fruit punch to cool you down," said Alex. "Would anyone else like some?"

Aunt Olivia and the brigadier declined and he strode off to the table laden with a cold buffet.

"Are you enjoying yourself, my dear," said the brigadier, patting his daughter's hand.

"Oh yes, very much Papa," Melody answered. "Everything is perfect. It's been a remarkable day, hasn't it? What with my contract with The Cork Street Journal and then being here with everyone."

Olivia gave her brother a knowing look. "She's talking about Alex in the main."

"No, Aunt. I'm talking about being here with you all, although Alex is special and I'm not afraid to admit that."

The banker had finally released Celia and she now joined them. The brigadier stood to give her his seat and she sat down elegantly next to Melody.

"Do you think he'll ask me to dance?" Celia whispered behind her fan.

Melody knew exactly to whom she was referring. "I don't know. Why don't you ask him?"

"Oh, I couldn't do that! What a thing to suggest."

The alarm on her face caused Melody to giggle, "Well I would, if I wanted to dance with a particular gentleman."

"You've no shame, Melody Kinsman. No shame at all."

Alex returned with two glasses of punch. Seeing Celia sitting next to Melody he volunteered to return to the table to get another, but Melody had just spotted Christian Jenner coming towards them and had decided to take matters into her own hands.

"I'm so glad you're here, Christian. Celia was just saying how thirsty she is and how much she'd like a glass of punch." She smiled pleasantly ignoring the look of horror coming from her friend.

"Certainly," said Christian, giving a polite bow. He went to fetch the requested drink.

"I suppose you'll ask him to dance with me next," said Celia incredulously.

"I might at that."

"Please don't, Melody. I'll die of embarrassment." But even Celia could appreciate the impish side to her friend's behaviour and she burst into laughter.

"I've just heard something about your Mr Wyngate, Melody. From Lady Delmont," said Alex.

"He's not *my* Mr Wyngate."

"Please tell," said Olivia, ignoring her niece.

Christian returned with the drink and handed it to Celia. "It seems his uncle is Sir Jack Wetherby, the proprietor of *The Evening Chronicle*," continued Alex. "Wyngate worked for him during the war and when he came back to England he decided he wanted to set up his own newspaper."

"The Cork Street Journal," nodded Melody.

"Yes, but there seems be something of a rift between them."

"What kind of rift?" asked the brigadier.

"Sir Jack didn't want Wyngate to leave. He was his best reporter, you see. Not to mention the fact he was a war hero and that sort of thing sells newspapers. Also, Wyngate is in line to inherit the paper when Sir Jack is gone, as the old gentleman has no children."

"It's so sad when there's a rift between members of a family," said Olivia.

"It certainly is," her brother agreed sadly.

Melody pondered on this fresh piece of news about her employer, but Christian Jenner suddenly diverted her attention. Throughout the conversation he had been gazing around the ballroom as though completely disinterested in Alex's revelations. However, Melody couldn't help noticing the muscles tighten in his jaw and he had a look of a man who had the weight of the world on his shoulders. She wondered if Doctor Jenner and the editor of The Cork Street Journal might know each other in some way.

The orchestra struck up with a waltz and Alex held out his hand to Melody. "Would you like to dance?" he asked.

She smiled with pleasure and allowed herself to be led once more onto the floor. Once in each other's arms it was as if they were oblivious to those around them. Alex didn't seem to be aware that there were others waiting to dance with Melody and she didn't seem to care that they were waiting.

The group they had left smiled after them.

"Celia, would you care to dance?"

Celia jumped with surprise when she realised Christian was speaking to her. "Thank you. I'd love to."

Picking up her full skirt, she let herself be swept away on a cloud of optimism.

"That leaves only you and me," said the brigadier.

"I'm afraid not, dear brother. I've promised this one to the Reverend Ansell."

As Melody twirled around the ballroom, nothing mattered but that moment. Life couldn't be sweeter and she looked forward to the future with an elation that almost took her breath away. She was in Alex's arms and his very closeness was awakening a desire in her that she could barely understand. The thought that she might be falling in love was making her head spin. This had never been part of her grand plan in life.

But it was the end of the old year and the start of a new one and as far as Melody was concerned, 1865 was going to be a wonderful year. Unfortunately, life at Hyde Park Gardens was about to change. Five days later the telegram arrived.

CHAPTER SIX

Melody wasn't at home when the telegram came. It was addressed to Celia, who immediately handed it to the brigadier. Tearing it open he read only eight words:

HIS LORDSHIP SERIOUSLY ILL STOP
PLEASE COME HOME QUICKLY STOP

It was from Mrs Carr, the housekeeper at Monkswood.

By the time Melody arrived home, Celia and the brigadier had already left, catching the afternoon train to Guildford.

"It must be critical if Mrs Carr felt it necessary to send a telegram," said Melody, reading the message for the second time.

Olivia frowned. "She's certainly not a woman to get in a flap over nothing."

"I wonder what he's ailing with."

"Your father said he'll write as soon as he's assessed the situation."

The following week seemed endless for Melody, as she waited for a letter from her father. But on the premise that no news was good news, she kept up her spirits and concentrated on her work. She had now settled into a steady routine, going where the editor sent her, but also keeping her eyes and ears alert for any groundbreaking news. She still visited Scotland Yard and pestered Police Sergeant Dallimore for any bits of information. And she was slowly building up a network of reliable sources.

Through all this, she and Alex tried to meet every day. Sometimes they would have luncheon together or go for a walk in the park. Alex was a frequent visitor at

Hyde Park Gardens and he in his turn, had given her the 'royal tour' of Saint George's showing her with great pride, the new laboratory for investigating diseases.

The brigadier had been gone nine days when the letter finally arrived. Melody had been reporting on a society wedding and it wasn't an assignment she enjoyed. But Henri Careme who usually wrote the Society Page, had had to have a tooth extracted and was away for the morning, so the editor had asked her to go instead. Melody smiled to herself as she made her way to meet Alex in the park, glad that they had arranged to see each other, even for an hour. It had been a tedious duty writing an account of the wedding; of how the bridegroom looked down on his new wife in a condescending manner and she kept her eyes on the ground in demure complacency. Not to mention having to describe not only the wedding gown but also the clothes of the female guests. Henri was much more adept and Melody hoped she hadn't let him down.

Melody found a bench overlooking the Serpentine and wrapped her thick woollen coat more closely round her. It was a cold day and the wind coming from the north-east, chased away any warmth from the insipid winter sun and sent stormy clouds scurrying across the sky. The trees swayed and bent and now and again a fragile branch would snap and tumble to the ground. She watched as two little girls competed with each other in their skipping abilities, while their nanny looked on in attentive admiration.

And then she saw Alex hurrying down the path towards her. He greeted her by taking her hands and kissing first her fingers and then her forehead. "Sorry I'm late," he said. He looked around. "Shall we walk, it's rather chilly for sitting?" She agreed wholeheartedly. The few minutes on the park bench watching the two little girls had already made her shiver with cold. They walked slowly, arm in arm. Alex suddenly squeezed her hand. "Melody, do you think that editor of yours would give you some time off?"

"Why?" she asked.

"I'd like you to come with me to visit my parents."

"I'd love to, Alex. But the paper is busy at the moment."

"You're still entitled to some leave, surely. He can't make you work constantly."

She didn't answer at first. She had never considered having any time away from the paper. After all, she had been employed for barely two weeks and she wanted to make a good impression. Somehow taking time off made her feel uncomfortable at the moment.

"It would be nice to meet your parents," she said, after a few minutes. "But I'd rather wait until Papa's letter arrives. It should be here very soon."

"Poor Celia. I wonder how she is?"

"Papa will take care of her and Mrs Carr is an exceptional housekeeper. She's been with the family since before Celia was born."

"Let's hope all is well. However, my parents have been asking about you and they're eager to meet you."

They walked in silence for a while and Melody thought of what Alex had told her about his family in Colchester, Essex. His father was a prominent doctor, has had been his father before him. Alex was the youngest of three children; his older sisters both married. He had also told Melody that he had inherited money on the death of his grandfather and some property that he was letting at the moment. She would like to meet Alex's family but at present there seemed to be so much to do.

"My goodness, is that Tilly?" said Melody, startled out of her troubled thoughts.

The maid came hurrying towards them, holding onto her cap for fear of it being carried away by the wind. Her mouth was moving but her words were being blown from her. It was only when she was nearly on them that they could hear her frantic words.

"Miss Melody, you must come home straight away. Madam has a letter from the brigadier. It's not good, miss. Not good at all."

Alex took Melody's hand and they hurried through the park and along the Bayswater Road. They were soon at Hyde Park Gardens and rushing through the door, went straight to the sitting room where Aunt Olivia was sitting on the couch, a piece of paper held limply in her hand. She didn't say anything, but simply handed the letter to Melody. Alex read it with her, his hands resting lightly on her shoulders. It was short and to the point.

The baron had died. It seemed he had developed a tumour in his stomach but had refused to send for Celia, not wanting to distress her. When his illness had become advanced, he had finally agreed that his daughter should come home. By the time she arrived he was so weak he could hardly speak and kept drifting in and out of consciousness. He had passed away peacefully his daughter holding his hand. They were now in the process of organising the funeral and Melody and Olivia were required at Monkswood.

"It looks like you're going to need that leave after all," whispered Alex.

The editor of The Cork Street Journal showed his displeasure at Melody taking time off and she winced at his dark expression. However, when she explained about the death of the baron and how her friend needed her, he sighed and giving a half-smile conceded that he would hate to be the cause of friction between friends.

The following day, Alex accompanied Melody and her aunt to Paddington Station to see them off on their journey. The whole vast area was a bustling hive of activity, with passengers hurrying about and porters trying to keep up with them while pushing trolleys loaded with luggage. All around was the noise of steam engines and the acrid smell of smoke. Melody and Olivia were swathed in yards of black crape, proclaiming to the world that they were now in mourning, but they kept their tears to themselves and even laughed with pleasure when Alex managed to find them a compartment to themselves. As the train pulled out of the station, Melody yanked down the window and called farewell until she could see him no longer.

They spoke very little on the journey into Surrey, both women alone with their thoughts as the countryside passed by at a stately sixty miles an hour. Just over an hour later, they were in Guildford and there the brigadier waited for them with the carriage, ready to take them to Monkswood.

A short time later they were travelling along the drive and drawing up in front of the great doors of Celia's ancestral home. As the footman unloaded the luggage and carried it indoors, Melody looked around at the late baron's estate.

Once a Tudor manor, then a Stuart palace, Monkswood had slowly evolved into a Georgian monstrosity. It had been some time since she had last visited and she could see that things had become more rundown than ever. She noticed a broken windowpane on the top floor and the whole structure was in need of new plaster and a lick of paint. Once inside, she sighed at the peeling wallpaper and the patches where portraits by Van Dyke and landscapes by Rubens had once hung, now sold to pay debts.

Celia's joy at their arrival was overwhelming and her tears began to flow freely once more, as she hugged and kissed them. Mrs Carr made them comfortable in the best bedrooms and welcomed them with an excellent dinner. Melody watched with great respect, the tall, thin woman with greying hair pulled back from her face and tucked under her cap. The housekeeper knew her days at Monkswood were numbered, as did the rest of the staff. There was a resignation about the place, a peaceful finality that had settled on the old house as if it had been awaiting the end and now it had come, it was sighing with relief.

After dinner, Melody and Aunt Olivia went to pay their respects to the baron, who was lying in state in the morning room. A large oak coffin stood on the mahogany table, a fat church candle flickering at each end. Flowers adorned the room and the flag bearing the coat of arms had been spread partially over the casket giving an appearance of faded grandeur. Melody and her aunt had to admit the baron looked peaceful and for some strange reason, at least ten years younger.

"The funeral is on Wednesday," the brigadier informed them after they had joined the others in the parlour. "And there will be a big turn out with estate workers, tenants and people from the surrounding villages. The baron was well thought of that's for sure."

"There will be a service in the church," added Celia. "And Papa will be interred in the mausoleum. Then there will be refreshments back here at the house."

"Have you thought what you'll do after the funeral?" Melody asked quietly.

The brigadier answered for her. "It's been agreed that the house should be sold, hasn't it Celia?"

She nodded sadly. "There's no money to keep it going and the staff are well aware of the situation. They'll all get excellent references. Mr Gunn is coming the day after the funeral, to read Papa's will and then I'll know how much income is available to me."

Aunt Olivia directed the next piece of information to Melody. "But at least we know where Celia will live." Aunt Olivia threw a smile at the young girl sniffing into her handkerchief. "At Hucknall Garth with us."

Seeing his daughter's surprised expression, the brigadier explained. "I never thought it worth mentioning to you because, well, I really believed it wouldn't be necessary. The baron asked me last year, if I'd be Celia's guardian until she reaches the age of twenty-one, if anything should happen to him."

"Do you mind, Melody?" asked Celia.

"Certainly not. It'll be wonderful. We'll be like sisters," she said, but then she had a dreadful thought. "I suppose your time in London is over now. You can't go dancing and to the theatre after losing your father. Society doesn't allow that."

"Yes, that's true."

"But what about the house in Hyde Park Gardens? Your Papa was paying the rent." Melody suddenly realised that the baron's death would have repercussions on her own situation. She now had a commitment to The Cork Street Journal and she needed somewhere to live. "I'll have to find lodgings."

"You will not," said her father. "I'm not having my daughter living alone in lodgings."

"But what else can I do, Papa? I have no choice."

"I'll take over the lease of Hyde Park Gardens, Melody. But you, my girl, will have to cover all the running costs, including Tilly's wages."

Melody thought for a moment. "I'm sure I can do that."

"And what about propriety?" Olivia protested. "She'll only have Tilly with her. I can't return to London. I must return to Hucknall Garth with Celia, while she completes her mourning. Is it right for two young girls to live alone without a chaperone?"

The brigadier burst into laugher at his sister's confusion. "I think Melody and Tilly will be a force to be reckoned with, don't you?"

"It still doesn't seem right."

"Oh, please don't worry, Aunt. Tilly and I will do very well," said Melody.

Melody's reassuring words didn't satisfy Aunt Olivia in the slightest. Her thoughts went to Alex Courtney and she prayed that the young doctor would behave appropriately towards her niece. In fact, it would be convenient if he proposed very soon and then she would have to give up this silly idea of being a journalist and become a wife and mother, as all women should.

The day of the funeral was cold and crisp, but the sun was making an effort to shine and there even seemed to be a small amount of warmth in its rays. The brigadier looked towards the western sky and frowned at the heavily laden rain clouds coming their way, but his worries were unfounded as the rain stayed away for most of the day. And the funeral, although desperately sad, was a satisfactory conclusion to the life of a well-loved and respected man who had brought much happiness but very little prosperity.

As the cortege made its way to the chapel, the estate workers and villagers stood beside the road, caps in hand and heads bowed. The vicar gave a passionate sermon and the brigadier a touching eulogy, during which there was many a 'God bless him' coming from the congregation who packed the small medieval building to the door. And then it was to the mausoleum to lay the baron in his final resting-place. During the entire time, Melody held Celia's hand and whispered words of comfort and support as the young girl wept into her lace handkerchief.

"I need a breath of fresh air," said Melody. "I think I'll take a walk in the garden." It was the day after the funeral and they were just finishing their breakfast.

"Mr Gunn will be arriving soon, so don't go far," advised her father, flicking over a page of his newspaper.

"I'll come with you," said Celia. "We could walk round to the side gate and then through the orchard to meet him."

Melody agreed it was a good idea and after dressing warmly, they set off on their walk with arms linked and breathing in the heavy scent of damp grass in the crisp, clean air.

The rain from the previous evening had only been spasmodic, but it was plain to see that the storm clouds were gathering and a torrential downpour was on its way. Melody and Celia walked through the garden that was devoid of flowers and rather overgrown and then passed through the side gate and into the orchard. Many times they had come here and picked the apples, to be made into pies by the cook. But now the branches were bare and they knew they wouldn't be at Monkswood to see the next harvest.

They strolled down the lane that snaked between the meadows and woodlands owned by the late baron, taking their time. In the distance they could see the village of Sutton Green with the church spire just visible and as they reached the crossroads, they spied a horse and buggy coming towards them.

"Good timing, I say," smiled Melody.

"Mr Gunn doesn't seem to be alone. I wonder who he's brought with him." Celia shielded her eyes trying to see the lawyer's companion.

Melody suddenly gave a cry of delight. "It's Alex. Alex is with him."

The buggy pulled up opposite them and Alex sprang down and caught Melody in his arms, swinging her almost off her feet.

Mr Gunn chuckled with delight. "Found this young man at the railway station. When he said he was coming to Monkswood, I thought it only right to give him a lift." He smiled at the couple greeting each other as though they had been apart for years.

Melody shook her head in disbelief. "What are you doing here?"

"Couldn't stay away from you a minute longer," laughed Alex.

"Please be serious."

"Actually he's got a good business proposition for Miss Celia," said Mr Gunn.

Alex let go of Melody and bent to kiss Celia's hand. "How are you? I do hope yesterday wasn't too much of a strain," he said softly.

"No, it went well and everyone has been so kind." She was smiling but her eyes suddenly filled with tears. "Oh, this is so silly." She pulled out her handkerchief and quickly wiped them away.

"Celia why don't you travel with me and let this young couple walk back to the house. I'm sure they've got plenty to talk about," said Mr Gunn.

Alex helped Celia into the seat. "And tell her about my idea, sir," said Alex.

"I certainly will." Mr Gunn whipped up the horse and set off towards the gates of Monkswood.

Melody and Alex began the short walk back.

"So, what's this idea of yours?" asked Melody.

"Saint George's is looking for an establishment that will serve as an isolation hospital; a sanatorium for treating patients with Tuberculosis. A country house would be perfect and I thought that if Monkswood was to be sold, then it would be ideal."

"And you suggested Monkswood?"

"Of course, I didn't know if Celia intended to sell her home, so that's why I came here myself to discuss it with her."

Melody thought for a moment. "Uncle Tom, Aunt Olivia's husband, died of consumption. I didn't know him as he died before I was born, but my aunt did tell me about his illness and how the doctors couldn't do anything for him."

"Well, we're making great strides in the treatment of diseases but we haven't discovered what causes Tuberculosis yet. We will one day, I assure you, but until that day comes we believe giving the patient peace, quiet and plenty of fresh air does help to alleviate the symptoms."

"Uncle Tom and Aunt Olivia went to Italy. The doctors told them that a drier climate would help."

"That's true, but not all patients can go abroad, so a hospital in the country might be their only chance of recovery."

She squeezed his arm. "And will you be working at this hospital?"

"Goodness me, no. I want to go back to Colchester and set up there in private practice."

"Oh, do you," she said in surprise. "I thought you intended staying at Saint George's and working with the poor and disadvantaged."

Alex tried to suppress his laugher. "The hospital was only temporary until I became a fully-fledged physician. And yes, I'll still help the poor and disadvantaged." He gave her a crooked smile. "But I still have to pay my bills and a few rich patients won't go amiss."

She gave him a push and while he tried to regain his balance, she gathered up her skirts and sped away, running up the drive towards the house. He was hot on her heels and they raced for the door, reaching it at the same time. Once there, they remembered the seriousness of the occasion and quickly composed themselves before allowing the footman to let them in.

"You're to go straight to the parlour, miss. Lawyer is just about to read the will," the footman said, giving a slight bow.

Melody and Alex did as they were told and joined the rest of the household waiting to hear the last will and testament of the late tenth Baron Sinclair.

The reading of the will was a mere formality since except for a few bequests to members of staff, including Mrs Carr, the bulk of the estate passed to Celia. After everything was completed, Mr Gunn brought Celia to tears once more by giving her an envelope addressed with the words, *To my dear daughter - To be read after my demise* in the baron's neat copperplate handwriting. She put it aside to read later as a discussion started up about the possibility of selling Monkswood to Saint George's Hospital.

The brigadier rubbed his hands together with glee. "I think it a splendid idea."

"It could be the answer to all your problems, Celia," Mr Gunn agreed.

Melody thought for a moment. "But would Saint George's buy this place? It's quite rundown."

"Well, they're looking for a suitable place without breaking the bank," said Alex. "I don't think you'll get the full market value, Celia. But it all depends on how quickly you want to sell."

"I'd like to sell as soon as possible," said Celia. "I want to get it over and done with."

"Then if I write to...What's the name of your professor?" Mr Gunn turned to Alex.

"Professor Sweeting, sir."

"So, if I write to this Professor Sweeting, he could get the ball rolling?"

"Yes, indeed. Of course, he'll have to come down with the rest of the governors of the hospital to look the place over, but that'll give you the opportunity to negotiate the price."

The lawyer nodded with satisfaction. "Then I'll write immediately."

"Actually, sir, I was hoping to travel back to London with Melody and if you give me the letter, I'll put it into the professor's hands personally." Mr Gunn nodded in approval. Alex turned to Melody. "When do you intend returning to London?"

"Tomorrow. Mr Wyngate wants me back at my desk very soon. He'll have kittens if I stay away any longer."

"Mr Wyngate sounds like a tyrant," murmured Alex, more to himself than Melody, but she heard.

"He has a business to run," she said quietly.

The assembled company began a heated conversation as they exchanged their views on the fate of

Monkswood and how Celia might come out of it very nicely after all.

"I'm surprised you let that one go." whispered the brigadier to his sister.

"Let what go?" she asked.

"Alex accompanying Melody back to London. What about propriety?" he said, trying to look nonchalant.

Olivia looked around the room, hiding the content of their conversation with a pleasant smile. She so enjoyed a conspiracy.

"Oh, that. Well, I can't see anything happening on a train journey. Besides, they have to have a little time alone together to give Alex the opportunity."

"Opportunity for what?"

"Wait and see."

She turned her attention to the young couple chatting away on the couch. There was no denying their fondness for each other, but was it strong enough to lead to marriage? She sighed and decided to take her own counsel and wait and see what happened. Mrs Carr announcing that luncheon was now being served interrupted her thoughts.

After the meal, Melody suddenly felt a twang of nostalgia and decided to take a stroll around the house and say a final farewell. As she moved along the corridors and wandered in and out of the staterooms, she was keenly aware that she would never see this house again. She lightly touched the tapestries and trailed her fingers along the walnut cabinets and tables remembering the happy times she had enjoyed here with Celia and her father. This is a wonderful old building, she sighed sadly, a strange composite of everyone who had lived in the house for the last three hundred years.

She passed the library and met Mrs Carr coming out carrying a pile of books.

"Mr Gunn's inheritance," the housekeeper laughed, nodding towards her burden. "His lordship had already put these aside in the tallboy for him."

"He'll enjoy reading them, I'm sure," said Melody. She wrinkled her nose at the titles and wondered at Mr Gunn's interest in the subject matter of some of them.

She was just about to carry on with her sentimental journey when the housekeeper seemed to have an afterthought.

"Miss Melody, could I have a word?" Melody nodded and they stepped into the library. Mrs Carr closed the door quietly. "Please forgive my impudence, miss. But I couldn't help overhearing your conversation the other night, when your aunt spoke of the predicament of you living alone in London with just a maid for company?"

"Oh, yes," said Melody, smiling at the memory.

The housekeeper took in a breath. "Well, it's like this, miss. I've obtained a position as a companion to a Mrs Bryant, widowed twelve months since." Melody winced knowing that that was an unenviable occupation. For Mrs Carr, a respected housekeeper, it would be intolerable to be at the beck and call of a cantankerous and spoilt woman. It seemed the housekeeper could read her thoughts and she smiled. "Please don't worry Miss Melody, I have accepted my situation and the widow wants to see the world, so by becoming her paid companion, I'll see it also."

"That's a positive attitude to have I suppose," said Melody.

"The problem is, my new employer planned to set off on her travels next month, but she's been taken ill and now intends leaving England in May. This means I have four months to fill before I take up my new position."

"So, what are you suggesting?"

"Perhaps your father and aunt would consider my going to London with you while I wait out my time?"

Melody gave a sigh. "I'm so sorry. It's a wonderful idea but my papa has told me that I must cover the cost of running the house and to be honest, I couldn't afford your wages."

Mrs Carr looked crestfallen. "I'd only need food and a place to sleep."

Melody's heart softened. "You're willing to work without wages?"

"Yes, miss. It wouldn't be for long and I do have a little money of my own."

"Leave it with me. Give me time to speak to my aunt and papa. I'm sure they'll agree to it. After all, it would mean they could go back to Hucknall Garth with an easier mind."

Mrs Carr gave a broad smile. "I'd appreciate that, miss. But I won't be able to leave here until everything is completed. I'd like to see Miss Celia on her way to her new life in Kent."

"I understand."

Melody left the library wondering how Mrs Carr would fit in at Hyde Park Gardens and especially how she would cope with Tilly. She walked slowly back to the parlour where her family had gathered after luncheon. Aunt Olivia was busy with her cross-stitch and deep in conversation with Alex. Her father was helping the lawyer sort through some paperwork. She noticed that Celia wasn't there so she decided to broach the subject of the housekeeper with Aunt Olivia.

To say that her aunt was enthusiastic was an understatement, she was beaming with satisfaction and brought the brigadier into the conversation to confirm the arrangements. By the time Melody left the parlour the details had been decided. Mrs Carr would live at

Hyde Park Gardens until such time as the widow needed her services and Aunt Olivia would speak to the housekeeper herself and organise everything.

So, thought Melody, as she climbed the stairs to look for Celia, it will be the three of us at Hyde Park Gardens and when Monkswood is sold, Celia will travel with the brigadier and Aunt Olivia to live at Hucknall Garth. What strange twists and turns life has for us.

However, Melody was about to experience a further twist in her life and this one would force her to pay a heavy price.

CHAPTER SEVEN

Melody tapped lightly on the bedroom door and a soft voice answered. Celia was sitting on the bed, her head bowed over the letter she had received from Mr Gunn.

"Are you all right?" asked Melody, sitting down beside her.

Celia nodded, her cheeks streaked with tears. "Yes, I am. It's just that reading this, has brought back so many memories."

Melody put her arm round her. "Memories are important at times like these."

They sat together quietly for a few minutes. Celia broke the silence. "Papa says in his letter, how much he…loves me and…how I've enriched his life." Her voice started to choke. "He says that he's so sorry…that he's left me very little, but he advises me to…be guided by Mr Gunn and accept any help from…your papa. He believes that the income I get from the sale of…the estate, should last me for the rest of my life, if it's wisely invested."

"He was a lovely, kind man and a good father. Try to remember him that way."

Celia quickly wiped her eyes and took in a deep breath. "You're right. I must stop all this wailing or I'll wear everyone out." She gave a watery smile. "So, you're leaving tomorrow?"

"Yes, I'm catching the morning train back to London."

Celia clutched her hand. "I really wish you could stay longer."

"I can't. I must get back to the Journal. I've signed a contract, remember."

Celia sighed sadly. "It was nice that Alex came here to see you."

"He didn't come to see me. He came to tell you about the business opportunity with Saint George's Hospital."

"No, he came to see you, Melody. You heard what he said about not being able to keep away from you."

Melody tried not to laugh in case she caused offence. "I don't think he meant that."

"Oh, yes he did. I sincerely believe he loves you." She leaned closer. "I also think he'll propose marriage very soon."

Melody felt a pang of unease. "I don't think I should consider marriage at the moment."

"Why not?" asked Celia. "It would be wonderful. And I'll be your bridesmaid." Melody moved away from her. Celia felt puzzled. For her, marriage was all she thought about. It was the fulfilment of a woman's dream, her only goal in life. "I know you have reservations about marriage, Melody, but I thought that was because you hadn't met anyone you wanted to marry. Now Alex has come into your life, surely you must be thinking of matrimony?"

"Certainly not. I have too much to do," she answered nonchalantly.

"Is your work as a journalist so important?"

"Yes, it is."

Celia looked around her bedroom as though for the last time. "If I met someone like Alex, I would be so overjoyed."

Melody gave her a comforting hug. "And one day someone will come into your life and he'll make you very happy."

"Perhaps he already has," Celia answered quietly.

Melody was startled by this revelation. What was Celia implying? Had she met someone whilst nursing her dying father? She scrutinised her friend's expression and noticed a sparkle in her eyes. She needed to know more.

"Please tell me, Celia." Seeing her mysterious smile, she pursued the subject. "Say something you scamp!"

"When I've settled at Hucknall Garth," said Celia slowly, "do you think your father and aunt would let me invite Doctor Jenner to dinner?"

Melody felt her throat constrict. "Has he been to visit you here, at Monkswood?"

"No."

"Has he been writing to you?"

"No."

Puzzled, Melody shook her head. "I don't understand, Celia. Why do you want to invite Doctor Jenner to dinner?"

"Because I'm sure he likes me a great deal, but he's too shy to say anything. If I invite him to dinner then it'll make it easier for him."

Melody tried not to laugh. Yes, Christian was reserved, but shy he certainly wasn't. "I don't think he'll take up your invitation," said Melody, trying to be honest.

"Why not? Oh, I know. Because he's too busy at the hospital?"

Melody didn't answer. After a few seconds she felt compelled to ask, "Tell me, how do you know he has feelings for you?"

Celia thought for a moment. "Oh, that's easy. At the ball on New Year's Eve, he held me very closely. And he laughed at all my witty remarks."

"Don't you think he was just being polite?"

"He was being more than polite. He was very attentive." Melody winced, realising why and how he had gained those skills. "Oh, Melody, don't you think he's the most beautiful creature you've ever seen. So tall and elegant and his golden hair like a halo." Her eyes lit up with delight. "That's what he is. My angel."

Melody looked away and then down at the hands she had clenched in a tight fist. "Please don't get too enamoured of Doctor Jenner," she said slowly.

"Why ever not?" said Celia, frowning in bewilderment.

"I don't think he's the right man for you."

Celia shuffled uncomfortably. "I don't think that's for you to say," she replied.

Melody decided to try a different argument. "You're a very pretty young woman, Celia, and there are dozens of men who have given you attention. Remember that banker? He was very handsome and he followed you round the ballroom all evening."

Celia wrinkled her nose; she didn't really want to talk about her other admirers. "All he talked about was the banking business in the city."

"Well, there were others. There was that…"

Celia interrupted her. "Melody, it's Doctor Jenner who has stolen my heart and I want him to come to dinner when I've settled at Hucknall Garth."

"You're in love with him?" she asked reluctantly, knowing what the answer would be.

"Yes, and I'm sure he wants to return my love, but he doesn't know how."

Melody stood up and walked into the middle of room, fighting her demons. She debated desperately with herself. Should she tell Celia about Alex's revelations? Would she understand?

She turned to face her friend. "I wish you weren't in love with him, I really do," she said.

"And why is that?"

"Because I know Doctor Jenner much better than you and he is incapable of returning your love. He's shallow, Celia, shallow and insincere."

Celia also rose to her feet, her eyes flashing with anger. "How dare you say that. He's a wonderful man and I think it's terrible that you should say such cruel things about him."

Melody came towards her, her hands outstretched, begging her to understand. "It's true, really it is."

"You don't want me to be happy!"

"Of course I want you to be happy."

"No you don't. You don't believe in marriage. You think it ties a woman down and prevents her from having a life of her own."

"That's not strictly true. I believe that society's perceptions of marriage prevent a woman from having a life of her own, not marriage itself."

Celia waved her hand in a gesture of dismissal. "It's all the same. But that doesn't mean you should prevent me from having the man I love."

Melody tried to keep silent, but the words spilt out before she realised it. "But he doesn't love you." She instantly regretted saying it when she saw the stunned look on Celia's face. "What I mean is…"

"How do you know that? You're lying," shrieked Celia, her cheeks flushing scarlet. It was all getting out of hand and Melody knew she had said too much. She turned away and opened the bedroom door. But before she could leave, Celia grabbed her arm. "Tell me how you know he doesn't love me." Melody shook her head, pressing her lips together. "I want to know."

When the words came they were slow and deliberate. "Because you're not what he's looking for."

"What do you mean."

"He's attracted to women who have wealth and influence and are able to advance his medical career. You have neither, so you're of no interest to him."

Celia looked at Melody through narrowed eyes. "What an evil thing to say! I don't believe you. Who told you this?"

"It doesn't matter."

Celia broke away from her and stood perfectly still, glaring at Melody in a way she had never done before.

Melody felt numb with shock. But worse than that was her growing sense of disappointment in herself. Why had she said anything? She should have kept quiet and let Celia discover for herself about Doctor Christian Jenner. But as was her silly inclination, she had to protect her and look out for her as she had always done. Now her meddling had turned on her.

She tried desperately to make amends. "Celia, I'm only trying to help you. I don't want you to get hurt."

"There's only one person here who's hurting me," said Celia.

"I'm sorry. I shouldn't have said anything."

Celia put her hands to her face, the pain in her pale blue eyes very evident. "I want you to leave, Melody. I want you to leave Monkswood immediately."

Melody felt stunned. "You don't mean that," she said. "You're upset."

Celia shook her head. "I can't bear you spending another night under my roof."

Melody tried to answer but her mouth was painfully dry.

Alex suddenly appeared in the doorway. "Aunt Olivia says tea is being served in the parlour," he said, smiling. But his smile faded when he sensed the atmosphere.

Celia tossed her head indignantly. "Alex, I've asked Melody to leave and I'd be grateful if you'd accompany her back to London on the next train."

Alex glanced first at Melody's white, strained face and then at Celia standing in the middle of the room, fists clenched and chin held defiantly. He decided it was better to stay silent and stood to one side as Melody ran past him and headed for her own room.

Soon he was standing in the doorway of her bedroom, watching her throwing her possessions into a carpetbag.

"Do you really have to go now?" he asked.

"You heard her," she said, fighting back the tears that threatened to overwhelm her.

"Come and have tea first."

"No, I want to go." She turned on him, anger causing her eyes to flash. "Why don't you come in and stop dithering in the doorway?"

He shook his head slowly. "A gentleman doesn't…"

"Oh, for heaven's sake."

Licking his lips, he took in a controlled breath. "Let me check on the next train and tell your father and aunt you're leaving." He left and her heart went with him.

Melody sank down on her bed, the pain she felt in her chest making her gasp. Angry tears filled her eyes and she wiped them away with the back of her hand. What had she done, how could she have been so stupid? She had offended Celia and the shame she felt had made her snap at Alex, hurting him. When would she learn to hold her tongue?

Her thoughts were interrupted by the appearance of her aunt, her expression showing her anxiety. Although she questioned her niece, Melody brushed it off as a small difference of opinion and nothing to worry about. She wanted to go back to London and that was that. Her aunt, knowing her niece well, decided to let her go and then sort out the problem later.

Within half an hour, the brigadier and his sister were at the main door to see Melody and Alex off on their journey. Mr Gunn had offered to give them a lift to the station in time for the four-thirty train and as the buggy pulled away, Olivia called out that she would write and let her niece know how things went. Melody could do no more than raise her hand in acknowledgement and then continue waving as the couple standing at the door became smaller and smaller until they melted into the fabric of the building. And then Melody kept her eyes on Monkswood until the buggy turned down the lane and she could see it no longer.

It was dark and the lantern on the vehicle creaked backward and forwards casting strange shadows on the surrounding vegetation, making it look like forbidding creatures from a mythological world. The open countryside stretched in front of them for the next thirty minutes, until the outskirts of Guildford came into sight and finally, they pulled up at the entrance to the station. Alex jumped down and helped Melody from the buggy. They said their goodbyes to the lawyer, Alex shaking his hand and then they made their way into the station.

They sat silently on a bench while they waited for the train. Alex desperately wanted to ask Melody what had happened, but sensing that she needed time to think things over, decided to delay his questions until they were back in London.

The journey home was melancholy and although there was small talk between them, the periods of long silences caused Alex to drift off to sleep, his head resting on Melody's shoulder. Melody stayed fully awake, the tension in her creating a restless ache. She looked out of the window but it was too dark to see the scenery, only her pensive face reflected in the glass. Sighing, she pulled down the blind. How could events have turned so sour?

She glanced at Alex and smiled. He seemed so like a small boy, so peaceful and untroubled yet she knew that he carried a great deal of responsibility at Saint George's and worked long hours. She caressed his face, as she watched him sleeping. She would tell him about her rift with Celia in time. Realising that the train was slowing, she pulled up the blind and saw they were approaching the outskirts of London. She gently shook Alex awake.

Melody returned to The Cork Street Journal the following afternoon much to the surprise of the editor and staff of the newspaper, who hadn't expected her back so soon. They showed their pleasure at seeing her, but their smiles of welcome couldn't hide their glances of alarm at her appearance. With her ashen face and the dark shadows under her eyes, she was well aware that she didn't look her best. In fact, Tilly had begged her to stay home the day after she had arrived back, telling her with a severe wag of her finger, that she would make herself ill, if she didn't get more rest. Melody had shrugged it off, saying she was quite well and going back to her work would perk her up.

Guy Wyngate greeted her with a nod and a smile that changed briefly to a frown as his gaze quickly swept over her pale complexion and vacant eyes.

"You don't look too well. Are you sure you should have come in?"

"I'm ready to go back to work, sir. I just feel very tired, that's all," she said, trying to smile.

She was still wearing mourning dress and she knew the black crape made her seem more dismal. Melody felt uncomfortable under his scrutiny and was unable to prevent the blush creeping into her cheeks.

"Funerals can be depressing," he said gently.

Melody shook her head. "On the contrary. The baron's funeral was unbelievably dignified. Very touching and somehow quite beautiful."

"Well, perhaps you'd like to write an account of it, with a short résumé of his life in Surrey?"

"Yes, I'd like to do that," she smiled.

"Excellent!" His concerned expression returned. "But if you start feeling weary, you have my permission to go home."

Melody went to her desk to start the task, knowing that she would have to hurry since the paper would be going to press very soon. As she sat working, a sense of elation filled her. Writing always made her tremble with exhilaration, almost like a drug, comforting and consoling her. But this time she was exorcising her doubts and rationalising her self-reproach. Perhaps matters weren't as bad as they seemed. Perhaps Celia would also think it over and come to the conclusion that the entire incident had been blown out of all proportion. Yes, thought Melody feeling more hopeful, she would get a letter soon from her friend, and everything would be resolved.

As her pen flew across the paper, she was relieved that she could conclude her mourning very soon. She wore black out of respect but society didn't expect her to wear it for long since the baron was not a family member. To wear cheerful colours would help her overcome her wretchedness.

But a letter didn't arrive, although Melody waited every morning and asked Tilly every evening, if there was anything in the post from Monkswood. There was nothing left to do but throw herself into the routine of daily life, going to the newspaper every day and meeting Alex when he was able to free himself from his hospital duties. And then the day finally came when Mrs Carr arrived at Hyde Park Gardens.

It was the end of February and it seemed as if it had been raining for weeks. Mrs Carr stepped into the hall dripping from head to foot, her black bonnet soaked and stuck to her head. She had brought all her worldly possessions packed in a large trunk and she and Tilly carried it between them to the room allocated to her.

At first, Melody wondered if she had made a mistake in allowing the housekeeper to come to Hyde Park Gardens, as Tilly seemed to resent her presence. The maid was used to organising the household in her own way and felt that the young mistress didn't trust her to do the job properly. Even when Melody explained it was for the sake of propriety that Mrs Carr was there and was going to act as chaperone, Tilly still pulled a face and told her firmly that she wouldn't tolerate any interference.

As far as Mrs Carr was concerned, the last thing she wanted to do was to interfere. Her only aim was to be of use until she took up her position in the widow's service. Realising that the housekeeper would only be there until the spring quietened Tilly's misgivings.

But the greatest joy of Mrs Carr's arrival was that she had brought a letter with her. It came from Aunt Olivia, detailing the events of the last four weeks. She described how the Board of Governors from Saint George's Hospital had visited Monkswood and after a great deal of wrangling, a price had been agreed. As Alex had predicted, it wasn't the full market value but Celia and Mr Gunn thought it acceptable under the circumstances. The farms and land still belonged to

Celia and would give her an annual income. All in all, everything had gone very smoothly and Miss Celia Sinclair would be financially comfortable although not wealthy by any means.

And so the furniture had been auctioned, the staff dismissed and the departure of Mrs Carr coincided with the departure of the remaining residents of Monkswood. Her aunt's letter concluded with a P.S. written on the train to Kent. *Celia was very distressed as we locked the door for the last time,* she wrote, *and we had to take a walk round the garden so she could say goodbye to every tree and shrub.* Her aunt then went on to describe how the tenants had collected at the gate to say their final farewells and Celia had been presented with a bouquet. *By the time you read this letter, my dear niece, we will be back at Hucknall Garth and hopefully Celia will settle quickly into her new life with us.* She finished the letter by sending their love and hoping that everything was going well in London.

Melody read the letter eagerly, hoping that some mention would be made of Celia's thoughts on their quarrel, but her aunt either chose not to say anything or had nothing to say. Sadly, she folded the letter and placed it in her dressing table drawer. She was convinced that she would hear more in time. Her aunt would surely speak to Celia and get to the heart of the problem. Tilly's scream from the kitchen interrupted her thoughts and alarmed, Melody ran from her bedroom and down the stairs.

"It's indecent!" screeched Tilly. "We can't have that in the house." Melody entered the kitchen to be confronted by the horrified face of the maid and the amused expression of the housekeeper. "Oh, miss, do tell her we can't have that here." She pointed to a small picture propped up on a chair and Melody smiled with delight.

"Why it's the *Bather* by Ingres," she said, picking up the frame and examining the portrait closely.

"Miss Celia sent it for you," said Mrs Carr. "She knew you always admired it and thought you would like it as a memento of Monkswood."

Melody's heart soared and she laughed gleefully. Whether this meant Celia had forgiven her or not she didn't know. But a gift from her was wonderful.

"But miss, she's got no clothes on," persisted Tilly. She might be working class but she had her standards.

"It's all right, Tilly," said Melody, trying to soothe the maid's doubts. "It was painted by a famous French artist called Jean-Auguste Dominique Ingres at the beginning of the century. It's only a copy, the original is in Paris."

The maid sniffed in disgust. "Well, only a Frenchie would paint someone in the all-together."

"She's bathing," laughed Mrs Carr. "You have to take your clothes off if you're intending to bathe. Anyway, you can only see the back of her."

"Well, don't think I'm going to dust her," said Tilly. She reached into the cupboard and threw some potatoes into the sink. Doctor Courtney was coming to dinner and there was still much to do.

"I'll dust her," said Mrs Carr, smiling contentedly at the portrait. "After all, I've done it for twenty-five years and a few more months won't make any difference."

She joined Tilly and started to help her prepare the meal. Melody smiled, her doubts melting away.

"She's charming, absolutely charming," said Alex, looking up at the picture. "I've seen the original, but this is a good copy."

He had arrived for dinner and he and Melody were standing beside the fire admiring the portrait that had been hung above the mantelpiece. In the gleam of the oil lamps, the naked flesh of the young woman sitting on the bed, seemed to glow with a beautiful amber vitality.

"Tilly doesn't like her one bit," said Melody. "She won't come in here without closing her eyes first, I'm sure."

Alex chuckled. "What did she think of Mrs Carr?"

"I was rather worried at first, I must admit, but they seem to be getting on very well."

"And what about you?" He placed his hands on her shoulders, turning her to face him. "How are you feeling now you're back in London?"

"I've been through worse things."

She smiled but Alex could see the pain in her eyes and placed his arms round her. He bent his head and kissed her lips. She gasped with surprise at the feelings that swept through her.

There was a polite cough from behind them. "Excuse me, ma'am, sir, but dinner is served."

Mrs Carr stood in the doorway, her expression one of utter disapproval. The brigadier and his sister had given her explicit instructions and she would follow them with rigid determination.

They took their seats and Melody realised that Alex had kissed her on the lips for the first time. It had been exciting and suddenly she became overwhelmed by the strangest desires. She wanted more of his kisses, she was certain about that.

Over dinner, Melody finally told Alex about the quarrel she had had with Celia and she was relieved that he chose not to make any comment. She didn't need to be told that she should have remained silent and she had already punished herself enough with guilt.

"You can see why she fell in love with him, can't you?" said Melody, thoughtfully. "He is very beautiful and almost aristocratic in his bearing."

"Ah, that was the enigma about Jenner at Eton. He was a good friend of mine right from the start but there was a certain mystery about him."

Alex paused dramatically and Melody leaned forward in anticipation.

"Go on, Alex, tell me more."

"Well, there he was at a prestigious school and yet he seemed to come from humble beginnings. His grandmother brought him up on a hop farm in Kent and I actually went with him to visit her. She has a quaint name, Mrs Hunneybell. Lovely lady she is, round as a barrel with a cheery manner that made you feel right at home."

"What of his parents?" asked Melody.

Alex thought carefully. "His mother died when he was at Eton, but I got the impression that there was only the three of them living at the farm before her death."

"No father?"

"That's the mystery." He held up his glass and studied the blood red liquid. "As you say, Jenner has an aristocratic bearing, so rumour was rife that his father was from foreign nobility and that Jenner had been born on the wrong side of the blanket, so to speak."

"The money for his schooling must have come from somewhere," Melody said, wondering at the story she was hearing. "I don't think a hop farm would bring in enough to pay for that sort of education."

"Not to mention his medical studies," added Alex.

"Where is this hop farm?" Melody asked.

"If I remember it's near Staplehurst."

"Goodness, that's not very far from Hucknall Garth. In fact, when I was a young girl we used to go there to have picnics on the banks of the River Beult."

"Sounds lovely. Perhaps we could all do that again in the summer and invite Jenner along."

Melody shrugged her shoulders. "I'm not sure, Alex. Now that Celia is living at Hucknall Garth and I've spilled the beans about Christian, I'd be embarrassed to invite him anywhere where she might be."

Alex decided to change the subject. "Talking about invitations, my parents are still asking when you'll visit them." He chucked her under the chin. "They want to meet you, Melody, and I want you to meet them."

She smiled and rose from the table. "I'll think about it. I don't want to be away from the paper too much. Come on, let's go into the sitting room where it's more comfortable." She smiled mischievously. "I'm afraid Mrs Carr will be sitting crocheting on the far side of the room."

Alex pushed his chair back from the table. "Damn Mrs Carr," he said under his breath.

CHAPTER EIGHT

Guy Wyngate closed the front door and stood for a while in the hallway. The noise of the printing press seemed to echo all around the building and the faint smell of ink swept over him. He loved this life, it was all he had ever known and The Cork Street Journal had been his venture, his child that he had nurtured and cherished for the last eight years. He walked slowly up the stairs to his office.

Marsh jumped to his feet as he entered. "How did it go, sir?" he said.

Guy shook his head. "Not good. Where is everyone?"

"The Frenchman is here and Eric too." He scanned down his diary. "Holbrook has gone to collect the latest news about the end of the war in America and this terrible assassination of President Lincoln. And Miss Melody is taking tea with Lady Palmerston."

"The prime minister's wife?" Guy asked incredulously.

"The very same."

"Why has she gone to visit her?"

Marsh thought for a moment. "She said something about behind every successful man there's a good woman, or words to that effect."

For all his troubles, Guy couldn't help chuckling. "She could be right about that. When everyone is back, gather them together and I'll speak to them in my office."

"Don't know what's to become of us all," muttered the secretary, as his employer shut his office door behind him.

Melody left Downing Street feeling very satisfied with herself. Her interview with Lady Palmerston had been a great success, more so in that the lady didn't usually conduct interviews with newspapers. But she had heard of Miss Melody Kinsman, reporter with The Cork Street Journal and was curious to meet this remarkable young woman who was starting to make her mark in journalism. Melody jumped aboard the gig, adjusted her skirt and straightened her bonnet. The spring sunshine warmed her and a sense of well being suddenly flooded through her. For a few minutes she held her face up to the rays, enjoying the simple pleasure of just being alive.

The prime minister's wife had been a great delight and had asked as many questions of Melody as Melody had asked of her. There were times when she had to remind herself who was interviewing whom. Not that she had gone there to ask about political matters, Melody didn't want that kind of information.

Instead she had wanted to know the intricacies of being the prime minister's wife, the duties involved and the problems faced. Lady Palmerston had given her a wonderful insight into the trial and tribulations as well as the loneliness of coping with the long hours her husband worked. Now it was done and Melody was keen to get back to Cork Street to write up her column. She shook the reins and Sultan pulled forward.

When she arrived she immediately went to her desk and sat down. Flicking over the pages of her notebook she began to transcribe the interview and then she heard Eric calling her. Without looking up she called back and he appeared in the doorway.

"Meeting in five minutes, Melody, in Mr Wyngate's office," he said.

"What about?" she asked, still not looking up from her work. He remained silent. Melody lifted her eyes from her writing and was shocked to see the usual high-spirited Eric with an expression that would have befitted an undertaker. "Goodness me, what's the matter?"

Eric shook his head and walked away.

Ten pairs of eyes turned in his direction as the editor entered the room, the conversation dying instantly at his appearance. He looked at them closely and then perched himself on the edge of the desk.

"Miss Melody and gentlemen," he paused and then cleared his throat, "this afternoon I spoke at some length to the bank and to put it bluntly, the paper's readership has steadily declined this last year and the costs cannot be sustained. The money has finally run out and I have no choice but to put this business into the hands of my bankers who will sell the assets. I would like all articles into print by Friday's evening edition after which this paper will cease to exist."

A low murmur filled the room and Melody quickly looked around. A tight knot had suddenly formed in her chest restricting her breathing. She had been with The Cork Street Journal barely five months but it had become everything to her. How could it be dismantled and cease to exist?

Standing near the door, she could see Henri Careme, the Frenchman deep in conversation with Eric, debating the consequences of the paper closing, the younger man leaning back, his hands thrust deep in his pockets. Dear, awkward Eric, who loped about with a constant cheery grin and words of encouragement. By the window, Holbrook with his quiet dignity studied his nails. The five men from the printing room, in their long green aprons and wearing black false sleeves to protect their shirts, also seemed shocked into silence.

Close by was Marsh, who she knew had a grudging admiration for her even if he did mutter objections behind his whiskers. She looked back at the editor, a man who had striven so hard to make his business successful, a man who had given her the chance to make something of herself, when others had sent her on her way.

Henri shrugged his shoulders. "*Oui*, I could go back to Paris."

"I know *The Times* is looking for more reporters," remarked Holbrook, without any enthusiasm.

The others just watched their employer, as though expecting him to perform some kind of miracle, but he remained silent. A short while later Marsh ushered them from the room and as Melody glanced over her shoulder, she could see the editor still perched on the edge of his desk, the pain in his eyes distressing to see.

Hyde Park Gardens just off the Bayswater Road and a stone's throw from the park, was a delightful cul-de-sac of select houses. Melody brought the gig to a standstill and leaned forward in the seat, resting her elbows on her knees. She played absently with the reins, as she contemplated the house she had lived in for the last eight months.

The houses looked the same, constructed of warm brick that gleamed in the spring sunshine, and all sporting doors of oak with shining doorknockers. Every window sparkled, but there again they would, every household had at least four servants. She only had Tilly and Mrs Carr yet they were managing very well, despite the brigadier and Aunt Olivia's concerns. Melody had even put her friction with Celia to one side, deciding that nothing could be done about it just yet. She and Aunt Olivia had exchanged numerous letters and although she had asked her aunt to intervene on her behalf, the advice coming back was to let time pass.

Melody looked about her with sadness. She had fallen in love with Hyde Park Gardens as soon as she had set eyes on it. It had been the middle of September and the cobbled area had been ablaze with autumn flowers, lavish displays of lobelia and petunia filling window boxes, while baskets of geranium flourished around the doors. Now it was spring and cherry and apple blossom adorned the area, lilac and hyacinths filled the air with their sweet scent. In a few weeks roses would replace these.

The dreadful idea of leaving London and returning to Kent came into her mind. How could she go back to Hucknall Garth and become financially dependent on her father? The thought pulled her up with a jolt. What was she thinking of? She was an independent woman and guarded that fact jealously, struggling to be self-sufficient. And now she was contemplating putting herself into a position of dependency. Melody began to feel angry with herself for simply having the idea. She wouldn't lose the life she had made for herself, not without a fight.

There was so much to think about now that the Journal had finished. The chances of being taken on by another newspaper were very remote and she had to make other plans for her future. Sultan neighed and tossed his head, agitated at his mistress's sudden halt in the wrong place. He knew the stables were just round the corner in the courtyard and wanted to get in where it was comfortable and food was waiting to be chewed. Melody sighed and clicked him into a slow walk.

After leaving the horse and gig with the stable boy, Melody walked across the court to the kitchen door of her own house. Since buying her own mode of transport she had got into the habit of entering by the kitchen door instead of the front door. In fact, many things had changed since Aunt Olivia and Celia had left Hyde Park Gardens, the most notable was that the mistress of the house now ate in the kitchen with the staff.

At first Tilly had objected, but when Melody pointed out that she would feel lonely eating in the dining room on her own, the maid agreed. And so Melody had her own seat at the kitchen table, and on an evening the three would sit together and swap stories of their day. Only when Alex came to dinner was the meal made more formal, the table in the dining room adorned with the best glasses and cutlery and all etiquette conformed to.

Melody came through the door untying her bonnet as she went. Mrs Carr was sitting at the table and jumped to her feet when she heard her mistress enter, hurriedly stuffing a piece of paper into her apron pocket.

"Oh, Miss Melody, you're home early," she said sounding breathless. "The evening meal isn't ready yet, Tilly's not back from the market."

Melody brushed her concerns aside simply telling her that she had finished her day's assignments sooner than she had expected. As she turned to make her way into the hallway and upstairs, the housekeeper gave her the letter that had arrived that morning. Melody took it eagerly, recognising her aunt's bold handwriting. She suddenly realised that Mrs Carr seemed rather agitated, the housekeeper's hair, usually so tidy under her cap, was hanging in loose grey strands down her cheeks.

"Have you told her, then?" Tilly's voice came from behind them, making them jump with surprise. The maid dropped her basket down on the table. "I hope you did or I'll tell her."

"Hush up, will you," Mrs Carr snapped back.

Melody looked at each of them in turn. The housekeeper sank down onto a chair and put her head in her hands. Melody looked at her for a few seconds before turning to Tilly.

"What's this all about?"

"She got a letter this morning, miss..." Tilly started, but was interrupted by the housekeeper.

"Who's she, the cat's mother?" Mrs Carr glared at her. "I'll tell her, it's my problem."

"Please yourself," said Tilly, picking up the basket of fruit and vegetables and flouncing off to the pantry.

Melody sat down next to Mrs Carr and waited patiently. The housekeeper drew a crumpled piece of paper from her pocket and offered it to her. The writing was so illegible that Melody had to take it over to the window to read it and then she saw it was from the widow who was to employ the housekeeper as a companion on her travels. Except that the widow had decided to remarry and was seeing the world with her new husband, thereby not requiring Mrs Carr's services after all.

"I don't know what I'm to do now, Miss Melody?" Mrs Carr said, running her fingers through her hair and almost dislodging her lace cap. "I've nowhere else to go."

Tilly returned from the pantry. "I've told her you'll let her stay here. You will, miss, won't you?" She smiled in anticipation of her mistress's answer.

"I don't know," said Melody slowly. She had been caught unprepared for this problem. The colour drained from her cheeks as she battled with a terrible dilemma.

"But you must," wailed Tilly, seeing her mistress hesitate. "She can't be thrown out in the street. It's not her fault the widow decided to get married again."

Mrs Carr threw her a look of disapproval. "Miss Melody can't afford my wages. I'll have to look for a new position."

Melody knew she was right. Even if the Journal hadn't closed, she would have been hard pressed to find the money to pay two servants. She looked down at the letter and then back at Tilly and Mrs Carr.

"Give me time to decide what to do," said Melody quietly. Handing the letter to Mrs Carr, Melody made her way up to her bedroom.

She sat at her dressing table, her mind lost in a jungle of uncoordinated and confused thoughts. She hadn't had time to tell them that The Cork Street Journal no longer needed her services, that in essence, she had also lost her income and her own future was far from secure. Melody stared at her reflection in the mirror and saw a pensive face staring back. And little wonder, she thought ruefully, she had taken on the responsibility of a household and now she couldn't fulfil her obligations.

Suddenly she remembered Aunt Olivia's letter that she had tucked up her sleeve. Quickly tearing open the envelope she started to read. It was a much shorter letter than the usual weighty package she usually received, and simply stated that two weeks earlier the brigadier with Celia had set off for the Continent, accompanied by the Reverend Ansell and his wife. Since the brigadier thought a holiday would benefit the young girl and the reverend had always had a desire to see Rome, it had been decided they would all go together. But they intended returning in July at the latest. Aunt Olivia concluded the letter by saying how much she missed her niece and looked forward to her visiting Hucknall Garth if her employer would give her leave to do so.

Melody sighed and went to the window. It had started raining, a gentle spring rain that washed the cobbles and made them shine. At the entrance to the cul-de-sac, she could see people hurrying along the Bayswater Road, some carrying umbrellas, some with their collars turned up against the sudden shower. She had all the time in the world to go to Hucknall Garth now, but what of Tilly and Mrs Carr? She couldn't abandon them. By the time she had washed and changed for the evening meal she had reached a decision. The following day she would search out every newspaper editor in London and find another position. She wouldn't give up yet, not when she had come this far.

The clock in the hall chimed two. Melody raised herself up on her elbow and punched the feather pillow for the hundredth time. She turned over onto her back and stared at the ceiling, watching the shadows of the swaying trees dance in the moonlight that streamed through her window. She had left her bed thirty minutes before in order to open the curtains so she could see the stars. Her mind was buzzing like a hive of bees. She had come to bed exhausted and had fallen asleep almost immediately only to wake up within the hour. And now she couldn't settle down back to sleep, even though she had tried to concentrate on closing her eyes and resting. But the more she tried the more restless she became and the hall clock kept counting the hours away.

She cursed its melodious chimes, hating its very existence. It was too early to get up and she didn't want to disturb the others. Melody plumped up her pillows and put them against the headboard pulling herself up into a sitting position. She contemplated the day ahead. She had decided not to tell Mrs Carr and Tilly about the closure of the Journal, not yet, not until she could also tell them that she had found another position elsewhere.

That would mean getting up in the morning as usual but instead of going to Cork Street she would do the rounds.

Melody gave a sigh; this was exactly what she had done before Guy Wyngate had given her the opportunity of proving herself. Now she was back to square one. Her thoughts turned to the editor and she wondered how he must have been feeling that night. Was he walking the floors of his room? Perhaps not, she thought ruefully, he could go back and work for his uncle at *The Evening Chronicle*. Her mind pondered on the various newspapers of London. Before Christmas she had been unknown but now she had something of a reputation. Even Lady Palmerston had been impressed; perhaps others would be also.

Hugging her knees, Melody formed a plan of action. She would start with *The Daily Mail*, then *The Evening Chronicle* and follow this with *The Times*. She shuddered at the thought of facing the editor of that particular newspaper again. He had been very rude to her when she acted as governess to his three obnoxious children. Perhaps she should miss him out, she thought, no use causing herself more grief than was necessary.

Her mind went back to *The Evening Chronicle* and she groaned at the fact that Sir Jack Wetherby, although the owner of the paper, was not the editor. By reputation he was known to be a jovial elderly gentleman who had taken semi-retirement some years before and only went into the office a few days a week, *'to keep his hand in'* Eric had told her one day when she had become curious about her employer's family connections. Perhaps Sir Jack would have given her a chance too, after all, there must be some similarities between uncle and nephew.

Melody sat bolt upright shocked at the idea slowly forming in her mind. But would she dare do it? Would it work? She snuggled down under the covers as the annoying clock struck four. The sun was starting to rise and Tilly would be up in an hour, but Melody knew that now she was resolved to carry out her plan, there would be no sleep for her.

"You don't seem to have slept well, Miss Melody," said Mrs Carr, watching her mistress yawn over her breakfast. "Why don't you take the day off?"

Melody smiled and wondered why people such as Tilly and the housekeeper thought that a 'lady' could work at will, with no obligations to an employer.

"Lots to do today," she said, a mischievous glint in her eye.

"Well, don't overdo it or you'll make yourself ill," said Mrs Carr. She paused for a moment before adding, "I don't wish to bother you, but have you considered what's to become of me? If you want me to leave, then so be it. All I ask is a little time to find another situation."

"I'm afraid I haven't decided yet, Mrs Carr. But I will sort something out," she answered adamantly. She was rewarded with a generous smile from the housekeeper.

The ride through Hyde Park and Kensington Gardens was delightful and Melody was buoyant with hope. It was a beautiful day with just a few white clouds majestically sailing across a sparkling blue sky, washed clean after the early morning rain. She let Sultan travel at his own pace and since he was getting on in years, his pace was just a little faster than a walk but not as fast as a trot. Melody didn't mind at all since she knew Sir Jack, when he did go to his office, rarely left his house until eleven.

To her utter delight, Alex appeared in view and she reined in Sultan. "What are you doing here?" she said, jumping down from the gig.

He gave her a quick kiss on the cheek. "Coming to see you, would you believe. I have some news."

She tied the reins to a bush and they sat down on a bench. "It must be important if you're coming to see me this early in the morning," she said, slipping her hand through his arm and giving it a squeeze.

"My mother's arrived in London, quite unexpectedly. She came to visit an old friend and is staying in a hotel. But she asked to meet you. So, I'd like you to come to dinner with us tonight."

Melody thought for a moment. "Why don't you bring her to Hyde Park Gardens instead. Mrs Carr and Tilly can cook one of their special meals and I can impress her with my hostess skills."

He kissed her hand. "I hoped you'd say that," he laughed. "A hotel isn't the ideal place to meet someone. I thought of asking my landlady to rustle up something for us, but meeting my mother in your home would be excellent."

Before Melody climbed back up into the gig, Alex pulled her closer to him than propriety allowed in a public place. She responded by giving him a brief kiss on the chin and a firm push to send him on his way.

"Seven o'clock then, and don't be late," she called, as he made his way through the trees towards the hospital. He answered with a brisk wave of his hand.

The owner of *The Evening Chronicle* lived in Chelsea on the far side of Hyde Park, in a large Georgian house with white Corinthian pillars each side of the door. Melody pulled up at the main entrance and jumped down, surveying the home of Guy Wyngate's uncle.

She paid a penny to a young boy of about seven years of age, dirty and wearing rags, who volunteered to look after the horse and gig for her. She knocked on the door and when a tall, dignified butler answered she asked if she could see Sir Jack Wetherby. To her utter surprise, Melody was shown into the parlour almost immediately.

"Well, goodness me. If it isn't Miss Melody Kinsman in person," he said, rising from his armchair.

Eric had been right, for Sir Jack was certainly a jolly old soul. For some reason she recognised the same characteristics of her father in him. He was small in stature but rotund, his large frame dressed in good quality clothes including a beautiful silk waistcoat adorned with a gold pocket watch. He sported whiskers that were neatly trimmed and yet appeared strange, as they were the only hairs he had on his head, since he was completely bald.

"You sound as though you were expecting me," laughed Melody, offering her hand that he kissed with a flourish.

"Well, obviously I wasn't. But I was talking to Lady Palmerston only last night and she was full of admiration for the young lady journalist from The Cork Street Journal. I think because you refuse to write any scandal. You say it as you see it. You've certainly left an impression. Do sit down." He offered her a seat and after seeing her comfortably settled rang the bell and ordered coffee. Then he took the armchair opposite her continuing with his convivial conversation. "I must be honest, I was very curious about meeting you myself."

The irony was not lost on Melody. "I wish your editor had been just as curious, Sir Jack. I might have been offered a position with *The Evening Chronicle* if that were the case."

"Ah, my editor has full authority to do as he sees fit and I'm afraid he's against female journalists."

"Unlike your nephew."

"Guy has what I call a progressive outlook and I admire him for it." He gave her a broad smile. "Now what can I do for you?"

They were interrupted by the appearance of the maid with a tray of coffee and after she had served them and left the room Sir Jack offered his guest a plate of ginger biscuits. She accepted one politely and took a small bite. His reassuring and friendly manner gave her confidence and taking a large breath she started on her ambitious project.

"I suppose you've heard about the misfortune that's befallen The Cork Street Journal?"

Sir Jack's round face showed bewilderment that caught her off guard. "No, I can't say I have. What misfortune?"

"Oh dear, I thought you would have known." She sipped her coffee allowing herself to collect a moment of courage and then carried on. "Mr Wyngate told us yesterday afternoon that the newspaper has run out of money and must close at the end of the week."

"Did he, by George!" Sir Jack leaned forward in his seat. "I haven't heard a word yet. Mind you, I was going to my club this morning and no doubt I would have been told then." He pursed his lips. "Poor boy. He's worked so hard to keep that paper going. I did warn him it would be difficult, but would he listen? No, he had to follow his own star."

Melody's courage grew. "Perhaps your nephew and I have much in common."

"You certainly seem to." Sir Jack suddenly thought he had the reason behind Melody's visit. "My dear Miss

Kinsman, you're here to ask for a position on *The Evening Chronicle*, are you not?"

"No, Sir Jack, I'm here to ask for financial help."

Sir Jack sat back in his chair and surveyed the young woman opposite him, hardly believing what he had heard. Seeing her eager expression that made her eyes shine a brilliant blue, he realised she was in deadly earnest.

"Please elaborate," he asked slowly.

Melody put down her coffee cup and clasped her hands together. "Put simply, the Journal is in debt and needs money to help it continue. Sir Jack, I'm asking you for that money." He didn't answer so Melody continued. "It's a wonderful newspaper and deserves to succeed."

A smile hovered on his lips. "Yes I know. So, you want me to give you money?"

"No, I want you to make an investment. A loan repayable with interest."

"Has my nephew sent you to see me?"

"Certainly not," Melody said, showing obvious horror at the suggestion. "It was my idea. Mr Wyngate knows nothing of my visit to you this morning."

"How much were you thinking of?"

Melody's heart skipped a beat and she thought rapidly. She had overheard a conversation between Eric and Marsh and a figure of thirty thousand pounds had been mentioned.

"Thirty thousand pounds," she answered carefully. Now that she had said it, it seemed a great deal of money.

"At what interest?"

She bit her lip. Sir Jack certainly got down to business when he wanted to.

"Two per cent."

"Far too low. Ten per cent."

"Four per cent, Sir Jack. After all, he is your nephew."

Sir Jack let out a laugh that resounded round the parlour and made his corpulent stomach wobble under his waistcoat. "My dear Miss Kinsman, you drive a hard bargain. How about seven per cent?"

Melody shook her head. "Five per cent and that's my final offer."

Sir Jack studied her for a moment. "You must care about my nephew a great deal, to go to all this bother for him."

It had been said softly, almost a whisper, but Melody's mouth became dry. She quickly took another sip of her cooling coffee. "N...No," she stammered. "I care for The Cork Street Journal and my position with it."

Again, Sir Jack didn't answer for a few seconds but studied her closely. "All right, my dear lady. Thirty thousand pounds it is, at five per cent interest per annum." He stood and went to a writing desk in the far corner. "I shall write a cheque now and if you could ask your employer to sort out the repayment details with his bank, I'd be very grateful. I won't put a time limit on this loan, he can pay it back as he wishes. As you say, he is family." She rose from her seat as he finished his task and took the piece of paper he handed to her. She accepted it as if in a dream, hardly believing her quest had succeeded. "How is my nephew?" he asked and Melody detected a hint of sadness in his voice. Suddenly she remembered that there was a rift between uncle and nephew.

"He seems in good health," she said.

"I'm so pleased to hear that."

He walked her to the main door himself and out into the sunshine. Taking the reins of the horse from the raggedy boy, he pressed a coin into the small grubby hand. The child's dirty face lit up at being paid twice and with a whoop of joy, ran off home.

"Someone else made a good business deal today," laughed Melody, watching him race across the small park in front of the house.

Sir Jack shook his head sadly. "It won't go far. His mother will drink it away if I know anything about it." He took her hand and kissed her fingers in his elegant style. "Goodbye, Miss Kinsman, and if you ever feel in need of a change, then I think I could persuade my editor to take you on at *The Evening Chronicle*."

"Thank you, but I'm very happy where I am," she answered.

He could see she spoke sincerely. "I believe my nephew is a very lucky man to have someone as loyal as you."

CHAPTER NINE

Her dream like state seemed to exist all the way back to Cork Street and Melody couldn't believe that in her purse was a cheque for thirty thousand pounds. The Journal could carry on publishing, she would keep her position, Tilly was assured of a home at Hyde Park Gardens. Of course, Melody had her qualms about Mrs Carr. Whether she could afford the housekeeper's services was still in doubt. Even so, it was a wonderful day.

When she entered the premises in Cork Street everything was the same. The sound of the printing press echoed around the hallway and she could hear Eric's laughter coming from along the corridor. She made her way to Marsh's office, but he wasn't there. The door to the editor's office was ajar and from beyond she distinctly heard the voices of Guy Wyngate and his secretary. She tapped lightly before stepping into the room.

The editor was going over some paperwork with Marsh when Melody appeared and he smiled when he saw her standing in the doorway.

"Ah, Miss Melody, we were just talking about you," said Guy, handing a file to Marsh. "It looks like your interview with Lady Palmerston has been a great success." He picked up a bundle of papers from his desk. "Letters of compliment and admiration." He gave a lopsided smile. "So, what can I do for you?"

"I've come to talk about the future of the paper, sir." She suddenly felt nervous and was conscious of her trembling hands. She glanced at Marsh who took the hint and gathering up the paperwork left the office closing the door behind him.

"You'd better sit down," said the editor, pulling back a chair for her.

Melody sat down and waited until he had made himself comfortable. Without speaking, she pulled the cheque from her purse and placed it in front of her employer. Ever since the plan had hatched itself, Melody had striven towards one single purpose, to get the money and save the Journal. Nowhere in her thoughts had she considered the reaction of the editor. If anything, she believed he would be relieved that the paper was saved and excited about the prospect of new investment. But now, watching Guy Wyngate pick up the cheque and read it, she began to have doubts.

His expression froze into concealed anger and his eyes became darker. "What's this?" he said coldly.

"It's a cheque for thirty thousand pounds from…"

He interrupted her sharply. "I can see what it is, Miss Kinsman. I can also see whom it's from. What I want to know is why it's here and why you've given it to me?"

She gasped at the fury in his eyes as he glared at her. "I…I went to see Sir Jack Wetherby this morning and asked him…" She tried to continue even though his stare was cutting through her like a knife. "I told him about the plight of the Journal and he offered to…" It was getting harder to speak, her throat starting to constrict.

Slowly, Guy rose to his feet and looked down on her. "How dare you!" He came round to her side of the desk and she jumped to her feet backing away from him.

"Mr Wyngate, I went to see your uncle for the sake of the newspaper, to help you."

"All you've done is humiliate me. How dare you go to my uncle and beg for money! Who the hell do you think you are?" Suddenly he lunged out and grabbed her by the arm, pulling her over to the window. "Look down there, Miss Kinsman, what do you see?"

Bewildered she stared down on the busy street below. "T...Traffic. Horses, wagons, carriages."

"What else?" he demanded.

"People..."

"That's right, people. People living their daily lives and trying to get by. Some of them will succeed and some of them won't. But win or lose, it's all part of life's chances."

"I don't understand. What have I done wrong?" She struggled against him but he tightened his grip on her.

"I tried to make this newspaper successful and I failed. That's life and I don't need charity from my uncle to help me when I go wrong. This was a venture I tried on my own, not with the benefit of family connections."

Melody now realised what he was saying and she pulled away from him breaking his hold. "Now I understand what this is all about. It all boils down to your stupid male pride," she said. Her anger was causing large teardrops to trickle down her cheeks. "You think you're too high and mighty to accept help. And it wasn't charity, it was an investment repayable at five per cent interest per annum. People invest in companies all the time. It's a natural way of going about things. I thought you'd have appreciated that."

A stony silence fell between them and Melody heard the outer door open and close. She knew that she and Guy had been shouting and Marsh must have heard everything. No doubt he would have gone to spread the news.

"I didn't ask you to do this," said Guy, taken aback at her vehemence and the sound sense in her reasoning.

Melody hissed through her teeth. "For God's sake, come down from your high horse and accept help when it's offered. If not for yourself, then at least do it for us, your employees. We have responsibilities too."

He moved away from the window and went back to the desk. "I'm surprised you didn't ask my uncle for a position with *The Evening Chronicle* while you had the chance," he said flippantly.

Melody didn't care for his sarcastic tone. "Actually, he made me an offer," she said, picking up her purse that had fallen to the ground with her struggling. She had had enough and wanted to go home.

"And what did you say?"

"I declined."

"Why was that?"

"Because, Mr Wyngate, I care too much about your damned newspaper to desert you now."

She turned on her heel and fled the office, almost colliding with Eric who was just coming through the door. Without hesitating she continued her journey, past the press office and the kitchen and then down the stairs and into the street. She was almost at running speed as she made her way along the roads and avenues that eventually led her to Hyde Park. It was only when she was in the park that she suddenly remembered Sultan and the gig, still stabled across the road from The Cork Street Journal.

Melody slowed down once she was among the trees in the park. She needed to slow down since her breath came in great gasps, her heart pounding in her ears. She felt stupid and embarrassed. Not only had she made a scene with her employer, she had shown herself up in front of her work colleagues and also left her means of transport behind. Poor Sultan, she thought, he'll wonder where she is when it gets to the evening. Melody shrugged, no use worrying about it now and besides, the horse would be well cared for in the stables overnight, she could always collect him the following day. She decided to go straight home.

When she arrived at Hyde Park Gardens no one was at home. Then she remembered it was Tuesday and Tilly always visited her mother on Tuesday afternoon and Mrs Carr was probably out on an errand of some kind. Melody ran upstairs and changed into a plain lilac housedress and then back in the kitchen she tied an apron round her waist and tucked her hair in a mob-cap. She quickly cut herself some ham and placed it in a sandwich, washing it down with a glass of milk.

"Now then, cleaning duties and laundry detail," she said, rolling up her sleeves. She thought of her girlhood at Hucknall Garth when the brigadier had given her tasks for disobedience, or insubordination as he called it. And Aunt Olivia had always advocated the benefit of useful work when Melody was either feeling sorry for herself or she was being rebellious.

"Take your temper out on that rug, milady," she would say, flinging a carpet over the line and handing the young girl a beater.

Melody spent the next two hours sorting out the possessions belonging to Aunt Olivia and Celia, so abruptly left behind after their sudden departure. Tilly and Mrs Carr had suggested doing it, but Melody had told them that she wanted to do it herself. But she had never found the time. Now she had time and set to work, clearing drawers and cupboards and folding clothes. Then everything was placed in boxes and chests and stored away in a spare room to await the hired men and wagon her aunt was sending very soon. By the time she had finished she was exhausted.

Tucking a loose strand of hair back under her cap she made her way into the kitchen and lifted the copper kettle onto the stove to make a well-earned pot of tea. While she was waiting for it to boil, she opened the kitchen door and let in a breath of fresh air, enjoying the soft breeze cooling her burning cheeks. Leaving the door open, she sank down at the table and rested her head on her arms, tiredness overwhelming her.

She heard a footstep just outside and looked up to see a dark figure framed in the doorway.

"Oh, Mrs Carr, you're back," she said, rubbing her eyes.

"May I come in?" His voice was soft and for a moment Melody didn't recognise him. "I took the liberty of searching out your address so I could bring Sultan home."

Guy stepped into the kitchen and Melody was surprised not only that he was standing there, but also that he was smiling. She stared up at him and then rose slowly to her feet.

"Thank you. I was wondering what I should do about him. He's not happy being away from home too long." She suddenly remembered her manners. "Please sit down. I was just making a pot of tea."

He took a seat, watching her. She looked absolutely charming in her apron and cap and although she appeared weary, he couldn't help thinking what a beautiful woman she was.

"Are you all right?" he asked.

"I'm just a bit tired. I didn't get much sleep last night." She gave a wan smile.

In fact, she was finding it difficult to keep her eyes open and when she reached up to get some cups from the dresser, the effort made her dizzy and she swayed a little. Guy was on his feet in a moment and putting his arm round her, guided her back to her seat.

"You sit and I'll make the tea," he said firmly.

He took off his jacket and hung it on the back of the chair and then started setting out the teapot, teacups, milk jug and sugar bowl.

Melody watched with fascination. "You're the first man I've seen making a pot of tea," she told him.

"Well, my housekeeper has an invalid mother and can only work a few hours a day, so I've learned to manage a couple of domestic chores on my own," he explained, lifting the kettle and pouring hot water onto the tea leaves. He carried the tray to the table and set it down. Melody smiled; his efforts would have pleased Mrs Carr.

"Wonderful," she said. "Just what I need."

"What you need is a good night's sleep, so I'll have my tea and then leave you in peace." Melody relaxed as she watched him pour out the tea and put in the milk. She took the cup he offered and sipped it. "I'm surprised you've not asked why I'm here," he said after a few seconds.

"To bring back Sultan, wasn't it?" she said, leaning her elbows on the table, cup held between both hands.

He shook his head. "No, I came to apologise. I went too far this morning and it was very rude of me. You went to see my uncle in good faith and I was too stupid to see it." He took a gulp of tea. "Will you forgive me?"

Melody could see he was finding this difficult. "There's nothing to forgive."

"I think there is. And I want you to know that I am grateful and I hope you'll return to the Journal."

"You accepted the money?"

"Yes, I did and with it I can continue the newspaper." He reached out and covered her hand very briefly with his. "You're my best journalist, Melody. I need you."

She thought for a moment. "I liked your uncle. I thought him a kind and generous man."

Guy nodded. "Yes, he is and well, to be honest, I went to his club this afternoon and we had a long talk."

Melody's tired expression turned to delight at the news. "I'm so glad you've spoken to him."

"It wouldn't have happened if it hadn't been for you." He gave an embarrassed cough. "We had an argument some time ago and hadn't spoken for many years."

Melody thought of Celia and her heart sank. "It's terrible to have a rift with someone you care for," she said softly.

Guy caught her sad expression and knew she was struggling with her own burden. He wondered who could have caused such sorrow to one so young.

"Well, there's no problem now. He was so pleased to see me. Slapped me on the back and called me 'my boy'. It was just like old times." He smiled at the memory. "And of course, we discussed the investment and finalised the details for the repayments." He finished his tea. "All I want to know is that you're coming back to the Journal."

Melody gave him a mischievous look. "Is it that important to you?"

"Yes," he said, watching her.

She gave an exaggerated sigh and fluttered her eyelashes. "Oh dear, I was planning to visit my Aunt Olivia in Kent."

He smiled and collecting up the cups, took the tray and placed it by the sink. "Despite your independent ways, you're not above using your feminine wiles on a man, are you? Well, it's up to you. But I can only pay you commission when you submit articles for publication."

"Then I'll do enough to cover my absence," she said. The thought of spending some time with her aunt at Hucknall Garth suddenly seemed wonderful.

He nodded and sat back down again. "Whereabouts in Kent does your family live?"

"Just near Staplehurst."

"I've heard of Staplehurst."

"Oh, it's such a lovely village on the River Beult. There's a bridge across the river and when I was a little girl I used to watch the trains and count the carriages." She grinned as she reminisced. "I didn't like the steam engines though. I thought they were black, fire breathing dragons."

"Did you expect a knight on a white charger to come riding by, sword in hand to slay the dragon?"

She gave an attractive giggle that made him smile. "Oh, no. If anything, I was on the white charger and I would have used the sword if I'd been given the chance."

"I'm certain of that," he said, standing up and pulling on his jacket. "I'd better go and I really think you shouldn't come into the office tomorrow. You need to get some rest."

Melody knew he was right. "I feel as though I've done enough today to fill two working days," she said, trying to stifle a yawn.

"Then stay away and when you return on Thursday, I should have some interesting information for you."

Grateful that she now had time to catch her breath and too tired to question his mysterious remark, Melody showed him to the door and with the briefest of goodbyes he left. She watched him stride down the cul-de-sac and then turn the corner, her feelings a mixture of confusion and warmth for him. There was something very special about Guy Wyngate and yet, she couldn't quite work out what it was. Her thoughts were interrupted by the appearance of Mrs Carr.

"Miss Melody, I didn't expect you back so soon," said the housekeeper, hurriedly untying her bonnet as she followed her mistress into the house.

"I came home because I was rather tired," lied Melody but then stifling yet another yawn, realised that she was very weary.

"Why don't you go and lie down for an hour or so. Tilly will be back soon and I can wake you when dinner is ready," she said kindly. "Give me your apron."

By now, Melody couldn't stop yawning and tired tears ran down her cheeks. She untied her apron and removed her cap, handing them to the housekeeper.

"I think I will. Thank you, Mrs Carr."

She forced herself up the stairs, every bone in her body aching. With relief she took off her dress and lay down in her petticoat, resting her head on the feather pillows that seemed so lumpy the night before and yet were soft and welcoming now. In a very short time she was fast asleep.

"Miss Melody, please wake up." Tilly's voice seemed to come from far away and Melody found it hard to stir herself, but the maid persisted. "You must wake up."

She slowly opened her eyes. "Is it time to eat already?" She rolled over and closed her eyes again. "I think I'm too tired to eat, Tilly. Tell Mrs Carr I'll have mine later."

"It's not that, miss," said Tilly, shaking her by the shoulder. "It's Doctor Courtney. He's just arrived with his mother. He says they're expected for dinner."

CHAPTER TEN

Melody swung her legs over the side of the bed, horror making her head spin. She trembled with the effort of trying to collect her thoughts. How could she have forgotten that Alex was bringing his mother to dinner? She cursed herself. It was an important occasion and now she had let him down and for the second time that day, humiliated herself. Only this blunder, she realised with a grimace, wouldn't be so easily forgiven as it had been with the editor of The Cork Street Journal.

"Where are they?" she said, pulling herself to her feet.

Tilly's expression was impassive as she busied herself around the room. "Don't worry, miss. Mrs Carr put them in the sitting room." She went to the wardrobe. "Now, I've brought you some hot water, so you must hurry and get ready. I'm afraid I can't help you dress, I must be away downstairs to set the table."

"What about the meal?"

"Mrs Carr is doing more vegetables to pad it out and there's apple pie for dessert. What dress do you want?"

"The green one," Melody said without thinking.

Tilly pursed her lips and then shook her head. "You already look too green. I think the white one would be better, then you'll seem all innocent like and win her over."

Melody jerked her head in the maid's direction. "Is she that formidable?" She began to pull the pins out of her hair letting it fall in auburn ripples down her back.

"She knows what's what," Tilly said, her expression grim.

Left alone, Melody hurried to wash and then change into the white lace dress, Tilly had lain across the bed.

She then brushed her hair, piling it on her head and holding it in place with the sapphire comb the brigadier had bought her for her eighteenth birthday. Taking her gloves and fan, she tried to descend the stairs gracefully, hoping that her demeanour would look calm and elegant and not betray the fact that every nerve in her body was on edge.

She glided through the door and saw Alex standing by the fire. He smiled as she entered the room and taking her hand, lightly kissed her fingers. He then led her across the room to the woman sitting on the couch. Melody couldn't take her eyes off her. Mrs Courtney didn't move as Melody came towards her, but her regal bearing was plainly evident, her manner superior even in a seated position. With her beautiful burgundy gown spread around her, her diamonds glittering at her throat and wrist and osprey feathers in her hair, she oozed style and breeding.

She held out a limp hand to Melody, who took it firmly.

"Mrs Courtney, it's so nice to meet you at last," she said, trying to sound confident and sincere.

Alex's mother barely smiled. "I've heard much about you, Miss Kinsman. We thought you might have come to Colchester to visit us there, but my son says you are in the newspaper business."

"I'm a journalist with The Cork Street Journal."

Mrs Courtney didn't answer, but instead flicked out her fan and wafted her face. Melody knew immediately she didn't approve and wondered what her son had told her.

Alex saved her from pondering any further uneasy thoughts. "Mother is amazed how a young girl of your class can be so dedicated in having an occupation."

Melody was about to answer when Tilly appeared saying that dinner was now being served.

Alex escorted the ladies into the dining room and seated them before taking the wine and filling each of their glasses. Tilly brought in the first course and placed it in front of the guests. It was leek soup and Melody could see that Mrs Courtney was not impressed. Nor did her manner alter with the serving of the lamb and vegetables or the apple pie and cream that concluded the meal.

Melody's indignation grew, knowing that Tilly and Mrs Carr had done their utmost to serve up a good dinner at short notice, even giving up their own meal for the sake of the guests.

"You run a simple household, Miss Kinsman. I can see your cook is not up to formal dining. My cook was trained in Paris and can produce the most exquisite dishes," she said, picking at the food on her plate. She cast her eyes round the room as if calculating the quality of the furniture and fittings.

Melody remained silent.

Tilly served coffee in the sitting room and Mrs Courtney took the opportunity of walking about and looking at the pictures and ornaments that adorned the shelves and cabinets, making comments as she examined them. At first, Melody felt irritated at the woman's audacity, but then realised she was doing it so her hostess could get a good view of her and perhaps admire her deportment. Yes, that is what she's doing, thought Melody, she's showing off her figure.

Although in her middle years, Mrs Courtney was a handsome woman, tall and slender with a waist pinched in with corseting. Alex should tell her how dangerous that is, Melody grimaced, perhaps she ought to mention it to him.

During the evening, Alex chatted happily to both women seemingly unaware that there was coolness from one and unease from the other. In fact, he seemed content to fill his glass at regular intervals while his mother looked on in disapproval. Finally, she stayed his hand as he was pouring himself another drink and told him firmly that the carriage was due and it was time to go. Melody showed them into the hallway and Tilly appeared to help the guests with their cloaks. She then saw them to the door and then out into the cool spring night where the carriage was waiting.

Mrs Courtney climbed aboard first, helped by the liveried coachman while Alex lingered for just a short time in order to plant a kiss on Melody's forehead.

"I'll call for you tomorrow evening about seven o'clock," he said, his words slurring slightly. "Mother is travelling back to Colchester in the morning, so I thought you might like to see the *Marriage of Figaro* at Covent Garden?" Melody murmured her approval and watched as he climbed in next to his mother. As he took his seat, he leaned out of the window. "I've something to ask you tomorrow, dearest." The carriage lurched forward and rumbled down the cobbled cul-de-sac.

Melody waved until it was out of sight her heart in her shoes. The evening had been a disaster and it had been all her doing. She went back into the house and made her way to the kitchen where two pairs of eyes turned in her direction as she entered. Tilly and Mrs Carr were tucking into some ham and cheese for their supper and their conversation died as they saw Melody's expression.

"Did your guests enjoy their dinner?" asked Mrs Carr.

"I think Doctor Courtney did and I certainly did," said Melody. She slumped into a chair. "But I don't think anything would have pleased Mrs Courtney. What a horrid woman! Such a snob. I didn't like her at all. But thank you ladies for all your efforts. You both pulled me out of a terrible mess. I can't believe I forgot that Doctor Courtney was bringing his mother to dinner."

Mrs Carr went to fetch a cup for her mistress and poured out some tea for her. "Sometimes things seem worse than they really are. She probably enjoyed herself more than she's saying."

Melody shook her head. "I think she was very disappointed with me. Thank goodness Doctor Courtney didn't seem to notice how icy her manner was."

Tilly decided to be practical. "Look, miss, as I see it, it's no good worrying over it tonight. There's plenty of hot water, why don't you have a bath and soothe all your worries away."

Melody gave a cry of approval. "That would be lovely."

"Then we'll put the bath in your room in front of the fire and you can soak to your heart's content."

Tilly and Mrs Carr carried the bath up the stairs and it was filled with steaming hot water and then lavender salts were sprinkled on the surface. As Mrs Carr helped Melody undress she felt compelled to ask the question she had been desperate to ask all evening. And that was her fate in the household of Hyde Park Gardens.

Melody slipped into the water and thought for a moment. "I want you to stay, but I'm not sure if I can afford your wage. I wondered if I should write to my aunt and ask for an allowance for you. After all, you are acting as chaperone and you should be paid for that."

Mrs Carr nodded. "I'll leave it to you, miss." She had dreaded the idea of finding another situation and leaving her present address. She had settled into the life at Hyde Park Gardens and although she wondered at

Miss Melody's enthusiasm for the journalistic life, she accepted that her mistress had a wonderful way with words. Miss Melody Kinsman could change the world with her writing, she was sure of that, and she wanted to be around to see it happen.

The following day a note arrived from Alex saying that plans had changed and he couldn't take Melody to the theatre that evening. His mother had decided to delay her return to Colchester and had expressed a desire to attend a performance of Handel's *Messiah* at the Crystal Palace. It seemed Mrs Courtney had a great deal of influence over her son.

Melody decided to spend the morning shopping in Bond Street and then impulsively went into the Cavendish Hotel for luncheon. She had gone there many times with Aunt Olivia and Celia and was known by the staff. Hoping that an unchaperoned lady wouldn't cause too much comment, she took a table near the door and after scanning the menu, ordered a light meal and a pot of tea. The restaurant was busy and a few pairs of eyes strayed in her direction making her feel uneasy. She might like to buck convention but she soon regretted her hasty decision to eat alone in public.

She drank the last of her tea, pulled on her gloves and gathered up her shopping. A hand gently touched her shoulder and she looked up to see Guy Wyngate.

"Miss Melody and looking in better health, I see," he said cheerfully.

She smiled. "I've just finished luncheon, but the waiter could bring you something."

He took a seat next to her. "Thank you, but I've just eaten," he nodded. "I've had a meeting with my banker, so it's been a busy morning and I must get back to the office. I suddenly spied you as I was passing through the lobby and wondered how you're feeling now."

"I'm feeling much better, thank you. I'll be back at the Journal tomorrow."

"Good," he said and rose to his feet. "Let me take those packages and escort you to your vehicle."

As he helped her aboard, Christian Jenner stood at the corner watching them, a smug smile hovering round his mouth.

The rain clouds raced across the sky and threatened a downpour as Melody arrived at The Cork Street Journal the following morning. But although the weather had changed dramatically from the previous sparkling spring day, she felt ecstatic to be back in Cork Street. She had had a day of rest and had benefited from it, but now she wanted to be at work.

Her first stop was Marsh's office where he sat as usual at his desk transferring information from sheaves of paper into a large ledger. He looked up as she entered and took off his spectacles wiping the lenses on his handkerchief.

"Have you heard the news, Miss Melody?" he said innocently. "The Journal is saved and our positions are secure."

She smiled and nodded. "Yes, I did hear. It is good news, isn't it."

She remembered that Marsh had overheard her heated argument with the editor two days before and everyone at the newspaper must now know why the paper was saved from closure. She wondered if he would mention it, but obviously the conversation was at an end as he bent over his work again.

"Mr Wyngate is expecting you," he murmured, dipping his pen in the inkwell.

Melody sat opposite Guy for a full thirty minutes as they discussed her work for the months ahead. He was eager to get her opinion on an idea.

His face lit up with delight that now he could make plans. "As I said, I received numerous letters regarding your interview with Lady Palmerston and I don't see why you shouldn't search out other society notables for interview."

"Are you thinking of men or women?"

He nodded. "Women mostly. Especially those in the public eye and there are quite a few."

"But are you really willing to give these women a chance to speak?" She couldn't believe that a man would allow such an exciting and yet innovative project in his newspaper.

Guy chuckled. "I want my newspaper to reflect society and women are part of society." He came round to her side of the desk and as was his habit, perched himself on the edge.

Melody nodded. "They're also fifty percent of the population, but completely overlooked."

"At the meeting on Tuesday," he continued, smiling, "when I informed you all of the fall in readership, I wasn't being strictly accurate." Melody watched him with interest, noticing how his intense brown eyes reflected his every mood. "In fact, the readership had started to increase slightly in the previous few months, but the bank thought it had come too late to save the paper."

"Because more women are reading The Cork Street Journal?" she whispered.

"More to the point, I sincerely believe that it was your articles that were attracting female readers. And because of this I've decided to give you a section of your own. Every week you can write a feature on the current affairs of women. And you will get a special commission for this as well as your normal fee for any news articles."

Melody gasped with surprise. "My own column and more pay," she smiled. Suddenly she realised that Mrs Carr could stay with her, since now she could afford to pay her wages.

"Yes, but I'll expect value for my money."

Melody thought for a moment, her face animated with excitement. "In the last few months I've been doing a great deal of research. There are many women who are trying to make a stand against the restrictions in society. Perhaps I could contact them for an interview. I could be their spokesperson."

"Who are you thinking of?"

"Well, there's Lydia Becker who is campaigning for a woman's right to study scientific subjects and Josephine Butler who's advocating higher education for women. Also, I'd like to interview Florence Nightingale."

Guy pulled a face. "I'm not so sure she'd agree to one. She's a very private person and has turned down every other newspaper."

Melody sighed but then had a further idea. "Alex told me about someone called Elizabeth Garrett who hopes to qualify as a medical practitioner this year despite prejudiced opposition. She had to train privately as no hospital would entertain the idea of a female medical student. I've heard she's planning to open up a dispensary treating women only."

"Alex?" Guy queried.

"Oh, a friend of mine," said Melody impatiently, her mind firmly fixed on her own plans. "There are so many women who want to speak and are held back by society's conventions. Not just the famous, but the poor and downtrodden too. Women from the East End.

Perhaps I could search out those women and let them have a voice."

She rose to her feet as if eager to get started. Guy stopped her, a worried frown crossing his face.

"I wouldn't like you to go to those parts of London, Melody. It would be far too dangerous."

"I was there when I reported the Fetter Lane murder."

"That was different. You didn't work for me then. I'm responsible for your safety now."

"Couldn't I take Eric with me?"

He let out a sigh of resignation. He knew that if Melody had an idea, there was no stopping her.

"We'll discuss it in more detail later. In the meantime, get your material from the mainstream of society and we'll see how that goes first."

She made for the door but then turned abruptly. "One day I'd like to write a book about the lives of women and their struggle to have their say."

"And what would you call this book of yours?" he asked, smiling.

She thought for a moment. "Perhaps something like 'The Silent Voice'."

He gave an incredulous laugh. "Show me a woman who is silent and I'll publish the book myself."

"I might hold you to that," said Melody, her cornflower-blue eyes sparkling with enthusiasm.

After she had left, Guy returned to his desk deep in thought. Alex? Was that male or female? Since the marriage of the Prince of Wales to Princess Alexandra of Denmark two years previously, many baby girls had been given that name. It had become popular. But Alexander could be a man's name also. Playing absently with his pen, he sucked in a deep breath. Why had his heart lurched when she had said the name? It wasn't his place to pass judgement on her friends. Damn it, he thought angrily, she's my employee and nothing more. He bent his head to his work, but found he couldn't concentrate. Rising from his chair, he collected his hat and coat. He would go to his club and have a drink in the company of male colleagues. Perhaps that would quell his disturbing thoughts.

The next three weeks were busy for Melody as she put her plans into action for interviewing the women making their mark on society. There were letters to send, appointments to make and numerous journeys backwards and forwards to addresses in London. She needed to write enough for her section, not only for the following weeks, but also for the time she would be away in Kent.

Time passed quickly and she began to count the days when she would be leaving London, her joy at spending time with Aunt Olivia, overwhelming her. She hadn't seen her since the baron's funeral and as the time drew nearer, she suddenly realised how much she had missed her. The brigadier and Celia were not due back from Italy for a further month, giving Melody the opportunity to speak with her aunt. She had to find a way to make amends for the terrible pain she had caused Celia and somehow restore their friendship.

When Melody found herself thinking of Celia, she also found her thoughts returning to Christian Jenner. For all his elegance and beauty, Melody knew that he was a person to be wary of. In many ways she was glad she had warned Celia about him. She had done it with the best of intentions and no one could fault her for that.

Alex had been full of apologies about his aborted plan to go to the theatre explaining that his mother had insisted on his company for a day longer and he thought it easier to comply. But his mother had returned to Colchester urging him to bring Melody to visit them as soon as possible. At first Melody had been surprised that his mother should want her to visit, especially after the disastrous meal at Hyde Park Gardens. But when she had tentatively questioned Alex about that evening, it seemed she had been right, and that he had been unaware that there was a problem. In fact, he thought it a successful evening and complimented her on her skill as a hostess.

However, he never mentioned what it was he wanted to ask her. Although they enjoyed each other's company, Melody would often catch him staring at her, as if struggling with some sort of dilemma. His manner was certainly more restrained. And she in turn, was too afraid to remind him that he had wanted to ask her something. She had an idea what it might be and felt happier pushing the notion to the back of her mind. She cared a great deal for Alex, there was no doubt about that. She even felt sure she loved him. But her life had become exciting and she didn't want it to change.

And so most of their conversation concentrated on their forthcoming holiday to Kent. It had been decided that Alex would accompany Christian to his grandmother's farm and in this way he could visit Melody at Hucknall Garth, situated only five miles away. They could even organise a picnic by the River Beult if the weather stayed fine. All in all it would be a delightful holiday and Melody felt sure that every problem would be resolved by the time she returned to London.

And then the day finally arrived when Melody caught the train to Staplehurst. She would be gone for two weeks and had given Tilly and Mrs Carr permission to close up the house if they wished. The maid had decided to visit her mother and younger siblings, but Mrs Carr said she would stay on at Hyde Park Gardens and 'keep an eye on things'. Tilly had confided in her mistress that the housekeeper had nowhere to go since she had no family whatsoever.

Hucknall Garth, the home Melody had shared with her father and aunt, was an old, rambling house set back from the main highway running through Staplehurst just eight miles from Tunbridge Wells. It stood in twelve acres of ground, mostly comprising beds of elaborate hardy perennials and robust shrubs. On the border of the estate stood the beech and lime trees, which shielded the house from prying eyes. The brigadier had always enjoyed his peace and solitude and although entertaining very occasionally, these rare events were more often instigated by his sister, than by the gentleman himself.

Melody strolled down the drive. The gardener had collected her from the station, but she asked him to drop her off at the gate. As she approached the house she slowed her walk even more and took in the full view of the home in which she had been born and, except for attending finishing-school and working in London, had spent her entire life.

It had been built in the mid-eighteenth century in a classical style; the Greek columns either side of the door enhancing the sash windows and warm brick. She turned to walk by the side of the building and made her way past the Garth, the small courtyard still containing the old stone bird table from where Grandma Hucknall had fed the birds and from where the house got its name. The house had belonged to her mother's family for a hundred years and her father had inherited it on his marriage, growing to love the house as much as Melody. But the brigadier's pride and joy was his rose garden. It consisted of fifteen beds filled with the perfume and beauty of red, white and pink blooms.

The brigadier's rose garden was special although frowned upon by his gardener, who complained bitterly that roses were not meant for bedding but destined for the shrubbery or climbing the stone walls round the house. The beloved geranium was for planting out, he believed, not the large rose shrubs which became straggly and untidy. The fact that the brigadier's late wife loved roses passionately and the garden was in her memory, didn't quell his annoyance.

The arguments that raged between master and gardener had continued ever since Melody could remember, and deep inside she felt that the two elderly men enjoyed bantering over the shape, style and display of the garden. It broke up what might have been a very dull existence for the people living at Hucknall Garth and had become part of life in the old house.

Melody examined the roses and sighed. She couldn't remember her mother, but had been told that although not beautiful, she had an elegance and style the envy of their close knit community. Her generosity to those in need was well known and her death had been mourned in many homes. It would have been lovely to have known her, thought Melody sadly, but she was still here, in this garden. Her father often came out and talked to the roses, but Melody knew to whom he was really speaking and she loved him for his devotion. She knew the brigadier didn't like to show his feelings and would grope for his pipe when his emotions threatened to get the better of him. He prided himself on his strength of character and had tried to engender the same in his daughter.

In Melody he saw the dynamic personality of his wife, the strength of character of the woman he had won so late in his life. His darling who had lived with him barely five years. But what years they had been. And out of their love had come Melody, to make their days bright and meaningful, to make them laugh and cry.

And when his wife was finally taken from him and he had sat alone in his study, it was the two-year-old Melody who crawled up on his knee and hung her chubby arms about his neck to comfort him. He held her tightly and for the first time in his adult life, Brigadier Liam Kinsman shed pitiful tears of grief.

Melody spun round as someone called her name. Passing round the rose garden and lifting her carpetbag against her, she walked faster to where Aunt Olivia stood waiting.

CHAPTER ELEVEN

It was extraordinary how familiar objects somehow appeared strange when a person had been away from them for a time. On that first day at Hucknall Garth, Melody rushed through every room, even into her father's bedroom, breathing in the smells of the old house. She touched everything she could, kissing the ornaments, hugging the cushions and reuniting herself with all the things she had taken for granted during her childhood. It had been a happy home and she was back, at least for the next two weeks.

For all her joy at being home again, Melody couldn't help noticing Celia's presence in the house. It wasn't just her room, although she didn't venture there. It was the sight of her outdoor clothing hanging in the hall, her shoes on the shelf, and the half-completed tapestry frame left on a table, that reminded Melody that her friend was now living at Hucknall Garth.

Alone with Aunt Olivia that first evening, Melody decided to broach the subject of her quarrel with Celia.

"Did she say anything to you?" asked Melody. They had finished their dinner and were sitting in the parlour together.

Her aunt nodded. "Not at Monkswood. I think she was too distressed over her dear father's death and losing her home to speak of anything. But once she was settled here, I decided to mention it and very slowly she began to reveal her feelings."

"And was she still very angry?" said Melody.

"No, not really. Quite a few weeks had passed and the anger had diminished somewhat. But she did feel hurt that you could destroy her dreams."

Melody felt stunned. "Her dreams?" she echoed, not quite understanding.

Aunt Olivia picked up her cross-stitch. "She had built up a fancy, as young girls do, of settling down and marrying a handsome eligible bachelor. And for some reason, she had fixed her mind on Doctor Jenner."

Melody sank back against the cushions of her chair. She had forgotten how shy and secretive Celia could be and her friend obviously had more desires than she had confided in Melody. They had always told each other their secrets, but as the years sped by, it was Melody who had monopolised their lives, fulfilling her dreams. And Celia had been left behind to hope and wish that her dreams would also come true.

"Did she tell you what I said about Christian?" asked Melody. She felt sick to her stomach that she had shattered her friend's allusions.

"Yes, she did. And although I agreed with you, because my dear, you will remember that I too saw Doctor Jenner for what he is, I didn't want to compound the problem."

"So, what did you say?"

"I told her that if this young man thought anything of her, then he would call on her himself and make moves to get to know her better." She gave a knowing smile. "In other words, I put the ball in his court. Of course, I knew he wasn't interested in Celia, and believed we would not hear from him again."

"That's for certain," sighed Melody.

"Not quite true," said her aunt.

Melody sat bolt upright. "Do you mean to say he visited Hucknall Garth?"

"He certainly did. About a week after we arrived back. But it was a courtesy call, simply to ask how she was and to bring some preserves from his grandmother, who has a farm near here I'm led to believe."

"Yes, Hunneybell Farm. Alex and Christian will be arriving in a few days to spend a week there."

"And Alex will be coming to see you?"

"Of course, although I hope he doesn't bring Christian too often. I'm not sure I like him."

Aunt Olivia looked up from her stitching. "Oh dear, don't tell me you've fallen out with him too."

"No, I just feel wary of him," said Melody, pulling a face.

"I've met his grandmother, you know. She and Christian were at the market in Tunbridge Wells and he introduced us. Mrs Hunneybell is a really delightful woman."

"I'm pleased about that. We've been invited to visit the farm while I'm here. And Alex wants us to have a picnic down by the river."

"That would be most agreeable." After a few seconds of thought Aunt Olivia added, "Shall we invite them to dinner? Alex naturally, but also Christian and his grandmother."

"It would only be polite," said Melody. She gave a huge yawn. "I think I'd better go to bed."

"I hope you haven't been working too hard, my girl. I was hoping Mrs Carr would keep an eye on you."

"She and Tilly look after me that's for sure. But I have been busy."

Aunt Olivia put down her needlework. "Before you retire for the night, I did want to ask you about Alex. In your letters you are so full of the newspaper, of Tilly and Mrs Carr and even of Guy Wyngate. But it seems you speak less and less of Alex. Is everything all right?"

Melody had risen from her seat but slowly sank back down again. "Remember the letter I sent you about Mrs Courtney and that terrible evening?"

Aunt Olivia tried to suppress a smile and failed. "When you forgot she was coming to dine? Yes, I remember."

"Well, Alex has been rather subdued since then, although he still thinks that evening went remarkably well. Sometimes I wonder if he's just saying that not to hurt my feelings."

"In your letter you thought his mother didn't like you."

"Aunt Olivia, I know she didn't like me. It was so obvious. And I wonder if this has influenced Alex."

"Are you expecting him to propose?"

Melody felt tiredness sweeping over her again. "I don't know what I'm expecting, Aunt. I really don't know. Sometimes I'm afraid he will propose and sometimes I'm afraid he won't."

"Yes, it's a very confusing time for a young girl."

Melody stood and kissed her aunt on the cheek. "Confusing or not, I'm too exhausted to think about it tonight."

As Melody climbed the stairs to her room, her thoughts were with Alex. But that night for some strange reason she dreamed of Guy Wyngate.

A few days later Alex arrived at Hucknall Garth and any reservations he seemed to have completely evaporated as he held her hands, kissing her fingers, her cheeks, her forehead, telling her how much he had missed her, although it had only been three days since they last met.

Arm in arm, Melody showed him around the home she loved and then the gardens. They sat for a time on the swinging seat and Aunt Olivia brought them some of her special lemonade. It had been a warm day, and the coolness of the evening was refreshing. The gardener had informed them that the weather was going to be remarkably hot this summer, and since he was never wrong, they planned the days ahead on the strength of it. There seemed such a great deal to do, especially since Alex only had one week before he had to go back to the hospital. But Melody knew the following week would be wonderful and she looked forward to everything with a childlike enthusiasm.

The day finally came when Melody, accompanied by her aunt, visited Hunneybell Farm and to her surprise, Christian couldn't have been more amicable. With great pride he showed his guests the oast house, newly renovated and ready to dry the harvest of hops that year. Its white conical tower gleamed in the bright sunshine and seemed to spread its charm over the Kent countryside and the fields of growing hops.

The farmyard was filled with machinery and implements of all shapes and sizes as well as a wagon. In the barn, two cows sedately munched the hay, staring at the visitors with inquisitive brown eyes. Christian told them that they were usually kept company by the horses, but they were out working with the farm hands at the moment. Outside the kitchen door, chickens clucked and bickered as they pecked the corn scattered about and just on the far side of the farmyard was a pen in which half a dozen pigs were kept.

Melody's impression of the farm was that it was fairly prosperous and wondered if Christian's education had, after all, come from the proceeds of hop farming. When they all finally entered the kitchen, they were amazed to see the table groaning under the weight of hams, chickens, fresh bread, tomatoes, baked potatoes and all manner of food waiting to be consumed. Christian, rather sheepishly, felt compelled to explain that Gran always provided enough food to feed an army.

They sat round the table tucking into the feast as best they could, while Mrs Hunneybell ambled backwards and forwards, filling up their glasses and cups with whatever beverage they wished. She couldn't have been more hospitable, tending to their every need, her plump face flushed with pleasure. While they ate, they talked incessantly of the farm, of their lives in London and any topic of conversation that came to mind. It was a most congenial party that met together that evening in Mrs Hunneybell's comfortable kitchen and Melody suddenly felt she liked Christian after all. She watched as he and Alex chatted together, reminiscing over their school days and vying with each other over the best and worst times.

"I'm surprised that Christian had ambitions to become a doctor," asked Aunt Olivia, looking around the spacious kitchen. "I would have thought farming would have come naturally to him."

"Oh, Christian always wanted to be a doctor," said Mrs Hunneybell. "He takes after my Grace for that. She went off to the Crimea with Florence Nightingale, you know. But it took its toll on her and she came home after six months. She died a year later." She sighed. "My girl wasn't strong enough really, but she insisted on going."

Christian stopped talking to Alex as he heard his mother's name mentioned. "She shouldn't have gone," he said acidly.

"You must have been quite young when she left," said Melody, realising that he was still hurting deeply over his mother's death.

"I was about twelve or thirteen when she went out there although I was away at school at the time."

"I remember you receiving the letter telling you she was dying," said Alex thoughtfully.

Christian took a gulp of wine. "Gran's right. Mother wasn't strong enough to withstand the rigours of working in a military hospital. The war was a terrible waste of life."

Melody thought the conversation was turning rather melancholy and decided to lighten the topic.

"Has Hunneybell Farm been in the family long?" she asked the elderly woman who was busy dishing out slices of cherry cake.

"Goodness me, yes. The Hunneybell family has owned it for the last two hundred years. And they've sold their hops to Shepherd's Brewery in Faversham for the last hundred years."

"And now Gran's doing her best to keep the nation tiddly," said Christian, grinning at his grandmother.

Mrs Hunneybell gave a chuckle that seemed to come from deep down within her. "Of course, Mr Hunneybell was my second husband, God rest his soul. Grace's father died when she was just a babe and we came to live here when she was only five years old, but Mr Hunneybell loved her like his own, he did."

"But you are from Kent too?" asked Melody.

"My family and that of my first husband come from Tunbridge Wells."

"Oh, what was the name of your first husband? We might know his family." Melody smiled broadly at her aunt.

"Jenner was his name," said Mrs Hunneybell softly.

"Oh, so you have your mother's maiden name?" Melody said, turning to Christian and then she felt the colour drain from her face, as a stunned silence went round the table.

Melody realised with horror that she had unwittingly exposed Christian as illegitimate.

Alex gave an apologetic cough. "This is wonderful cake, Mrs Hunneybell," he said, taking a large bite and casting Melody a piercing glance.

"Is that why you wanted to be a doctor, Christian?" asked Aunt Olivia, trying to retrieve the situation. "To make up for your mother's death."

He gave a bitter laugh. "No, I believe there's more money in medicine."

"I just wish you wouldn't ask so many questions," Alex sighed. He and Melody were in the cellar at Hucknall Garth selecting the wines for the forthcoming dinner. "I know you didn't mean to embarrass Jenner, but your inquisitiveness can be so damaging at times."

They had entered the cellar down stone steps that led from the kitchen to the storeroom where the eggs, bottled fruit and preserves where kept. Adjoining this room was the cellar filled with casks of cider, barrels of ale and what seemed like hundreds of wine racks, the higher shelves being reached by a ladder. The brigadier chose to have a wide selection of wine even though he didn't like entertaining. Alex steadied himself on the ladder, slid out a bottle, read the label and passed it to Melody who was already holding two others.

She jostled the bottles into a better position. "That's a strange comment to make to a journalist, since asking questions is what I do," she answered rather indignantly.

Alex glanced down at her, smiling at how beautiful she looked in the glow from the lamp. Her auburn hair was fastened with a small spray of artificial flowers and her rose pink silk gown swished around her emphasising her slender figure. He had gasped when he had stepped into the parlour and seen her and he would have taken her in his arms and kissed her, if her aunt hadn't been in the room. Instead, he had bowed politely over her hand, with Olivia's eyes on him.

"I know that, dearest, but what I'm saying is can't you keep your questions for the newspaper business and behave in a more demure manner in company?"

Melody raised her eyebrows. "Demure!" she snapped. "You'll be saying next that I should keep my eyes down and only speak when I'm spoken to."

"Don't be silly. You know I don't mean that." He selected the final bottle and descended the ladder. "But it would be nice if you could keep your conversation on a lighter level when in company and not interrogate everyone as if you're the Spanish Inquisition."

Melody smiled despite her indignation. "Is that what it seems like? As though I'm interrogating people?"

Alex smiled too. "Yes, it does."

He took the lamp in one hand and carrying the wine in the other, he led the way out of the cellar. Suddenly he stopped and leaned over to kiss her lips tenderly. A pleasant shudder went through him and he couldn't prevent himself from stealing a second much longer and lingering kiss.

"Are you all right down there?" Cook came to the top of the steps.

"Yes," called Melody. "We're all finished here."

She too had felt a quiver race through her and had been shocked how her lips had parted as his mouth had pressed on hers.

But she couldn't let go of her resentment. "I'm surprised Christian and his grandmother accepted our invitation to come to dinner if I'm that horrid," she said.

"You're not horrid. Just overpowering at times. Anyway, they were delighted to be invited."

Melody let out an audible sigh. "I really didn't mean to embarrass Christian or upset his grandmother. I could have bitten out my tongue when I realised what I'd said."

He tried to be philosophical. "Well, it confirms one thing, that the rumours at Eton were true and Jenner's parents weren't married. Can you manage those bottles?" Melody nodded. "Then let's go back upstairs and please try and behave yourself."

"I hate you Alex Courtney," hissed Melody through her teeth.

Alex grinned and gave her a wink.

They made their way through the storeroom and up the stone steps. In the kitchen they past Cook, her face hot and flushed from her labours as she chided the two maids, sending them scurrying in all directions. Melody and Alex quickly went into the dining room, leaving the bottles of wine on the beautifully prepared table and then through into the parlour where Aunt Olivia was offering sherries to the guests who had arrived only five minutes before. As soon as Mrs Hunneybell spied Melody, she enfolded her in a warm embrace and even Christian was smiling as he stepped forward to kiss her hand.

With great relief, Melody realised she needn't have worried, as the dinner was a great success and everyone enjoyed themselves tremendously. Nothing was said of Melody's *faux pas* and as the evening ended, they said their goodbyes with the next outing planned, the picnic by the River Beult. It would take place the day before Alex returned to London and with his departure, Melody would only have four days left of her own holiday.

She wondered if the picnic might give Alex the opportunity to propose. For now she was certain that that was what he intended doing. During the dinner, she had caught him smiling at her over the rim of his wineglass and afterwards, in the parlour, his hand had constantly brushed against hers. Her heart pounded with the prospect of being asked and she hadn't dared contemplate her answer. She wouldn't think about it, she decided, she would wait for the moment and her feelings would tell her what to say. It never occurred to her that feelings can be deceptive, even transient and what seems right one day, can feel very wrong the next.

CHAPTER TWELVE

The party from Hunneybell Farm arrived at Hucknall Garth just before midday. Christian turned the wagon in at the gate, with his grandmother sitting next to him, and Alex perched at the back. The vehicle was loaded with all the paraphernalia needed for a good picnic, including a large hamper, folding chairs and blankets to spread on the grass. Olivia had also prepared a hamper and contributed bottles of wine and two parasols, as they were certainly in the throes of a heat wave and the sky was completely devoid of any clouds.

They loaded up the wagon and then Melody climbed into the driver's seat of the carriage with Alex next to her and Olivia sitting serenely in the back. The carriage led the way as the wagon and its occupants followed them down the country lane and towards Staplehurst and the River Beult. Just as the cottages of the village appeared, they turned towards the river, where many others had obviously had the same idea. The riverbank was filling with people, young and old, determined to make the best use of the coolest place in the area. Picnics were being laid out on colourful tablecloths, boats of all shapes and sizes bobbed on the water and children ran up and down, some paddling in the shallow parts, pantaloons and skirts hitched up above their knees. Everywhere was the noise of people enjoying a day out.

They found a place and set out the chairs and parasols. It wasn't long before Alex and Christian wanted to eat and the picnic was spread out on a tablecloth and a bottle of wine was opened. After they had eaten, Olivia and Mrs Hunneybell sat chatting while Christian stretched himself out on a blanket and enjoyed a doze in the sun, his hat over his eyes.

Alex had no desire to do either of these things and instead suggested that he and Melody take a walk beside the river. Melody slipped her hand through his arm and they strolled along the path, sometimes meeting an acquaintance that Melody would introduce to Alex and after a brief conversation they would say their goodbyes and move on. When Alex realised they could hire a boat, he expressed a wish to go out on the water and Melody agreed enthusiastically.

They walked slowly towards the man hiring the boats, allowing the wonderful weather and the charming scene to drift over them. Despite the beautiful day, Melody was growing increasingly concerned by Alex's manner that was becoming more subdued the further along the bank they went. If he was going to propose, she thought, he was finding it difficult. Suddenly she wondered if she had misread his intentions. Perhaps it wasn't a proposal he was considering but an end to their courtship? Perhaps his mother had filled his head with too many doubts! But there was no mistaking his behaviour at Hucknall Garth. He had been unbelievably affectionate towards her and had even stolen a third kiss as he had said goodbye.

They finally arrived at the small hut where the man who hired out the boats usually sat. There was already a few rowing boats wobbling about, crewed by a motley assortment of oarsmen in various stages of skill.

"Are you sure you want to go in a boat?" said Alex smiling.

"Absolutely," said Melody. "Do you want me to row? I can. The brigadier taught me when I was ten."

"No, I'll row," he answered.

The man at the boating hut pushed the craft into the water and helped Melody step in. She made herself comfortable and when Alex jumped in and took the oars, she settled herself back to enjoy the extraordinary day. He pulled on the oars steadily, making the small vessel skim smoothly through the water, concentrating on his task of aiming for the middle of the river. They reached the centre and he leaned on the oars, studying her. She noticed.

"What are you looking at?"

"I'm looking at you. I think you're the loveliest woman I've ever seen," he said softly.

"Thank you," she said, fluttering her eyelashes.

"I'm serious." He dipped the oars and manoeuvred the small boat out of the way of another trying to get by. "And I enjoy your company very much."

"Then why the sombre expression?"

"I'm not sombre, just thoughtful."

"What are you thinking about?" Melody looked down at his hands gripping the oars. They were physician's hands, gentle hands, trained to heal and help people. And yet she could see that the knuckles were white with the pressure of his grip. She sat forward and put her hand over his. "What is it, Alex? Please tell me."

He breathed in and held it for a moment. "I have something to ask you. I want to know if you would consider…"

He stopped and turned his head away, biting his lip. Melody couldn't help bursting into spontaneous laughter. But seeing he didn't care to join in with her amusement, she put her fingers over her lips.

She gave a gentle cough and tried to control herself. "Sorry. I didn't mean to laugh. It's just that you're being so mysterious."

He nodded. "Yes, I know." Summoning courage he added, "I've been giving it a great deal of thought Melody and I want you…"

A large object whistled past them, missing the boat by inches, and hitting the water with a resounding splash. It had come from the iron girder bridge that was directly above them and they looked up, hardly daring to breathe, wondering what had happened. From another boat, a man's cry of alarm echoed over their heads; sending a swan hastening into the water, its magnificent wings outstretched ready for flight.

"Are you all right down there?" They looked up again to see a face peering over the bridge. "That was my bloody hammer. Is it gone, mate?"

Alex looked into the water's depths. "Afraid so," he shouted back.

"They must be working on the railway line," said Melody. "I can't say I noticed."

Alex picked up the oars again. "You wouldn't. The workmen will be hidden behind the ironwork." He began to pull for the shore. "I think we'd better get back. It's getting rather dangerous with missiles hurtling around."

Alex steered the small boat back to the moorings, surprising the hiring man as they still had thirty minutes left.

"Can't give you a refund," he grunted, but Alex had already turned away and taking Melody's arm, guided her towards the rest of their party still sitting on the riverbank.

"What's the time?" asked Melody.

"Nearly two-thirty," said Alex, looking at his watch.

She thought for a few seconds. "If I remember, the Folkestone to London train is due soon. I hope it doesn't run into the workmen."

Alex smiled. "I'm sure they've done enough maintenance work to know when to stand aside as it passes."

They reached the others and made themselves comfortable. As Christian passed them each a glass of wine, a high-pitched whistle sounded in the distance and Melody put down her wineglass and jumped to her feet.

"I thought so," she cried. "It's the London train and right on time too." She ran down to the river so she could get a better view.

"You'd think she'd never seen a train before," smiled Olivia to Mrs Hunneybell.

Alex and Christian joined her and they looked in the direction of the whistle, their hands shading their eyes. In the distance they could see a small black object and the glint of glass and polished wood of the coaches. It was coming closer and they could now hear the wheezing of the engine as it clanked its way over the lines. Soon, the engine with smoke pouring from the funnel, the tender and coaches could be easily seen.

"Dear Lord, what's that?" said Alex, pointing up at the bridge.

Melody caught her breath. "It's a red flag." She narrowed her eyes. "Why are the men stopping the train?"

The engine was getting much closer and Melody watched mesmerised, first at the train and then at the red flag waving frantically, and then back at the train. She froze as she heard the chilling screech of brakes; the engine hurtling onwards unable to stop. What happened next, Melody would remember for the rest of her life.

The engine reached the bridge and then seemed to jump the line, taking the tender and first coach with it. The remaining coaches suddenly lurched to one side and then with a frightful sound of splintering wood and shattering glass, sprang upward and over the bridge to start their terrifying descent into the waters below. The last coach broke from its couplings that saved it from following and teetered on the edge, gently rocking backwards and forwards.

Melody gave a gasp as the coaches floated on the surface for a brief moment, but then rapidly filling with water, disappeared beneath the river. People had risen to their feet, children had stopped playing, all with expressions of utter bewilderment mixed with horror. A deathly stillness filled the air; there seemed to be no sound except the occasional barking of a dog and the hissing from the engine high up on the bridge.

And then a passenger from the submerged coaches broke the surface of the water, splashing, gasping for air and screaming in terror. Someone echoed her piercing screams on the riverbank and the spell was broken. Mayhem followed as instructions were shouted. People ran towards the coach on the bridge, others waded into the water to pull out the survivors that were slowly rising from the depths and lift them onto the bank. Some able young men pulled off their jackets and shoes and dived into the river, risking their lives by swimming down to the coaches to see if they could rescue any trapped passengers.

Alex and Christian immediately set to work treating the injured, tearing up tablecloths to bind wounds and make tourniquets. Others too, went from casualty to casualty wrapping them in blankets and tending to minor cuts and abrasions, offering comfort where they could.

The casualty numbers were growing and when the first body came floating to the surface and was carried to the riverbank, Melody knew it would be the first of many. Luckily, the coach suspended on the edge of bridge hadn't moved its position and the workmen were able to evacuate its passengers and lead them down to the riverside were the doctors could treat their injuries.

Melody also discovered that no one had been below the bridge in a boat. In fact, she and Alex had been directly in the path of the falling coaches and had they stayed ten minutes longer they would have undoubtedly been among the number of fatalities. The very thought made her hair stand on end.

She worked steadily for the next two hours doing all she could, sometimes assisting Alex or Christian, who would call her over to help them to dress a wound or stem bleeding. Her pride in Alex at his calm and confident manner in dealing with the casualties, was equalled by her growing respect for Christian. Never had she seen two doctors work so tirelessly dealing with people in such desperate circumstances.

Residents came hurrying from Staplehurst and soon the 'walking wounded' were escorted back to homes willing to care for them until they were well enough to complete their journey or be collected by relatives.

Melody knelt beside a young girl, holding a cloth against a large cut on her shoulder. She had been pulled from the river, her dark hair dank and matted, her clothes torn and muddy. Alex had already examined her and said her injuries were not life threatening and the bleeding would stop if Melody applied pressure. This she did until the child's mother, who had been searching for her, cried out in relief when she discovered her daughter lying on the ground. Leaving the girl in her care, Melody looked about her.

People seemed to be everywhere, and a terrible sort of order pervaded the scene. The constabulary had arrived and a police sergeant was coordinating the rescue effort, writing information in his notebook at regular intervals. Over on the grassy bank, a tidy line of bodies, covered respectfully, was being laid out ready to be taken away for identification. For Melody, it seemed like a battlefield and yet it was obvious that everything that could be done was being done. She didn't feel she could do any more and wondered if now was a good time to do what she had been yearning to do.

Going over to the place where they had been sitting before the accident, she found the picnic basket and pulled out her notebook and pencil. Well, she thought with a shrug, this is news and she was a reporter. Soon, she was talking to the survivors who were able and asking them about the accident, scribbling their statements down as fast as she could. She met a ganger who had been working on the line who told her that they had been pulling up about forty-three feet of rail, since they thought the train had been diverted. It was he who had run down the line with the red flag and tried to stop it, but it was going too fast to brake in time. The engine, tender and first coach had miraculously jumped the gap in the line, but the remaining coaches had been thrown over the bridge by impacting on the girders.

"There'll have to be an inquiry about this," he said, wiping the sweat from his brow with a dirty hand. "Someone will have to explain his negligence."

Melody saw a tall, thin, middle-aged man trying to help a younger man who seemed to have a serious head injury. She decided to help him and saw immediately that the wound looked critical and called Alex over. Noticing the elderly gentleman biting his lip at the condition of the casualty, Melody questioned him.

"Is he your son?" she said.

"Oh no, just someone I came across and thought I could help," he answered softly. They moved away so that Alex could examine the patient.

"That's very kind of you." She looked about her. "But there's been a great deal of heroism today. I don't think any of us will forget this afternoon in a hurry."

"I certainly won't. I was on my way back to London from Paris and this happens. What a way to finish a holiday."

"Where were you seated on the train?"

He pointed to the snorting funnel above him. "The first class carriage behind the engine. I called to everyone to keep still, until we knew what was happening. I've never been so afraid in my life."

Melody nodded and then started asking him what actually happened at the moment of the crash.

The gentleman answered her questions without hesitation but frowned when he saw her writing in her notebook. "Why are you writing this down? If I hadn't been a journalist myself, I would have said you belonged to that profession, but I know there are no female reporters."

She looked at him closely, at his thin face, receding hairline and wispy beard. "You were a journalist, sir?"

"Many years ago. I'm an author now."

She held out her hand and shook his warmly. "Then I must contradict you, since there is one female reporter. May I introduce myself? Melody Kinsman from The Cork Street Journal."

The gentleman was at first startled and then smiled. "I've heard of you, young lady. You have something of a reputation, or so I'm led to believe."

"Yes, I've been told that myself. I keep hoping it's a good one."

He smiled but then became serious and taking her arm, led her over to a quiet area of the riverbank. "Am I to understand, Miss Kinsman, that you intend publishing my comments in your paper?"

"Yes, if you'll allow me."

He looked around at the disaster and then took in a deep breath. "Then I must tell you that my name is

Charles Dickens." He shook his head slowly. "And I beg you to leave my name out of your newspaper."

Now it was Melody's turn to gasp in surprise. "The famous novelist?"

"Yes, indeed. And mention of my name will have terrible repercussions."

"Why is that?"

"I'm not travelling alone." He indicated two women sitting on the riverbank that Melody had not noticed until then. "The younger one is my...companion. The other lady is her mother. I hope you understand that if it becomes known that I have been to Paris with this young woman, I will be hounded out of the country."

Melody didn't need further explanation and closed her notebook. "Sir, I wouldn't do that to you for the world."

He took her hand and kissed it. "I will be forever in your debt."

"I have always admired your work and it was you who inspired me to become a journalist in the first place," said Melody, hardly believing she was speaking to the great man himself.

"It's a worthy profession for any man...or woman and one to be proud of."

Melody looked at the devastation about her. "Bringing the news to the people is one thing, sir, but one day I hope to follow your example and write about social reform and the equality of women."

"You do that, young lady. Always hold onto your dreams and never let anyone discourage you from your true destiny. Oh, how I envy your youth. You are just starting out on the big adventure. I wish you every success."

Kissing her hand once more he left her and hurried across to the two women who greeted him with relief.

Melody knew she would never betray his trust, not even to Guy Wyngate, but whether the editor would understand or not, she had yet to discover. She noticed there seemed to be reporters everywhere, mostly from the Tunbridge Wells newspapers. Melody grimaced, they might not be so discreet and it would be better if Mr Dickens and his party left the area as soon as possible.

Her aunt called for her assistance and she went to help her.

They travelled home slowly that evening, even the horses hung their heads as if weary to the bone. Waving goodbye at the gate of Hucknall Garth, Alex, Christian and his grandmother continued onwards to Hunneybell Farm, while Melody and her aunt made their way round to the stable and then into the house.

For all that she could hardly keep her eyes open, Melody was determined to write up her report on the train accident. It had been decided that Alex would take it with him the following morning when he returned to London. The editor had to get it first thing, if it was to make the evening edition.

Once her head was bent over her task, it seemed as if the pen flew across the paper. It was still not known how many bodies were trapped in the coaches submerged in the waters of the River Beult but lifting gear had been arranged and it would arrive the following day. Melody intended to return there to finalise her report, although she knew that by then she would have to jostle with the sightseers who always flooded to an accident scene.

She raised her head thinking over the events of that day and of her intended journey back to the River Beult. It would be a melancholy scene and she knew what to expect. She would try and speak to someone in authority; perhaps a friendly police sergeant might be available. Then she would get a full account, including the number of casualties and fatalities.

Melody sighed and realised what a wonderful, magical place the riverbank had been for her. A place she had visited with Aunt Olivia and her father as a child. She had run up and down the riverbank with her hoop, she had hitched up her skirts and paddled and the brigadier had taught her to row and skim stones across the surface of the water. But now it would all be changed, not just for her, but for everyone. It was a place of death and carnage. People wouldn't be able to picnic there, lovers wouldn't be able to woo, and children wouldn't be able to play, without remembering the terrible events of that June afternoon. Everything had been swept away in a moment of unbelievable horror.

The article finished, she then wrote a note to Guy Wyngate, telling him that she would send further news as it developed and also added, off the record, that she had met someone he would be interested in hearing about. She had hardly signed her name, when her head dropped on her arms and she fell fast asleep. It was Olivia who found her and put her to bed.

The following morning, Melody was awake early and by eight she was in the trap, urging Halley to move as fast as possible. She had to get to the farm and pick up Alex for his ten o'clock train to London. Next to her on the seat was the envelope in which she had put her news report and letter.

Driving into the farmyard, she saw the kitchen door open and outside stood Mrs Hunneybell feeding the chickens who clucked around her as if she was Mother Hen.

Melody drew to a halt as Alex and Christian appeared at the door. "I came as fast as I could," said Melody. "But I think we'd better go immediately. I've heard the trains are disrupted after yesterday's havoc."

"I'm all ready," said Alex, throwing his bag into the trap and climbing aboard. "Thanks for your hospitality, Mrs Hunneybell and I'll see you in a few days Jenner."

They waved as Halley lurched forward and soon they were on their way to the station. Their conversation en route was invariably about the accident. It seemed impossible that workmen could pull up the track without informing the railway to stop the trains. Alex said he would be interested to read the inquiry report and in fact he had had to give his name to the police sergeant and would most probably be called as a witness.

"For the second time in twelve months," grimaced Alex, remembering his day in court before Christmas.

"But this time your evidence might help improve matters."

"Who knows? An injured workman told me that the timetable had been consulted. Obviously someone had looked at the wrong day. Can human error be eliminated?" Melody shook her head slowly and Alex smiled. "But in the meantime I must get back to what I do best. Give me that report of yours."

Melody passed it to him and he pushed it into his bag. "Please make sure the editor gets it," she said. "You know where Cork Street is, don't you?"

"Yes I do. Don't worry, I'll put it in Mr Wyngate's hands personally."

They arrived at the station and were soon on the platform where they were told that the London train would be on time. The South-Eastern Railway Company always did their best to keep their trains running. Eventually the engine steamed into view.

"I'll expect you back at Hyde Park Gardens in a few days, dearest," he said, pressing Melody to him.

She nodded. "We'll have dinner together as soon as possible."

The train stopped with a squeal of brakes and the passengers started to clamber aboard. Alex hesitated and then turned Melody round to face him, his hands on her shoulders.

"I didn't want to do it this way, but...Will you be my wife? Please marry me."

Stunned, Melody swallowed hard as she looked into bright, eager eyes waiting for her answer.

"Yes, I'll marry you." She could hardly believe it was her words leaving her throat. Alex's face broke into a rapturous smile and he pressed a hasty kiss on her lips before pulling open the door of an empty compartment but Melody stopped him. "Please travel in the end coach," she said.

For a moment he frowned, but then realising her concern, acquiesced with a smile. They walked along the platform and he jumped into the last carriage.

"Goodbye," he said leaning out of window and giving her another kiss. "I'll miss you while we're apart, but I have some wonderful news to take back with me."

She blew him a kiss as the whistle screeched and the engine began to pull its load away from the platform. Melody stood there until the train was out of sight and when she turned to leave, tears dripped down her cheeks.

She had accepted Alex's proposal when marriage had always been something she had been wary of. But she loved Alex and they would be happy together. Yes, marriage did have a place in her life after all. But if anyone had told her that just seven months ago, she would have laughed at the very idea.

CHAPTER THIRTEEN

It was far too hot to do anything the following day and Aunt Olivia and Melody spent the morning relaxing in the garden. They were sitting below the steps of the wide terrace that led down to the lawn where the croquet hoops were set up. This had always been Melody's favourite place since it overlooked the grounds at the back of the house. Beech and alder framed the lawn giving the shade so necessary on hot summer days. A long flower border, a riot of colour, adorned the terrace where all the windows were left open to allow any breeze to circulate through the house. Pots and hanging baskets speckled the terrace and everywhere was the sweet perfume of summer blooms.

Along with the swinging seat and three cane chairs, a hammock had been strung between two trees and Melody had always loved lying in it and swaying gently from side to side. Her aunt was content to sit close by and read. As the sun rose higher, the air became still and even the birds stopped singing. Only the sound of a bee could be heard humming among the hollyhocks and foxgloves and now and again a butterfly would flutter by, land on a blossom and then after a few seconds continue its lethargic journey.

Melody looked up at the leaves in the tree, her thoughts drifting into space. She felt relaxed and at peace with the world. The train accident had made her realise how lucky she was to be alive. She and Alex had come very close to being killed and if it hadn't been for the clumsiness of a workman and Alex's astuteness at removing them from under the bridge, they certainly would have stayed on the river. A falling hammer saved our lives, she thought with wonder. And now they were engaged to be married. For all her reservations, Melody felt happy. She couldn't understand why. Was it just the sheer joy of being alive after so many others had not lived to see this beautiful day? Or was it because she was now ready for marriage? After all, at the end of the year she would be twenty-three and many girls were married long before that age.

Melody sighed and contemplated how fragile life could be. And short! Too short to let a silly misunderstanding spoil a special friendship.

She turned to her aunt. "Before I leave for London I'm going to write a letter. Would you make sure Celia gets it when she comes home?"

Olivia smiled and put down her book. "Oh, my dear, I'm so pleased." She stood and stretched herself. "Well, I think I'll organise luncheon. Would you like Sarah to bring out some iced tea?"

Melody closed her eyes murmuring her approval. Silence enveloped her and with one arm flung over her forehead she began to drift off to sleep.

She barely heard her aunt return five minutes later, or realised that a second person accompanied her. It was only when she heard her name called that she opened her eyes and looked across to the terrace. She saw her aunt with a man whose easy stride seemed very familiar and although he wore a hat, he had taken off his jacket and was carrying it over his shoulder in a casual manner.

"We have a visitor," her aunt said, smiling with pleasure.

Melody tried to lift herself from the hammock. "Goodness me, it's Mr Wyngate," she said in surprise. Her actions were too quick and she fell back as the hammock's swinging motion caught her off balance.

"We seem to have a damsel in distress here," said Guy, taking her hands and helping her from the captive canvas. "I hope I'm not intruding but I was in the area and thought I would call in to see you." His eyes crinkled into a smile.

"Not at all," she stammered. "You're always welcome at Hucknall Garth. You've obviously met my aunt, Mrs Olivia Timme."

"Yes, and I'm pleased to meet you at last Mrs Timme," he said, giving a slight bow.

Aunt Olivia nodded. "And I've heard so much about you, Mr Wyngate, I'm rather disappointed you turned out to be a mere mortal." Seeing Melody's horrified expression, she added quickly, "I was just organising some cold drinks. Could I offer you a glass of cider or ale?"

"Cider would be wonderful," he said. "It certainly is a hot day."

Melody gave her aunt a warning glance, before turning her attention to the editor. "Is this just a social call?" she asked. "I'm rather intrigued as to why you should suddenly visit me here at Hucknall Garth."

"It's part business, part pleasure. I have something to discuss with you." He turned to Olivia. "That's if you don't mind, Mrs Timme? It shouldn't take long."

"Of course not, do make yourself comfortable and I'll send Sarah out with the drinks. You'll not be disturbed." She started walking towards the house but turned to call over her shoulder, "Will you stay for luncheon?" But she didn't wait for his answer.

Melody indicating the cane chairs under the tree and they sat down. Guy flung his coat over the back of his seat.

"I hope you'll forgive me for appearing in shirtsleeves. I know it's polite for a gentleman to wear a jacket in company, but I would find it unbearable."

"When have I ever bothered about convention?" laughed Melody. She looked towards the house. "In fact, I'm surprised my aunt left us alone out here. She's usually very strict about protocol."

He smiled. "Perhaps it's because I'm a lot older than you as well as being your employer."

"I don't think you're that much older?"

"I was forty-one last birthday," he sighed.

"Oh, that's ancient. I'm amazed you're still able to get about without a stick."

He raised his eyebrows at her impertinence and chuckled at the mischievous glint in her eye.

"It'll be a relief when this hot weather breaks and we get some rain," he said, taking off his hat and fanning his face.

"I've been told it's to last another week at least," she said. "But I'm sure you don't want to talk about the weather. So, Mr Wyngate, what are you doing in my neighbourhood?"

He smiled at her, noticing how pretty she looked with her hair tied back with a single red ribbon.

"Perhaps when we're in private, you could call me Guy?" She nodded as a small spot of pink coloured each cheek. "I was visiting Sir Jack at his country home near Hastings."

"You said you were in the area. Hastings isn't exactly in the area," she said, narrowing her eyes with suspicion.

He put up his hands in surrender. "Very well, if you want to know the truth, I decided to come and see you about this." He reached into his jacket pocket and pulled out a piece of paper. She recognised it instantly as the letter she had sent him with the account of the train wreck. "It's about the accident, or more accurately, your mysterious statement that you met someone I'd be interested in hearing about."

The maid came trotting across the lawn, bringing a tray of cold drinks that she placed on the table. Guy took his glass of cider and had nearly drunk half of it before she had time to bob a curtsey.

"You came to see me about that?" said Melody in bewilderment.

"Why not?" He smiled roguishly. "I received your account and letter just before I left London and since I was in no hurry to return because of this intolerable heat, I thought it would be delightful to see Hucknall Garth." He looked about him. "And I must admit, it's as lovely as you described it."

"So, you couldn't wait to hear my story?"

"Your account of the train wreck was excellent, but your letter held a mystery that I had to investigate for myself."

Melody relaxed against the cushions remembering the terrible events of the accident and the people she had helped, and the people she hadn't been able to help.

"Well, I wouldn't have called it a mystery exactly. The truth is, I met Mr Charles Dickens. He was in the first class carriage at the front of the train, so managed to escape relatively unscathed."

Guy leaned forward in his seat. "You talked to him?"

"Yes, I did."

Guy puzzled for a moment. "He wasn't mentioned in your account of the accident."

Melody scrutinised his expression hoping he would understand. She bit her lip nervously. The look in his eyes stirred doubts.

"I made him a promise that I wouldn't mention him because of the circumstances."

"What circumstances?"

"Would you like more cider?"

"No, thank you. What circumstances?"

Feeling very uneasy, Melody shuffled in her seat. "He wasn't travelling alone. He had a female companion with him and if that had become public knowledge then his reputation would have been destroyed."

"You made him a promise?"

"Yes, I did. But I thought…"

Guy interrupted her. "You shouldn't have made that promise, Melody. It's my decision what is news and what is not."

Her eyes flashed with indignation and she gripped the arms of her chair. "I disagree. I had to make a decision. I was there and you were not. I sent you an accurate account of the event; I just left out certain details. I intended to tell you when I returned to London. I wasn't hiding anything from you."

"Perhaps, but those *details* you talk about would sell newspapers."

Melody shuddered with alarm. "What do you mean?"

"The public love scandal and the mistress of Charles Dickens would make headlines. Did you get her name?"

Horror swept through Melody, the shock of what he was suggesting numbing her mind.

"N…No, I didn't," she stammered. "I didn't ask her name."

"Pity, but that's easily remedied. I'll get Holbrook on to it as soon as I get back to London. And as for you, I'll treble your commission for this story, it will certainly make my fortune."

Melody rose to her feet slowly, nausea welling up from the pit of her stomach. She looked down on him, her face creased in distress.

"Please, please don't do this. I promised him and I've told you in confidence."

He looked away from her and fanned his face once more with his hat. "That'll teach you to make promises you can't keep."

Melody couldn't believe what she was hearing. How could he betray her confidence? How could she look herself in the mirror if she allowed this to happen? Her gaze fixed on him as her eyes filled with angry tears.

"You must do what you believe is right, but so must I. I can't continue working for you if I have betrayed a trust. I don't condone his behaviour but I will not be party in destroying the reputation of a great man who has done so much for this country." She blinked away the tears and raised her chin proudly. "Therefore, I think it would be better if I resigned from The Cork Street Journal."

Melody couldn't bear the way he was looking at her, his deep brown eyes seemed to pierce her heart. She turned away from him holding her face in her hands. She prayed he would leave; all she wanted was to be left in peace. She heard him rise from the chair and step over to her. He turned her round to face him and to her astonishment his smile was gentle, his eyes now showing a strange tenderness.

"I've been in the newspaper business all my adult life and I've seen good reporters sell their souls for a sensational headline or the right payment. I had to know if you could be bought too."

She looked at him aghast. "You were offering me thirty pieces of silver?"

"Yes, you could say that." He smiled and touched her cheek lightly. "But I did it for a purpose. I'm proud that the Journal is a reputable paper. I'll not print scandal just to sell copies and I want my staff to reflect my values."

Melody shook her head. "You were testing my integrity?" she said.

"I'm afraid so." He took her hand and kissed it. "Now, I must confess that I've known for some time that Charles Dickens had a mistress. Her name is Ellen Ternan and I've been a friend of her family for many years. She's a lot younger than Mr Dickens and comes from a theatrical family so only a few of us know of his friendship with her."

Melody felt startled. "You knew they were on the train?"

"No, I didn't know that, although I heard they were in Paris." He led her back to her chair and they sat down.

"If other newspapers find out then they might not be so discriminating," said Melody thoughtfully.

He blew out a gentle breath. "I was thinking that myself."

"We'll just have to hope it doesn't happen."

"But in the meantime, we're both party to his guilty secret."

Melody sighed sadly. "He's lucky to be alive, Guy. Ten people died that day with an estimated forty casualties. It's a day I'll never forget as long as I live."

"Would you like to tell me about it?" he said.

"It was all in my report."

"No, that's the version for the newspaper. I'd like to hear it from your own personal viewpoint."

Melody knew he was asking her to reveal her true feelings. She heard the gardener shouting at the stable boy who had obviously disrespected one of his flowerbeds. And then she saw Aunt Olivia crossing the lawn towards them.

"I'd like to tell you, but not here," said Melody.

"Shall we go for a walk?" he said. "Perhaps it would be cooler up there." He pointed to a distant hill covered with trees.

He rose to his feet as Olivia approached.

"Luncheon will be ready in ten minutes. It's only sandwiches and fruit but I think that's all that's manageable on a day like today. You will stay won't you Mr Wyngate?" said Olivia.

"I'd be delighted to," he answered, giving Melody a charming smile. "My train isn't until eight."

"We were thinking of going for a walk, Aunt, would you mind?" asked Melody.

Olivia squinted at Guy. "I'm not sure. Can you be trusted with my niece Mr Wyngate?"

Guy placed his hand on his heart as if stung by her remarks. "Mrs Timme, you can trust me with her very life."

She pulled a face. "It's not her life I'm worried about."

Their meal was packed in a small wicker basket along with flasks of lemonade and cider and also a few apples. A bowl of strawberries covered by muslin was also tucked away.

"The strawberries are for Miss Garlick. If you're going for a walk, you might as well head in her direction," said Aunt Olivia. Melody nodded as Guy picked up the basket. "And you look after my niece, sir."

He gave his charming smile. "I'll bring her back safe and well, I assure you."

Melody and Guy made their way down the lane towards the hill, where they could get the best view of the countryside. As they walked Melody elaborated on the details she had already sent him in her account of the terrible events of the ninth of June. The horror of seeing the carriages lurch over the side of the bridge, the shocked faces of the onlookers and the trauma experienced by the passengers. She told him not only of the courage she saw that day, but also about those who had been caught going through the pockets of the dead and were now languishing in prison awaiting their punishment. Guy listened intently and made only the occasional comment.

They finally reached the foot of the hill that gave them shelter with the trees and yet they could look across the landscape. A gentle wind caressed them and they could hear the birds and the lowing of cattle. A stone wall bordered a field and Guy lifted Melody onto it, while he stood at her knee surveying the beauty spread about him.

"I think I've been in the city too long. I hadn't realised how stuffy London can be until I went to visit my uncle," said Guy, shielding his eyes to get a better view.

"When did you last leave London?" she asked.

"Oh, it must be over a year." He quickly glanced at the young girl sitting on the wall and took in a slow breath. In the sunlight, her hair shone and her cornflower-blue eyes sparkled with life.

"Well, perhaps you should visit Sir Jack more often. I'm sure he'd appreciate your company and make you very welcome," she said, smiling.

"I know he would," he said. He paused a few seconds before saying, "The Journal hasn't been the same while you've been away."

"Hasn't it?" She was genuinely surprised, but seeing colour rush to his cheeks quickly added, "Then it's a good thing I'm returning soon." She hesitated before saying, "I've enjoyed working for you."

"I'm pleased about that. I thought I'd given you a difficult time."

"Oh, you have, you have," she laughed. "I don't think I'll ever get over the shock of this afternoon. But it was all part of my apprenticeship, I suppose."

They looked out over the beautiful Kent countryside; the hot June afternoon making them feel sleepy and contented. The swallows and larks soared above them; a slight breeze murmured among the leaves of the trees bringing a little coolness with it.

Melody pointed further up the hill. "Cobweb Cottage is just up there. That's where Miss Garlick lives."

"And who's Miss Garlick? Your aunt didn't say."

"She used to be my governess, but she's retired now. She taught me from when I was six until I went to finishing-school at sixteen."

Guy showed obvious surprise. "I can't imagine you tolerating a finishing-school."

"Well, it was Aunt Olivia's idea and the brigadier went along with it. I spent a year at a ladies academy in Brighton and learnt music, dance, deportment and painting. My aunt thought it would turn me into a lady and make me accomplished enough to enter society." She leaned towards him and whispered, "Do you think it worked?"

"Yes, I think it did," he said, suddenly finding his heart racing. He gave a slight cough before saying, "But I get the impression that Miss Garlick made you what you are?"

"Well, she taught me a great deal. She even borrowed a telescope once and we trained it on the moon. It was wonderful to see. Aunt Olivia taught me French and literature and the brigadier taught me to ride a horse and drive a buggy."

"Then I must certainly meet this Miss Garlick and one day I must meet your father." He thought for a moment. "Do you always refer to your father as the brigadier?"

A look of surprise passed over her face. "Occasionally, when it's appropriate. As I was growing up he disciplined me in army ways and gave me cleaning and laundry detail when I misbehaved."

He couldn't help laughing. "He sounds a very interesting fellow."

"You'll have to wait to meet Papa, he's in Italy at the moment. But I'm sure Miss Garlick will be at home. I must warn you, she's quite old and a bit hard of hearing."

"I've always found it easy to make myself understood," he chuckled.

Melody, perched up on the wall, suddenly remembered the food in the basket. They ate until all they had left were the apples. She offered one to Guy and they started munching. After Guy had finished, he threw the core up into the air and they watched it climbing higher and higher until it turned and started its journey back to earth.

"You eat your food very quickly," she said with a giggle.

"Something I learned in the Crimea. You had to or you didn't get your share."

For a few seconds she resisted the temptation to ask more and instead demurely brushed the crumbs from the front of her skirt. But her inquisitiveness finally got the better of her.

"The brigadier said you were a hero in the war."

"Did he?"

"He said you were invited to Buckingham Palace to meet Queen Victoria."

He thought for a moment. "Then your father is quite right."

"Tell me about it," she asked.

He looked away and smiled. "Have you brought your notebook and pencil, Miss Kinsman?"

She nodded and reached into her basket. "I never go anywhere without it."

"Always the journalist," he laughed. "But you can keep it tucked away this time." He sighed gently. "What do you want to know?"

"What was it like, seeing the queen?"

"Pleasant. She was a very gracious lady."

"And she commended you for your bravery in the war?"

"You seem to know about it already," he said.

"No, I don't. Please go on."

"Well, she said some kind words and then presented me with a medal. And that was that."

He glanced at her, smiling at her enthusiasm. Silence followed as they watched a flock of starlings circle over the trees and then climb away to an unknown destination.

"You find it difficult to talk about the war, don't you?" she murmured.

"It was a long time ago."

"I was only a child when it was all going on."

"Yes, you must have been." He chucked her under the chin.

"What happened, Guy. What did you do to win a medal and be invited to Buckingham Palace?"

"Do you really want to know?"

"I wouldn't have asked if I didn't."

He stared out at the countryside although his mind was far away. "It was just before the Battle of the River Alma. I was a correspondent sent out to report for *The Evening Chronicle*."

"That's when you worked for your uncle?"

He nodded. "One night I decided to sneak a look at the Russian encampment, but instead found myself in the middle of a covert operation by the Welsh Fusiliers. I became embroiled in a battle I wasn't meant to be in. I wasn't a soldier, my job was to report on the action, not get involved in it." Melody remained silent letting him continue his story. "They were trying to destroy a Russian gun and a grenade went adrift. It fell at my feet and I instinctively picked it up and threw it at the gun emplacement."

"And it exploded?"

"Yes, killing six men."

"But they were Russian soldiers, our enemy."

Guy turned towards her and she was stunned to see the pain in his eyes. "They must have heard me and they looked in my direction just seconds before it exploded. I saw their faces. They didn't seem like enemy soldiers. Just six very tired young men, heartily sick of the war and wanting to go home to their families." He rubbed his hand over his face as if trying to wipe away the memory.

"What you did was courageous. You could have been killed too."

Guy shook his head sadly. "I've been haunted by those young faces for nearly ten years. Some hero, eh?"

She placed a tender hand on his shoulder. "It was war and you did what you had to."

Their attention returned to the view.

"You're the first person I've ever told that story to," he said in surprise. "I've never wanted to talk about it before. You certainly have a way about you, Miss Melody."

"I'm glad you told me. But what did…"

He held up his hand to stop her. "You ask too many questions."

"You said that a good journalist asks as many questions as possible."

A soft smile played on his lips. "*Touché*," he whispered. Suddenly he stooped to pick up a poppy growing by the side of the wall. He twirled it in his fingers before leaning towards her and caressing her cheek gently with its soft, red petals. "Just like you. Wild and untamed and yet so vibrant and beautiful."

She took it from him and put it in her hair. "Yes and I've been chastised for being wild and untamed quite a few times."

He shook his head. "Not by me. You're charming just as you are."

Suddenly Melody felt embarrassed. "Thank you for saying so," she said.

"You feel uncomfortable about receiving compliments, don't you?"

"About me personally, yes. But you can praise my abilities as a journalist until the cows come home, if you wish."

"You're so unlike the young girls of today. So refreshing and different," he murmured.

"That's not been to everyone's liking either," she smiled.

"Who doesn't like it?"

Melody shook her head. She remembered that Alex had often tried to discipline her for her inappropriate behaviour. Thoughts of Alex made her remember their engagement and the fact she would have to tell Guy about it at some time.

He broke into her troubled thoughts. "We'd better visit this Miss Garlick before it's time for my train," he said. He gave a chuckle. "Why is it called Cobweb Cottage, by the way?"

She smiled. "Because there's not a cobweb in sight."

"I suppose there's a strange logic in that."

She held out her arms and Guy lifted her to the ground. For a brief moment he pulled her up against him and through his thin linen shirt, she could feel his heart pounding. She slipped her hand through his arm and they made their way up the hill.

CHAPTER FOURTEEN

By the time Melody arrived back at Hyde Park Gardens, she had decided to tell Mrs Carr and Tilly her news straight away.

"Oh, we're so please, aren't we Tilly?" said Mrs Carr full of smiles. She turned to Tilly. "But we've been expecting it."

Tilly nodded. "I guessed Doctor Courtney would pop the question while you were on holiday."

Mrs Carr licked her lips. "Circumstances will change, Miss Melody, once you're wed. You'll probably need more staff if you should want to live in a larger house."

Melody knew she was fishing and smiled. "We'll not be living in a larger house, we'll be living here."

"Here, miss?" said Mrs Carr and Tilly together.

Melody nodded. "Yes, here. Doctor Courtney has rooms with Doctor Jenner and I couldn't possibly live there, so my new husband will move in here with me. We'll be perfectly comfortable."

"And we'll be retained?" asked Mrs Carr.

Melody felt stunned that she should think otherwise. "Of course. I couldn't do without you." She gave a merry laugh. "I only hope you are both happy with a new master in the house." She left the kitchen to go to her bedroom and change out of her travelling clothes.

Mrs Carr pursed her lips. "But will the mistress be happy having a master in the house?"

"That remains to be seen," sniffed Tilly.

In her room, Melody sat on her bed to read the note Alex had sent. The inevitable had happened, he wrote, the hot summer months had caused a cholera epidemic in some areas of the East End, but mainly Camberwell.

There was no need to worry just yet, since the number of cases was relatively small. However, it was the usual epidemic expected at that time of the year and it was hoped the fatalities wouldn't increase. The main objective of his note was to impress on her to keep out of the area. He added that he was very busy at the hospital at the moment, but was still walking on air at the idea they were to be married. Jenner sent his kindest regards and couldn't wait to be best man. He concluded his letter saying he loved her and would call to see her in the next few days.

Melody considered the note carefully, remembering that terrible day when she had reported the murder in Fetter Lane. The dilapidated dwellings of Whitechapel with its overcrowding, the bad sanitation with the exuding cesspools and rotting refuse, the very foetid stink in the air, all pointed to death and disease. That was probably why it was called Fetter Lane, she thought grimly. The court of King Cholera. Placing Alex's message on her bedside table she considered his warning. He asked her not to go to that area. Of course he would be worried about her, but she was a journalist and a potential social reformer and there was work to be done. She smiled to herself. Alex meant well, but he would never understand the driving force that inspired her to search out the truth.

"I'm really against you going, Melody. Not with a cholera epidemic," said Guy, leaning against the edge of his desk.

Melody let out a slow breath of exasperation. "Please let me investigate what's happening there," she said. "I just want to talk to the residents."

He gazed down at her, knowing her so well, and shaking his head that he couldn't persuade her otherwise once her mind was made up. "Would you be offended if I accompanied you?"

"I don't need a wet nurse," she snapped.

"How about an interested observer?"

She knew he had won. "All right," she smiled. "But don't get in my way."

"Would I dare!" he said, collecting his hat from the stand in the corner.

Out in the street the heat seemed to bear down on them. The stable doors, front and rear, had been left open to allow a cool breeze waft through. Sultan neighed when he saw his mistress and as she stroked his nose, he nuzzled her shoulder. The boy led him out and hitched him to the gig.

"It's getting a bit oppressive, don't you think?" said Melody, as Guy helped her into the driver's seat and then jumped up beside her.

"It could herald a change in the weather. We need a thunderstorm to clear the air," he said.

Melody shook the reins and Sultan pulled forward. She let him travel at his own pace knowing the heat would affect him. He would need a good drink when he arrived in Camberwell.

"It might be better to leave your horse and gig at a public house I know," said Guy. "The landlord will take good care of them for you. I wouldn't trust the young rascals in Camberwell, you might not see Sultan again."

Melody nodded in agreement suddenly grateful for his company.

The landlord at the Merry Jester couldn't have been more affable and Melody and Guy spent twenty minutes drinking a cool glass of cider before setting off on their quest. Although in the midst of a cholera epidemic, the people of Camberwell were still going about their daily business. The street sellers called out their wares; the urchins ran backwards and forwards doing any errands that would earn them a penny; shopkeepers stood in their doorways and housewives hung out their washing.

Melody approached a shopkeeper and he directed her down an alley to a family who had already seen one death and had others stricken. The woman opening the door looked tired and ill, but admitted Melody and Guy into her humble home. She was more than glad to tell the lady reporter about how the illness had come to her, how her small child had died and two were still sick. Melody asked her questions about her diet and what medicine the doctor had prescribed and then after offering their condolences they were directed to the next home.

For the next two hours they went from house to house, each affected family directing them to the next. Guy followed at Melody's heels and as promised only observed the situation. And the situation was deplorable. The rundown homes and dreadful sanitation would often make them put their hands over their noses. Stepping over the refuse in the alleys and streets, Melody needed to lift her skirt to keep the hem away from the stinking debris that consisted of anything that could be discarded by the residents of Camberwell.

Then Melody decided she had collected enough information and to Guy's immense relief suggested they return to the Merry Jester.

"Would you like to eat?" asked Guy, as they rounded the corner and the public house came into view.

"Here? At the Merry Jester?" She couldn't hide her amazement at his suggestion. "I've never eaten in a public house before."

"We don't have to eat in the saloon. The landlord has a private area upstairs. It's a small room set aside for such occasions. It's for the coach travellers, but I'm sure he'll not mind us using it."

Melody thought for a moment. "Well, if you think it's acceptable. I'm certainly in need of a cold drink."

"Then I don't think you'll find it a problem," smiled Guy.

The landlord ushered them into the select room upstairs and to Melody's surprise, it was small and cosy and could have been a sitting room in an average middle class family home. Before leaving them to fetch their meal, he opened the windows wide and with a cry of delight Melody found herself looking into a delightful courtyard filled with boxes and hanging baskets crammed full of flowers. Pansies and geraniums mingled with marigolds and wild roses and Melody almost believed she was looking into a fairy dell. She leaned on the window ledge watching a cat meticulously grooming itself on the courtyard wall until the landlord came in once more with a tray filled with ham, cheese, tomatoes and chunks of bread that looked like door wedges. With him he also brought tankards of ale and cider that his guests drank thirstily.

The meal was one of the best Melody could remember. The simple fare, the good company, the interesting conversation with her companion all added to her enjoyment. Guy talked of his ambitions for The Cork Street Journal and Melody told him that she intended to start on her book very shortly.

"Ah, yes. Are you still thinking of calling it The Silent Voice?" he asked, trying to conceal his amusement by taking a gulp of ale.

"That's just the working title. I might change it yet," Melody answered crisply.

The landlord came in to clear away the dishes but suddenly bent and whispered something in Guy's ear.

Guy gave the merest shake of his head and looked down at his hands. Melody got the impression he was trying not to laugh.

"What did he say?" asked Melody.

Guy shrugged and glanced towards the window. "He just asked me if we'd enjoyed our meal," he said casually.

"Oh, I think not," she said. "You shook your head, so tell me."

Guy turned his face towards her, his eyes full of mischief. "He asked if I required a room."

"Why would you want a room?" she said, frowning. Suddenly she realised his meaning and jumped up nearly knocking her chair over. At first she was lost for words but then blurted out, "So that's your game! How dare you bring me here under false pretences…"

Guy was on his feet in a second. "Steady on. I brought you here for luncheon, nothing more, I assure you."

Melody glared at him for a moment, but his expression showed such alarm she couldn't help bursting into laughter. She placed her hand over her mouth, suddenly realising the unacceptability of the situation they were in.

She shook her head. "I suppose I was wrong to accept your invitation, but I wasn't considering my reputation at the time."

Guy came round to her side of the table and took hold of her hands. "Neither was I and it was very remiss of me to suggest we do this. I've compromised you." He looked down at her fingers. "Please forgive me. But I so enjoy your company." His gaze became tender. He licked his lips. "Melody, I…thought…I hoped…"

He stopped as she pulled her hands away. She put them behind her back as if to hide the fact that his very touch caused them to tingle uncomfortably.

"Well, I think we'd better leave while my reputation is still intact," she said, averting her gaze.

He gave a polite bow. "Said like a young lady of true virtue."

Melody gave him a half-smile. He was a rebel too and she liked that.

Guy drove back to Cork Street, giving Melody a chance to look over the facts and figures she had collected in Camberwell. Their moment of disquiet had passed and they were back to their usual friendly relationship.

"There's something here I can't quite put my finger on," she said, frowning as she flicked the pages backwards and forwards. "A sort of pattern, but it's eluding me."

He gave a chuckle. "I know that state of mind very well. Don't worry, it will suddenly occur to you, probably at two in the morning."

She glanced at his strong, reassuring profile, pleased that he was there at her side. A slight breeze started up and she shook her hair back from her face.

"Goodness, that feels nice."

He scanned the western sky. "I do believe we're going to have a thunderstorm. Those clouds are looking very ominous."

"I hope it doesn't come this afternoon. I've an appointment with Miss Nightingale." The look on her employer's face was a sight to see and Melody couldn't help giggling.

"How on earth did you manage that?" he said.

"I just wrote to her and told her about my intended book and the column I write," she said, sounding as nonchalant as possible.

"Well, I'm astonished. I tried to get an interview with her ages ago and she turned me down flat. She wrote to you, then?"

"Not exactly. She sent me a telegram stating the date and time she could see me, which is in an hour so we'd better get a move on."

"I'm impressed," smiled Guy.

Guy Wyngate might have been impressed but unfortunately Doctor Alex Courtney wasn't. He listened quietly to Melody's account of her morning in Camberwell, although she thought it better not to divulge Guy's part in it.

After she was finished, he leaned back against the bench. "I did ask you not to go to that area, Melody," he said. "I'm very disappointed that you chose to disobey me."

They were sitting in their usual place beside the Serpentine and although not wanting to spoil their short time together, Melody's eyes flashed in annoyance.

"Disobey you! I'm sorry, but I didn't take it as a military order. What are you going to do? Put me on a charge? Clap me in irons?"

He shook his head in dismay. "It was for your own good. I was looking out for you."

She winced at his expression. He really was worried about her. "I know, but I had to go. It's my job."

"Why is it your job? There are good men out there investigating the epidemic. All right, we don't know why this one happened but the conditions of the East End are an obvious factor."

"Perhaps my efforts this morning might bear some fruit. Something might be revealed they haven't thought about."

"I doubt it," he said, but then seeing the hurt in her eyes added, "Sorry, dearest, I didn't mean it to sound…What I mean is that I don't want to discourage you. It's just that…Well, you report for the newspaper and let the inspectors report for the hospital board."

Melody tried to swallow her disappointment. She thought Alex would have been proud of her, after all, her account when written up and printed, would embrace the medical side of a story. But Alex didn't see it like that. For him, Melody realised with mounting alarm, she was only interfering in his line of work. Waves of doubt began to grip her and no matter how hard she tried to ignore them, they just seemed to scream at her even louder.

Alex took her hand and kissed it. His smile softened as he whispered, "I have something for you." He went into his pocket and pulled out a box and opening it, revealed a diamond and sapphire ring.

"Oh, Alex. It's so beautiful."

"It's actually a family heirloom. It belonged to my grandmother."

He slipped it on her finger and it was obvious that it was too big. "What a shame," murmured Melody. "Your grandmother must have had larger fingers."

He slipped it off and put it back into the box. "I thought it might be too large. We'll visit a jewellers and get it altered."

Suddenly lightning streaked across the sky and ten seconds later was followed by an almighty crash of thunder. The hot weather had finally broken and the storm had arrived. Melody jumped to her feet.

"We must go," she laughed. "Or we're going to get thoroughly drenched."

He pulled her close and pressed his lips on hers. And then they ran in opposite directions. He to his evening duties at the hospital and she towards her home.

By the time she reached Hyde Park Gardens it had become steadily darker. She ran into the house as a lightning bolt lit up the trees and rooftops again followed by a crack of thunder that was almost ear splitting. And then the rain started, a deluge that drummed on the houses and cobbles and in no time, was running in small rivers down to the lower end of Hyde Park Gardens.

"This will do a great deal of good," said Melody to Mrs Carr. "It will be so much cooler now."

"It certainly will, miss," she laughed. "However, we have a bit of a problem. Tilly's barricaded herself in the pantry and won't come out till this storm's passed. So, dinner will be a little later with veg being in there with her."

It was going to be a beautiful day. Melody knelt on the seat and opened the window, looking up at the sky. It was now the end of July and a very important occasion had arrived. Drinking in the fresh, clean air she surveyed the wonderful scene before her. There were a few clouds about, but none threatening rain. The sun caressed the rooftops and the cobbled road shone as if newly polished. There was perfume in the air from the vibrant marigolds, clematis and roses that filled the flower boxes. It was a wonderful mixture of scents and sights and sounds that made Melody feel that the world was heaven.

"Damn and blast this cravat!" The doors had been left open and the sound came from her father's room just across the hall. Closing the window, she climbed off the seat and made her way to him.

"Now what's the matter?" she sighed.

"I hate new cravats. I can never get them to fold properly. Can't I wear one of my others?"

"No you can't," she snapped, slapping his hand to stop him tugging at his collar. She straightened everything out. "There now, you look very smart. The Beau Brummell of London."

He looked down at her, a smile spreading across his face. "One day I'll be taking you up the aisle."

"Yes, Papa."

"When you and Alex decide to set a date, that is. You'll make a beautiful bride and it'll be the proudest day of my life."

"Well, just for today we'll be your honoured guests at the Guildhall," she said quietly. "It's your day and I want everything to be perfect for you."

"What stuff and nonsense. I only did what I thought I should. After your mother died I decided to continue the work she had started."

Melody picked up the letter from the governors of The London Hospital, a charitable establishment and always in need of funds.

"Papa, it says here that you've raised over one thousand pounds this year with your continuous appeals and publicity campaigns. Not to mention the donations you've squeezed out of people and the dinners you've organised to raise funds."

The brigadier lifted his chin. "All done for love of your mother."

Melody shook her head at his humility. "You've worked hard and deserve the honour." She kissed him on the cheek and decided he needed something practical to do. "Why don't you fill your pipe?" The brigadier needed very little persuasion and started for the door. "But do it outside. Remember Aunt Olivia doesn't like you smoking indoors."

Back in her room, Melody began to dress, struggling into her new gown and trying to fasten the buttons.

Aunt Olivia appeared in the doorway. "Tilly is helping Celia, so I thought you might need some assistance," she said, smiling at her niece's contortions.

"Why do we have to wear such stupid garments," said Melody "Surely fashion shouldn't be so uncomfortable."

Although complaining about the vogue of the day, Melody was pleased with her blue and white dress with a royal blue mantle trimmed with lace and braid. She had bought a new bonnet to match and at the ball that evening she intended wearing a peach dress of silk trimmed with Honiton Lace that brought out the lustre in her complexion. She would adorn her hair with small cream silk rosebuds and dance the night away, so proud of her wonderful papa.

Her aunt fastened the buttons and tied the laces after which she helped her put up her hair. When she was finished she turned her round to look in the mirror. "All done. Goodness, you look lovely. I'm sure Alex will want to marry you immediately."

Melody pulled a face. "But not yet, Aunt." Olivia followed her out of the room and they met Celia on her way downstairs. "You look beautiful," said Melody, slipping her hand through her friend's arm.

"So do you," said Celia.

They continued on to the sitting room, where the brigadier was waiting and in a state of agitation, puffing away on his obnoxious pipe. Olivia frowned. No matter how often she reprimanded him, he never listened.

"Brigadier, we're all ready for inspection," said Melody.

He spun on his heel and his mouth fell open, his pipe clattering to the floor.

"Oh, Liam, you are a nuisance," his sister grumbled, watching the grey ash tumble out of the bowl.

The brigadier looked them up and down, inspecting them closely. Celia giggled as he adjusted the ribbon at her sleeve and folded the collar on her gown. "The most beautiful young women I've ever seen. Better be on our way. Don't want to be late," he said, his eyes glistening.

Olivia stooped to collect the pipe ash in her palm. Silly old fool, she thought, what's he going to be like the day Melody weds? She sighed. That day would soon arrive if she were any judge of character. Alex was keen to set a date, that was obvious and when he looked at Melody, she could see a longing in his eyes. But what were they waiting for? It was now six weeks since they had become engaged. Why didn't they get on with it? There was something else that troubled her and it didn't matter how much she tried to push that demon to the back of her mind, it insisted on tormenting her. And the demon's name was Guy Wyngate.

He had had a similar expression when Melody was in his vicinity. Olivia had seen it the day he had come to talk 'business' with her niece at Hucknall Garth. And when they had returned from their walk, Olivia had regretted giving them permission to go in the first place. But she had thought Melody safe with an older more experienced man. Not that Melody had come to any harm. On the contrary, it seemed Mr Wyngate had kept his word and taken good care of her. But Olivia had noticed a change in her niece during the last day of her holiday. Melody had been distracted and her expression was often troubled.

For all the brigadier's reservations, the ceremony at the Guildhall went very well and he was presented with a pocket watch to honour his hard work, many standing up to sing his praises, making him flush with embarrassment.

The ball that evening in his honour was a great success. As the evening wore on, the waltz was played more frequently and holding Melody in his arms and guiding her round the floor, Alex became overwhelmed by the occasion. It was time they set a date and made plans, he decided. And October would be a good month, before the winter set in. Yes, he thought, life in Colchester would be perfect with a wife at his side.

CHAPTER FIFTEEN

The manuscript was started, at least the introduction was well on the way. Melody sat back in her chair and smiled at her efforts. She had not reached a firm decision about the title and so for now, the working title of, The Silent Voice, graced the top of the page.

She was sitting at a walnut writing desk, a present from Celia that she had brought back from her holiday in Italy. Not that anyone could see the wonderful pattern of the wood, as it was covered with numerous pieces of paper from which she was gleaning her information. Her interviews, research material and the odd assortment of books lay all about her.

The house was peaceful, the family having gone shopping and sightseeing. Aunt Olivia and Celia were taking advantage of the larger stores in Bond Street and the brigadier had accompanied them intending to visit the Tower of London, a place he had never had time to visit.

During their visit, Melody and Celia had been absorbed in catching up with all the news, their rift now healed and their hearts mended. Celia regaled her friend with her adventures in Italy and Melody told Celia about her engagement to Alex.

"I always knew he would propose," Celia had said. "When are you getting married?"

"We haven't decided yet although you must be my bridesmaid."

Celia had clapped her hands with glee, her eyes shining. "Oh, it's so romantic. How I wish that would happen to me."

Melody had just grunted in reply. She knew that everyone was waiting for her to set the date for her wedding and it was annoying her. There was just too much to do. The Journal was now very busy and it was all she could do to cram everything into a day. Sometimes she wished the hours wouldn't go so fast.

To her delight, she had managed to get an interview with Elizabeth Garrett, the first female physician who was in the process of setting up her own practice at number twenty Upper Berkeley Street London.

Melody had been amazed at the doctor's candid answers to her questions, as they sat in the makeshift room that was her surgery. Miss Garrett pointed out the main problems she was facing concerning women's health; the excessive childbearing and ignorance of symptoms leading to late diagnosis of illness with dire consequences. And her patients in the lower classes suffered from utter exhaustion and negligence on matters of hygiene.

Doctor Garrett grimaced. "Unfortunately, one of the fundamental factors leading to ill health is the total absence of consideration by the husband when it comes to the intimacies of married life."

"Is that so? And how do you remedy that?" asked Melody, taking a sharp breath.

"Well, I try to speak to the husband!"

Her answer had been so vehement that Melody couldn't help laughing. "Doesn't that cause a problem?"

"I don't care if it does. My patient's health is more important." Melody scribbled away, but nearly snapped her pencil with the next comment. "Of course, when it comes to venereal disease, I really lose my temper."

"Venereal disease?"

The doctor grinned. "I'm sorry. I forgot you're unmarried and probably don't know much about sexually transmitted infections." She pursed her lips. "Not that being married is a doorway to knowledge."

"But I'd still like to be informed, married or not."

"Well done. Usually young women from your class shy away from something so nasty."

"I'm a journalist and there are no boundaries."

Doctor Garrett smiled at the young woman sitting opposite her wearing a burgundy skirt and jacket with a tiny Empire bonnet perched on the back of her head and looking every inch the businesswoman.

"Miss Kinsman. It's a sad fact of life that men stray from the marital bed. And when they do they pick up certain infections such as syphilis. They carry this infection back to an innocent wife who ends up in my surgery complaining of symptoms they don't understand."

"Dear Lord. Do you confront the husband about this?"

"I certainly do. And they get on their righteous horse and bellow about the sanctity and privacy of marriage. And I shout back that if they considered it sacred and private then they should save their pricks for their wives only. That usually does the trick." Melody couldn't help erupting into laughter. If only Alex was here, how appalled he would be at the conversation. He wouldn't approve at all. Miss Garrett broke into her thoughts. "I see you're engaged to be married, Miss Kinsman."

"Yes, to a doctor at Saint George's Hospital."

"Well, may I offer my best wishes. I believe that marriage isn't all that bad despite our discussion today. I wouldn't wish to talk you out of it especially since your future husband obviously approves of your work."

Melody bit her lip and murmured, "And that's what you need, isn't it? An understanding spouse."

Yes, Doctor Elizabeth Garrett had been a revelation and Melody had decided to devote an entire chapter to her work. Her thoughts turned to the doctor's disclosure of wayward husbands and the frightful infection of syphilis. She wondered if she should include a chapter on prostitution, but then realised this would mean researching in the more dubious areas of London. She had overheard Eric talking about the girls forced into this line of work, some as young as nine and even younger. It was a grim thought to have to question the women on the streets, but it would be worth it. Their opinions were just as important. She cast her eyes over her manuscript and grinned. She would ask Guy to accompany her. That would be her revenge for his mischief at the Merry Jester. She placed a big question mark against the note on including this chapter. After all, she wanted her book to be read and appreciated, not held up as a work of moral degradation. Society was a strange animal, she mused to herself, all politeness and convention on the surface, but beneath lay a world of utter brutality and ill treatment.

She rummaged through her papers and discovered the notes on her investigation into the cholera epidemic. The article had been written and published weeks ago, but she had kept the notes for her book and also because she still had a strange feeling that there was something hidden in the figures. She stared at the line of numbers indicating the fatalities and sickness in each home.

Melody lifted her head from her writing and looked at the clock standing on the mantelpiece. Sometimes she was so busy that she forgot the time. There was a tap on the door and Tilly came in carrying a tray of tea.

"Oh, Tilly. I have a little errand for you. I want you to go to Mr Parfitt's shop with this note. Show it to him and he'll give you what I want." She placed a sovereign into the girl's hand. "And please hurry because I need to get back to the Journal very soon."

It was fifteen minutes before Tilly returned, quickly flinging her coat over a chair in the hall and hurrying into the room, her face red with exertion.

Time passed in deep concentration as Melody bent over the map spread out on the table. She had asked for a detailed street plan of the East End and after finding Camberwell, she carefully put an ink spot on every address that had been infected with cholera. After she had finished, she straightened herself, holding her back and wincing from the pain of being in one position for so long. She screwed up her eyes to focus on the pattern of dots and then gasped with surprise. It had been there all the time! All she had to do was put it into some kind of order. She quickly flicked through her figures once more and almost shouting with delight, folded the map and crammed it into the leather pouch along with the notes.

Melody hurried through the kitchen to the bemused smile of Mrs Carr. "I don't think I'll ever get used to that."

"You will," said Tilly, grinning.

Sultan had to travel a little faster than normal as Melody urged him through the streets. When they finally arrived at Saint George's Hospital she left him at the main door with the porter and rushed through the entrance hall and down the corridor where she knew the doctors' office was situated.

Only Christian Jenner was there, busily writing at the desk. "Good afternoon, Melody," he said, putting down his pen and rising from his chair. "If you want to see Alex, he's setting a broken leg at the moment."

"Will it take long?"

Christian pulled out his watch. "Well, he was called away only a few minutes ago," he said. Melody's agitation was obvious and Christian gestured to his chair. "You can always wait here if you wish."

"I haven't got time," she said. "I have something to show him."

"Why don't you show me, and then I'll show him when he comes back."

She let out a sigh and accepted his offer. She pulled out the sheet of paper from her pouch and spread it on the desk.

"What do you see?" she said, pointing to the map.

"A map of the East End," he said bewildered.

"A map of Camberwell to be exact."

"And a lot of black dots," he ventured.

"Each dot represents a home that was infected with the cholera in June. Do you see a pattern?"

Christian scrutinised the dots. "I suppose I do see a kind of circular pattern."

"Yes, the pattern is circular. Three concentric circles actually." She took the notes from her bag and began to read. "The inner circle has eighty-nine dots, the next circle has thirty and the outer circle has only ten." She waited for recognition but none came so she felt compelled to explain. "The circles are surrounding the source of infection."

"And that is?"

Melody began to feel exasperated. "The pump is in the centre! The place where the residents go to collect what they believe is clean water."

"And the residents always go to the pump that is nearest to them," said Christian, rubbing his chin thoughtfully.

"Yes, exactly. That's why the outer circle has only a few cases. Most of those people used another pump." She looked down at her notes again. "I discovered that many of the cases are children, who usually drink water. The adult cases are fewer because they drink ale, especially the men. And very few men contracted the disease."

She was almost breathless with elation. But Doctor Jenner seemed very casual. "So, the pump is the culprit. I'm not sure which company provides that water, but we'll find out," he said, smiling at her. "May I keep this?"

"Yes, of course. And you'll tell Alex?"

"I will," he promised, folding the map.

Melody suddenly felt uneasy, but brushing her qualms aside, she said her farewell and quickly left the hospital. She was meeting the brigadier, Aunt Olivia and Celia for tea at the Cavendish Hotel and didn't want to be late. And after that she would call at Cork Street and tell Guy of her findings. She also wanted to tell him another morsel of news. One she had been putting off since June and one she knew he would not be happy about.

Guy listened as Melody told him of her discoveries and how she was convinced that there was a strong correlation between the incidents of cholera and the water pump. She told him she had been to the hospital and left the information with a member of the medical staff. Her employer's expression had been one of amazement and then of silent approval. Agreeing that the investigation into the water supply would make interesting reading, he accepted her weekly article. Thinking that the interview was over, he waited for her to collect her gloves and umbrella, but she sat quietly, not moving.

"Was there something else?" he asked.

She fidgeted with her gloves. "I need to tell you…that…"

"Yes."

"I'm engaged to be married."

She glanced up to see his eyes darken and her heart skipped a beat. She knew he would be angry, this was just what he didn't want. To lose her to marriage when he depended on her.

He looked down at her hands. "I've not seen you wearing a ring."

"I decided not to wear it to work."

He leaned back in his chair. "So, you'll want to tender your resignation."

She shook her head. "Oh, no, we've not set a date yet. It might be next year...or the year after."

"Your fiancé is obviously not in any hurry."

"Actually, I'm the one who's not in any hurry."

He rose from his chair and went to the window. She watched him and noticed his face muscles tense. He was very upset with her, she could see that.

"So, when did this all happen?" he asked quietly.

"Do you remember the day you visited Hucknall Garth?"

"How could I forget."

"It happened the day before."

He nodded, not taking his eyes from the traffic below the window. "Will you let me know when you do set a date?"

"Naturally. I'd like you to come to the wedding. And everyone at the Journal, of course. You've all become so dear to me."

He turned and gave a half-smile. "I must say I'm astonished," he murmured. "I didn't think you considered marriage as a viable option."

You're not half astonished as I am, she thought. Even after all these months, she still couldn't get used to the idea of becoming Alex's wife.

Guy left the window and perched himself on the edge of the desk. "So, tell me about this young man you're betrothed to."

Melody was a little taken aback, wondering why he would be interested in such matters.

"You've already met him." Seeing his puzzled expression she added, "I'm talking about the young man who brought you my article on the train accident."

Guy frowned. "Goodness, that spotty youth with the big ears."

At first Melody didn't understand and then she realised what had happened. "He must have sent a porter from the hospital." She couldn't hide her disappointment that Alex hadn't delivered her report in person as he had promised. "His name is Alexander Courtney. He's a doctor at Saint George's Hospital."

Guy nodded. Alex. The friend she had mentioned back in the spring.

"Well, may I congratulate him and give you my very best wishes. And how do you feel about being a doctor's wife?"

"I've not really thought about it."

He raised his eyebrows. "Really? Where do you intend to live?"

She began to feel uncomfortable. "At Hyde Park Gardens. Nothing will change in that respect."

"Well, it seems you'll be experiencing a different way of life from the one you have now, being a married woman and running a home."

"I already run a home," she said quietly. His words had jarred her. "Isn't it possible for me to go on working for you? Many married women do work."

"Only through necessity. And would your new husband agree to that?"

"I think I could persuade him."

"If anyone could, you could."

Melody gathered up her gloves and umbrella and rose to her feet. "I'd better go. We're having a family dinner tonight and I want to…em…do a little more on my manuscript…before I need to…" Her voice trailed away in confusion.

He watched her from the window as she jumped aboard the gig and set off down the street. What was it about this woman that stirred his soul as well as his body? He had never understood the effect she had on him. Returning to his desk, he dallied with his pen, unable to concentrate. Ever since the day she had swirled into his office and cajoled him into printing that first article, he had been confused by his feelings for her.

His mind returned to their first meeting. At first, he had felt overwhelming annoyance at her brash interruption of his busy day, although her charms were not lost on him. Her cornflower-blue eyes held him in a steady gaze and his attention had been drawn to her auburn hair glowing like burnished copper.

He had never considered employing a woman and it had been a good hour before he had actually read her report. And then the quality of her work had amazed him and instinctively he knew her journalistic abilities couldn't be ignored. From then on, he had thrown every obstacle in her path expecting her to lose interest in the newspaper business. But she had come through with enormous success. Some of the tricks he had played on her had made him feel ashamed and his admiration for her had grown.

Even after he had given her the contract he had tried to stay aloof, he was the editor and she was just one of the reporters on his paper. Until that day when she had presented Sir Jack's cheque and he had seen her dedication to the Journal. Was that the day he had fallen in love with her? He couldn't remember. The feelings had grown slowly but relentlessly, like ivy along a wall. And when he had visited her at her home in Hyde Park Gardens and then again at Hucknall Garth, he had met the woman behind the journalist. Beautiful and vivacious. Courageous and determined.

Guy sighed and leaned his elbows on the desk, resting his chin against his clasped hands. A wild poppy, he thought sadly. And Doctor Alex Courtney would have the joy of plucking this brilliant wild flower. He tried to work but knew that his heart had broken in two.

Melody couldn't believe her ears. She didn't say anything, because she didn't want to embarrass her family and humiliate Alex, but the hurt she felt was running deep.

Alex hadn't been able to attend the family dinner the evening before and Melody had been very disappointed since she wanted to know the outcome of her findings in Camberwell. His note had said that he needed to stay at the hospital due to 'unavoidable circumstances' and so she had been forced to wait a further twenty-four hours until the farewell meal, as the brigadier, Aunt Olivia and Celia were returning to Hucknall Garth the following morning.

And then she had listened, her heart in her mouth, as he told the assembled company how his friend, Doctor Christian Jenner, had produced irrefutable evidence that a water pump was the main source of the cholera outbreak. She listened, hardly raising her eyes from her entwined fingers held in her lap, to how he and Christian had confronted the professor and he in turn would be speaking to the General Board of Health as soon as possible. Full of enthusiasm, he acknowledged that if the water was contaminated, and it pointed that way, then it would change the way society regarded its supply of clean water.

"It's simple really, but then it is simple once you know the answer," he added. He took a gulp of wine and then raised his glass to look at the amber liquid. "What we drink is very important and we mustn't take fresh, clean water for granted."

Celia giggled. "Thank goodness for men like you and Doctor Jenner," she said, flicking out her fan and wafting her face.

Alex gave her a polite bow. Melody fought back the desire to hit him over the head with a wine bottle.

"Well, this is all very pleasant, but I'm in urgent need of a pipe of tobacco," said the brigadier.

"Outside!" warned his sister.

"But of course," he answered, standing and stretching himself.

"And I'm off to my room," smiled Celia. "I've still a bit of packing to do."

"I shall go to the kitchen and compliment Mrs Carr on her excellent meal," said Aunt Olivia. She wagged her finger at Alex. "But I shall return in ten minutes."

"Do you think they'll leave us alone after we're married?" asked Alex, watching the aunt's retreating back with great amusement.

Melody went to draw the curtains. The sun had set and there was just a glimmer of light in the western sky. "My family have their own way of doing things," she said turning to him. "Just like Christian Jenner."

Alex came to his feet and made his way over to her. "What are you talking about, dearest?" He put his arms round her waist.

"Did he say anything about my visit to the hospital yesterday?"

"No, he didn't. Why did you come to the hospital?"

"To bring you the map and my notes on the investigation I made on the cholera epidemic." She could see by his astonished expression she had hit home. She added tersely, "By the way, I'd appreciate the notes back, if you please. I need them for my book."

"You discovered the source of the epidemic?" His amazement didn't pacify her one bit and she fought to keep her temper under control. "Jenner didn't say a word."

"Well, now you know," she murmured, turning away from him.

He stopped her and turned her back towards him. "Now look, Melody. To give Jenner credit, he didn't actually say the map or the information came from himself."

"And what's that supposed to signify?"

Alex thought for a few seconds. "Professor Sweeting is an excellent doctor and has a great deal of influence. But he doesn't agree with women in male occupations. If he had known a woman was behind the information, he would have dismissed it out of hand. It could be that Jenner simply had your best interests at heart."

"Is this professor so bigoted?"

"I'm afraid so." He kissed her on the cheek. "I'll ask Jenner tomorrow and we'll get this all sorted out."

"But he could have told you and sworn you to secrecy about its origin. Why did he keep you in the dark too?"

"I can't answer that. Tomorrow everything will be made clear, I'm sure."

"I just wish…"

He didn't let her finish before raising her chin and placing a tender kiss on her lips. "My dear love, you do get hot-headed sometimes." He caressed her, running his hands down her back. "I have something special to ask you," he said softly. Melody caught her breath. Feeling uncomfortable, she tried to ease herself away from him. "I think it's time we set a date. I want us to marry in October."

A tidal wave of emotion washed over her as she heard the words. This was something a young girl dreamed of, to plan her wedding. But Melody knew she wasn't in the right frame of mind to set a date, she still smarted with Christian's deception.

"October? Oh, Alex, it's too soon," she stammered. "The paper is so busy at the moment."

"Damn the paper! That has nothing to do with us getting married."

"But I would have to leave. Can't we wait a little longer?"

He shook his head and led her over to the couch. "Melody, we've waited long enough. I'm tired of waiting. I want you to be my wife."

"Are you sure about that?" she said, taking a seat.

His eyes widened in surprise. "I wouldn't have proposed if I wasn't. Dearest, I want us to start our life together and I want to join my father in his medical practice."

"You're adamant about living in Colchester?"

He took a seat next to her. "But you've known that from the start. I've not hidden the truth from you."

She squirmed. "I know, but I thought you might live here with me."

"Here?" He looked about him as if seeing the room for the first time. "Oh, no, Melody. I never intended staying in the capital."

"But the paper…"

"Oh yes, The Cork Street Journal. All you seem to think about is that blasted paper."

"I've worked hard to get where I am. You don't know how I struggled…"

"But when you're my wife you'll not work. You must understand that."

Melody felt anger rise up inside her. "But you've seen what I can do and how I can help. My work as a journalist is important. Besides I don't know Colchester. I don't know if I'll be happy there. Please can't we stay in London? You could always set up in practice here." She knew her voice had risen in desperation.

"No, Melody," he said, taking her hand once more. "My mother is looking forward to introducing you as her daughter-in-law."

He seemed to have it all worked out and she felt like a trapped animal.

"Colchester seems so far away," she insisted.

"Goodness, it's only Essex. We'll be able to visit your family regularly."

"But since your mother's visit," she continued, "I've been worried. I really believe she doesn't like me."

A strange look crossed his face. "Why do you think that?"

"Her manner towards me was so cold."

He started laughing. "My mother is like that when she's making a decision."

"And she was deciding about me?"

"Yes she was. I told her I wanted to marry you and she was looking you over."

Melody stood and walked over to the mantelpiece concentrating her mind on the dahlias standing so tall and proud in a vase.

Alex rose to his feet, watching her. "Are you that worried about my mother?"

"I'm sure she doesn't like me," she repeated.

Alex gave a chuckle. "You silly goose." Taking two steps towards her, he wrapped her in a warm embrace. "She thought you very beautiful but rather free spirited.

But as she said, a year amongst Colchester society will calm you down."

He went to kiss her lips but she drew back from him in horror. "Your mother said that?"

Alex realised that he had made a mistake by divulging his parent's comments. In fact, Mrs Courtney had expressed it in much stronger terms, calling Melody wild and uncontrolled and totally unsuitable for her son. But when Alex had insisted that he wanted her as his wife, she had sighed in compliance and said that Colchester society would tame her and teach her to 'kiss the rod'.

"What she means is that *she* will turn me into a fine doctor's wife," added Melody bitterly.

She pulled away from him, anger causing her cheeks to flush. It was obvious he didn't understand what restrictions this sort of life would place on her.

"My mother simply wants me to be happy."

"But I must be happy too."

He tried to draw her back into his arms. "And I will strive to make you happy." Melody didn't respond and in fact, remained motionless, not returning his embrace. "I thought you loved me," he asked hesitantly.

"I do love you. But you're asking me to love you unconditionally."

"What's that supposed to mean?"

"I mean that it's me that has to give up everything. My life, my work. Everything I've striven for."

"But your life will be with me. As my wife." Disquiet passed across his face. "Have you had second thoughts about us marrying?"

Melody couldn't answer. She turned away from him her mind spinning. She did love him and there were times when she had felt happy with him. She had had wonderful feelings when she had been close to him. When he had kissed her, she had felt certain stirrings.

Was this the first flowering of passion? And if it were, would this passion, this love she had, survive if he put such tight controls on her life? But then, shouldn't she be content with making her husband happy? To be satisfied with only that? These thoughts had hardly formed themselves when she saw for the first time, that she couldn't settle for anything less than her heart's desire. All her life she had been zealous about fulfilling her dreams. And this fervour must be evident in her married life. The man she chose for her husband must touch a need deep inside her, his very presence able to move her. But most important of all he must want to walk the same road as she.

Melody tried to blink away tears that had suddenly welled up. "Please, Alex…"

He gripped her arms in sudden shock and made her turn to face him. He could read something in her eyes. Something he didn't like at all. "Melody, tell me. Do you still want to marry me?"

"I don't want to be…just a wife," she said.

His hands dropped to his side and he turned away from her. "It's Wyngate, isn't it? You love him," he said in a hoarse whisper.

This time it was Melody's turn to be shocked. "Don't be silly, he's my employer, that's all."

His eyes narrowed with suspicion. "Jenner said he saw you both coming out of the Cavendish Hotel together."

"Yes, I was taking luncheon and he happened to be there."

"Why was he there?"

"He had a meeting of some kind. It was a pure coincidence."

"Was it?"

Melody thought for a moment. "What is Christian implying? That I was secretly meeting him?" Anger for Christian began to surge through her. That man had done more than enough damage to her for one evening.

"Perhaps that's the truth."

"That's preposterous. Guy is my employer. As I said, he was simply passing by and saw me and decided to…"

"Guy! You call your employer by his first name?"

"No, no, of course not." She saw a look on his face that frightened her. "Well, yes, but only in private. We've become good friends."

He came closer to her, almost threatening. "When are you in private with him?"

"In his office. And other times. But not often…" She suddenly remembered the delightful walk she and Guy had taken when he had visited Hucknall Garth and the meal they had shared at the Merry Jester.

Her expression told Alex everything. "Are you involved with him?"

"No, Alex. No, I'm not."

He straightened up and his hazel eyes seemed harsher than she had ever seen them. "I think I'd better leave," he said, trying to control his voice.

Not trusting herself to speak, Melody stayed silent, unable to move. She barely saw him go, her eyes were so misty with tears. All she heard was the front door closing.

"Was that Alex leaving so soon?" Aunt Olivia entered the room and gasped at the look on her niece's face. "What's the matter, my dear?"

Melody gave out a sob. "Oh, Aunt Olivia, what have I done?"

CHAPTER SIXTEEN

Work became her solace over the next two weeks. Melody refused to let her estrangement with Alex interfere with her daily routine. In the office she was as vivacious and as happy as she could be, forcing smiles and a demeanour that she didn't feel. But she couldn't hide the look in her eyes, now dark and filled with deep sorrow. She chose to say nothing, but bent her energies to her work with a fervour that started to worry her employer. The editor had always admired dedication but not to excess, and especially not to breaking point. Often he would find her still sitting at her desk as he was locking up the premises and would have to usher her out into the street.

"I don't want that young man of yours to think I'm a slave-driver," he admonished her on one occasion. "Get yourself home and spend an evening with him."

"What do you think of my manuscript?" she asked, watching him lock the front door. She had been bringing in the completed chapters for his opinion.

Guy smiled. "Excellent. You've dealt with the subject with great sensitivity and also with humour. I liked that."

"Eric says he'll do the illustrations for me."

"Good! Illustrations always make the narrative more interesting."

"I'm still considering a section on prostitution. But I'll need company if I'm to go into those areas of London. Eric says he'll go with me."

"I bet he did," Guy chuckled. "No, I think I should go or perhaps Holbrook. When were you thinking of going?"

"As soon as possible."

Guy thought for a moment. "I could chaperone you the day after tomorrow. Would that be all right?"

Melody smiled in approval. She had hoped that Guy would accompany her. The women on the street would have eaten Eric alive.

It was difficult keeping up the pretence that all was well. In fact, her estrangement from Alex was still not public knowledge. After Alex had left so suddenly, Melody had sat with Aunt Olivia and told her everything and then sworn her to secrecy. On no account must she tell either the brigadier or Celia, or Mrs Carr and Tilly for that matter. Melody didn't want any sympathy or recriminations, all she wanted was to get on with her work, her book and her life.

Although it crossed her mind that Alex might call on her, the end of each day convinced her that he was gone for good. She refused to cry, believing herself too strong to give in to it. And so the pain remained and if the tears seemed to well up inside her, she would swallow, take a large breath and push forward in her indomitable way. She slept fitfully and would rise in the middle of the night and continue with her writing. Frequently, Mrs Carr or Tilly would find her bent over her manuscript and then chastise her for ruining her eyesight. It became obvious to the housekeeper and maid that Miss Melody had broken her engagement, as Doctor Courtney never called again.

"Are you ready for this?" said Guy, jumping up next to Melody.

She nodded and urged Sultan into a walk. "Yes, I'm looking forward to it."

"You're a remarkable young woman, Miss Melody Kinsman. Not many girls of your class would want to speak to those kind of women."

"They're still people with feelings and dreams."

"Shattered dreams I should think."

Melody smiled. "It'll be interesting. I haven't actually thought how to go about it. Have you any suggestions?"

"We'll start at the Ten Bells. That's where they congregate." He turned away as he asked, "Do you actually want to go out in the street?"

"If I get enough information at the public house, then I'll just observe their working methods."

Guy looked at her aghast. "I beg your pardon!"

She threw back her head and gave a gleeful laugh. "I mean I'll watch how they pick up their clients."

Guy blew out a breath. "Well, we'll have to be very discreet. And we'll have to be wary of the pimps. They're very suspicious of anyone on their patch."

Melody gave him a sidelong glance. "Know the area well, do you?"

Guy shook his head trying to keep his face straight. "A prostitute was murdered about five years ago and I went to report on it."

Melody smiled and thought of how the profession of journalism could send a person anywhere and into any situation. No wonder Alex disapproved. The thought of Alex made her swallow hard.

They were just turning a corner when a large figure appeared and called to them. Melody reined in Sultan.

"Police Sergeant Dallimore," she cried with delight. "I haven't seen you at Scotland Yard for quite a while. Where have you been?"

"Got sent up to Newcastle, miss. Just to observe their ways for six months."

"Could I introduce you to Mr Guy…"

"It's all right, miss. Mr Wyngate and me go back a long ways."

The two men shook hands. "Sergeant Dallimore was dealing with the murder I was telling you about," said Guy, smiling. "Although he was just a constable then."

"And where are you off to?" asked the sergeant. "Not on any social call, I reckon."

"Back to Whitechapel. Where everything first started for me," said Melody, grinning at Guy.

"Whitechapel? What business have you there, if you don't mind me asking?"

"I'm writing a book on the plight of women and I want to do a chapter about the women on the streets. I'm going to ask them some questions about their lives."

"Miserable lives, I should say," the big man said, biting his lip. "I really think you should keep out of that area."

"There's no point in persuading her to do otherwise," said Guy, shaking his head.

The sergeant thought for a moment. "Look. I'm just coming off duty and I've got the time. Why don't I accompany you? Where are you starting?"

"At the Ten Bells," ventured Melody.

Sergeant Dallimore nodded. "Good place to start, I guess. Plenty of them in that place. Yes, I'd like to accompany you, if you don't mind. But I must pop home first and tell my better half. She'll only worry if I don't turn up."

It was decided that the police sergeant would meet them at the public house and urging Sultan forward, Guy and Melody continued their journey. The area they were going into brought back memories of the Fetter Lane murder. Melody looked around at the dilapidated dwellings, the poverty and squalor and worst of all, the thin, ragged children playing in the streets amongst the rubbish and household waste. She spied a young girl standing on the corner, obviously waiting for a customer to pass by. She must have been fifteen and her excessive makeup and low-cut blouse gave her an odd appearance. She looked like an actress from a badly written play, who was trying to act a part meant for someone much older. Melody bit her lip apprehensively. It wasn't safe for a young girl to stand about like that. As if to answer her misgivings, an older woman approached the young girl, perhaps in her twenties, but age was deceptive in this profession. She was dressed in the same manner, although it was obvious she was much more experienced. Speaking to the girl in a compassionate way, Melody saw her caress the young girl's cheek as if to comfort her.

"They seem to look after each other," she said, nodding in the couple's direction.

"Yes, I think there's a kind of sisterhood or camaraderie amongst them. Which is a good thing," said Guy softly.

Thankfully, there was a small stable at the back of the Ten Bells and they were able to leave Sultan and the gig with a scrawny stable boy. Guy promised him a guinea if he cared for the horse and vehicle and didn't let anyone near them.

The boy doffed his cap and smiled showing decaying teeth.

"That's very generous," said Melody to Guy.

"Money talks in this place," he answered grimly.

"Money talks everywhere," Melody chuckled, taking his arm.

At the door of the Ten Bells they met Sergeant Dallimore and although Melody was grateful of Guy's company she knew that no harm would come to them now. A big man like the sergeant would make anyone think twice. Besides, she soon discovered that he was well known in the tavern and the landlady clapped him on the back and offered them the best part of the saloon. Drinks were put in front of them and Melody looked about her.

The gas lamps around the wall hissed and spluttered and gave off a pungent smell. The place was none too clean, with food and spilt alcohol on the floor where straw was scattered about to absorb some of the debris. There was a lot of noise as people filled the place for an afternoon of drinking and anything else they could find to entertain themselves.

Melody spied a table on the far side of the room, around which were seven women and by their manner of dress it was obvious what they were. She pulled out her notebook and pencil eager to start.

"I'm going over there. Won't be long," she said, rising from her chair and lifting her skirt away from the filth on the floor.

Guy and the sergeant watched her.

"She's got some pluck, 'as that young lady," said the sergeant, taking a gulp of his ale.

"She certainly has," murmured Guy.

Melody approached the table cautiously. Seven pairs of eyes turned in her direction. Eyes that had seen too much, in expressions that were all alike.

"Ladies, I'm sorry for intruding…"

"Hark to 'er calling us ladies," said one who seemed older than the rest.

Unperturbed, Melody introduced herself. "I'm Melody Kinsman from The Cork Street Journal. May I sit with you?"

The women looked at each other and then at the well-dressed woman with a notebook in her hand.

"Aye, dearie," said one of them. "Why not."

In a short while Melody had explained her mission. She told them about her book and the chapter she wanted to write on their particular profession. She assured them that she wasn't going to pass judgement on them, only speak on their behalf. At first they were wary, but as they gained confidence and Melody worked her magic on them, the words poured out of mouths bright red with lip-rouge. It seemed many of them had been in domestic service first; some had been maids, one had been a cook. Another had been a lady's maid for a countess, but had fallen for the charms of the earl and after he had finished with her, she had lost her livelihood, her home and then her pride.

"But it's not a bad life," she said. "I have my friends and some of the clients are acceptable."

"I wanted to be a florist and own my own shop," said one girl.

"I just wanted to marry and have kiddies. But it wasn't to be," said another.

Melody kept scribbling, interested in all she was hearing and yet filled with the awful awareness that these girls had fallen to the bottom of the pile simply through misfortune. It could happen to any woman who fell on hard times. They had had their dreams too. Shattered dreams Guy had said and how right he was.

Guy and the sergeant watched from a distance, sipping their ale and falling into easy conversation. A young man sauntered across and took a seat next to them.

"Afternoon Eddie. What can we do for you?" said the sergeant, eyeing him up and down.

"You could buy me a drink, sarge."

Sergeant Dallimore called for three more glasses of ale and then introduced Guy to the rather attractive, but arrogant young man with large, cat-like eyes. Yes, thought Guy, he's just like a cat. Sleek and agile, with a slow, easy manner.

Eddie leaned back in his chair. "So who's the bit of skirt talking to my girls?"

"Mind your manners! She's a lady and not 'a bit of skirt'," snapped the sergeant. "And for your information, she's Miss Melody Kinsman from The Cork Street Journal. This 'ere, is her employer Mr Guy Wyngate."

Eddie nodded at Guy, who returned the nod but didn't offer his hand, deciding it was better to keep some distance between them.

"What's she doing?"

Guy explained. "She's writing a book on the lives of women and she's including a chapter on girls working the streets."

Eddie's laughter echoed round the tavern. "Now why would she want to write about a load of whores and sluts."

"Well, you've done quite well out of them," said the sergeant.

Guy scrutinised the young man sitting at their table. He was certainly wearing clothes of good quality, a lot better than the girls were wearing. A gold earring glinted from one ear and he had an impressive ring on the middle finger of his left hand.

Eddie watched Melody for a few seconds and then blew out a breath. "Gawd Almighty, I could make my fortune out of that one. She's a real beauty." He pursed his lips. "Well, time to get them back out working." He gulped down his drink and jumped to his feet.

"Does he view every woman as a potential money earner?" asked Guy.

"His mother was a whore," said the sergeant grimly. "He's not known any different."

They watched him stride over to the table and urge the girls out. Protesting loudly that they hadn't had long enough, he dismissed their complaints and steered them towards the door. Melody followed them.

"You coming too, darling?" he said, chucking her under the chin.

"I thought I'd just see what happens," she said, giving him a sweet smile.

The sergeant and editor left the table and came across to her.

"I don't think you should," said Guy, gripping her arm.

"Just a little look," she said. "There's no harm standing with them for a short while."

Eddie grinned. "Not too long, though. The punters will get distracted from the real merchandise."

Outside, the girls went their separate ways, but Melody decided to stay with two who remained on the corner, still asking her questions. Guy and the sergeant stayed by the door, looking around at the people milling about. It wasn't long before two men approached the women. To Guy's horror they went straight to Melody, touching her face as though she was already theirs. She rebuffed them with a polite word.

Eddie gave a lewd laugh, his eyes showing his pleasure. "What did I tell you? Thirty seconds that was and she's already got customers."

"Enough," murmured Guy, not finding the situation amusing one bit.

"Yes, let's get her out of here," nodded the sergeant.

If Melody had been delighted with her excursion to Whitechapel, her reaction to the report on the water supply in Camberwell, was in stark contrast. To Guy's amazement, he might as well have shown her a pamphlet advertising the new fashion in bonnets. She showed no interest whatsoever and simply gave him a misty smile.

"Aren't you eager to read the report? The company responsible for the supply has removed the handle from the pump, so the residents can't use that particular water supply and the General Board of Health think there might be contamination from sewage."

Melody looked down at the report but her face remained impassive. "That's good. I'm pleased about that."

Guy frowned. "But it was all your doing. You prevented more illness occurring."

"I'll read it when I get home," she said, taking the bound document and rising to her feet.

It was only after she had left the office that he realised her name wasn't mentioned in the report. In fact, no one's name was mentioned and Guy decided he would check further and find out why.

The brigadier was in a rush. He didn't care for tardiness in others never mind himself, and he was late. His appointment was at two o'clock prompt and he needed to drive at full speed to be there in time.

Celia noticed the papers lying on the hall table and picked them up. With alarm she realised he had left without them and when he arrived at his destination, his journey would have been pointless. She ran to the window and glanced down the drive, he was just turning the trap at the gate and if she took a short cut through the kitchen she could meet him on the main road. She looked down at her feet frowning at the house shoes she was wearing. She really shouldn't go outside without wearing her boots, but there was no time to put them on.

Picking up her skirt, she was through the house and out into the kitchen garden running towards the small gate that led into the main thoroughfare.

"Brigadier! Brigadier! You've forgotten the papers."

There was only fifty yards between them and he heard. Peering over his shoulder, he pulled on the reins and brought the vehicle to a halt. "What's that, Celia? What are you saying, girl?"

She reached him, holding her stomach to ease the stitch in her side. "The papers. You left them on the table," she gasped.

She pulled herself up onto the running board and as she did so, her shoe slipped from her foot and clattered into the road. She looked down at it in dismay.

"Better check they're all here," said the brigadier, carefully examining the documents and counting each page.

Celia waited patiently, watching him in his task.

"I believe this belongs to you," said a soft voice to her left. She looked down in surprise. Alex slipped the shoe on her foot and took her hand to help her alight from the running board.

"Why Alex," she said, "What are you doing here? Melody is still in London."

"Found myself in the area, so I thought I'd call in and see you. Good afternoon, sir." Alex held out his hand to the brigadier who shook it warmly.

"Good to see you again, my boy, but I'm in rather a hurry. Perhaps you could stay for dinner?"

Alex nodded. "Yes sir, that would be delightful."

"All present and correct, Celia, so I'll be on my way," said Brigadier Kinsman. "I'll have to leave you and Olivia to entertain the good doctor." He whipped the horse into action and was gone.

Celia gave an embarrassed giggle. "Aunt Olivia will be so pleased to see you again," she said, trying to hide her blushes.

"I'm looking forward to seeing her." He suddenly became pensive. "And then you and I must have a long talk. I have something to ask you." He offered his arm and they walked back to Hucknall Garth.

The letter was terse and to the point. Professor Sweeting from Saint George's Hospital had never heard of Miss Melody Kinsman of The Cork Street Journal. And he certainly had no knowledge of her involvement in the findings of Camberwell. However, if Miss Kinsman would like to produce evidence that it was through her efforts the infected water supply was discovered, then he would be happy to consider her case, although he couldn't guarantee that her name would be mentioned in future reports.

"I'm sorry, Melody, the man was extremely unhelpful," said Guy, folding away the letter.

Melody shrugged. "It doesn't matter who discovered the problem. It's being dealt with and that's the important fact."

He gave a slight smile. "I remember a young lady who sat in that very chair and whimpered that only her initials had been included at the bottom of her article."

Melody grimaced. "That seems a long time ago."

"Even so, you're still entitled to some recognition. Would you like me to write a section on your findings, to be printed in the next edition of the Journal?"

She shook her head. "No, that will only cause controversy," she said quietly.

"Since when did you care about controversy," Guy laughed, but when he saw her pensive expression he stopped. After a moment of silence he added, "I could see Sir Jack. He has a great deal of influence and could sway the opinion of this Professor Sweeting."

Melody raised her hand in a gesture of disapproval. "Please don't, Guy. Leave it be." She suddenly smiled and he was relieved to see that radiant glow light up her face once more. "We can't all be heroes and win medals."

He smiled with her but then said, "You are all right? I mean, there's nothing worrying you?"

"You're very kind to consider my welfare, but I'm doing very well."

Guy paused, suddenly feeling uncomfortable. "You've certainly had a busy year. But an interesting one I hope?"

She realised he was trying to be a friend to her. "Yes, it's been very interesting. And it's all thanks to you for giving me the chance to prove myself."

"You've been an asset to me. The editors from the other papers said I was a fool to take you on. Now they admit they let a prize slip through their fingers."

"Even the editor of *The Times*?" she asked in surprise.

Guy nodded. "He more than the others. He said you were the governess to his children?" Melody nodded. "He now realises that his prejudices have cost him a great deal."

She couldn't contain her glee. "How wonderful."

"And Sir Jack has had words with his editor. Told him to broaden his mind, or something like that."

"Sir Jack is such a lovely man."

Guy gave an embarrassed cough. "I've noticed you're not wearing an engagement ring to work. I'm certainly not against it and I don't think the others will mind."

Melody looked down at her hand and sighed. "I don't want to wear it in the office."

"Well, it's up to you. Have you set a date yet?" She shook her head. Puzzlement passed across his features. "That fiancé of yours must be a very patient man. I doubt I'd have such patience."

She scanned his face and knew he meant it.

A few minutes later, Melody left the editor's office. Guy picked up the letter from Professor Sweeting and smiled sadly.

Brigadier Kinsman nearly dropped his pipe in delighted surprise.

"Alex! Have you brought Melody with you?"

"N…No, sir. I wished to speak with you," he stammered, bewildered that the brigadier should suggest such a thing.

The brigadier frowned. "Is there something wrong?"

"No, it's just that I've made plans for the future and I wanted to…Well, actually sir, I need to ask you something."

"That's splendid," said the brigadier. He knew what this was about, it was about his Melody. A wedding date was forthcoming. "Let me offer you a drink, my boy."

Alex was saved from replying by the timely appearance of Aunt Olivia, but her expression made him uncomfortable and he looked down at his shoes gathering his courage.

"Oh, Alex, it is you. Sarah told me you were here but I thought she must be mistaken. To what do we owe the pleasure of two visits in one week?"

"I believe that Alex and Melody have finally named the day and he's come to tell us all about it," smiled the brigadier. "Sit down, my boy. And here's your drink."

Alex took his drink but remained standing.

Olivia felt uneasy. Melody had forbidden her to tell the brigadier about the estrangement and he was still under the impression that a wedding was imminent. She remembered their farewell dinner at Hyde Park Gardens and its aftermath. And she would always remember that Melody, although putting on a brave face, couldn't hide the pain and confusion she was feeling.

"Yes, sit down, then," she said softly.

Alex accepted a chair, his quiet and reserved nature suddenly becoming a hindrance to him. He coughed. "I'm sorry, sir. But Melody and I...we called off our engagement."

A kaleidoscope of emotions passed across the brigadier's face. "You and Melody are not getting married. I don't understand this." He turned to his sister. "Why didn't you tell me?"

"She didn't want you to know," she whispered. "It was too painful for her."

Alex caught her last remark. "Melody was hurting?"

"Of course she was, Alex," snapped Olivia.

He shook his head. "But it was she who didn't want to marry! She couldn't give up her life in London." He swallowed the brandy in one go and placed the empty glass on the occasional table.

"That didn't stop her heart breaking. For goodness sake, Alex! She's not made of stone."

Alex pondered on this for a few seconds. He remembered the beautiful woman he had held in his arms. Her sweet kisses and the hopes and dreams he had had for their future together.

The brigadier took in a breath. "Well, young man. Why are you here?"

Alex cleared his throat. "I've always wanted to join my father in private practice and with my inheritance and a good income, I believe the time is right for me to move to Colchester."

"So, what's this to do with us?" said the brigadier dryly.

"I still want to marry and as her guardian, I feel it only right to ask you for my future wife's hand in marriage."

The brigadier's mouth fell open. "Who are you talking about?"

Aunt Olivia sat back and frowned. "I think I have an idea, Liam. It can only be one other person," she said, her face flushing.

"Who? Goodness, you don't mean…"

"She's waiting in the hall," said Alex quickly, wanting to get this over and done with.

"Is she? Well, you'd better tell her to come in," said the brigadier.

Alex rose from his seat and disappeared through the door. Moments later he returned, his arm round Celia. "I would like permission to take Celia as my wife, sir."

The brigadier stared at the pair of them but then questioned Celia. "Are you happy about this, my dear?"

"Oh, yes. Very happy," she smiled.

The brigadier thought for a moment. "You do realise that Celia is still in mourning?"

Alex nodded. "Of course. And society frowns on a wedding in the family during the first twelve months. However, we hoped that if we married quietly as soon as the banns are read, then a simple, private ceremony in All Saints' Church would be acceptable."

Celia's voice was firm. "We are to honeymoon at Alex's parents' villa in Nice. When we return we'll be settling down in Colchester." She added curtly, "Papa would want me to be happy."

The brigadier took her hand. "Then as your guardian I can only wish you the same happiness."

"You must stay for dinner, Alex," said Olivia. She thought it only polite to suggest it, but was relieved when the invitation was declined.

Ten minutes later Alex left to catch the London train.

"Do you think you could explain what that was all about?" the brigadier asked his sister when they were finally alone.

Olivia stood and walked over to the drink's decanter. Pouring out another good measure of brandy, she handed it to her brother. It was going to be a long evening. And then she would have to write to her niece.

CHAPTER SEVENTEEN

Melody made her way to Cork Street. It was now the end of September and the summer was slowly dying, although the weather was staying pleasantly warm. The trees were hinting at the coming autumn with the occasional leaf showing a shade of gold, brown and orange.

She went straight to her desk and opening her leather pouch she pulled out the sheaves of paper, ready to prepare her article. She had started to feel better the last few weeks, burying her pain deep inside her, refusing to let herself think of Alex and if the memory of him threatened to engulf her she would push it to the back of her mind.

The Times newspaper was folded on the table and Melody decided to glance through it before getting down to her own work. The front pages were full of the continuing reports from America on the aftermath of the civil war and the assassination of President Lincoln. She quickly read that the estimated numbers of dead in the war was over six hundred thousand, a number far greater than the figures for the Crimea. Breathing a heavy sigh Melody turned to the society pages to scan the engagements and social events.

It was only a small section and she would have missed it except that it had been circled in thick, black pencil. The report said that the wedding had taken place the previous day, between The Hon. Celia Sinclair only child of the late tenth Baron Sinclair and Doctor Alexander Courtney, at All Saints' Church, Staplehurst in Kent.

Melody let out a cry and gripped the paper tighter until her fingers hurt. She was hardly aware of Guy entering the room, until she heard him say her name and looking up saw his form quivering in a misty haze. Removing the paper from her shaking hands, he scanned the page finding the announcement.

"I don't understand," he said frowning.

Melody shook her head. "Why didn't Aunt Olivia write and tell me," she gasped. "Why didn't she say something?"

The secretary appeared at the door. "Mr Wyngate, a messenger is here from your uncle."

"Deal with it Marsh," Guy snapped at him.

"Sorry, sir, he needs a reply from you."

Guy gave out an audible groan and biting his lip, turned to Melody, alarmed at her ashen face. "I'm leaving for just ten minutes. Stay here until I come back. Do you understand?"

She nodded as if in a daze. He quickly made his way to his office to dispense with the annoying business as soon as possible. But when he returned she had gone.

Melody couldn't remember how she got to Hyde Park Gardens, only that Sultan had brought her home. But once he was in the stable, she had no desire to go into the house. Instead she walked towards the Bayswater Road and from there through the gate into the park. A slight breeze kissed her burning cheeks and there was a feeling of impending rain in the air. Melody didn't care, but kept on walking along the paths, between the flowerbeds, until she reached the Serpentine. Here she found the bench that she and Alex had always shared and sank down against the cool, wooden frame.

The rain started to fall and people hurried past eager to find shelter. But Melody didn't move from the bench. She untied her bonnet and slipped it off. Tilting her face to the grey, sombre clouds scurrying across the sky, she closed her eyes. It was on a day like today she had first met Alex. She remembered filing past the steps of the library. She had turned to look at him, he had smiled and the sun had come out.

Tears sprang from behind her closed eyelids and began to trickle down her face, mingling with the rain that caressed her cheeks. And once they had started there was no stopping them. She gasped as the pain bubbled to the surface and relief came only in anguished crying.

She had never been one for self-pity. Even as a child, she had rarely cried. But now it was all she could do but pour out her sorrow and loss. Finally her tears subsided and she opened her eyes to find herself quite alone, the park now deserted. The rain continued falling and she watched fascinated, as the ducks bobbed about on the surface of the Serpentine. She was getting wet and yet she felt no discomfort, in fact, she felt peaceful, as if her spirit had left her body and was soaring above the trees. She rose from the bench and walked to the edge of the water.

It was now nearly nine months since she and Alex had met for the second time and those months had been filled with joy and sorrow. They had gone through so much together and yet their paths had rarely run side by side. Ever since he had given her that first smile, she had thought of him as a talisman, someone who made her life better. But now, realising the restrictions he would have placed on her, she knew that life with him would have been impossible.

The feelings she had for Alex were nothing more than a young girl's infatuation. They didn't run deep enough to be his wife. The man for her must have the ability to reach into the very depths of her soul and lift her to the heavens. And there was no man alive who could do that. She took a step closer to the water.

Guy spent five minutes searching the building for Melody. He felt confused. What was Melody's fiancé doing marrying another woman? Why hadn't she told him that their engagement was over? He crossed the street to the stable and discovered her gig was missing. Hoping that she had gone home, he hired a horse and turned its head towards Hyde Park Gardens, intending to take a short cut across the park. He pulled up when he saw a lone figure standing by the side of the lake.

His heart in his mouth, he dismounted and leading the horse forward secured him to a post, stroking his nose to keep him quiet. He approached Melody silently until he was within speaking distance. She was staring into the lake and he licked dry lips when he saw how close she was to the edge.

He spoke her name softly and she turned in his direction. Her eyes were heavy from crying, but her expression was serene.

"What are you doing here?" she said, startled by his sudden appearance.

"I've come to take you home," he answered and then added, "Please would you step away from the edge."

She lifted her chin and smiled. "It's all right, Guy, I've no intention of throwing myself in. What would be the point? I'd only frighten the ducks."

He came towards her and she went to meet him. He breathed deeply as he took her hands; thankful she had come to no harm. The rain had stopped and the sun emerged from behind the clouds flooding the park with its warming rays. The trees and grass seemed to glisten with a vivid green and the raindrops caught in the foliage, sparkled like diamonds. She looked up and smiled at the rainbow that now spread its glory across the sky.

"I've been so worried about you," he said, kissing her fingers.

"You're very considerate."

He shook his head. "I wouldn't want anything to happen to my best reporter." He gave a tender smile. "Tell me if you don't want to talk about it, but I wondered…that announcement in *The Times*…?"

Melody shrugged. "It's all right. I don't mind telling you."

"You obviously broke off your engagement?" he said, watching her.

"Yes, about seven weeks ago."

"Seven weeks! And he's married someone else?"

She grimaced. "It seems I'm easy to forget."

"Then he's a fool," he said. He regained his composure. "But his…new wife. Isn't she a friend of yours? I recognised the name."

"Yes, she's a friend of mine. I went to her papa's funeral at the beginning of the year."

Guy nodded and placed a gentle hand on her elbow. "I'll take you home."

He took the horse's bridle and with Melody on his arm, they made their way down the path. The sunshine had brought people from their shelters and now the park was filling rapidly. They watched two children running by chasing a small puppy, being followed by their parents who were laughing at their antics and calling for them to slow down.

Guy squeezed her hand. "The sunshine always makes things seem better."

Melody gave a watery smile. "Why does society think only in *families*?"

"Because that's the way it is, I guess."

"It's difficult to be on your own," she said. "But I've realised that great strength can come from that very courage you need to be alone."

"Who says you're going to be alone? Goodness me! Someone else will come into your life and you'll be happy again."

She looked up at him. "Alex was pushing me into marriage and children. I had to tell him that I'm not ready for that yet. I have such a lot of plans, so much I want to do. I have a long road to travel and if he had been willing to walk by my side while I travel that road then I'd have known how important I was to him." She sighed. "It looks like I'll be travelling that road on my own."

Guy stopped walking and turned to face her. "Melody, I won't have you wallowing in self-pity. It's not like you to feel sorry for yourself."

"I'm not feeling sorry for myself."

"Yes, you are. Now, stop it. I've told you, someone else will come along one day. "

"I'm not sure if I care for someone else to come along. In fact, I shall be content to remain a spinster for the rest of my days."

"No you won't. You'll change your mind when you meet the right man."

"You're a fine one to talk. You chose not to marry, to live your life alone. So, why shouldn't I? Or are only *men* allowed to live as bachelors, while spinsters are viewed with contempt?"

Her tone was brittle and Guy smiled to himself. He knew that her bravado was shielding her pain.

"What makes you think I've never married?"

Melody looked at him askance. "No one ever mentioned it to me."

He shrugged. "Ah, well. Just because no one's told you, doesn't mean it hasn't happened."

"You've been married?" she whispered.

He glanced around. The sun was warm on their backs and it was pleasant to stand and enjoy the sights and sounds of the park. The scent of moist grass and autumn flowers wafted about them.

"I married Constance three months before I left for the Crimea."

"What happened to her?"

"She knew that I'd be away a long time and she accepted it as part of the work I did. Letters between us were few and those I did receive told me nothing of the true situation back in England. By the time I returned home, I found that she was dead and buried."

"Oh, Guy, I'm so sorry."

"She had died in childbirth. The doctors thought there would be complications and her life might be threatened, but she decided not to tell me. She didn't want me to worry while I was so far away from home."

"She must have been a kind person."

"She was, but in truth, I never had the opportunity to get to know her properly. We met only two months before we married." He gave a wistful smile. "She left me a daughter."

Melody's eyes became wider. "You have a child?"

"She was christened Charlotte."

"But where is she?"

Guy let out a long sigh. "She died from scarlet fever when only three years old."

Melody couldn't help taking his hand and pressing it against her cheek. Tears stung her eyes.

"Oh, dear Lord, all the pain you've suffered and here's me moaning about my insignificant troubles and grieving for a man who wasn't right for me in the first place."

He caressed her face. "It still hurt you and you need to recover from that pain."

They carried on walking and Guy went on to tell her about the little girl with dark curls and big, brown eyes, his special angel that he had lost so long ago.

And Melody listened, engrossed in his story and by the time they reached Hyde Park Gardens, Doctor Alexander Courtney had been swept from her heart.

The letter arrived a day later. It was from Aunt Olivia and was handed to Melody in a sorry state. Frayed and grubby, it had obviously been dropped, stepped on and then sent to every address that side of Hyde Park. Scribbled across most parts of the envelope were further possible destinations, until the Post Office had succeeded in delivering it to the right house.

Melody opened it to find the date three weeks old and she read that Celia and Alex were to marry on the twenty-seventh of September. Her aunt's tone was rather subdued and Melody knew that she would have found it difficult to write, realising what a shock it would be to her niece. Melody smiled to herself and decided that one day she would tell her how she actually discovered about the wedding.

It was Marsh who had unwittingly placed *The Times* on her desk knowing that Melody had some connection with the late tenth Baron Sinclair and might therefore, be interested in such an event. When Melody returned to work, he was all of a fluster for his misplaced kindness, apologising profusely for causing her such distress.

The next few weeks passed and daily life at the Journal continued. Melody had slipped into a contented routine. Her book was coming along satisfactorily and her weekly section was generating a great deal of interest, with letters from readers arriving every day. Guy would often bring the mail to her personally and then linger to make conversation. The staff watched with amusement and began to get used to him walking along the corridor or through the press office.

"Never sits at his desk these days," grunted Marsh. "There was a time when he hardly left the office except to go out. Now he buzzes around the place like a bee from flower to flower."

"Aye, but there's only one flower. And that happens to be our Miss Melody," said Eric, grinning from ear to ear.

September moved into October and the weather stayed remarkably warm. 'An Indian summer' quoted Eric, but then added grimly that it might be a ghastly winter.

Melody came into the office that Saturday morning to Henri studying the latest fashions from Paris. It was his job to write the Society Page and it suited him since he loved the gossip and intrigue that followed the upper echelons of 'polite society'.

"Ah, Mademoiselle Melody," he said, in his heavy French accent. "Fashions are on the change, it seems. The crinoline will be expanding in the next few years."

Melody wandered over to his desk. "What do they expect us to wear now?" She looked at the illustration and gasped. "Oh, no! I'm not wearing a skirt that wide. Goodness, I'll not get through the door."

"*Oui*, I have a cartoon here that will amuse you."

He rustled through the pamphlets on his desk and pulled one out. Turning to the required page he passed it to Melody who burst into laughter. The cartoon depicted a fashionable couple coming downstairs, with the man walking on the outside of the banisters since the lady's skirt took up the whole width of the staircase.

Melody shook her head, giggling with delight. "Well, that decides it. I have a good mind to remove this damned hoop right now."

Eric entered the room. "What's keeping you two amused?" Melody handed him the illustration and he too chuckled. "My ma insists on wearing one that takes up the entire length of the couch. So I just sit on her dress. She gets very annoyed with me."

Melody gathered up her leather pouch. "Well, can't stand around here all day. I need to see Mr Wyngate and then I'm off to interview Miss Susan Anthony."

"Who's Miss Susan Anthony when she's at home?" asked Eric.

Melody gave him a withering look. "She's an American and she's here doing a series of talks on equality for women. She wants equal pay for female teachers, women's suffrage and also the right of a woman to keep anything she owns after she's married, instead of it going to her husband."

Eric and Henri looked at each other.

"No point in marrying a rich widow, then," said Eric gloomily. Melody headed for the door. Suddenly he remembered. "Oh, Mr Wyngate isn't in today. Apparently he's ill."

Melody spun on her heel. "He's ill? What's the matter with him?"

Eric thought for a moment. "Holbrook told me and Marsh told him that it's influenza."

"Influenza," whispered Melody, her heart starting to beat rapidly. "But that can be serious."

Eric shrugged. "He's usually in a good health, but I suppose he has to be ill sometimes." He and Henri went back to looking at the pamphlets.

Melody travelled to the tearoom at Claridge's where she was to meet Miss Susan Anthony, but the journey was marred by the dreadful thoughts running through her mind. She remembered the influenza epidemic when she was twelve and how some of the residents of Staplehurst had ended up in the churchyard. True they had been mostly elderly and four or five small children. But folk of any age could be afflicted and die.

Susan Anthony turned out to be a bubbly, talkative woman with an American drawl that would have suited a southern plantation owner. She was full of information and pointed out that she also worked for the anti-slavery and temperance movements. Melody tried to concentrate on what she was saying but found her mind wandering.

"Have you ever been to America, Miss Kinsman?"

Melody smiled. "No, I haven't. I've not even thought of travelling to the Continent."

"Well, I hope your book is published in my country. I think it'll be a great success. We Americans are far more liberated than you serious and may I say, quite conventional English."

"Yes, I suppose we are too conventional."

"And if you ever do decide to cross the Atlantic, then come and visit me. I live in New York City now and I've a roomful of people who would love to meet you."

Melody smiled. At the moment the last thing on her mind was travelling to New York City. As she climbed aboard the gig, she knew that she couldn't go home. The anxiety that had started in the press office had now intensified to a frightening level. She snapped the reins and headed for Mayfair.

Melody drew up outside number four, Hill Street and climbed down from the gig. She looked around her at the row of Georgian buildings, three storeys high. They were all whitewashed with wrought iron fencing enclosing small front gardens. Large windows dominated each house and grand oak doors made impressive entrances into fine buildings. She had never been to Guy's home and, she realised, shouldn't be there now without a chaperone. It wasn't seemly for a young unmarried girl to visit an unmarried gentleman alone. But when had she ever bothered with propriety? Even so, she couldn't stop her heart from racing at what she might find. What would she do if she discovered he was desperately ill?

She quickly tied Sultan to a post. A stern, middle-aged woman wearing black answered her knock.

"I'm Miss Melody Kinsman and I'll like to see Mr Guy Wyngate if you please."

The woman sniffed. "He never mentioned about visitors calling."

"Mr Wyngate is my employer. I've come to ask after his health."

"His health, miss?"

"May I come in please?"

The woman pulled a face and held the door open. Melody stepped into a pleasant hallway. A magnificent grandfather clock stood in the corner and on a small walnut table was a vase of flowers. Sunshine flooded in from the open door and leaded window above, sending colourful rays of light bouncing off the oak panelling on the walls.

"Are you alone?" said the housekeeper.

"I'm afraid so, but I'm sure Mr Wyngate won't mind that."

The woman sniffed again. "I've heard of you. You write the woman's column, don't you?"

"I certainly do."

She closed the door. "I suppose he won't mind seeing you. Although I don't hold with young girls coming to the homes of unmarried gentlemen. Master's in his study."

"Why is he in the study?" asked Melody. "Shouldn't he be in bed?"

The housekeeper grunted and led her upstairs, ushering her into a room just off the landing.

"Miss Melody Kinsman, sir." She glanced over her shoulder. "And she's alone."

Melody saw him rise from his place at the desk. He was in his shirtsleeves and reached for his jacket, quickly slipping it on.

"Melody? What are you doing here?"

She stepped into the room feeling embarrassed. "I don't understand. I was told you had influenza."

The woman cleared her throat. "Shall I stay, sir?"

"Yes. Yes, Mrs Talbot," he frowned. "You must act as chaperone."

"Indeed, sir," she said, coming further into the room.

"Influenza? Who told you that?" He scanned the figure standing in the middle of the room, dressed in an emerald green skirt and jacket with a pretty matching hat perched on auburn curls.

"Eric told me."

"And who told Eric?"

"I think it was Holbrook. Who got it from Marsh." She swallowed hard. "Oh, dear."

His eyes crinkled in amusement. "I think the story has become rather twisted in the telling. It's Sir Jack who's got influenza. That's why I didn't come into work, because I went to see him."

"And he's recovering?" asked Melody, feeling very alarmed. She was fond of Sir Jack and didn't like to think of the elderly gentleman being ill.

"The doctors have no cause for alarm."

"Oh, good."

She glanced around the room and then back at the man standing by the desk, realising that her mission was now complete. She had discovered he was well and there was no reason for her to remain. They stared at each other. Melody couldn't help noticing how handsome he looked in his dark blue jacket and trousers, with a lighter blue and white waistcoat and a white cravat tied neatly about his neck. He was watching her with that tender expression he often had, as though he was waiting for something wonderful to happen. Suddenly she didn't want to go. She had had such a fright thinking he was ill, perhaps dying, that the thought of leaving him made her shiver. Melody gasped as her true feelings began to gush to the surface.

The next words came tumbling out before she realised it. "I've just discovered some groundbreaking news," she said.

She found it hard to breathe. What was she saying? What was she doing? She should leave right now.

"And you wanted me to know straight away?"

"It couldn't wait."

"Of course not. A good story can never wait." He stepped towards her. "So, what is this groundbreaking news?"

Melody licked dry lips. "I've just heard, from a very reliable source…that Miss Melody Kinsman…is to be married."

Guy blinked hard. His left hand clenched and realising that the housekeeper had noticed, deftly flipped back the edge of his jacket and thrust his fist into his trouser pocket.

"Is that so?" He let out a breath. "Did your reliable source give you the name of the gentleman she intends to marry?"

She clasped her hands together in a tight knot. "Oh, yes. You've probably heard of him." She choked on words that would hardly leave her throat. Run, she thought. Run away now, before you say it. But like a runaway train, she found she couldn't stop. "He's the editor...of The...Cork Street Journal. Mr Guy...Edward...Wyngate."

Guy looked down at his shoes. "Yes, his name does sound familiar," he said softly. He turned to the housekeeper. "Mrs Talbot, do you think you could make us a pot of tea please?"

"Certainly, sir." She was glad to leave. Newspaper folk had a strange way of talking.

Guy came closer. "And does your reliable source say how this all came about?"

"It came about very quickly, actually." Tears began to well up in her eyes. Would he be offended? Had she done a terrible thing? "It seems that Miss Kinsman has only just realised that she...cares for Mr Wyngate very much. No...not just cares. She loves him desperately...and can't live without him."

"And does Mr Wyngate feel the same way?" he whispered.

"I...I hope so. I do hope..." She gasped for air and looked towards the door.

Guy stepped across the rug in three strides and holding her face between both his hands, pressed his mouth down on her lips. She responded as tears trickled down her cheeks.

When he finally released her, his eyes were shining with elation. "Oh, my angel," he said. "When you break with tradition, you certainly do it in a big way, don't you?"

"You're not angry with me?"

"Why should I be angry? I've wanted to ask you, but I thought you hadn't recovered from Doctor Alex Courtney."

"I don't give him a moment's thought," she murmured.

Guy smiled and kissed her again. "You've made me so happy." She made to answer but he placed a finger over her lips. "And before you say anything else, please don't think that because you're my wife you can break your contract with the Journal. If I remember correctly, there's still over a year to run on that. Also, you have a book to finish and Sir Jack wants us to visit him to discuss publication."

Melody gave out a cry of surprise. "He wants to publish my book?"

"Yes, he does," he said, chucking her under the chin. "I've already shown him the first chapters and he agrees that it will be successful."

Melody smiled up at him and she knew her love for him came from the very depths of her soul, a woman's love for a man.

"What about Mrs Carr and Tilly?"

"My housekeeper has wanted to resign for some time because of her mother's ill health. So, they can either live with us here or I can move in with you at Hyde Park Gardens. You can choose."

She gave him a sly look. "That all depends on what your home is like. I haven't seen much of it."

"I'll give you the grand tour as soon as we've had our tea."

Melody bit her lip. "You are sure about this, aren't you? I haven't forced you and…"

He didn't let her finish, but wrapped his arms round her and his kiss told her everything she wanted to know.

Mrs Talbot struggled in with the tray and as she placed it on the table she spied her master in a tight embrace with the young lady who had come to the house unaccompanied. She sniffed once more. What was the world coming to?

Melody responded to the kiss passionately, sinking against him, oblivious to the housekeeper setting out the cups. Only when she heard another sniff and a gruff, "Tea is served, sir," did she try and unwrap her arms from about his neck. But Guy didn't break his hold and still pressed her close. The woman he loved was in his arms at last. And no grunting, sniffing housekeeper was going to spoil his enjoyment.

CHAPTER EIGHTEEN

The housekeeper climbed the stairs with the small, cream silk rosebuds clutched in her hand. One bud had become loose and she had been to sew it back into place.

"Hurry up, Mrs Carr! He'll be here any minute."

Mrs Carr sighed and didn't hurry in the slightest. There was a full fifteen minutes before Mr Wyngate was due and time enough to finish getting her mistress ready. Melody stood before the mirror in her room surveying her appearance in a way she had never done before. She and Guy were attending a dinner at Sir Jack's home to celebrate their engagement and this was their first official social event.

It had been five days since she had stumbled into Guy's study and taken ten years off her life by proposing to him. Melody smiled at the memory. Where had she got the nerve? Even in her wildest imaginations did she ever expect to do anything like that. But she had done it and it had turned out to be the most wonderful moment of her life.

The last few days had been unbelievable. They had snatched luncheon together at the Cavendish and then gone to the jewellers to choose a ring. For the second time that year, Melody was wearing a betrothal ring, but this one was a simple diamond solitaire and they had chosen it together.

Now, staring at herself in the mirror, she wanted to look perfect. And so for their first official dinner she had decided to wear the peach silk dress trimmed with Honiton Lace that suited her complexion and she had even decided to wear the rosebuds in her hair. She had been dismayed to find that one had become loose, but in her calm manner, Mrs Carr had sewn it back in place. Now she was pinning them amongst the auburn curls.

Tilly clapped her hands with glee. "Oh, miss. You look like a fairy princess, you do."

"Do I, Mrs Carr? Do you think he'll approve?"

"Miss Melody, I've never seen you in such a state over your appearance."

"But this is the first time he's seen me in evening dress. I've always worn a skirt and blouse to the office." She suddenly had a thought. "Oh, he saw me in a day dress at Hucknall Garth and there's that day he visited here and I was wearing an apron and mob-cap."

"Well, this is going to be a big improvement on an apron and mob-cap. I think he'll like what he sees," smiled Mrs Carr.

The sound of the doorknocker reverberated round the house and Melody let out a squeal of dismay.

"He's here," she gasped.

"Compose yourself, my dear. I'll go and let him in and he can wait in the sitting room while you make your grand entrance."

She tried to calm herself, but her heart was pounding fit to burst. She descended the stairs, carrying her fan and gave herself another quick look in the hallway mirror. Then she opened the door and stepped through. Guy was standing by the fireplace, looking smart and elegant in his evening suit. He was staring up at the painting of the *Bather*.

"Now that's what I call a very seductive pose," he said, without turning his head. Then he spun round. A look of surprise crossed his face and he gave a polite bow. "Oh, I do beg your pardon. I thought you were Miss Kinsman." He looked towards the door. "You don't know how long she'll be, do you?"

Melody glanced down at the rug trying to keep her face straight, but then she was running towards him and he caught her in his arms.

"You clown," she cried, stroking his face as he kissed her cheeks, her nose, her lips.

"You look so beautiful," he murmured, drinking in the sight of the woman he was going to marry. "Beautiful and young...and alluring and young... and innocent and young. Have I told you how young you look?"

"Four times! Are you slightly worried, by any chance, about our age difference?"

"I'm old enough to be your father."

Melody shook her head. "You'd have been a very *young* father. Come on, let's go."

Sir Jack's house in Chelsea was ablaze with lights when they arrived. He had sent his carriage to pick up Guy and then he, in turn, had travelled to Hyde Park Gardens to collect Melody. It was wonderful riding through the park as the sun was setting, the western sky glowing with scarlet and orange flames. Guy had kept his arm round her all the way and now and again, she would feel him briefly caress her shoulder or neck. It seemed so intimate and very different from the inexperienced embraces she had received from Alex. Guy's touch sent small shivers of pleasure up and down her spine and sometimes these sensations reached places that were deemed private. It made her feel so sensual. At one point, he bent his head and kissed her lips. She responded passionately and didn't care that they were in an open carriage for all to see.

To Melody's amazement, there were twenty diners sitting down that evening, some of them quite prominent in the newspaper world. She was introduced to all of them and knew they remembered her from her daily excursions to their companies trying to sell her articles. Mr and Mrs John Delane were there and Melody was delighted that Mr Delane bowed over her hand and kissed it politely.

As Sir Jack guided her round the room, she knew he was finding it amusing to present her to men who had sent her away from their doors with derisive comments. All the time she could see Guy, his drink in his hand, watching her steady progress from person to person, a satisfied smile flitting across his face. And then the gong summoned them to dine.

The dinner was remarkable, the table set with crystal wineglasses and silver cutlery. The food was served on Wedgwood plates and there was more food than anyone could have possibly managed. But Sir Jack liked to be a congenial host and nothing was too much trouble for him. At the end of the meal, he proposed a toast to the newly betrothed couple and Melody found herself blushing. How stupid, she thought. I'm a grown woman, not a simpering girl of seventeen.

Unfortunately, after the meal the ladies retired and left the gentlemen to their gossip, cigars and port. Melody always grimaced at this little tradition but once in the drawing room she was grateful for the segregation as Lady Palmerston took her to one side.

"My very best wishes, my dear. I can see how much he adores you and you can't go wrong with a man whose devotion is so apparent. But will you be able to settle down as a wife?"

Melody leaned closer to her. "I know it's not normal practice, but I will continue as a journalist even as a married woman. Guy insists on it."

"Until you become a mother and then you'll need to give it up."

Melody hid her blushes behind her fan as the gentlemen joined them.

Guy came to sit next to her. "By the look on your face, you've been up to no good."

Melody feigned offence. "Oh, we've been discussing married life."

He kissed her hand. "Well, these ladies will keep you well informed," he whispered.

A few days later, Melody and Guy travelled by train to Hucknall Garth to visit Olivia and the brigadier. Melody had already written to them and told them the news and this was a special trip so that Guy could finally meet Melody's father. The weather was still mild and as she looked out of the window, she couldn't believe that the month of October could be so beautiful. The trees wore their autumn colours and leaves fluttered past, pulled off the branches by the wind turbulence from the carriages.

They had managed to find an empty carriage and at every station, Melody prayed that no one would join them. She leaned against Guy who kept his arm round her. Now and again he would kiss her hair.

"I know you've been down this road before, angel, but I'd rather not have a long engagement."

She looked up into serious brown eyes. "Do you want us to set a date?"

"Yes. I think it would be fair to your aunt and father if we can tell them exactly what we're doing."

"Mmm. Let me think." She turned her head to watch the scenery passing the window. Suddenly she grinned. "How about the twenty-fifth of March?"

He puzzled for a moment. "You came out with that date quickly. You've obviously been thinking about it."

She shook her head. "I've just seen an old poster for this year's Tunbridge Wells Easter market. And it seemed a good day to get married."

"It sounds like a wonderful day to get married," he laughed. He lifted her chin and placed a gentle kiss on her lips. The second one was more ardent. The third one was passionate and Melody felt herself melting into him as his tongue explored her mouth. Even in such a short time, her sexual feelings were growing every time he caressed her.

"How long is it to the twenty-fifth of March?" he whispered, when he finally lifted his head.

"Five months," she murmured.

"Oh God," he groaned.

The brigadier met them at the station and shaking Guy's hand, his gaze took in the age of the man his daughter wanted to marry, but any misgivings he had, he certainly didn't want to voice at that moment. During luncheon, Guy answered all the questions that the brigadier put to him and by the time they had eaten, he was convinced that his daughter had picked the right man this time.

That afternoon, Melody challenged Guy to a game of croquet on the lawn. The weather stayed kind and the sun warmed them, as their happy laughter drifted over to where the brigadier and Aunt Olivia were sitting under a beech tree. Olivia smiled at them knowing that her niece, although she didn't realise it yet, was more in love with this man than she would ever think possible.

Sitting next to her brother, she contemplated the idea of Melody becoming the wife of Guy Wyngate. She knew he was the perfect husband for her, a man who would understand her needs and encourage her ambitions. As for Guy, life certainly wouldn't be dull with Melody as his wife. There were some things to be thankful for in this world, she nodded happily, a loving child was one of them and a soul mate through life was another.

The following day it was decided that Olivia would travel to London at frequent intervals and help Melody organise her wedding. Nothing elaborate, definitely no bridesmaids and the service would be held in Saint John the Evangelist, the church ministered by the Reverend Wilfred Ansell and within easy travelling distance of both Melody and Guy's home. Afterwards, the wedding breakfast would be held at the Cavendish Hotel, since the lengthy guest list prohibited either home being used.

Melody had decided to live in Mayfair. Her tour of the house had delighted her and it seemed more practical to give up the lease at Hyde Park Gardens. As for the honeymoon, they had decided to take up Sir Jack's offer of using his summer retreat on the Isle of Wight.

Unfortunately, for all their happiness, for all their plans, they had forgotten that life is never that simple. A twist of fate can change plans; a sudden turn of events can crush dreams.

CHAPTER NINETEEN

Guy had always liked the view from his office window. In times of doubt or frustration, or even just to contemplate his thoughts, he had often wandered over to it and studied the hustle and bustle below. His interest in people had made him observant and he had enjoyed watching the daily routine of the people who lived in Cork Street. Old Mr Penn who owned the tobacconist across the road, would frequently stand outside his shop and puff away on his pipe. Then there was Mrs Rafferty who made delicious cakes and pies, always chasing away the urchins that gathered round her door. But not before giving them an enormous pie to share. And then there were the incidents that would suddenly erupt, causing mayhem to the steady routine of the day. Incidents such as the constable chasing a pickpocket along the cobbles, his whistle blowing and his truncheon waving in the air like the conductor of an orchestra.

But when another incident occurred, one that would affect his life in an unimaginable way, Guy was sitting at his desk, absorbed in reading the proofs for the evening edition. The sound of horses neighing and a man's voice crying out, did make him turn his head for an instant. But these were normal sounds and he was too busy to investigate.

Melody stared at the letter in amazement. The address of Marlborough House was clearly printed at the top of the page and embossed in silver. It was from the secretary of Princess Alexandra, the Princess of Wales, who requested the presence of Miss Melody Kinsman at a date to be decided. It wasn't an interview, the Royal Family didn't like to be interviewed. The Princess was simply interested in the young woman who had stirred up London society and was writing a book on the social and moral conditions of women.

She turned the letter over in her hand and then passed it to Mrs Carr.

"It's genuine, that's for sure," said the housekeeper.

"She wants to speak to me?"

"Well, why not? Royalty have as much right to be interested in you as us ordinary folk." She gave out an incredulous laugh. "I don't know, Miss Melody. One day you're interviewing women of dubious character and the next you're taking tea with the highborn."

"She's not asked me to take tea," mused Melody.

"But she'll offer you a cuppa, surely?"

As Melody travelled to the Journal, she felt as if her head was in the clouds. Not that the clouds were particularly inviting that morning. It was two days before her birthday and November had been the usual mix of rain and bitterly cold wind. She wrapped her skirts round her knees and urged Sultan into a brisk trot. He might be old but it was far too chilly to saunter along at the stately walking pace that he preferred. Melody was keen to get to Cork Street and tell Guy about her invitation to Marlborough House. How surprised he would be. And delighted.

Melody smiled at the memories of the last month. It had been a wonderful month and the plans for their wedding were underway, the church and wedding breakfast booked. Aunt Olivia was arriving in a few days and they were to see the dressmaker to discuss her gown. Melody grimaced at the thought of wearing a crinoline. She remembered the cartoon Henri had shown her, depicting the couple walking down the stairs with the man being forced to walk on the outside of the banister because of the width of the lady's dress.

Throwing back her head she let out a merry laugh, startling a dog sitting in a shop doorway and causing him to stand and bark furiously. The image of the brigadier having to clamber over the pews while she swished up the aisle in a ridiculously wide hoop had suddenly popped into her head. No, she would keep her dress to a reasonable width, perhaps wearing many petticoats so that the skirt had a certain amount of volume. Probably with puff sleeves and...watered silk would be nice, trimmed with Brussels Lace.

Melody eased the gig into the stable and ruffled the boy's hair as he took Sultan's bridle and led him further into the vast space to unhitch him. She stepped out into the street. She must finish the next two chapters of her book...write to Marlborough House and organise an appointment with the Princess of Wales...then there were the wedding invitations to send...

The horses seemed to come out of nowhere. Giant, snorting, black beasts that towered over her like the Horses of the Apocalypse. She didn't have time to cry out, although she knew that someone had. A man's voice, deep and clear above the neighing of the monsters just above her. Instinctively, she raised her arms, but they weren't enough to protect her from the first, strong, sharp hoof that hit her shoulder sending her spinning into the second, even harder hoof that caught her a sickening blow in the centre of her back.

"Mr Wyngate, sir!" Eric's face was white under his freckles, as he ran into Guy's office. "I think you'd better come outside."

Guy rose to his feet. "What is it, Eric?"

"It's Miss Melody, sir. Please come quickly!"

Guy hurried downstairs hardly aware that others were going in the same direction. In moments he was out in the chill, November air and what he saw made his blood turn cold. Melody was lying on the uneven cobbles, Mrs Rafferty bending over her. A man, his clothing that of a coachman, was kneeling the other side of her, biting his lip anxiously. Many other people were standing about, their eyes wide, shaking their heads, mouths moving as they told their neighbour how they had seen a young woman step into the path of a coach and four.

Guy dropped to his knees next to the slender form lying so still.

"I'm so sorry, sir," said the coachman. "She just walked out in front of me. I didn't have time to rein in the horses."

Guy stared at him, his mind numb with shock.

A police constable appeared. "We need to send for a doctor," he said, taking control. He saw Eric standing nearby. "You there. Run to Saint George's and fetch one. Tell him to hurry." He looked around. "Can't leave her in the street. Must get her in the warm, but her back might be broken."

"We'll carry her into the Journal," whispered Guy.

The constable, Guy and two other men slipped their arms under her and lifted her from the hard surface of the road. They tried to keep her level, so that no further damage would be done to her injured back, but the movement caused severe pain and she regained consciousness. She let out a cry and her eyelashes flickered. They carried her through the entrance and hallway and finally to an alcove, where a couch became her resting-place.

Guy stayed with her, kneeling on the floor to remove her bonnet and unbutton her coat. He brushed the hair away from her pale face.

"Don't worry, angel," he whispered. "The doctor is on his way."

Eric burst in, this time his face red from running. Behind him hurried a tall, elegant young man with blond hair, his blue eyes narrowed in concentration. He carried a medical bag and placed it on the ground as he knelt beside the couch. Guy stood to give him room. A brief examination showed that the patient had minor cuts and bruises to her face but he detected no broken bones. However, the injury to her back gave him more cause for concern.

"I need to examine her spine, but her coat and gown will have to be removed. It might be better if we could get her home."

Guy turned to Eric, who was staring down at Melody as though she were a corpse. "Help Marsh get the wagon round to the front door."

He started visibly at the order but then quickly recovered and ran to find the secretary. They both disappeared to the rear of the building where the wagon was kept. It was used for carrying the bundles of newspapers to the vendors and while Eric rushed to the stable to fetch the horse, Marsh cleared away the string and paper debris still remaining from the previous evening's batch. He found some sacks and old blankets and spread them over the bottom of the wagon. By the time he had finished, Eric was leading the horse in and they were hitching him to the traces.

Guy looked down at Melody and gritted his teeth. Her complexion was grey, her lips parted as small groans came from her throat.

The doctor went into his bag. "I'll give her some laudanum to calm her down and help her sleep on the journey."

Guy nodded and then turned round to see the entire staff of the Journal assembled in the hallway with spectators from the street crowded round the main door and trying to peer in. When they saw they had his attention, a barrage of questions filled the air.

"How is Mademoiselle Melody?" said Henri.

Guy shook his head. "The doctor is dealing with her. I'll let you know as soon as I find out. Where's that damned wagon!"

"They say the horse gave her one hell of a kick," said Holbrook.

Eric careered through the front door, his long arms and legs uncoordinated in a frenzy of activity.

"We're all ready for you, sir."

The editor turned to his staff. "Holbrook and Henri can help carry her out. Eric, I want you to drive. The rest of you, please go back to your work." They went about their business reluctantly. Guy watched as the doctor held a vial to Melody's lips and encouraged her to drink. "The wagon is outside," he murmured to the doctor.

"The laudanum should take affect very quickly," the doctor smiled back.

Melody had drifted away into semi-consciousness and was only vaguely aware of the four men lifting her from the couch and carrying her outside to the wagon. Eric was already in the driver's seat and set off immediately, trying to drive with care over the ruts in the road. She was forced back to consciousness on the journey home, potholes jolting her out of her drug-induced sleep and then the pain was unbearable. She knew that a horse had kicked her, but the pain ripped through her as though it had been a cavalry of horses. She prayed to be in her home, wanting to lie in comfort on a soft mattress, where perhaps she would find some blessed relief from the agony that made her feel sick.

Mrs Carr showed her horror as Melody was carried in and taken up to her room. Once there, the housekeeper removed Melody's coat and gown, trying to cause as little jarring as possible. Now, lying in her petticoat, the doctor noticed the injury to her shoulder, already swollen with an angry blue and red bruise. He turned her over onto her side and the scream that burst from her throat, made everyone wince. He felt down her spine, talking to her gently as she gave out short groans and gasps.

The doctor went downstairs where Guy waited, pacing the floor. "I think the horse's hoof hit her spine, or more accurately the nerve running down the spine. Her back is very bruised. I'm going to send for Sir Charles Piper. He's a leading authority on spinal injuries."

Guy nodded. "Thank you, doctor." He smiled at the young man whose expression reflected his own frightful concerns. "I'll have to telegraph her family immediately. I'm Miss Kinsman's fiancé, Guy Wyngate. Owner of The Cork Street Journal."

The young man shook his hand. "Doctor Christian Jenner."

Even the soft mattress didn't bring relief and in fact, the torture intensified. Sights and sounds became mixed up and Melody fell into a state of confusion, through the pain and discomfort. She was sure she had seen Christian Jenner's face and that worried her. An older man hovered into view, his eye hugging his monocle as he peered at her. That made her angry. And then there were the faces she wanted to see; Aunt Olivia, the brigadier and Guy. They were all blurred, their words incoherent as if she was listening to them in a vast, echoing chamber that reverberated, first softly and then with an ear splitting boom.

In her own invincible way she persevered, fighting the pain, knowing that she would recover soon. She had a manuscript to finish, she was to visit Princess Alexandra, but most of all she was to marry Guy in the church of Saint John the Evangelist on the twenty-fifth of March.

Sir Charles Piper collected the family together in the sitting room. Christian stood with him since they had worked together on this case, although Sir Charles had taken the lead because of his seniority and expertise.

"I concur with Doctor Jenner that Miss Kinsman has sustained bruising to her spinal cord. I'm afraid the nerve membrane has now become inflamed and although we can treat her with a poultice for the bruising and of course, laudanum for the pain. It's just a case of waiting for it to heal on its own accord."

Guy cleared his throat. "How long will that take?"

Sir Charles shrugged. "Who can say? An injury of this kind can take months or years to heal. It all depends on the patient and her willingness to recover."

Olivia's face brightened at this news. "Then it won't take long knowing Melody. She'll be back on her feet by the end of the week."

Sir Charles coughed apologetically. "No, dear lady, I'm afraid not. Even after the inflammation has subsided, we don't know if the patient has sustained permanent damage to her spine."

A stunned silence went round the room.

The brigadier spoke up, his voice husky. "Are you telling us…Are you saying that Melody, my Melody, might be confined to a…Bath chair?"

Sir Charles nodded. "There is that possibility, sir."

The brigadier groped for his pipe and for the first time in years, his sister remained silent as he filled and lit it.

After Sir Charles had left, Christian Jenner remained. Olivia had introduced him to Guy once more, only this time as the friend and work colleague of Alex Courtney. Guy had felt frustrated at Sir Charles's opinion. It had been too vague and he needed more information. But when the young doctor sat down with them and said confidently that he believed that Melody would get better very soon, Guy's admiration for him soared. Christian tried to allay the family's fears somewhat by explaining that Melody's thick winter coat had actually prevented her from receiving a far worse injury. Had it been summer and she had been wearing only a thin day dress, the horse's hoof might have severed her spine causing permanent paralysis or even death.

"I believe that she will make a full recovery," he said. "I know Sir Charles's prognosis was rather dismal, but I believe she'll walk again within a few months. She's a feisty girl and I'm sure she'll fight this all the way. I'm just relieved she sustained no injuries to her head."

But despite his assurances, there didn't seem to be any improvement. Every day, Guy sat by her bed with either Olivia or the brigadier and watched Melody in restless sleep. Her inflamed back made her life wretched and even the poultices didn't seem to work. Only the laudanum knocked her out long enough to give her some rest.

The house began to fill with flowers. Letters, cards and telegrams containing best wishes came in sacks from the Post Office. Olivia and the brigadier couldn't believe where some of them came from. Even the Princess of Wales had sent a personal message, saying how sad she was to hear of Miss Kinsman's terrible accident. She hoped her recovery would be swift and she looked forward to meeting her in due course.

The card from Mr Charles Dickens, along with a beautiful pink orchid, was placed next to Melody on the bedside table. But she was unaware of them. She was lost in her own world, where pain was her only companion and the frequent drugged journey into darkness, her only solace. And when she surfaced from the abyss and cried out for Guy, he was there, holding her in his arms bringing comfort and reassurance, until the black void claimed her once more.

CHAPTER TWENTY

"It's not fair!" said Melody, through her teeth. "Why did this have to happen to me. And why now?"

Aunt Olivia straightened the bedcovers round her and sighed wearily. "I don't know, my dear. It's happened and there's nothing we can do about it."

Melody lay back against the pillows, her face creased in a disgruntled frown. "It's not fair," she muttered again.

It was now two weeks since her accident, the pain had subsided and she could sit up and eat. Sleeping wasn't too much of a problem either, but staying in bed was unbearable. She had rarely been ill and now being a prisoner in her room was making her desperate. She ached to go downstairs; she wanted to walk outside. More than anything, she wanted to go back to work. She had almost forgotten what the place looked like. Sir Charles Piper visited twice a week and Doctor Jenner made daily visits, feeling her back with soft, gentle hands as he probed her spine. He never mentioned Alex and Celia, much to Melody's relief. She felt too bad tempered to hear news of their life in Colchester. She felt too miserable to hear any news. And she had missed her birthday! Turning her face to the wall, she sank into her own mire of suffering, oblivious to those around her.

She didn't notice how her aunt trekked up and down the stairs to fetch and carry for her so that she could be washed and changed into clean linen. She didn't notice Mrs Carr bringing her meals on a tray made pretty with a dainty cloth and a small vase of flowers. She didn't even notice Tilly scurrying about with hot water preparing the hip-bath so she could find relief in the soothing water. Miss Melody Kinsman had lost control of her life and Miss Melody Kinsman didn't like it one bit.

Sir Charles examined her back, pressing the knobs of bone. "Does that hurt?"

"It's more uncomfortable than painful."

He nodded in satisfaction. "Well, the inflammation has subsided. And that's good." He helped her roll onto her back. "Now then. Let's look at these limbs of yours." He and Olivia folded back the covers and the aunt lifted the cotton nightdress above the patient's knees. There then followed a serious of gentle blows on parts of her legs. "Can you feel that?" Melody nodded. "Good!" He gripped her foot. "Now I want you to press against my hand." She tried but there didn't seem to be any strength in her leg. He asked her to repeat the exercise with her other leg, but again, it wouldn't move. Sir Charles stroked his chin. "Obviously the spinal cord was damaged enough to cause immobility, but I'm hoping its not permanent."

Melody spirits lifted. "Does that mean I'll be up and about soon?"

Sir Charles shook his head. "Not soon, I'm afraid. Your condition will improve and I'm certain that one day you'll walk again."

Melody glanced at her aunt in alarm. "What do you mean one day?"

"I can't put a specific time limit on it, dear girl. It might be years before it happens."

"Years," whispered Melody. "But I'm getting married in March."

"There's nothing stopping you from getting married, providing you feel well enough. And as long as your husband doesn't mind coping with an invalid and pushing you around in a chair."

She hated Sir Charles Piper from that moment on. His plain speaking and forthright manner was not very encouraging and when he left, Melody found herself sobbing in her aunt's arms as though her heart would break.

Guy stooped to kiss her and pulled back at her cold manner. "Oh dear, I see we're not in a good mood this evening."

She glared at him. "I've nothing to be in a good mood about."

"You're alive, Melody. That's something to be thankful for." It didn't pacify her one bit. He drew his chair closer to the bed and took her hand. "Angel, we have to discuss our wedding plans."

Melody pulled away from him. "What is there to discuss?"

He leaned forward and rested his hands on the bed, his fingers linked. He had to keep the situation amicable. He had to make her understand. "As I see it, we have two options. Either get married as planned, or wait until you're back to your old self."

"What do you want to do?" asked Melody dryly.

He let out a breath. "I really want you to decide. Sir Charles says we can get married…"

"As long as you don't mind pushing me down the aisle in a Bath chair"

"I don't mind doing that."

"I do! I want to walk down the aisle on your arm."

"Then we need to wait until you're fully recovered."

"And that could be years."

Guy stayed patient. "We need to work with what we've got," he said softly. "Not with what you'd like us to have."

"It's all right for you." Angry tears stung her eyes. "You're not in this bed. You can walk about, go to work, do anything you want to do."

He bit his lip. "True and if we could change places, I would."

"No, you wouldn't."

"I would, believe me."

Melody ran her fingers through her hair. The long, auburn locks fell over one shoulder and although her features were creased in a scowl, Guy couldn't stop himself smiling.

"What are you smiling at?" she snapped.

"At you. You still look very beautiful, even when you're bad tempered."

"I don't feel beautiful," she said sullenly.

He sat back in his chair. "So, we've established that you'll not get married sitting in a Bath chair, you're too impatient to wait until you're well again, you don't feel beautiful but you do feel extremely sorry for yourself. I'm pleased we've got a few things clear."

His facetiousness annoyed her. "Have you come here to cheer me up or just add to my bloody discomfort?"

Guy clicked his tongue. "I shouldn't have allowed you to interview those women of easy virtue. You've picked up some unladylike language from them." Melody had heard enough. Picking up the vase containing Mr Dickens's pink orchid, she made to throw it at him. He caught her arm and took the vase from her, placing it back on the bedside table. "If you want me to leave you only have to ask," he said.

"Yes, go. Leave me alone."

He stood and looked down at her, his eyes dark with anger. "Then I will. And when you're in a better mood, please send me a message. Because I don't want to keep company with a sulky girl who spends her days throwing tantrums…or vases. Perhaps one day, you'll take a good look around you and notice how your aunt is exhausted with caring for you. Your father is so worried he's wearing the rug out with his pacing and downstairs there's a pile of cards and letters from sympathetic people who have taken the time and trouble to tell you how much they care." He turned and walked towards the door. "Good night, Miss Kinsman."

Melody glanced at the orchid in the pretty glass vase, realisation sweeping through her. Everything he said was true. She had been so absorbed in her own misery that she had totally ignored everyone around her to the point of taking them for granted.

"Guy, please don't leave. I'm so sorry." He stopped in the doorway and half-turned. "I've been so selfish and thoughtless. I want to get better. But I can't if you're not here to encourage me. Please come back."

He faced her slowly and she could see the anger had gone, replaced by a tender look that told her how much he loved her. He shook his head in defeat and smiled. She held out her arms and then he was there once more, holding her and kissing the tears from her cheeks.

"I suppose there's some good points in being an invalid," Melody giggled.

It was Christmas Eve and Guy was carrying her downstairs to spend time with the family. She had been sitting by the window in her bedroom watching the snow gently falling, covering the cobbles and rooftops with soft, white flakes. And when he finally appeared, she had hung onto him, nuzzling his neck and teasing him mercilessly.

In the sitting room, everything was ready for the festive season. The tree glistened with silver garlands and white candles, underneath a pile of gifts waited for

Christmas Day. Holly and ivy adorned the mantelpiece and even the *Bather* had her own laurel of ivy round the frame. Guy placed Melody in the armchair by the fire and wrapped the blanket round her knees.

The last month had been difficult, but Melody was learning to accept her situation. Guy had carried her up and down the stairs so that she could join in with the company and this alone had lifted her spirits. He had also started writing a weekly bulletin in the Journal about her condition and this had become avid reading, producing more mail from people suffering similar afflictions often for many years. Her cheeks had been wet with tears as she had read of the experiences of the readers and the knowledge she wasn't alone gave her some encouragement.

She had also continued with her manuscript and with a writing board resting across the arms of the chair and wads of paper all over the floor, she had scribbled away to her heart's content. And when she had had enough and her back ached she would be carried upstairs to lie on her bed.

Visitors to the house had been numerous and like a queen surrounded by her court, she had entertained in regal style. Sir Jack called to discuss publication of her manuscript and brought with him an azure blue cashmere shawl. Lady Palmerston had sent her a gaily-wrapped basket of fruit and Police Sergeant Dallimore brought her a box of chocolates. The staff at the Journal arrived, bringing their little gifts. Eric had drawn her a very good portrait of Guy that she had framed and put on her bedside table and even Marsh and Holbrook had bought her books to read, while Henri dropped off a beautiful gift box of perfumed bath oils.

And then a case of wine arrived from Colchester, with love from Celia and Alex.

"Why a case of wine?" asked Guy, scrutinising the labels and nodding with approval at the vintage.

"It might be something to do with that last night. The night we ended our engagement," said Melody. Guy frowned and she explained. "It all started with a blazing argument about Doctor Jenner. Do you remember I told you that I'd left the information about Camberwell with a member of the medical staff?" He nodded. "I left it with Doctor Jenner and he passed it on to his professor."

"Without telling him that you had discovered the source of the infection?"

"Yes, but Alex pointed out how bigoted this professor is. And we know that's true."

"Even so, he shouldn't have claimed the credit himself."

"Well, he did," she said thoughtfully.

"So, the wine?"

"Alex said that night how important it is what we drink. And nothing's more important than fresh, clean water. I guess the wine is symbolic of drinking pure liquid."

"I'm surprised at Doctor Jenner, though. While he's been treating you, I've grown to admire him greatly. He's a splendid doctor."

Melody leaned forward and lowered her eyelashes, a smile hovering round her mouth. Guy always found this gesture very seductive and his pulse quickened.

"He's illegitimate, you know."

"Is he?" he said, watching her. "And how do you know that, Miss Kinsman?"

"Oh, I have my sources," she grinned. "As all good newspaper reporters should."

Christmas Day was wonderful and with everyone sitting round the dinner table, Melody began to feel happy again. True, she couldn't walk yet, but she knew she would one day. And when that day came, the brigadier would escort her up the aisle. Their wedding plans were 'pending' and a final decision would be made one month before the set date. That's plenty of time, thought Melody, anything can happen in the next two months.

"I've got some news for you," said Aunt Olivia, as they finished their Christmas dinner. "But I don't want you to get upset about it."

"What is it, Aunt?"

"I've had a letter from Celia. And it seems she's expecting a child in the summer."

"But that's wonderful, I'm pleased for her. And Alex of course. Why did you think I'd be upset?"

Olivia looked at her brother, who was studying his daughter anxiously. "I…We thought, that with your illness and everything, well, that you might take it rather hard," he said.

Melody threw back her head and laughed. "Everything I want in my life, is in this very room."

She reached across and squeezed Guy's hand.

For all her acceptance of the situation, Melody's only desire was to walk, run and even skip if she felt the urge. In her dreams, she did just that. And when she awoke she felt bewildered that she was still unable to move her limbs. She did feel stronger. Sir Charles Piper had stopped paying her calls, although Christian came every day.

She would often hear him in conversation with Guy and marvelled that they were striking up a friendship. She didn't know if she felt pleased about it or not. After all, Christian had denied her the accolade of finding the contaminated water supply. In fact, he had never even mentioned it to her and she didn't like to bring the subject up. Perhaps one day she would suggest they talk it over.

And she couldn't forget that he had caused trouble by telling Alex that she had been seen leaving the Cavendish with Guy. Melody puzzled over the mysterious and contradictory nature of this elegant, handsome boy. He had proved a skilled and compassionate physician during the terrifying train disaster as well as the dedication shown after her accident. His concern during her illness had been admirable. He was an enigma, Melody sighed and there was no use trying to make sense of it.

Miss Florence Nightingale sat heavily on the couch and surveyed the patient with large, brown experienced eyes.

"You're looking well," she said dryly. Her handsome face didn't smile. Miss Nightingale rarely smiled.

"I feel very well," laughed Melody.

She was very surprised that Miss Nightingale had paid her a visit, since the heroine of Scutari, Sevastopol and Balaclava, who had been called the Lady with the Lamp by the soldiers, rarely made social calls. When Melody had interviewed her she had been struck by this controversial woman who had given up a brilliant marriage to travel to the Crimea.

"Good!" Miss Nightingale looked around her. "So, you stay in the sitting room most days?"

"Yes, but the brigadier, my papa, takes me out in the carriage when it's not too chilly."

"You're engaged to be married I hear."

"To Guy Wyngate, the editor of the paper I work for."

"Mmm. And a hero in his own right. Or so I'm led to believe."

"He received a medal from the queen," said Melody proudly.

"Very nice, Miss Kinsman. And I appreciate that you're proud of him. But you have to earn your own medals, not share in his honours."

"I'm sorry I don't know what you mean."

Miss Nightingale sighed. "My dear young lady, I'm talking about your desire, or not, of wanting to walk again."

"But I do. Oh, I do," urged Melody.

"So, what are you doing about it?"

"Well, nothing. I'm resting and…"

"Nothing! Oh dear, nothing generally comes from nothing."

"Then what should I do, Miss Nightingale?"

"Every night and every morning you must order your legs to walk."

Melody giggled at the absurdity of what she was saying. Was it possible that this icon of British society had lost her mind?

"But how do I do that?"

Miss Nightingale shook her head in exasperation. "When you wake up in the morning and before you go to sleep at night, you must massage your legs. Start at the top and work your way down as far as you can reach. If you have a female member of the family handy, then get her to do it." She thought for a moment. "Or this fiancé of yours might be obliging."

"I'm sure he would. But I don't think it would be appropriate."

"Is Miss Melody Kinsman talking propriety?"

"N…No, it's just that…"

"I'm teasing you, my dear."

"So, I must massage my legs?"

"Yes, from the top to the bottom. And then from the bottom to the top. In firm, even strokes, mind. And while you're doing that you must think about walking."

"Think about walking?"

"Exactly! You must send messages from your brain down your back and into your legs. Remind your legs how to walk again. You must will the strength to come back into your limbs. Will yourself to move them." Her smile was challenging. "That's if you have the courage, Miss Kinsman, to stand on your own two feet."

Melody was put in the hip-bath that night and as the hot water soothed her and the scent of the lavender oils calmed her, she decided that she would attempt Miss Nightingale's treatment; there would be no harm in it, even though she thought her idea rather bizarre. But she wouldn't ask for Aunt Olivia's help, to explain would seem too ridiculous for words.

When everyone had gone to bed, Melody threw back the covers and pulled herself up onto the pillows. She began to massage her legs, all the time thinking of her legs moving, thinking of walking. At first it seemed silly, but as each day passed, she became more enthusiastic. Until one day a strange tingling started in her back and began to flow in soft waves down her legs. It was exhilarating and exciting all at the same time. It was also the beginning of February and there were only a few weeks to go before they made the final decision about their wedding.

The weather on Saint Valentine's Day was beautiful. Melody sat at the window and looked out at Hyde Park Gardens. The sky was a vivid blue with just the occasional fluffy cloud sailing across the sun's face. Blackbirds and sparrows fluttered amongst the bare branches of the trees, gathering twigs to start their nest building. Guy was coming for luncheon and Melody was watching for him. And when he appeared at the end of the cul-de-sac, she smiled. She threw off the blanket and gripped the arms of the chair.

Six days before, something wonderful had happened. She had been massaging her legs as usual and then settled down to sleep, but then she felt the strongest urge to stand. She knew she could do it if she only tried. Flinging back the bedcovers she eased her legs over the side of the mattress and tentatively put her feet on the floor. She stood for ten seconds, before she fell backwards, laughing, on top of the covers.

The following night she had done it again, only this time she had stood for much longer. And so it had continued, until standing turned into walking. Just a few steps at first, but eventually she could walk cautiously round her room. But today, Saint Valentine's Day, she was going to go much further.

It was easy to haul herself to her feet holding onto the arms of the chair, but then she stood a while to steady herself. Aunt Olivia had helped her into a pink and white day dress, putting her hair up with an ivory comb and the movement made the comb slip causing an unruly strand of hair to fall over her eyes. She quickly pushed it back in place and walked to the door. By the time she had reached it, opened it and stepped into the corridor, she heard the doorknocker and knew Guy had arrived. She made her way to the top of the stairs where she heard Tilly's greeting as she let him into the house. And then she saw him walking towards the sitting room. Guy would always spend ten minutes with Aunt Olivia and the brigadier before coming to fetch her.

The stairs looked frightful, like some giant staircase, leading to a vast hallway. Had she really run up and down them without giving it a second thought? She moved closer to the head of the stairs and holding onto the banister, stepped down. She brought her other foot over the edge to meet its partner. One step was complete. She tried the second step and then the third followed by the fourth. Slow and easy, she took her time. The clock chimed one o'clock. Her foot slipped to the fifth tread. Six...seven, then she stopped and rested. Eight...nine...ten. She was nearly there. Only two more. Eleven...and...twelve.

Melody stood at the bottom in triumph and suddenly caught sight of her image in the mirror. She looked weary and her cheeks had lost their bloom, but her hair still had a lustre as it curled round the ivory comb. All she had to do now, was walk to the door and into the sitting room. The hallway seemed endless, but step after step brought her closer, the voices becoming louder.

Guy's laughter echoed from behind the door. "I'll go and bring..." she heard him say, as he opened the door and then pulled up short, his hand still on the handle.

She had forgotten how tall he was, now that she was standing in front of him. He stared at her as if disbelieving his own eyes. "Dear Lord! Olivia, Brigadier, I think you'd better come and see this."

People surrounded her. Aunt Olivia gave out a scream and then burst into tears. The brigadier, his eyes watering, took her hand. Mrs Carr and Tilly ran from the kitchen and the neighbours could hear their cries of delight. And as for Guy? At first, his stunned expression remained, until his face broke into a smile. Putting his arm round her, he guided her to the table and as he made her comfortable in the chair, he couldn't stop kissing her hair, her cheeks, her lips. And Aunt Olivia didn't stop him. It didn't seem to matter any more. After all, they would be getting married very soon.

CHAPTER TWENTY-ONE

Melody's strength only lasted the duration of the meal. By the time they had eaten, the shadows under her eyes had deepened and her exhaustion was very evident. Guy carried her back upstairs, but she fell asleep in his arms before he reached her room. He lay her on the bed and Olivia tucked the blanket round her.

"The poor love, she must be worn out."

"She's done remarkably well and to think she's been holding out on us," he chuckled.

Melody had told them how she had been practising for a week, until she felt confident enough to join them for luncheon, laughing gleefully when recounting the look on Guy's face as he opened the sitting room door. "Such a picture," she giggled. "As if you'd seen a ghost."

"I thought I had seen a ghost," he laughed with her. "Or at the very least I was hallucinating."

Sir Charles was called that afternoon and when Melody awoke she found him bending over her. A quick examination confirmed that she was on the mend and his services wouldn't be required any longer. His bill would be sent in the post.

Doctor Jenner had a kinder approach. "I hoped you'd do it in three months," he said, as he examined her spine and did the reflex tests on her knees and soles of her feet. "But secretly, I expected six."

"But I'm getting married. I had to get better," said Melody, smiling. She had every confidence in Christian now, after all his care and attention.

But he grimaced in answer. "It's next month, isn't it?"

"The twenty-fifth," she breathed. "Just five weeks."

He became more serious. "Would you consider delaying it just a little longer?"

"How much longer?" Aunt Olivia asked.

"Oh, just a further six weeks. A good three months of convalescence will help you gain the strength you need." He had learnt how to win her round. "And you'll be more confident when you walk down the aisle."

Aunt and niece looked at each other.

"I suppose it makes sense, my dear," said Olivia.

"Oh dear, I had set my heart on marrying when the daffodils and tulips are in bloom," Melody sighed, but then became more cheerful. "But May will give us more time to finish the arrangements. Yes, we'll get married in May."

When Guy came that evening, he agreed that waiting was for the best and so the date was changed and arrangements were restarted for their wedding. It was still to be held in the same church with the wedding breakfast at the Cavendish Hotel, but now the day would be the fifth of May. And then they would travel to the Isle of Wight two days later after Melody had rested and gathered her strength for the journey.

Melody's strength returned with each passing day. On a bright March afternoon, when the sun was warmer than it had been for some time, Guy and Melody went for a walk in Hyde Park.

"I don't think I'll ever take life for granted again," said Melody, leaning on his arm.

"Do you mean the way you used to run about as though the end of the world was nigh?" he grinned, squeezing her hand.

Melody nodded. "These last months have taught me a valuable lesson."

"I think we've all learnt something from it, angel."

"What have you learnt?"

He stopped walking and turned her round to face him. "That you mean everything to me and I couldn't bear to lose you."

She reached up to caress his cheek. "There's one thing I'll miss about being an invalid."

"And what's that?"

"Being carried about in your arms," she laughed softly. "You'll have to carry me upstairs to bed after we're married."

Guy turned his head away. The thought that there would come a time when they would share a bed, made his blood roar in his ears. "Yes. Yes, if that's what you want, then I'd be pleased to," he murmured.

"Are you sure? You don't sound certain."

He put his arms round her and pulled her close. "Oh, I'm certain," he whispered, his lips against her cheek. "I'm absolutely certain."

As they left the park gates they saw Doctor Jenner coming down the Bayswater Road. He waved to them and when they met, he looked his patient up and down.

"Well, I can see you're improving and that's wonderful. Soon I won't have to make any more visits."

"You've been more than attentive. Sir Charles disappeared ages ago," said Melody with a grimace.

Christian smiled. "To tell you the truth this is not so much a medical call as a social. I've come to bring you these." He went into his pocket and pulled out a rather grubby map and some sheaves of paper.

"Are those my notes from the Camberwell enquiry?" asked Melody incredulously.

"They certainly are. I'm sorry it's been so long getting them back to you, but Professor Sweeting has only just released them."

Melody took them and cast her eyes over the state they were in. "It looks like every man and his dog have been chewing at them."

Christian couldn't help laughing. "I think that's the case." Suddenly his laughter died away and he became serious. "And I want you to know that I never intended to steal your glory. Alex was so enthusiastic when he saw them that he was running to the professor's study before I could pull him back or explain their origin. And once in the hallowed room I realised that the professor would put the whole damned lot on the fire, if I told him that you were behind the findings. He has no patience with 'mere females' as he calls them. So, I decided to stay silent." He stared down at the ground. "Will you forgive me?"

Before Melody could answer, Guy broke in. "I noticed that no one was named in the report."

Christian nodded. "The professor urged me to put my name to it but I declined. I knew it wasn't right...or honourable for me to agree to it."

Guy and Melody exchanged glances.

"Do you think I should forgive him," she said dryly.

"I think you should. After all, he's been a gentleman about it all." Guy grinned at Christian who returned the grin.

Melody placed a tender hand on his arm. "Then I forgive you."

The two men shook hands.

"Thank you for everything you've done for my future wife, doctor," said Guy.

"Not at all, I'm glad I could be of assistance."

They said their goodbyes and Christian watched them continue their walk down the road until they turned into Hyde Park Gardens. He smiled to himself. The evening before he had stood by the fire in his lodgings, staring at the wedding invitation leaning against the clock. Oh yes, Miss Melody Kinsman, he thought, I needed to make you well again. It suits me to see you as the wife of Guy Wyngate. I've got wonderful plans for you.

Melody couldn't believe how much it rained on the twenty-fifth of March. It had started in the morning and got increasingly worse as the day progressed. Now at nine in the evening it was coming down in buckets. She peeped behind the curtain and could see that Hill Street was deserted. The streetlights flickered and tried to cast their guiding rays across the road, but the rain obliterated any effort. It looked set to rain through the night as the clouds were dense and no moon could be seen never mind the stars.

She and Guy had had dinner together and were now in his cream and terracotta sitting room enjoying a coffee. Not that he was there at the moment as Melody was quite alone. Mrs Talbot had requested that she speak to him concerning arrangements after the wedding and he had gone to have a private word with her. Melody knew she intended leaving her employment to nurse her sick mother and agreement had been made that Mrs Carr and Tilly would move in. They had already looked the property over and been delighted at the prospect of living in a more fashionable area and working in a better-equipped kitchen.

Melody sighed as she watched the rain bouncing off the cobbles and running in rivulets down the street. It had been a lovely dinner and Mrs Talbot had left them alone to talk and make their plans. In fact, the family had left them together far more than they had done when she had been engaged to Alex. It must be because Guy is an older man, she thought with amusement and they trusted him. Why did she find that fascinating and provocative?

The plans for their wedding were well underway. Her dress was almost finished and replies to the invitations were arriving every day. Melody had not returned to the office yet, since Doctor Jenner had advised against it until she felt stronger. But she was working from home and hoped to spend a few days a week at the Journal after their honeymoon.

The brigadier and Aunt Olivia had remained at Hyde Park Gardens and after they had seen Melody and Guy married, they intended giving up the lease and returning to Hucknall Garth, to enjoy the summer months in the country.

When Guy entered the sitting room, he found Melody still looking out at the torrential rain.

"I don't think it's going to ease off tonight," he smiled.

She nodded. "And to think this would have been our wedding day. Perhaps it's a good thing that horse kicked me."

He came up behind her and put his arms round her waist, pulling her close. "Rain or not, I'd rather it hadn't happened."

"But I'm recovering now," she smiled.

"Thank the Lord." He led her over to the couch and poured out the coffee. He handed her a cup. "We'll just have to wait and see what the fifth of May is like."

"In just eight weeks' time," said Melody happily.

"The weather should be much better by then," he chuckled.

Melody turned her head to listen to the pitter-patter of the rain on the window. It was cosy in Guy's sitting room with the fire blazing and the oil lamps glowing round the room. A very masculine domain and yet she felt safe there, as if it was a fortress where the world couldn't impinge on the lives of the people inside its four walls. She would be contented living in this house, she knew that and she also knew that her life with Guy would be exhilarating. He would encourage her in her work, just as he had always done, allowing her to follow her own dreams.

"What did Mrs Talbot have to say," she said, sipping her coffee.

He took in a breath. "She'll stay until the day after we're married and then make way for Mrs Carr and Tilly."

"That sounds organised." She watched him over the rim of her cup. "Will you miss her?"

"Not her sniffing and grunting. But she's been a good housekeeper all these years."

"It will be nice having Mrs Carr and Tilly here. They're really looking forward to changing their address."

He glanced around the room. "If you want to change anything, please do."

"Change what?"

"Well, if you want to get decorators in, or buy more furniture, then I don't mind one bit."

She reached across and gently caressed his cheek. "It's lovely just the way it is."

He caught her hand and kissed it. "You've never really concerned yourself with household trivia, have you?"

"I don't think you should say that to a young woman who's just about to become a wife. It sounds as though she's lackadaisical."

He gave a boisterous laugh. "I take your meaning. But what I'm saying is that your mind isn't cluttered with meaningless facts about colour of curtains or style of rugs or pattern of cushions."

Melody pulled a face. "Whenever I've had to do anything like that, I've just got on and done it. I treat that kind of job as a necessity not as a pastime."

He smiled. "No, your mind has always been set on becoming a journalist," he murmured.

His eyes swept over her turquoise gown and the matching ribbons threaded through her auburn curls. He knew that she only gave herself a cursory glance in the mirror when she was dressing for the evening and yet she always looked stunning.

Melody smiled knowing what he was thinking. Her gown was the one she had worn for the New Year Ball at the Carlton Club the year before, when she and Alex had danced the evening away. And since her engagement to Guy, she had spent more time in front of the mirror than she had ever done. Whenever he was calling for her, she always wanted to look her best, fretting if her hair was not quite right or her dress the wrong colour. She had bought an entire new wardrobe for her wedding and had spent more time deciding on it, than she would have had the patience for in the past.

A dull ache started in her back and she bent forward massaging her spine. "Damn it! I wish that wouldn't happen," she groaned. "I forget all about it and then I start hurting and it reminds me."

Guy frowned and took the cup from her, placing it on the table. "Are you all right? Do you want to go home?"

"Not just yet." She gave a weary smile. "Christian said this would still happen until my back becomes stronger. But it seems to be taking longer than I expected."

He moved closer and put his arm round her, rubbing her back gently. "You just need to persevere. You're improving every day," he said.

"But I'm not running about yet."

"Society dictates that young ladies shouldn't run about."

"Does it really?"

"Not that you adhere to social rules."

"Neither do you."

He pulled her closer and kissed her hair. "You're quite right. I don't," he smiled.

She gave a mischievous grin. Suddenly the devil was at her elbow.

"In fact, I think a lot of society's rules are too discriminatory. There are rules for men and rules for women and that's always irritated me."

"Are you thinking of any rules in particular?" he murmured. He brushed his lips against her cheek, slowly making his way towards her mouth.

"The one that says that a young girl must wait until she's married before she's allowed to give herself to the man she loves." Guy jerked his head back to look at her. She ignored his dumbfounded expression and continued. "However, a young man can have as many lovers as he wishes."

"Are you suggesting that a young girl should…anticipate her wedding night?"

"Why not? Why does a bride have to be a virgin?" The devil had moved to her shoulder and was whispering in her ear.

"Because that's the way it is."

"But why? Why is it instilled in us that it's the right thing to do, to wait until we're married."

Guy sat back in his seat and narrowed his eyes. "I don't think I agree with this one, Melody."

"Why not?"

"Because I don't think it would be a good thing if women had that kind of sexual freedom. It would lead to unwanted pregnancies and God knows what."

"I've never heard you so conventional."

"I beg your forgiveness. But on this subject I feel I must be."

For all her vehemence she couldn't help teasing him further. The brigadier and her aunt trusted him. But how far could he be trusted? Should she put him to the test? She reached up and wrapped her arms round his neck. He smiled and resumed his original position, holding her close.

"Actually, I wasn't talking about loose morals," she whispered, pressing herself against him. "As I said, I was speaking about a young woman expressing her feelings for the man she loves…the man she's going to marry."

"But not wait until her wedding night," he moaned. Talking like this had a habit of exciting him. He pressed his lips against her hair once more.

Melody stayed quiet for a moment and then said, "I nearly didn't survive that accident."

"What a dreadful thought."

"And if I'd died, I would have died a virgin."

"I suppose you would have."

"And that's a dreadful thought too."

He raised his head and chuckled. "What are you saying, Melody?"

"You never know what's round the corner."

He blinked hard and pulled away from her, staring into cornflower-blue eyes that seemed to shine like stars. "Are you saying…?"

She pressed herself closer to him. "Mrs Talbot nurses her mother in the afternoons. I could always tell

Aunt Olivia I'm going to the office and instead I could visit you here. We could go upstairs and…"

He let out a gasp and pulled her closer, burying his face in her neck, biting her gently. She became alarmed, wondering if she had gone too far with her silly little game.

"You shouldn't make those kind of suggestions," he groaned. "Have you any idea what that does to me?"

"What does it do?" she whispered.

"Never mind."

"Please tell me," she urged.

He shook his head. "Melody, don't. I'm exploding as it is."

His last statement stirred memories. Suddenly she remembered a certain night in the finishing-school in Brighton, when the girls had collected in Dorothea Montgomery's room. Dorothea's father was an eminent physician and one afternoon she had sneaked into his study and examined his medical books. More specifically, the section on the male organ and how it enlarged during sexual arousal. Dorothea was more than delighted to tell the other schoolgirls this bit of titillation and at the innocent age of sixteen, the girls had either cried out in alarm or incredulity. Melody had belonged to the disbelieving group. Dorothea must have misunderstood, she told her. That couldn't possibly happen. How would it happen? Dorothea had shook her head and said she hadn't had time to read that part as the housemaid had suddenly come in to do the dusting. The girls urged her to find out and Dorothea said she would. But it had never happened.

Melody stayed silent as Guy breathed into her neck, still crushing her against him. And then his mouth was on hers and his tongue was gently exploring. Her hand slipped down his body, to his thigh and then, trembling, she inched across the front. She gave a yelp as she came into contact with his hardness and then she heard him give a soft moan, her fingers becoming trapped as he pressed himself against her clothing. His hand came round to cup her breast. Fear, tinged with excitement surged through her.

So, Dorothea had been right all along. It had taken seven years to discover the truth but she had finally arrived at it. She didn't dare move, overawed at the realisation that a man's body changed when impassioned and she had caused this passion, this change in him. How many times had it happened before and she hadn't known it? She wondered if it had happened with Alex. Oh God, she thought, no wonder it hurt on the wedding night. And no wonder Doctor Elizabeth Garrett had called it a 'prick'.

Guy moved slightly and she was able to free her hand. He raised his head and looked at her with eyes that were angry and yet bewildered. "Damn your inquisitiveness. And your teasing."

"I'm…sorry. I heard it happened and I wanted to find out for sure."

He held her away from him, studying her expression. She looked so innocent and a little frightened. He ought to think himself a lucky man. How often had he been at his club and heard the men complaining about their wives, their coldness and total lack of response in the bedroom. In the last five months, Melody had already shown that she could be very eager when it came to the physical side of married life. But she was inexperienced and it would be unfair to take advantage. For all her arguments she would have been terrified if he had led her upstairs. No, the marital bed was the best place and he was content to wait.

"Well, now you know," he smiled. "Did it alarm you?"

"No. Yes, but only a bit."

His smile became a grin. "Dear Lord, now I understand why unmarried girls must be chaperoned. We men are just not safe to be left alone with you!" Mrs Talbot knocked on the door and when Guy called for her to come in, she announced that the hansom cab had arrived to take Miss Melody home. He took his fiancée's hand. "Come on, I'll take you back to your father and aunt, before they start missing you."

In the cab, he sat holding her hand. They hardly spoke all the way home and although his goodnight kiss was tender, Melody knew that she had tested his endurance that night. As she crawled into bed she decided she wouldn't do that again. It wasn't fair on him. Perhaps he felt pain when that happened to his body. After they were married, she would ask him.

CHAPTER TWENTY-TWO

Sir Jack viewed himself in the mirror, turning from side to side. Although small in stature, he was a dapper gentleman and his new wedding clothes had already brought him many compliments. Setting his top hat at a jaunty angle he nodded with approval and collecting up his gloves and cane, he made his way outside into the bright spring sunshine. The fifth of May, Melody and Guy's wedding day and the weather was just perfect, he thought with a smile, climbing aboard the carriage.

Within fifteen minutes he was alighting outside number four, Hill Street, Mayfair. A dour and very flustered Mrs Talbot, answered his knock. "Oh, sir. I'm so glad you've arrived. I don't know what to do with him, I really don't."

Serenely, Sir Jack stepped into the hallway. "I take it you're talking about my nephew, dear lady?"

"Yes, sir. I've never seen him in such a tizzy. And he's getting me in a flap too."

"It's his wedding day and that can make any man nervous. But never fear, we'll have him straightened out very shortly. Where is he?"

"In the second-best bedroom, sir."

Leaving his hat and cane with the distraught housekeeper, he climbed the stairs. The second- best bedroom was at the end of the corridor and with a sharp rap on the door, he entered the room.

Guy was sitting on the bed in a state of undress, shoeless and trying to tie his cravat.

He breathedf a sigh of relief when he saw his uncle. "Damn it! I'm all fingers and thumbs today."

"Stand up, my boy," said Sir Jack. Guy did as he was told and stood patiently while his uncle tied his cravat.

"I wouldn't have thought a man who's seen enemy action, would be so jittery on his wedding day."

Guy grimaced. "I just hope I'm doing the right thing."

Sir Jack peered at him over gold-rimmed spectacles. "Had second thoughts, have you? Button your waistcoat and where's your shoes?" Guy pointed to the wardrobe and Sir Jack fetched the new leather shoes that went with the wedding outfit.

"Not about Melody," said Guy, slipping his feet into them. "I love her so much that sometimes I stop breathing when I think about her."

"Then what's the problem? Where's your jacket?"

Guy stepped over to the chair and lifted his jacket from the back of it. "No, it's the age difference. Am I too old for her?" He slipped his arms through sleeves that whispered as his linen shirt brushed the silk lining.

"What is it? Barely nineteen years? I was twenty-two years older than your aunt."

"Were you?"

"I was, indeed." He sighed. "Fifteen very happy years we enjoyed. Although I must admit, I always thought I'd go first. Never occurred to me that I'd outlive her."

"I want to wear my diamond tie-pin," Guy murmured, thinking about his late aunt and how full of life she had been. "You've got the ring?"

Sir Jack nodded and patted his waistcoat pocket as he fastened the tie-pin through Guy's grey silk cravat.

"Why are you in this room," said Sir Jack, looking the groom up and down and nodding in approval.

Despite his nervousness, Guy couldn't help chuckling. "Because Mrs Carr and Tilly spent the best part of yesterday making my room presentable for my bride. Not that there was anything wrong with it, but they wanted to give it a going over to make it 'softer and more feminine'." He laughed as he quoted Mrs Carr's words.

Sir Jack smiled too and then became more serious. "Mmm. Take it easy tonight, dear boy. You don't want to frighten the poor girl."

Guy opened his eyes wide in surprise. "Goodness me, Uncle, what do you expect me to do? Throw her on the bed and ravage her?"

Sir Jack straightened his lapel and brushed a piece of loose cotton from Guy's shoulder. "No, but it's not so long ago that she couldn't even walk."

"I'm well aware of that."

"And when did you last lay with a virgin?"

"Not since Constance," mumbled Guy. He glanced in the long mirror against the wall.

Over the last few months he had come to despise society's reticence at keeping a young girl ignorant about the wedding night. He had seen panic in Melody's eyes when she had been inquisitive about the workings of the male anatomy and that, in turn, had worried him. No wonder some women were repulsed for life, he thought with a grimace. It must be a terrible shock to them.

"So, you understand what I mean?" said Sir Jack, breaking into his thoughts.

"Yes, Uncle. I understand your meaning. And I wouldn't do anything to cause Melody distress, you know that."

"Well, I'm just saying that the first time for a young bride, can be quite alarming."

"I won't frighten her and I won't alarm her." He gave a playful grin. "Mind you, Melody is not what I'd call a shy virgin. She's shown a great deal of curiosity in that area throughout our engagement. In fact, I'd go so far as saying she's frightened me on a few occasions."

Sir Jack suspended his action of checking the groom's appearance now that he was dressed.

"Has she, by George. Well, if you do change your mind on the way to the church, then we can always trade places. I wouldn't mind marrying a girl like that."

Guy gave him a withering look. "Let's be on our way, Uncle. Let's be on our way."

"Turn round, then. I want to see you from all angles."

Melody turned slowly smiling that her skirts swished as she moved. The dress was beautiful, made from white watered silk and heavily trimmed with Brussels Lace. The sleeves reached just below her elbows with a small amount of the lace at the edges. On her head, she wore a veil of the same lace and it hung down the back, fixed to her hair with a circle of orange blossom. Her white satin shoes made her feel nimble despite the heaviness of the dress that flared out with the many petticoats.

The veil had been a big surprise. The brigadier had presented her with it as the dress was near completion. It had been her mother's and her father had kept it safely tucked in its box so that one day Melody might wear it at her wedding. And she was wearing it, with love and in memory of the mother she couldn't remember.

Aunt Olivia nodded in approval. "Yes, I think you'll do."

"I think she'll more than do, ma'am," Mrs Carr sighed. "She looks absolutely perfect."

"I think it's time to go downstairs," whispered the bride, her cheeks flushing prettily with excitement.

She descended the stairs and there in the hallway was her bouquet, a posy of pink and white roses, her mother's favourite flowers.

Tilly stood at the bottom of the stairs her eyes large in wonder. "Oh, miss. You look so beautiful."

The brigadier appeared.

"Ready for insp…" It was what she had always said in the past when she had been going to a social event, but this time the words stuck in her throat.

Her father smiled and seemed calmer than she had expected. "My dear girl. I always knew you would look like this. Guy is a lucky man."

Melody took up her bouquet, slipped her hand through her father's arm and they all went out into the bright sunshine of a sparkling May morning. The trees were covered with blossom and now and again a gentle breeze would stir a few branches and send flurries of pink petals floating in the air to land on the ground making a carpet of soft blooms. To her utter amazement the housemaids, footmen and cooks from the neighbouring houses were waiting to send her on her way.

Her aunt, Mrs Carr and Tilly scrambled into the first carriage and set off at a brisk trot in order that they would be at the church a few minutes before the bride. Melody and her father took their time getting settled into the seats of the second carriage, a vehicle festooned with garlands of flowers. Many of their neighbours appeared and joined the servants that had already congregated in the cul-de-sac. There was applauding and cries of 'bless you, my dear" and 'good luck' as the carriage pulled forward. Melody waved, a smile lighting up her face.

But if Melody had been surprised by the attention she had received from her neighbours this was nothing compared to her utter shock at the people waiting for her on the road leading to the church. There seemed to be thousands of onlookers, all waving and shouting their greetings. Young boys ran by the side of the carriage waving their caps and cheering loudly.

"I don't understand, Papa. Who are all these people? What do they want?"

The brigadier took her hand and kissed it. "They've come to see you, my dear girl"

"But why?"

"Everyone in London has heard of Miss Melody Kinsman and they want to wish you well and share in your special day."

The carriage pulled up in front of the eighteenth century building, where Police Sergeant Dallimore, in his best uniform, was waiting for her.

"Just keeping the crowd under control, Miss Melody. Then I'll go inside and find a seat."

Her father stepped down and helped her alight. The sergeant left his instructions with two constables and then disappeared inside the church.

Standing on the pavement, Melody looked around at the thousands of smiling, cheering faces, hardly believing that they were there for her. A young girl stepped forward and Melody recognised her as one of the girls from the Ten Bells in Whitechapel. Behind her, she could see the other six women, all grinning and waving to her.

"For you, miss. With all our love and best wishes for your happiness." She gave Melody a bunch of seven violets. Melody smiled and tucked them in the bouquet with the roses.

As she walked through the entrance of the church she turned and waved and was answered with a thundering roar.

The groom and best man heard it. "I think your bride has arrived," whispered Sir Jack.

Guy smiled. "Thank goodness for that. I wondered what I'd do if she didn't show."

The pews were packed to overflowing, with invited guests and those who wanted to witness the ceremony. Melody heart beat furiously as she peered through the beautiful screen that separated the front entrance from the nave. She tried to steady her breathing as Aunt Olivia and Mrs Carr pulled her dress straight and adjusted her veil. And then they were gone and it was just the bride and her father.

"Are you ready?" the brigadier asked. "Best foot forward and quick march."

"No, Papa," she said smiling. "We walk to the music. No marching."

The brigadier grinned and offered his arm. Melody slipped her hand through and took in a deep breath. The music started and the congregation rose to greet the bride. They started the walk up the aisle at a leisurely pace. She smiled as she passed the guests. Tilly and Mrs Carr; Miss Nightingale and Mr Dickens; Doctor Christian Jenner; Police Sergeant Dallimore. And all the staff from The Cork Street Journal, turning their heads and letting out a hushed 'ah' or 'oh' as she made her way to the man she loved and the one waiting at the altar for her.

Guy had turned when he thought his bride must be halfway and what he saw made him gasp with surprise. He knew that Melody would look beautiful, she always did, but to see her now, as a bride, was like looking at a vision.

"Sure you don't want to change places?" murmured Sir Jack.

"Never," said Guy, not taking his eyes off Melody.

"Oh well. It was worth a try."

Melody couldn't remember a wedding ceremony so beautiful as the Reverend Ansell's clear voice rose to the rafters, joining them together as man and wife.

She heard Guy's firm 'I will', and then it was her turn.

"Wilt thou have this man to thy wedded husband, to live together after God's ordinance, in the holy state of Matrimony? Wilt thou obey him, serve him, love, honour and keep him in sickness and health, and forsaking all other, keep thee only unto him, so long as ye both shall live."

For ten seconds Melody didn't answer. The church was hushed as the reverend waited patiently for her response. Guy turned to her in surprise. She mouthed the words 'obey' and pulled a face.

"I will," she said, giving him a sidelong glance.

The reverend exchanged relieved but amused smiles with the groom. Yes, thought Guy, the 'obey' part might prove to be very interesting in this marriage.

"Who giveth this woman to be married to this man?"

The brigadier stepped forward and took Melody's left hand and placed it in Guy's. His duty done he went to sit next to his sister.

"I, Guy Edward, take thee, Melody, to my wedded wife, to have and to hold from this day forward, for better for worse, for richer for poorer, in sickness and in health, to love and to cherish till death us do part, according to God's holy ordinance, and thereto I plight thee my troth."

Aunt Olivia held the handkerchief to her eyes. Oh Tom, she thought. Was it really over forty years ago that we stood at the altar? She quickly looked around the church. Some faces were missing. Not only her Tom, but also Melody's mother. But worst of all, no

Celia and Alex. They hadn't been sent an invitation. Melody just couldn't bring herself to invite them to her wedding. Somehow it didn't seem right.

The reverend turned to Melody and she repeated her vows.

"I, Melody, take thee, Guy Edward, to my wedded husband, to have and to hold, from this day forward, for better for worse, for richer for poorer, in sickness and in health, to love, cherish and to obey…" Melody looked up at Guy who squeezed her hand. "Till death us do part, according to God's holy ordinance, and thereto I give thee my troth."

The reverend asked for the ring and Sir Jack placed it on the Bible where it was blessed. And then it was offered to Guy.

"With this ring, I thee wed. With my body, I thee worship..." Melody watched as he slipped a band of gold on the third finger of her left hand.

The reverend placed his hand over their joined ones and pronounced them man and wife. A collective sigh rose up to the rafters as Guy kissed her on the lips. And then there was the Lord's Prayer and the final hymn, followed by the blessing.

The register was signed in the vestry and then the bride and groom walked down the aisle as man and wife.

"Now, isn't this better than you pushing me in a Bath chair?" Melody whispered, as they smiled at the congregation.

Guy had to agree.

Outside, there seemed to be even more people who cheered loudly as they appeared at the door.

"Good heavens!" exclaimed Guy. "Where did they all come from?"

"All over London, by the looks of it." She gave him a sly look. "My ladies came."

"What ladies?"

"My ladies from the Ten Bells. They brought me these." She pointed to the violets. Guy shook his head in disbelief.

They climbed aboard the carriage and then they were on the way to the Cavendish Hotel for the wedding breakfast. The banqueting hall had been prepared so that the guests sat round tables of twelve and now those tables were decorated with exquisite garlands of artificial pink and white roses and shining with cutlery and crystal wineglasses. Melody and Aunt Olivia had pored over the seating plan spending many days making sure it was just right.

The next three hours were spent with eating and proposing toasts. And then the musicians arrived and the dancing began. Melody danced with everyone, all the male guests ready to take their turn.

"She's a beautiful bride," said Sir Jack, offering Guy a drink.

He looked over to where Melody was waltzing with the brigadier. "She certainly is. I can't take my eyes off her."

"Neither can Doctor Jenner." He gestured to the far side of the room and Guy looked across to see the tall, blond figure of the doctor.

"He's probably worried she might overdo it."

"Mmm. Perhaps," said Sir Jack. But he knew the doctor's expression was not one showing medical interest and for some unknown reason, it set his nerves on edge.

He was saved from further comment by the newly married couple being called to cut the cake. And then there was more dancing. Finally, Melody found herself in the arms of her new husband.

"I can't believe you've been able to dance for so long," he said in amazement.

Melody nodded. "I was determined to enjoy myself and I love dancing."

He smiled as he whirled her round the floor. "I think you ought to sit down soon and rest."

"Is that an order I must *obey*?" She narrowed her eyes at him.

"No, angel, just a request from a concerned husband who's looking out for his new wife."

"Husband," murmured Melody. "That sounds so strange."

"You'll get used to it."

The dance finished and they went back to their table. Mrs Talbot made her way towards them.

"I'm going now, sir. Must stoke up the fires and prepare everything for your arrival."

"Thank you, Mrs Talbot," Guy smiled.

His life was certainly going to change from now on. His housekeeper would be leaving the following day and Mrs Carr and Tilly were keen to take up residence. He had led a solitary, bachelor existence for so many years that it seemed strange to have the house full of women. He looked at Melody sitting beside him and taking a rest as he had requested.

By the time the guests started to say their goodbyes, Melody was filled with trepidation and excitement. Soon she would be spending her first night with her new husband and her obligatory talk with her aunt concerning the intimacies of married life, had been very sketchy and devoid of detail. Melody hadn't found it very informative and had hesitated asking further questions, not wanting to embarrass Olivia. As they said farewell to their guests, Melody reached for Guy's hand and smiled when he gently kissed her fingers. She loved him, she thought contentedly and that's all that mattered.

Soon the last guests had left and Guy and Melody climbed into the carriage that would take them home. He placed his arm round her shoulders and pulled her close.

"You must be very tired," he said softly, as the carriage rolled along.

"No, I'm full of beans," she smiled. She leaned against him and watched the houses sweep by. Suddenly she realised they were going in the wrong direction. "Where are we going? Hill Street is in that direction."

"Just a small diversion. Nothing to worry about," grinned her new husband.

Melody sat upright and noticed that they were heading for Hyde Park. As they entered the gates, it seemed that the entire area was full of people and as she alighted from the carriage she saw all their guests collected around the Serpentine. On a platform, an orchestra was tuning up.

"I don't understand. What's going on?" Melody turned to Guy in bewilderment.

"Oh, a little surprise we kept to ourselves."

And what a surprise it was for Sir Jack had organised a firework display in honour of Guy and Melody's wedding. Drinks were flowing freely and as the sun disappeared below the horizon, lamps were lit and the entire place became a magical land of lanterns and flaring torches. Guy and Melody walked along the path and greeted everyone once more, everyone knowing about this special event, except Melody. Everything had been thought of and even Mrs Carr had brought

Melody's thick mantle coat, since in her wedding gown she would soon feel the cold. Guy placed it over her shoulders.

The orchestra burst into life and to Handel's *Water Music* and *Music for the Royal Fireworks*, the sky was filled with the sudden flash of bright and fizzing rockets that soared into the air showering the cloudless night sky with a cascade of brilliant stars. The colours were dazzling and bounced off the surface of the Serpentine, creating a shimmering reflection. People strolled around, laughing and shouting with delight as glittering fountains of light danced in the air.

Melody stood and watched in wonder, leaning back against Guy, his arms tightly round her.

"Happy, angel?" he asked, kissing her hair.

Melody nodded. "Very happy." She raised her face and he placed a deep, sensual kiss on her mouth.

And when he lifted his head she saw his eyes shining with joy in the light from the fireworks and his face, so handsome, so dear to her, melted her heart and filled her with longing.

CHAPTER TWENTY-THREE

Mrs Talbot helped her off with her veil and wedding dress, her expression one of utter sombreness.

"Is there anything the matter?" Melody tried to hide her amusement.

"Oh, you poor dear." She patted her arm. "But by tomorrow you'll know what's what." She sniffed and grunted as she left the room.

Melody watched her disappear through the door with a smile. She was such a strange woman. How Guy had managed to put up with her melancholy ways all these years was a mystery.

Her new husband came into the room carrying two glasses and a bottle of wine.

"May I come in?" It was almost a whisper.

Melody was still hanging up her dress, smoothing out the white silk. She was clothed in only her chemise, the ribbons tied loosely at the breast.

She quickly glanced at the floor, a blush tingeing her cheeks. "Of course. You're my husband now, so you have a perfect right to be here," she said, hoping she sounded confident. "Besides, it's your bedroom."

He shook his head. "No, it's our room now."

She sat at the dressing table. Guy watched her as he poured out the drinks and offered her a glass. Mrs Carr and Tilly had made the room very pleasant for the new bride. He looked around, marvelling how a bachelor domain could suddenly appear very feminine.

Melody sipped the sweet liquid and then placed it back on the dressing table. Reaching up, she released her hair from the pins, allowing the auburn locks to flow down her back. She shook her head, her hair springing round her face and then she picked up the hairbrush and started brushing in long sweeping movements.

Guy took a gulp of wine to steady his nerves. She was his and his breathing shuddered at the very idea.

"You looked so beautiful today," he said, trying to keep his voice steady.

"Do you think so?"

He nodded. "It's been a wonderful day."

"And the weather was perfect."

"Well, I did order good weather. Otherwise the fireworks wouldn't have been much of a success." He placed his glass next to hers and pulling a chair closer, sat down. In the flickering light of the fire and the glow from the oil lamp she looked stunning, her skin radiant with an amber hue. He suddenly realised he was trembling. "Good Lord, my hands are shaking," he said with a grimace.

Melody put down the brush and closed her hand over his. "Why?" She fluttered her eyelashes shamelessly. "This isn't your first time."

"It feels like it," he smiled. He paused for a moment. "What have you been told about tonight?"

She bit her lip. "Aunt Olivia has told me a few things," she said shyly, realising that a blush was covering her face and neck."

"But what has your aunt told you?" he whispered.

"That you'll want to kiss me, but you've already done that." He smiled and leaned over to kiss her lips. "And touch me."

He reached out and gently caressed her face and then hooked his finger under the strap of the chemise, slipping it off her shoulder.

"If I do anything you don't want me to do, then you must tell me."

"I can't imagine you doing that." He came closer and she saw a look in his eyes that she recognised. She suddenly panicked. "Do you like my veil?" she asked quickly.

"Yes, it's really lovely," he murmured.

"It was my mother's," she smiled,

"Really?" he said in surprise. "And you kept it for your own wedding?"

"Well, Papa did," she nodded. "He always hoped I'd wear it one day. It was my 'something old' in the 'something old, new, borrowed and blue."

"Do brides really do that? I mean, follow that superstition."

Melody gave a giggle. "If you're asking if *I* really followed that silly superstition, then the answer is yes, of course I did. No self-respecting bride would go against superstition."

Guy drank back the last of his wine. "So what was the 'something borrowed'?"

She unfastened the pearl earrings, set in an exquisite silver mounting. "Aunt Olivia let me borrow these. They were a gift from her late husband."

"And the 'something new'?"

"My dress."

He glanced round the room and then his eyes swept over his new wife. "I can't see anything blue," he smiled. She looked at him shyly and turned her face away. He waited before saying, "Well, are you going to tell me?" Melody suddenly remembered that he had called her a tease and tonight seemed a good time to let her nature have its way. Taking a breath, she lifted her chemise skirt revealing limbs encased in white stockings. Above her knees were blue satin garters. Guy realised his heart was thudding violently. He rose to his feet, knelt down in front of her and placed tender hands on her waist. "Melody, I want you to know how much you mean to me and I'll never do anything to hurt you," he said, trying to calm his breathing.

"I know that, Guy." She licked her lips apprehensively.

"But please remember, there's no written law that says that you have to make love on your wedding night. We have tomorrow and the next day and the rest of our lives. If you're tired or your back hurts then we can just go to sleep. I do understand."

She shook her head. "Oh no, I feel well," she said, stroking his face.

His hand slid under her petticoat, searching for the garter. Once found, he removed it and placed it on the dressing table and then he slipped her stocking down her leg. He continued fondling her thigh, caressing the smooth skin, as he removed the second garter and stocking. He leaned forward and undid the ribbons on her chemise, running his fingers along the lace and briefly touching the softness beneath.

"We're going to be very happy. I just know it," he murmured. He took her hands and kissed them. "If only you knew how much I love you."

"I do and I love you," she whispered.

Guy pulled her close, his mouth covering hers urgently, a hunger surging through him like a hurricane. His tongue was exploring and she gasped at the sensations that always swept through her when he kissed her that way. But in reality, Melody didn't know what to expect. Aunt Olivia had hesitantly told her what she felt she ought to know, but her concluding statement was that her new husband would guide her through the intimacies of married life. However, she must be prepared for some discomfort and pain.

Guy rose from the floor bringing her up in his arms and carried her towards the bed. As he helped her out of her chemise and removed his own clothing, his kisses and caresses were gentle and unhurried. And even when he slipped into bed beside her, he showed no signs of impatience.

Melody turned her face towards him and he raised himself up and kissed her throat and mouth. His lips moved down and over her breasts. When he took the nipple in his mouth and his tongue caused it to harden, she gave a moan of pleasure. This had happened before during their engagement when he had pressed sensual kisses on her mouth and the few occasions when he had briefly cupped her breast in his hand. She already knew that her body could leap into arousal at his touch and the knowledge fascinated her.

She felt completely relaxed and closed her eyes, letting herself drift away on a wave of sensations. It was only when he started touching her most intimate part, did she tense. He hadn't hurt her but the sheer panic at being caressed in what was known as a 'forbidden' place, had caused an instinctive reaction. He stopped immediately his face showing unease. Stroking her face, he kissed her lips.

"Don't you want me to touch you there? I won't if you don't want me to."

She stared up at him and knew that she had to trust the deep love she felt for this man.

"No, it's all right, really," she murmured.

Taking his hand, she moved it down, across her breasts and stomach and then to her thigh.

He lowered his eyelids and sucked in a breath. "I'll take my time and touch you very gently. If it's slow and easy, then the feelings will grow naturally and there'll be no discomfort." His voice was almost a whisper and so soothing Melody closed her eyes again. She was prepared for 'some discomfort, some pain' as Aunt Olivia had warned her, but when he moved between her thighs and pushed inside her, the sharp, stinging sensation made her give out a muffled cry and her body tensed once more. Guy raised himself up on one elbow. "Are you all right?" he whispered. Melody nodded. He smiled and kissed her lips. "It hurts only once. Just try and relax."

He adjusted his weight and began to move slowly. She clung onto him as the thrusts became more demanding and she could hear his breathing becoming laboured, as he pressed his face against her hair. It wasn't altogether unpleasant, just very intimate. Melody stayed still, not daring to move, not knowing if she should move. Suddenly, she realised he seemed to be struggling as if he was in a great deal of discomfort. Did becoming so hard cause him pain too? She had always wondered about that.

"What is it, Guy? What's the matter?" She held his face in her hands.

He gasped for a moment. "I've wanted you for so long, I'm...I'm finding it difficult to keep control."

"Why must you keep control?"

"Because I don't want to hurt you."

Melody raised herself up to kiss him. "I love you and I want to show you my love in every way that I can. It's your wedding night too. I'm not a china doll. I won't break. Do what you have to do."

Pulling himself up and supporting his weight on his hands, he started to move with more enthusiasm, pushing her into the mattress, his breathing coming through his teeth in sharp urgent pants. Melody had never imagined the energy a man used in the act of making love and found this display of extreme passion exhilarating as well as exciting.

She smiled at the noises he made that finally climaxed into an anguished cry of pleasure. His body stiffened as the ecstasy surged through him and then he collapsed to one side, sucking in his breath and blowing it out in a shudder.

They didn't speak as he tried to control his breathing.

"Oh, angel," he groaned. He took her hand and pressed a kiss into the palm. "You're so beautiful." She stroked his chest watching it fall and rise steadily. Finally, he turned over to face her. "You won't believe how worried I've been about tonight."

"Why have you been worried?"

He smiled. "I hoped it wouldn't be too frightening for you and that it wouldn't repulse you so much, you'd lock me out of the bedroom the second night."

"I wouldn't do that."

He kissed her lips and sighed. "I promise that one day, you'll find it just as exciting."

"I already have," she laughed.

"No, you don't understand what I mean, but one day you will."

Melody puzzled over this statement, but then grinned. "I think I need to ask more questions. I'll just get my notebook and pencil from the drawer. Would the editor like a brief account of tonight's events? I'm sure the readers of the Jour…Oh!"

He quickly rolled on top of her pinning her down under him. "There are some things that shouldn't be reported, Miss Kinsman."

"Mrs Wyngate, if you please," she smiled.

"Yes," he said, brushing the hair away from her face. "Mrs Wyngate."

She gave a long sigh. "And I'm glad we waited until our wedding night."

"So am I, angel. So am I."

Melody awoke the next morning to find him gone. At first she felt disappointed and wondered if he had decided to go to the office. But then she remembered that they had planned to spend the day visiting the Royal Observatory at Greenwich and later that evening, they were attending a production of Sheridan's *The Rivals* at Drury Lane.

She pulled herself up on the pillows and as the covers fell to her waist, she realised she was still naked. There was a slight soreness between her thighs, but not uncomfortably so. She smiled and glanced at the white satin nightdress lying over the back of the chair. She hadn't had time to put it on. It was so pretty and she quickly reached for it and slipped it over her head, smoothing out the folds and adjusting the short sleeves that fell loosely at the shoulders. She heard voices outside the door and scrambled under the covers.

Guy entered with Mrs Talbot close behind. "She's still asleep," he whispered. Melody tried to keep still as she heard them prepare the fire. They had obviously brought some hot coals up from the kitchen stove and thrown them onto fresh kindling, as she could hear the crackling as the wood burst into flames. "We'll have our breakfast sitting by the window, if you please."

"Yes, sir," said Mrs Talbot. "I'll bring a tablecloth up and some cutlery and crockery. Breakfast will be in about fifteen minutes."

Melody heard the housekeeper shut the door behind her and then the mattress dipped as Guy sat on the edge.

He gently pulled the covers down revealing a mischievous grin. "I knew you weren't asleep. I could see the quilt shaking," he said, laughing

"I was trying to hide from Mrs Talbot."

"Why?"

"I suppose I felt embarrassed."

He chucked her under the chin and then noticed her nightdress. "Goodness, that's lovely."

"Do you like it? I planned to wear it last night but I didn't get the chance."

"Was I that impatient?"

She shook her head. "Not at all." She leaned forward and kissed his lips. "But I wondered where you were this morning when I found you gone."

"I've arranged for us to have breakfast up here and I thought we needed a fire. The sun is out but it's still quite chilly."

She looked across to where the flames danced in the grate and snuggled against the pillows feeling contented. Guy watched her knowing that he had had an ulterior motive for removing himself that morning. He had awoken to find her sleeping peacefully, her hair flowing over the pillows in billowing curls. Gathering her up in his arms, he had kissed her beautiful face, his hands moving over her naked body, his desire for her torturous. But he realised that he mustn't make any undue demands on her, it was too soon and she hadn't fully recovered from her accident. Sir Jack had been right and he had to take his time. He had jumped out of bed and putting on his robe had gone in search of the housekeeper to organise a fire and some breakfast.

Now, sitting on the mattress, his eyes swept over the swell of her breasts as they rose and fell gently with her breathing. The smooth sheen of the nightdress enhanced her complexion and her eyes sparkled with health.

"You look good enough to eat," he murmured.

She smiled and leaned forward wrapping her arms round his neck, pressing her lips on his. His hand cupped the soft mound of her breast and he knew he would go insane if he fought his need for her. He was a lost man when it came to his new wife. He pressed her back against the pillows, his kisses becoming more demanding.

The following day they would catch the train to Southampton and from there take the ferry to the Isle of Wight. They intended to spend a week in Shanklin where Sir Jack's townhouse had been prepared for them. The housekeeper would call daily to cook their meals and clean, but otherwise they were to be left to their own devices and Guy wanted it to be a week of walking and talking, sightseeing and making love.

Mrs Talbot reached the bedroom door carrying a tray of cutlery and crockery, with a tablecloth flung over one arm. Placing the tray down on the side table, she was just about to raise her hand to knock when she heard the rhythmic sound of the bedsprings. She smiled to herself. If the master intended spreading his seed inside his young bride with such regularity, then she would be with child within a year. Oh well, she thought, breakfast will just have to wait.

CHAPTER TWENTY-FOUR

Marlborough House seemed enormous. Situated in Pall Mall, Melody had spent the entire journey in a state of excitement and as the hansom cab drew closer, she couldn't take her eyes off the impressive structure, its many windows glinting in the morning sun. Magnificent wings four storeys high flanked the main part of the building and the front door boasted a deep porch. The whole appearance of the building was pleasing to the eye and even the many chimneys seemed to add a certain charm about the place. She knew that the Prince and Princess of Wales had lived there since their marriage and amazement swept through her that she was moments away from being in the presence of the future Queen of England.

At the gate, the soldier on duty stopped the driver and Melody reached out and handed him the letter. He gave it a cursory examination and then saluted before letting them pass. Soon they were at the main entrance. The major-domo was already waiting for her and ushered her into the vast hallway and then into a reception room. While she waited she amused herself by walking around and looking at the objects in the cabinets, the portraits on the wall and then she picked up some books that were on the shelf and read the titles. There was movement behind her and she spun round.

A young woman stood in the doorway and after casting her eyes over the 'commoner' standing by the bookshelf, she walked across the floor towards her. She was tall and thin with large, blue eyes in fine, chiselled features. Her hair was swept up and held in place by an ivory comb. She had an aristocratic bearing and as she came further into the room, Melody could see that she still thought she had a book balanced on top of her head.

"Good morning. I'm Lady Louisa Hastings, one of Princess Alexandra's ladies-in-waiting. You are the journalist, Mrs Melody Wyngate?"

Melody could see straight away that Lady Louisa didn't approve of her, but answered with a pleasant smile.

"Yes, I am. I'm pleased to meet you." She held out her hand.

Lady Louisa declined to take it. "Before we go up, I need to clarify a few points of etiquette." Her gaze swept over the royal blue day dress and dainty Empire bonnet trimmed with matching coloured ribbons. She continued in a cold tone, "Her Royal Highness will offer her hand and you will take it and curtsey and you say 'How do you do, Your Highness. After that you always refer to her as ma'am. But you will not put questions to her. Do you understand?"

Melody took in a breath. Lady Louisa had obviously been given an odious task and although she was determined to do it well, the expression on her face told Melody that she would rather be elsewhere. Lady Louisa swirled round in rustling skirts and Melody followed her back into the hallway, where they then turned and walked up the thickly carpeted marble staircase and along a wide passage. They entered an opulent room of gold and red and then Lady Louisa went across to a second door and knocked before entering.

"Mrs Melody Wyngate, ma'am," she said and gestured Melody to come forward.

Melody stepped into a lime green room where a tall, elegant woman, dressed in a simple skirt and blouse, rose to her feet. She was beautiful and her beauty was enhanced by the enchanting smile she gave her visitor as she held out her hand in greeting.

Melody swept into the Journal and ran through the hallway and up the stairs. Marsh was at his desk as she burst into his office causing him to jump with fright, dropping the biscuit he was munching with his drink of coffee.

"Miss Melody! Do you have to rush in on me like that? It's enough to give me apoplexy."

The fact that she was now Mrs Wyngate had not quite registered with many of the staff who still insisted on calling her 'Miss Melody', much to Guy's amusement.

She danced round his office with delight. "I've seen her," she sang. "And she was so gracious and wonderful and kind and beautiful and interesting."

Marsh smiled and picked the pieces of biscuit off his lap. "I take it your audience with Princess Alexandra went well?"

"Oh, it went more that well! It was absolutely…"

The editor's door opened and Guy appeared. "I thought I heard you. Would you like to come in and tell me all about it."

Hardly able to contain her delight, Melody picked up her skirts and glided into her husband's office. Marsh smiled at her enthusiasm and then chuckled as he continued his work and ten minutes later when the door opened once more and Melody walked past him, patting him playfully on the head, he scowled and blurted out a disgruntled comment. Even so, he was pleased she was back although he knew she was working far more hours than Mr Wyngate wished, his entreaties to take it easy going unheeded.

Melody too, was overjoyed to be doing the work she loved and at that moment she was on her way to interview Josephine Butler who had written to her and told her about her fight to allow women into university and also improving the circumstances of prostitutes. The first item was close to Melody's heart, but the second interested her, since her journey to Whitechapel to visit the girls at the Ten Bells.

And then there was her book. She had now completed the last chapter and sent it to Sir Jack. The proofs were already arriving and Melody spent her time amending them before sending them back. The publishing date was set for September and Melody was impatient to hold the first copy in her hands.

Guy sat at his desk and tried to read the document in front of him. He wandered over to the window and smiled as he saw Melody climb aboard the gig. He would have to buy her a better horse. Sultan was long overdue for retirement. He sighed softly. If there was one thing he couldn't wait for, it was the evenings and nights spent with his wife. They had been married such a short time and yet it had been the happiest time of his life. And he knew Melody was happy too. He couldn't understand why he still felt apprehensive about their age difference since they had found harmony and contentment almost immediately.

During working hours, he and Melody went their separate ways and bumped into each other at the same rate as they had done before their wedding. But in the evening, when they were together, it was a different story. After they had eaten, they would spend their time in the sitting room, talking about their day or taking walks and making plans for the next. His social life had increased dramatically now he had a wife and invitations arrived every morning inviting them to dinners, soirees, balls and musical evenings. And then they hosted their own entertainment, but on a much smaller scale with quiet dinners followed by a game of cards.

Guy thought he would never get tired of Melody's presence as she rushed about the house, or when she was getting ready for bed. He loved watching as she brushed her hair and then her warm softness enveloped him filling him with uncontrollable desire. Sometimes it seemed he couldn't get enough of her and she in turn was beginning to respond to his lovemaking with all the passion and expertise she was slowly learning.

"There are two letters for you this morning, angel," said Guy, handing her the envelopes.

Melody took them and looked at the handwriting. "One's from Aunt Olivia and I'm sure this one…" She quickly tore it open. "Goodness, it's from Celia."

"How did she know our address?"

Melody let out a sigh. "I told my aunt that she could pass it on, if Celia ever asked for it."

"Did you think she would get in touch?"

"I thought she might. I haven't spoken to her since Papa received his honour. She went back to Hucknall Garth and then that's when everything happened." Her expression became sombre as she remembered.

"Well, what does she say," he smiled.

Melody read down the letter. "She wants to know if we're still friends and have I forgiven her." She shrugged indifferently. "Why does she want forgiveness? Alex and I had ended our engagement before they got married."

"Yes but he didn't waste any time," Guy sighed but followed this with a smile. "Is there a new member of the family yet?"

Melody scanned down the second page. "No, she says nothing about that. But she does say she'd like me to visit her."

"Would you like to visit her?"

"I've not really thought about it. I suppose I could. Would you mind?"

He tried to pretend enthusiasm. "Certainly not. You must go and get everything straightened out."

"I don't think there's anything to straighten out. She's married to Alex and seems happy enough and I'm married to you and I'm very happy."

He reached across and took her hand, pressing her fingers against his lips. "Well, that's all right, then. You go and visit her."

"I'll write immediately. I can catch the train to Colchester."

"Good! I'm glad that's decided."

Melody smiled to herself as she ate her breakfast. Did Guy really think she was fooled by his calm and confident manner? She knew him too well to be taken in like that. He was concerned about her meeting Alex. Did he think him a rival? She shook her head in amusement. He was trying to hide the fact he was jealous and it was an emotion she wasn't used to seeing in her husband.

More letters passed between Melody and Celia and with each one the situation became warmer. Celia spoke of her sadness at losing Melody as a friend and how she had wanted to write for a long time but lacked the courage. She hardly mentioned Alex except to say he was very busy working for his father. The baby was due at the beginning of July and Celia hoped she would pay her a visit before the birth. And so it was decided that Melody would travel to Colchester in the middle of June and spend three nights at Alex and Celia's home.

Melody climbed into bed and watched her husband shaving. The long blade glided skilfully over his face, sweeping away the soap and leaving the skin smooth. She had always been grateful that he preferred to be clean shaven and didn't choose to sport a moustache or the side-whiskers so common amongst professional gentlemen. He was such an attractive man, she thought, the shades of silver in his dark brown hair made his face seemed tanned, his smile enhanced by the laughter lines on each side of his deep brown eyes.

She snuggled against the pillows and fluffed up her thick, auburn hair that tumbled over the pillow. One sleeve of her nightdress slipped from her shoulder as she moved her arms about.

Guy tipped the mirror slightly and watched her through the glass. She noticed and smiled seductively.

"You really shouldn't do that?" he said, starting on the other side of his face.

"Do what?"

"Look at me in that way when I have a razor in my hand. If my hands shake it could prove very nasty."

"I can't help looking at you the way I do. I feel happy and I love you."

"That's good to hear," he smiled. He finished shaving and wiped his face and throat with a towel. "I shall miss you while you're away."

"It's only for three nights."

"We've never been parted that long since we married," he said, unbuttoning his shirt and hanging it over the chair. "And you'll be in the company of Doctor Alex Courtney."

It had happened at last. After a week of preparation for her visit and absolute support from her husband, she had finally detected the change in tone when saying

Alex's name. He had certainly kept up the pretence long enough.

"Are you worried about me seeing Alex again?" she asked innocently.

He started getting ready for bed. "I'm not worried," he said. "A little apprehensive, maybe. After all, he is your former suitor."

"And now you're my husband. And there's a big difference between a husband and a former suitor."

"You haven't seen him since you ended your engagement and he might still have feelings for you."

She shook her head and gave a quiet laugh. "That was ten months ago. Anyway, I'm going to visit Celia, not Alex."

"He's a young man," he murmured. "And no doubt a fine young man, for all his failings."

She held out her arms. "Oh, come and make love to me, you silly thing."

He smiled sheepishly and slipped into bed beside her. What a fool I am, he thought, as he wrapped his arms round her. She's right, I am being silly. I have the world in my arms and I should thank God. As he kissed her lips, her face, her throat, he resolved never to fret over his wife's young friends. Or the young admirers she was bound to attract.

The journey to Colchester took two hours and when the train finally approached the station, Melody couldn't contain her glee at seeing Celia once more. But on the platform she found an elderly gentleman waiting for her. Tall and dignified, he didn't need to introduce himself as she could see the likeness between father and son immediately.

"Mrs Wyngate? I'm Doctor Courtney Senior. I've come to escort you to Oaklands. Let me take your bag."

Melody smiled and handed him her luggage. Outside the station an elegant carriage waited and he passed the bag to the driver, who stored it under the seat. Doctor Courtney Senior helped her into the carriage and then took his place beside her. She remembered that Celia's letters had come from a house called Oaklands, but she was surprised that Alex's father should be accompanying her there. Somehow it seemed more appropriate if Alex had met her himself instead of giving the task to his father. Perhaps he was detained on medical business, she thought.

Shrugging it off as unimportant, Melody delighted at the sights and sounds of Colchester as they trotted through the streets and avenues. She and Doctor Courtney kept up a lively discussion, but when they took the road leading out of the city, she became puzzled.

"Where are we going? I thought Celia lived in Colchester."

Doctor Courtney grinned. "Oaklands is ten miles from Colchester. About halfway to Sudbury I'd say."

Melody looked around her as they journeyed into the Essex countryside. It was quite pretty with a profusion of wild flowers adorning the grass verges, the fields speckled with the black and white Friesian cows who turned their heads unperturbed and munched the grass as they watched them pass. The country air would certainly do Celia a great deal of good, thought Melody. Fresh air and exercise should help her have a healthy pregnancy. But how strange she had mistakenly thought that she lived in town.

"Is Celia well?"

"Indeed. We're very happy with her progress."

Melody thought for a moment. "Will Alex deliver the baby?"

"Me or Alex. Whoever happens to be available."

"But I suppose it will be Alex, since he's her doctor."

Doctor Courtney frowned. "Well, in truth, I've been looking after her during her pregnancy."

Melody felt puzzled. "Oh, so you must visit them often?"

"Visit, my dear? No, Mrs Courtney and I live at Oaklands. It's been our home quite a while."

She stared at him in surprise. "But I thought they intended living in Alex's townhouse in Colchester? The one he inherited from his grandfather?"

This seemed to amuse him. "No, Alex decided to keep his tenants on for that house. My son and his wife moved in with us after they came back from honeymoon."

Melody was filled with horror at this revelation. They were living with Doctor and Mrs Courtney! Celia would be constantly under the nose of that arrogant woman, always under scrutiny and liable to be criticised at every turn. If she, Melody, had married Alex then she too would have been in the same dreadful situation and that would have been intolerable. But there again, Celia was made from different material. Being more compliant might have made her more agreeable to Mrs Courtney. Perhaps the relationship was thriving if her mother-in-law approved of her the way she never would with Melody.

Oaklands loomed into sight thirty minutes after leaving the outskirts and the house itself was a delight, its impressive front emerging from behind the trees as they trotted up the drive. It had been the old manor when Alex's grandfather had bought it, Doctor Courtney informed her as they rumbled along and after considerable renovations, he had turned it into a fairly respectable family home. It had all the necessary main rooms and also numerous bedrooms. Surrounding it was the garden that three gardeners kept in immaculate condition. There were meadows and woodlands beyond and about two miles away there was a small village of about three hundred people.

As they pulled up at the door, a footman came out to collect her bag and then she was ushered inside. There didn't seem to be anyone about and at first Melody was surprised that there was no one to greet her.

"I'll just see where everyone is," said Doctor Courtney. "Would you like to wait in the parlour?"

Melody went through the door indicated and found herself in a spacious room decorated with pale green and blue wallpaper and olive green curtains at the window. It reflected Mrs Courtney's taste and although sumptuous seemed cold and unfriendly. Suddenly she missed the cream and terracotta sitting room she shared with Guy in Hill Street. And then she missed Guy. Was this visit really necessary? She and Celia hadn't seen each other for ten months so perhaps they weren't friends any more, otherwise they would have kept in touch.

"Melody," said a whispered voice behind her. "I'm so pleased you've come."

She spun round to see the swollen shape of a young girl who seemed vulnerable and so small, like a child who was lost and alone. Seeing her once more, filled her with the protective instinct she always felt and soon she and Celia were hugging each other and Celia was crying with joy at being reunited with a friend she thought she had lost forever.

Celia showed Melody to a small room, overlooking the courtyard and therefore, the stables. The curtains and rug were faded, the marble washstand old and discoloured, the bedspread frayed.

"I hope you don't mind," said Celia, showing her embarrassment with a scarlet face. "I wanted you to have one of the best rooms, but Mrs Courtney said they mustn't be disturbed for someone staying only three nights." She eased herself into an armchair, which had also seen better days.

Melody shrugged indifferently. "This will suit me very well." She finished hanging up her dress for dinner and turned to the young girl sitting in the uncomfortable chair. "When did you say you're due?"

"First week of July."

"Then you haven't long to wait."

Celia pulled a face. "I feel as though this pregnancy has been going on forever. Sometimes I think it'll never end."

"But it will and when it does, you'll have a lovely baby to care for."

Celia seemed disinterested. "Tell me about your wedding and your new husband. Are you happy?"

Melody smiled. "Oh yes, very happy." She suddenly felt uneasy and went to sit on the bed. "I'm sorry you didn't get an invitation to our wedding. It just...It seemed..."

"You don't have to explain, Melody. I understand perfectly. Why would you want Alex and me at your wedding after what we did to you."

"You and Alex didn't do anything to me."

"Yes, we did. We broke your heart," she insisted.

Melody shook her head. "No, you don't understand." She took in a breath. "It was never meant to be. Alex and I weren't suited at all. He didn't understand how important my work was to me and he wanted me to be a good wife who would support him in his career."

"As I'm doing," murmured Celia.

Melody gave her a sidelong glance. "Yes, but being married was all you wanted from life. I had other plans."

Celia turned pale blue eyes on her. "I was so surprised to hear of your engagement to Mr Wyngate. I didn't realise you thought of him in a romantic way."

"Neither did I," laughed Melody. "But when I did realise I loved him then it was like an explosion inside me."

"Your feelings were that strong?"

"So strong, I actually proposed to him."

"You didn't!"

"I did and then discovered that he had loved me for ages and was just waiting for the right opportunity to propose to me."

"Melody Kinsman! I always said you had no shame." For the first time Celia giggled and it brightened her face and made her look like the girl Melody once knew. But then the frown returned. "How strange that we both got what we wanted, but I wonder who's the happier."

"Did you get what you wanted? I thought you were intent on Doctor Christian Jenner." She chuckled at her teasing.

"A girl's fancy. Nothing more," sighed Celia.

"Aren't you happy?"

Celia paused before answering, "I love Alex and I believe he loves me. But he still thinks about you. I know he does, I can see it in his eyes."

"Well, that's sad as I hardly give him a moment's thought."

"That's because you found the man who could make you happy."

"Yes," breathed Melody, thinking of Guy. "He was there all the time and I didn't realise it."

"What's he like?"

"Guy? Oh, clever and handsome. Thoughtful and caring."

"He sounds remarkable. And he let you continue working?"

Melody threw back her head, laughing. "He's the editor and owner of the newspaper I work for. I'm helping him to become a wealthy man."

"But he's already wealthy?"

Melody thought for a moment. "He inherited property and money from his parents. But he's made a huge investment in the Journal, so he works very hard for every penny he has."

"And I've heard he'll inherit again."

"Well, he has an uncle. The brother of his late mother, wonderful Sir Jack and when he passes away and I hope that won't be for a very long time, Guy will inherit everything."

"Seems you have it all. A handsome, wealthy, war hero of a husband who adores you and allows you to live your life the way you choose."

Melody couldn't help detecting the bitterness in her voice. "But doesn't that put your mind at rest? The fact I'm happy means I'm quite content with you and Alex being together. I don't hold any grudges. Not that I should have since we had broken our engagement before you and Alex married."

"But not very long before. Alex wanted a wife and I…"

A maid came to the half-open door and announced that luncheon was being served. Celia accompanied Melody to the dining room where Doctor and Mrs Courtney waited for them.

Mrs Courtney held out her hand. "Mrs Wyngate. I hope you've settled in and made yourself comfortable."

"Thank you, I have. I must take a walk round the garden. It looks so beautiful."

Mrs Courtney answered with a superior smile and while Doctor Courtney pulled out a chair for Celia, Melody sat herself down without ceremony. She wondered where Alex was. No one had mentioned him.

The meal was delicious, although Melody's heart went out to Celia when she knocked over her glass of wine and her mother-in-law reprimanded her for spoiling the spotlessly white tablecloth. Celia turned her face away, her shoulders hunched. Melody began to feel dismay. She had never seen Celia this way, not even when they were at Miss Lawson's.

Halfway through the second course of veal pie, Alex finally made an appearance. He breezed into the room and kissed his mother first, then greeted his father, before dropping a kiss on Celia's forehead. Throughout this he didn't look at Melody. It was only after the formalities were completed that his gaze fell on their guest. Melody could see he looked uneasy. His hazel eyes darkened somewhat as he raised her hand to his lips.

"Hello, Melody. You had a good journey from London, I trust?"

"Yes, thank you. An excellent journey."

"Good." He sat down and the footman brought him his meal.

The conversation continued, but Melody didn't want to join in. Now and again she would sense Alex watching her, but when she turned her eyes towards him, he would look away. By the end of their meal, Melody was beginning to believe that this visit was a terrible mistake.

She was glad when the first day was at an end and she could escape to her tiny bedroom. She had spent the afternoon wandering around on her own, as Celia had gone for a sleep and the two doctors were cloistered in the study discussing some case notes. She had dressed for dinner that turned out to be a melancholy business and after a quick game of cards she had retired early.

She stood at the window and looked up at the silver brightness of the moon, wondering if Guy was looking up at it too. He probably wasn't. He was never much of a moon-gazer.

As she snuggled under the covers, she remembered his expression at the station as he helped her into a carriage where two ladies were travelling together. And as he had stored her bag and made sure she was settled, his face had shown his pain at her leaving. She had never seen him look so desolate. She had pulled down the window and he had held her hand even after the guard had blown his whistle and the train started to move. She had giggled and told him he had better let go or he would be coming to Colchester with her. He had released her with a grin and a comment that he hoped she had packed her notebook and pencil as she might pick up a good story. Her journalistic instincts told her that there was an interesting story in this house, but her humanity cried out that it would be a desperately sad story too.

Melody sighed as she pressed her cheek against the pillow. She had been married only one month, but she had already become used to sleeping next to her husband. She hoped she would be able to sleep without him, but then her eyes closed and sleep came with no problem.

The following morning was a brilliant summer's day. As Melody pulled back the curtains she could see the grooms working in the stable, feeding the horses and shovelling the night's manure into a cart. There was a knock on the door and when she called out a small, dainty maid entered.

"I've brought you some hot water, ma'am."

"Thank you." Melody watched her bustling about preparing the washstand. "What's your name?"

The maid bobbed a curtsey. "Sally, ma'am and I've been asked to attend to your needs."

"Oh wonderful. My own personal maid."

"Well, I'm only the under parlour maid really, but I think being a lady's maid would be quite nice."

"I'm sure it would." She thought of Celia. "I suppose Mrs Courtney has one?"

"Yes, ma'am. Her name's Bertha and she always travels with her." The maid's eyes shone with excitement. "That's what I'd like to do, one day."

"I didn't know Mrs Courtney travelled."

"Oh, she's travelled to Spain and France and many other countries including America."

Melody marvelled at this piece of information. "Even during her pregnancy?"

The maid stopped folding the towels. "I'm so sorry, ma'am. I thought you meant the mistress." She thought for a second. "We kind of forget that the young master's lady is also called Mrs Courtney."

After Sally had left, Melody pulled off her nightdress and washed herself from head to toe. As she did so, she wondered at Celia's position in the household and came to the conclusion she didn't have one. She might as well be invisible. Poor Celia. She must float about like a phantom and no doubt the family overlooked her very existence. It must be a lonely, melancholy life.

She went down to breakfast and discovered Mrs Courtney Senior sitting at the table alone. Melody greeted her hostess warmly, but Mrs Courtney simply inclined her head in answer. There followed a dismal meal albeit an excellently prepared one, during which Melody was informed that Celia wanted to stay in her room for the morning and the two doctors had gone into Colchester to buy some new equipment for their surgery.

Thirty minutes later, Melody climbed the stairs and after meeting Sally on the landing was directed to Celia's room. She was lying on her bed, still in her nightdress, but with a pretty shawl thrown over her shoulders.

"Are you feeling unwell?" asked Melody, noticing the pale face and listless eyes.

"Just very, very tired," said Celia. "I'm going to stay here for a while but I'll get up for luncheon. Alex will be back then." She sighed. "You'll have to amuse yourself this morning. I hope you don't mind."

Melody shook her head. "I shall do well. It's a wonderful morning and I'll probably take a stroll."

She set off on her solitary walk and made her way through the gardens, stopping to talk to one of the gardeners who was collecting great bunches of lavender that would be taken inside the house to freshen the air. Eventually she wandered into the meadow filled with poppies and hollyhocks, the fresh breeze making them dance and causing the humming bees to make precarious landings to collect the nectar.

Then she saw the swing. It was attached by strong ropes to the branches of an ancient oak and it had a sturdy wooden seat made from ash. Melody pulled on it and seeing that it was quite secure, made herself comfortable and began to swing gently backwards and forwards. It was so peaceful and she closed her eyes, leaning her cheek on her hand as she clutched the rope. Only the song of the birds filled her conscious mind as her thoughts drifted with the gentle movement of the swing.

It was now a year since she and Alex had become engaged. It was a year since that tragic train accident and her first encounter with Mr Charles Dickens. And a year since Guy had visited her at Hucknall Garth and they had taken that walk to visit dear Miss Garlick. That was when her feelings for him had started to blossom. He had called her a wild poppy and he had been right. She was wild and untamed and thank goodness he loved her for it.

"Marriage has made you even more beautiful and I really didn't think that would be possible."

She opened her eyes to see Alex leaning against the tree. "Have you been standing there long?"

He gave a charming smile. "I saw you from the road so I thought to join you and left my father to return to the house alone."

"There isn't room for two on this swing."

"You think not? My sisters managed it perfectly well. Anyway, I didn't mean join you on the swing."

Melody smiled too. "I know what you meant. I was only teasing you."

"Shall I push you?"

"Yes, but not too high." She laughed with delight as she soared into the air, her skirts billowing out behind her. Suddenly the wind pulled the pins from her hair and it tumbled down her back. "Stop! I've come undone." Alex grabbed the swing and brought it to a halt. Melody couldn't stop giggling as she tried to control her unruly curls, twisting them into a plait over one shoulder. Alex found some of the pins, glinting in the grass, but there wasn't enough to put up her hair. "Oh dear, I'll just have to leave it loose. What will your mother think?"

"Whatever it is she won't hesitate to speak her mind," he said dryly. His gaze swept over the meadow. "I played here often as a boy."

"You must feel about Oaklands like I do about Hucknall Garth?"

"I suppose I do." He gave a gentle smile. "But I never expected to come back and live here. At least not while my parents were still alive."

"Why did you, Alex? I thought you were going to take up residence in Colchester. That's what you told me."

He grimaced. "Mother suggested that I keep renting out the house in town and move here with Celia."

"And you thought it a good idea too?"

"At the time I did."

"But not now?"

He shrugged and didn't answer the question. Suddenly he changed the subject. "I followed your recovery from your accident with great interest."

"You did?"

"I came up to London quite a few times and Jenner discussed your case with me."

"Oh, I didn't realise you were on the team of doctors that treated me. You didn't send a bill."

Alex broke into a cheery laugh. "It was only professional interest." He became more serious. "Celia begged me to keep an eye on you. She burst into tears when Aunt Olivia wrote to her." Melody found swallowing difficult. She had never considered how Celia would take the news of her accident. "And as for me, I thought you'd be paralysed for at least a year, but Jenner reckoned on six months. I couldn't believe you did it in three. That was remarkable."

Melody smiled. "But it might have been six or twelve months if Miss Nightingale hadn't paid me a visit."

"Miss Nightingale? Florence Nightingale?"

"The Lady with the Lamp herself."

Seeing he was interested, Melody went on to tell him about Miss Nightingale's suggested treatment and how it had worked.

Alex bit his lip and stared down at the ground. "We know so little about the nerves and how they function. Is it possible to jolt injured nerves into working again?" Melody remained silent knowing he was lost in his own medical thoughts. He lifted his head and frowned. "When Jenner told me you had injured your spinal cord, I thought it a dire situation. But he was very optimistic about your recovery."

"Christian was wonderful. My opinion of him certainly changed over those three dreadful months."

"Yes, he seemed to become very fond of you," Alex grinned. "He even apologised for telling me that he'd seen you come out of the Cavendish Hotel with Wyngate."

Melody lips twitched. "I was not having an affair with Guy behind your back."

Alex's hazel eyes darkened. "I believe you although you seemed to get engaged to him very quickly."

"You were already married to Celia by then," she reminded him.

He paused for a moment before saying, "I knew you had feelings for him. Your expression changed every time you mentioned his name."

"Well, you knew more than I."

"I don't suppose it matters now."

"No, Alex, it doesn't."

He pulled his watch from his waistcoat pocket. "It's nearly time for luncheon. Shall we walk back to the house?" He held out his hand and in a husky voice said, "Friends?"

Melody slipped off the swing, nodded and shook his hand. "Always." She took his arm as her dissident curls became loose once more. "Oh dear, I must go to my room and tidy my hair. A married woman isn't supposed to have her hair down in the company of gentlemen."

"No," he murmured, watching her. "Even so, you look enchanting. Your husband is a very lucky man."

CHAPTER TWENTY-FIVE

The afternoon turned out to be one of the most delightful Melody had ever experienced. They decided to sit out on the lawn after luncheon, Mr and Mrs Courtney on the stylish wrought iron chairs with embroidered cushions, so different from the old cane chairs at Hucknall Garth. Celia appeared, now feeling much better and settled herself on the long garden seat, propped up with many pillows. Melody and Alex provided the entertainment by playing badminton and causing a great deal of laughter from Celia and Mr Courtney as they hit the shuttlecock over the net, shouting insults at each other with every volley.

Mrs Courtney didn't feel amused at their antics. "It's not right for a young woman to run about like that and especially not a married woman," she told her husband.

"Oh, for goodness sake, Davina, she's strong and healthy. I have to deal with too many sick people and a sight like this gladdens my heart."

"But we must always maintain decency and Mrs Wyngate…"

"Six months ago, Mrs Wyngate couldn't even stand on her own two feet never mind run about enjoying herself. Now stop complaining!" Davina Courtney pressed her lips together and turned her head away.

It wasn't often he spoke to her like that but sighing heavily, she knew she only had herself to blame. Her father had told her what would happen if she married beneath her. But her children wouldn't fall into the same trap, she had been determined about that. She had married her daughters well and her son had won the hand of a baron's daughter. Thank goodness Alex had told her that The Hon. Celia Sinclair also lived with Mrs

Wyngate's family and she had persuaded him to turn his attention to her instead. He had been all for winning back 'his darling Melody' after they had ended their engagement, even going so far as saying he'll stay in London so she could continue her work as a newspaper reporter. It had taken all her resolve to talk him out of it. And then there had been a further few fraught weeks before she could convince him that Oaklands was the proper place to bring his bride.

Watching Melody dashing backwards and forwards, she was now sure that her son, her 'baby', had picked the right wife. This young woman was too spirited and uncontrolled and would have made his life impossible.

"You're no match for me," yelled Alex, as Melody reached up and missed the shuttlecock flying over her head.

She placed her hands on her hips in irritation. "You do realise I'm rather hampered in these skirts."

"Why don't you take them off," called Celia, enjoying the spectacle.

"I've a good mind to do just that." Mrs Courtney sent her a withering look across the lawn and it was if the sun had disappeared behind a cloud. Melody became more subdued, but answered cheekily. "Next time I'll borrow a pair of trousers."

"Women wearing trousers! Whatever next," said Mrs Courtney contemptuously.

The fun was interrupted when tea was served on the lawn. Melody tucked into the scones filled with gooseberry jam, made by the cook who excelled in her pickles and preserves. Melody had already sampled the pickled onions, eggs and chutneys that flowed out of the nether regions of the house and had to admit that Mrs Courtney's pride in her cook was well-founded.

That evening, the cook excelled herself once again with her special dish of pheasant and wild mushrooms. And with the dessert of strawberry tarts, she produced a wonderful dish of asparagus in a decorated pastry crust, served with mayonnaise and eaten with the fingers. The conversation round the table that evening was more lively as Alex and his father pulled the asparagus out of the pastry shell and vied with each other on how many they could eat. After dinner, Melody suggested a game of charades and there followed two hours of complete enjoyment until they settled down for a hand of cards.

"I can't remember when I've had such an enjoyable evening," said Doctor Courtney as he and Alex went to fetch the ladies some refreshment from the sideboard.

Alex smiled in reply.

He looked over to where Melody was sitting at the card table, chatting with Celia. What was he doing with his life? It was as though he had been in a trance for the last ten months, allowing himself to be controlled like a puppet. He stared round the room and then back at Melody, wearing a rose pink gown, her hair fastened with a small spray of delicate silk flowers.

They were in the middle of a hand when a courier arrived with a message for Doctor Courtney Senior. He tore it open and read, his brow furrowed in a deep frown.

"It's from the hospital in Ipswich," he said. "It seems Bower's arm has become gangrenous and we'll have to amputate tomorrow."

"Oh, how sad. Is that the man who was injured in the rolling-mill?" asked Celia.

Alex nodded. "Yes, we've been fighting to save his arm for the last week. Looks like we've lost."

"But how will he support his family if he loses his arm?" said Melody.

Doctor Courtney shrugged. "No doubt something will be put his way. But first we must save his life." He turned to his son. "We must travel to Ipswich first thing in the morning."

Alex agreed.

Melody saw them leave. She was awoken early with the neighing of horses and the grind of carriage wheels. Peeping through her curtains she saw the grooms hitching the animals to the vehicle and then leading them round to the front of the house. Feeling inquisitive, she sneaked barefoot out of her bedroom and peered through the large window on the landing that overlooked the main entrance and watched the two doctors climb aboard. She wouldn't like to be in their shoes today. To amputate a limb! Thank goodness for chloroform to knock the poor man out, she thought.

Sally came up the stairs. "Oh, ma'am. You're already awake. I wondered if you'd like to take a bath this morning. There's plenty of hot water on the boil."

"That would be wonderful if you don't mind bringing the bath to my room."

"We don't do that in this house, ma'am. It's kept in a special room and the bather has to go to it rather than the bath go to them."

She was right for it seemed a special room had been set aside and a very large hip bath was placed in the centre. Against the wall was a rail of towels and nearby a large cabinet of jars and bottles of oils and bath salts.

"This is wonderful," cried Melody. "A room especially for bathing."

Sally laughed. "It was Doctor Courtney Senior who had the idea. I was carrying the bath with one of the housemaids and we dropped it on her foot. After that Doctor Courtney said it had to stay in one room for safety reasons." She gestured towards the fireplace. "On a cold day we can light the fire and it gets real cosy in here. And it's private. I'll go and bring the water up."

In a few minutes, Melody was soaking in a hot tub, the heady scent of jasmine and roses filling her nostrils.

"You still have to haul the water from the kitchen, though," she said, as Sally poured another jug into the bath.

"That's another thing that Doctor Courtney Senior talked about. The fact that there might be fresh, clean water piped to every house. Just imagine that."

Melody thought about this. "Well, gas is piped to major buildings and to streetlights. So why not gas and water to homes."

"It would certainly help my back if I could just turn a lever and water came gushing out," Sally nodded.

Melody went down to breakfast and joined Mrs Courtney who was reading a letter.

"I'm very angry with the dressmaker. She said she'd have my gown finished by today and now I get this message to say she's delayed and it won't be completed for three more days."

"When do you need it?" asked Melody nonchalantly.

"We're attending a very special function in two weeks' time and we will be introduced to our Member of Parliament, so everything must be perfect. I have a notion that my Alex will do well if he entered politics."

"You're attending a function so close to the baby's arrival?"

Mrs Courtney turned cold, blue eyes on her. "My dear Mrs Wyngate, babies do not always arrive on time and we cannot change our social engagements on that account. Celia will be well cared for." She poured herself another cup of tea from a silver teapot. "But I must speak to my dressmaker and insist she completes my gown immediately. I must have enough time to go into Colchester and buy the necessary accessories."

"Sometimes these things can't be helped," Melody sighed. She smiled at her. "Why don't you call me Melody? Celia and Alex do." Mrs Courtney declined to answer and went back to her breakfast. "Where's Celia?" said Melody, after a few uncomfortable minutes had settled on them.

"She rose early. I think she went out into the garden."

After breakfast, Melody decided to find her. She strolled through the flowerbeds, smelling the roses and when she reached the herb garden, picked a sprig of rosemary. Celia was in the herb garden, staring into the blue sky as if she wished to be up there flying with the swallows.

"You're up and about early," said Melody, reaching her side.

"I couldn't sleep so I thought I'd take a walk."

"Shall we continue walking?"

Celia nodded and they made their way along the path to the orchard. "Do you remember Monkswood?" whispered Celia. "And how happy I was there?"

Melody sensed her terrible sadness and put her arm round her. "Yes, but life moves on. You were happy at Hyde Park Gardens and Hucknall Garth too. They have all been happy homes for you."

"But not Oaklands. I'm not happy here."

Melody already knew that. "You must tell Alex and then something will be done."

"What for example?"

"Oh, I'm sure he'll have lots of ideas."

Celia shook her head. "Not if his mother has anything to do with it." Suddenly she stopped and gritted her teeth, a small, almost imperceptible groan coming from her throat. "I have a bit of indigestion this morning," she gasped.

"A common symptom during pregnancy, so I've heard." They carried on walking. An attack of indigestion occurred once more as they entered the orchard. "Do you want to sit down? You seem to be very uncomfortable." Melody guided her to a small arbour set in a stone wall, where geraniums entwined with ivy.

Celia leaned back against the seat. "If I die will you always remember me?"

"You're not going to die! Don't be silly."

"I might. Women do die in childbirth."

Melody smacked her hand playfully. "You've got two wonderful doctors looking after you. There's nothing to worry about."

Silence descended on them as they listened to the birds in the branches and watched a squirrel scamper up the trunk of a tree.

"You're going home tomorrow?"

"Yes. Back to the capital." Excitement surged through her. "Did I tell you that my book is due out in September? I must see Sir Jack…" Celia let out another groan. Melody glanced at her. "This indigestion is causing you a lot of pain. I think we ought to go inside and get you something for it. Aunt Olivia swears by peppermint."

Celia shook her head vigorously. "No, I want to stay here." More silence fell only this time it was an uneasy silence. Celia let out a louder groan and clutched her stomach. "Oh, God. It hurts!"

Melody stared at her in shocked awareness. "You haven't got indigestion, have you? You're in labour."

Celia turned wild, angry eyes on her. "I'll...I'll not have this baby. I'd rather die than let her have it."

"Who are you talking about?"

"Her! My mother-in-law. She's taken everything from me. My husband, my home and she'll take this baby. She won't let me be a proper mother to it. I just want to die and I'll take my baby with me."

Horror swept through Melody. "You've been concealing your contractions? Oh, dear Lord, how long have you been in pain?"

"Since the early hours," she gasped.

"Did you tell Alex before he left?"

"No, why should I? I don't want him anywhere near me."

Melody began to panic. "We must get you indoors and call for help."

"No, I've told you, I want to stay here."

For the first time in her life, Melody was glad of her superior height and strength over Celia. Jumping from her seat, she hauled her to her feet and forced her to move down the path, her arm guiding her along. Celia protested, but Melody was adamant. They left the orchard and reached the gardens. To her relief, she saw one of the gardeners and called out to him. Between them they helped the suffering Celia to the house and then a footman took over and managed to half-carry his young mistress to her room. On the way, Melody saw Sally and ordered her to find Mrs Courtney immediately.

In her room, Celia was placed on the bed and Melody, not knowing what to do, but wanting to do something, started removing her clothing.

Mrs Courtney appeared. "So, the baby's on its way?"

Melody nodded. "Yes, you must send…"

"I know what is needed, young lady. I've had three children of my own." Mrs Courtney stood perfectly still, her back rigid, as she watched her daughter-in-law being undressed.

Melody slipped the cotton nightdress over the squirming, groaning form on the bed. "I don't think there's much time. She's been hiding her pains so I think she's further along than we know."

"The groom has gone to fetch the midwife from the village."

"Good," breathed Melody. "Then she should be here soon and I will stay…"

Mrs Courtney bristled with indignation. "You will leave. And now. You have no place here."

Melody stared at her, hardly believing what she had heard. "You won't let me stay?"

"I don't think you'll be of any use."

Celia lifted her body from the mattress. "No, please, let Melody stay with me. I want her here."

Melody looked at Mrs Courtney through pleading eyes. "You heard her, ma'am, she wants me to stay."

Celia groaned and then erupted into a scream. Suddenly Melody was filled with overwhelming anger. Celia knew nothing of childbirth. It was one of the mysteries denied to women except those who dealt with it such as midwives and doctors. Just as a young girl knew nothing about the intimacies of married life until she was married, a woman knew nothing about childbirth until she was in the throes of it. Oh, what a stupid world we live in, thought Melody, where for women, ignorance is thought a virtue and knowledge corrupting.

"Please let her stay," begged Celia, clutching Melody's hand.

Mrs Courtney shook her head. "The groom will be returning with the midwife soon. Please go and wait in the parlour. You'll only get in the way."

Celia let out a scream and clutched Melody's hand even tighter. "It hurts. Oh, it hurts terribly. Stay with me Melody. I know I will die if you leave me."

Mrs Courtney stared at her, a smile hovering round her mouth. "To the parlour if you please."

Melody tried to hide her hostility and peeled Celia's fingers from her hand. With her friend's screams in her ears, she left the room and made her way downstairs. But there she couldn't settle and wandered about the hallway, listening and ready to respond if she should be needed. The midwife arrived and was bustled upstairs where Melody heard the bedroom door slam, but not before she heard Celia's anguished shriek of, "I don't want to die. Melody, I want Melody."

The next hour or so seemed to stretch to eternity. Melody strained her ears to hear anything of what was going on upstairs, but although the door opened and closed frequently, there was no sound of a baby's cry. Finally, Melody could bear it no longer and crept up the stairs to stand outside the door. Suddenly, the wail of a baby came from the room and Melody walked to the head of the stairs, tears pouring down her face. She would organise a cup of tea for the new mother; it was one thing she could do.

Sally appeared carrying soiled bed linen. "The baby's born ma'am. It's a boy." She took in a breath. "But young mistress isn't too well. She still has pains."

"And I guess that's not normal?" asked Melody.

The maid shook her head. "Midwife thinks there's another baby wanting to come out, but it's breech and Midwife can't reach it."

Melody swallowed hard. Was Celia going to die? There were voices in the hallway and Alex came running up the stairs. He barely glanced at the two young women standing in the corridor before rushing into the room, leaving the door open. Melody followed him. If Celia was dying then she had to be with her.

Alex took in the sight of his wife lying on her back, her eyes closed, small cries coming from pale lips. He pulled off his jacket and quickly rolled up his shirtsleeves, dipping his hands in a basin of water suffused with carbolic soap.

The midwife shook her head. "You have a son...But there's another baby there..."

Celia gave out a groan. "Oh, Alex, what's happened?"

"I'm going to examine you. Try and relax." He ran his hands over her stomach, before feeling inside her, his skilful fingers locating the source of the problem immediately. "Do you feel the urge to bear down?" he asked softly.

"Yes," she gasped. "But I..."

"You must trust me. Push when you need to. I'll do all the rest." The urge came and she started to strain. "That's it, you're doing so well. Just a little longer." She bore down again, holding onto the midwife's arm, concentrating on the instinct that was taking her over once more. "Good, one more should do it."

Melody watched from the door in amazement. She looked across to where Mrs Courtney stood in a white apron, a look of admiration on her face. Yes, she was proud of her son, but what of her daughter-in-law? Did Mrs Courtney have any empathy for Celia? Did she even care what she was going through? But Melody knew the answer. Poor Celia was just a vessel for producing the next generation of Courtneys.

A baby started crying and Alex wrapped the second child in a towel, a tiny, pink scrap of humanity, its skin still glistening from its birth. He placed the bundle next to the first infant lying in the cradle.

"Twins. A boy and a girl," he chuckled.

"Two babies," gasped Celia.

"Well done," grinned Alex, brushing her hair away from her damp forehead.

Melody stepped forward. "What do you want me to do?"

Alex smiled. "You can help Sally wash my wife and get her into a fresh nightgown. I need to give my son and daughter a quick examination."

Melody nodded and moved towards Celia, but Mrs Courtney prevented her. "Mrs Wyngate's place is downstairs. Perhaps she can order some tea for us all?"

Melody didn't ague but made her way downstairs to summon the footman for a tray of tea to be taken upstairs. It was twenty minutes later when she decided to venture back to the bedroom and only after she knew that the midwife had left and Mrs Courtney had gone to speak to the cook about the evening meal.

Celia was washed and dressed in a clean nightdress. The babies had also been cleaned up and wrapped in shawls, were in Celia's arms.

Melody peered down at them and frowned. "They're so tiny. Do you think they'll survive?"

Alex blew out a long breath. "I'd estimate the boy's weight at about six pounds. The girl is a bit smaller. But they're certainly healthy. The second child born in a set of twins usually gets the worst deal. But girls tend to have more stamina than boys." He squeezed her hand. "Thank you for all your help."

Melody smiled but then bit her lip. "I didn't do anything," she murmured.

Alex hadn't heard and went to sit on the edge of the mattress, helping his wife to take a sip of tea from the china cup.

Celia held the babies close, kissing each one in turn. "What shall we call them?" She looked at her husband. "How about Georgina, after your grandmother?"

Alex pondered a second or two. "Yes, Georgina sounds wonderful."

"Henry for the boy. After my father," said Celia.

Melody leaned across and stroked the babies' cheeks, delighting in the softness of skin that hadn't faced the harshness of the world yet.

"Georgina sounds beautiful and Henry is a noble name. Just like the baron," she nodded.

Alex rubbed his eyes. Now that his children had names, he felt overwhelmed. He gave a watery smile. "You must get some sleep now," he ordered, wanting to busy himself with practical details. "I'll take the babies and put them in the cradle." He suddenly chuckled. "They'll have to lie head to toe until we buy another one."

Celia snuggled down against the pillows and closed her eyes.

They watched her as she drifted off into contented sleep. Alex stepped closer to Melody and placed a gentle hand on her elbow.

"Now, Mrs Wyngate. I want to know why you were not with my wife in her hour of need. Celia has told me that you were sent from the room, on my mother's orders!"

CHAPTER TWENTY-SIX

Alex shook his head in disbelief. "Now she's gone too far!"

"I didn't want to tell you. She probably thought she was doing the right thing," said Melody.

"To deny my wife the company of her friend?"

"I was outside the door."

He frowned. "You should have been there, helping my wife. Celia told me that she wanted you there. And my mother kept you apart. It's intolerable."

The enormity of the event washed over her. "Oh, Alex, was Celia in great danger?"

"They could have died. All of them," he said, through gritted teeth. He ran his fingers through his hair. "Thank God I was already on my way home. One of the gardeners told me what had happened as I drove through the gate."

"But it all turned out right in the end," she tried to reassure him, not wanting to dwell on what might have been.

"That's no excuse, Melody."

He wasn't going to be pacified so there was no point in trying. She put her hand to her mouth and tried to stifle a yawn. "It's been a busy morning."

He noticed the shadows under her eyes and reached for her hand. "You go and rest," he said gently. "I'll wake you when luncheon is ready."

She turned to go. "Can I make a suggestion?"

"By all means."

"That little under parlour maid, Sally. I think she deserves a promotion. She should be the nursery maid."

Melody stumbled towards the door and upstairs to her room. Kicking off her shoes, she threw herself down on the mattress. In minutes she was asleep.

It must have been an hour later when her eyes opened again. She stretched and yawned and studied the room. It needed decorating and although clean, it looked like part of the servants' quarters. Perhaps in day's gone by it had been. How like Mrs Courtney to put her in a servant's room. She realised it must be time for luncheon and scrambled off the bed. Not wanting to be late and thereby adding to her sins, she straightened her skirt and blouse, pushed her feet into her shoes and glanced in the mirror. Seeing that her hair was untidy, she pulled out the pins and tied it back with a ribbon, before making her way downstairs.

Raised voices from the parlour told her that a heated argument was in progress. For a moment she listened at the door. The sound of Mrs Courtney's voice was piercing but the other voices were lower and not so audible. Then she heard her own name mentioned and decided to go in. What she saw stopped her from venturing too far into the room.

Mrs Courtney was sitting on the couch, her face twisted with distress, a white lace handkerchief held to her streaming eyes. Her husband sat beside her, a hand on her shoulder, trying to calm her. Alex stood by the fireplace, fists clenched, his expression thunderous.

Melody's appearance caused further uproar.

Mrs Courtney jumped to her feet. "There she is, the little viper! How dare you come into my home and turn my son against me."

"This has nothing to do with Melody," said Alex. "This is of your own doing." He turned to look at Melody, his colour heightened.

Mrs Courtney pointed an accusing finger. "Oh no, everything was going well until she arrived. I didn't want her here. But I allowed it because you and Celia wanted it."

Alex stepped forward. "Yes, and I'm glad Melody was here to give my wife the support, that I admit to my shame, I didn't give her. Nor you."

His mother waved her hand in dismissal. "Celia has had as much support as she needed."

Alex shook his head. "No Mother, she hasn't. We've neglected her. But thank God I've seen it in time."

Mrs Courtney glared at Melody, hate pouring from her. "Celia wasn't due for another three weeks. She went into labour after taking a walk with Mrs Wyngate. That makes me wonder what she was saying to my daughter-in-law. What nasty little mischief was she whispering in her ear? Something upsetting I shouldn't wonder. Something to cause Celia distress and start her contractions."

Doctor Courtney rose to his feet and shook his head. "No, Davina. Twins often come early. You can't blame Melody for that."

"Melody!" she screeched. "Oh, I see. She's got you wrapped in her coils now, has she." She stepped closer to the figure that had kept a dignified silence. "I want you to leave and leave now. One of the grooms will take you into Colchester."

Melody lifted her chin and slowly turned. She wanted to go home, what did one day matter.

Alex stepped across and took her arm. "No, you can't send Melody away when she's done nothing wrong."

Doctor Courtney cleared his throat. "Davina, I've been married to you for thirty-two years and it's time I took you in hand. God knows it's long overdue. I will not allow you to send Melody away from this house. I am the master here, not you. Do you hear me, woman!" Mrs Courtney stared at him as though she didn't recognise him and then fled the room, her eyes burning red with tears of humiliation. Doctor Courtney sighed and turned to Melody. "My dear girl, you can stay for as long as you wish. You will always be a welcomed guest in my house." He crossed the floor and took her hand and kissed it.

"Thank you, sir," she murmured. "But I think I would like to go home, if you don't mind."

"Are you sure, Melody? Why don't you stay until tomorrow?" urged Alex.

Melody shook her head. "There's a train from Colchester at four. It would be best if I were on it."

"You'll not go without taking luncheon and then Alex will accompany you to the station."

She agreed and they watched her as she turned and left the room. She must explain her sudden departure to Celia.

"That's a very remarkable young lady," said Doctor Courtney. "I must buy that book of hers when it's published."

Melody didn't need to give a full explanation to Celia since she already understood why Melody had to leave and held her hand until Sally came to say that young Doctor Courtney was waiting with the carriage.

"I've got this strange feeling of déjà vu," said Melody, as the carriage travelled through the countryside and the outskirts of Colchester came into sight.

"Why's that?" smiled Alex.

"People keep throwing me off the premises."

He chuckled, but then became serious. "But you shouldn't have been asked to leave Oaklands. Mother was in the wrong. In fact, she's been in the wrong about you right from the beginning and I shouldn't have listened to her."

She turned to look at him. "You don't regret marrying Celia do you? She's a lovely girl and now you've got a son and a daughter." She giggled. "You're a family man."

Alex smiled. "No I don't regret marrying her." He paused. "But I often wonder what my life would have been like if we had married."

"I would have refused to live with your mother," she said.

He kissed her hand. "And that's probably what I needed. Someone to tell me straight."

"Can I tell you straight now?"

"Why not. Fire away."

"I think you should leave Oaklands and find a house of your own. Celia needs to be mistress of her own home, to bring up her children the way she thinks best."

Alex nodded slowly. "I was thinking the same thing myself."

"Well, you already have a house in Colchester."

"I was thinking of London, actually."

Her mouth fell open in surprise. "London! You want to move back to the capital?"

"Yes, Jenner wants to leave the hospital. He's suggested we set up in practice together."

"That would be wonderful."

"Is the house in Hyde Park Gardens still for rent?"

"It was the last time I heard."

"Then I think I'll be taking a little trip to London in the near future."

Melody smiled with delight. Alex and Celia would be living on the far side of the park, in easy reach. She would be able to visit them and see the babies grow. They arrived at the station just in time for the train.

As Melody took her bag and climbed aboard she held out her hand. "Friends?"

He shook her hand. "Always."

It was gone six o'clock when the train wheezed its way into Paddington Station. Melody had spent the best part of the journey nodding off to sleep, only waking up as the engine clanked and hissed to a halt at every station on the way. The sun still had three hours before setting and the sky overhead was a glorious blue. But in the west, dark clouds were gathering and a rainstorm looked imminent. It wouldn't be long before the sun sank behind the ominous veil, plunging the city into premature darkness. Melody caught a cab and soon it was pulling up in front of number four, Hill Street, Mayfair.

She knocked lightly on the door and Tilly answered. "Oh, miss, we didn't expect you until tomorrow."

"I know, but I decided to come home early. Where's the master?"

"He's in the sitting room." She took Melody's coat and bonnet. "Dinner will be in forty minutes. I'll set another place at the table."

Melody stepped into the room and saw her husband in the armchair, his legs stretched out in front of him. It looked as though he had been reading as an open book lay on his lap, one hand resting on the pages. He had dropped off to sleep, his head slightly bowed. Melody knelt by the chair and holding his face between her hands, brushed her lips against his.

He stirred. "Dear God," he murmured. "My dreams are starting to feel real." His eyelashes flickered and then he opened his eyes. "Well, you look like my wife. But you can't be since she's in Colchester. So, who are you, madam?"

"Oh, just someone passing the door and wanting to spend the evening with you."

"And the night?" he whispered.

She tilted her head. "If you wish."

He sat bolt upright and pulled her into his arms and this time his kiss was passionate, demanding and full of the yearning he had had for her while she had been away.

CHAPTER TWENTY-SEVEN

Alex moved his family from Oaklands with breathtaking swiftness. Even while Celia was recovering from the birth of her twins, he had travelled to London and secured the lease on number fourteen, Hyde Park Gardens. He had also consulted with Doctor Christian Jenner and they had decided to set up in practice, renting three rooms on the ground floor in the same building where Christian already lived. It was accessed by a private door leading from an alleyway and as the two young doctors viewed what would be their surgeries and waiting room, they nodded with approval. It was agreed that Christian would organise the redecoration and refurbishment of the rooms, while Alex concentrated on his new family.

And only six weeks after Melody had left Oaklands, Alex and Celia were on their way to their new home. They didn't travel alone since a housemaid and footman came with them and Mrs Carr had obtained an excellent cook for them. Sally came too, but not as an under parlour maid but as the nursery maid of Henry and Georgina Courtney, the new additions to the Courtney family.

Losing her son pierced Davina Courtney like an arrow through the heart. All her pleading, all her arguments, had no affect on him whatsoever. He was determined to remove his family from her clutches and the day they left was met with tears and grasping hands that he removed gently but firmly from his sleeve, turning cold eyes away from her imploring face that had aged beyond recognition.

Everyone was there to meet them and help them settle in.

"Oh, I can't believe I'm back," cried Celia, as she danced around the sitting room that she had once shared with Melody and Olivia.

Melody looked about her. "It looks the same, but seems different too."

Celia burst into happy laughter. "That's because it smells of babies now."

Melody sniffed the air. "Is that what the strange aroma is? I was beginning to wonder."

"Don't you overdo it, Celia," called Olivia from the kitchen. "You still need to take it easy."

Celia took Melody's arm. "Thank you, thank you, thank you. I'm so happy."

"What did I do?" asked Melody in surprise.

"Far more than you'll ever imagine," said Celia, with a wink.

The surgery was also coming along well and with a fresh coat of whitewash, second-hand although serviceable furniture and the cabinets filled with new and gleaming instruments, everything was ready for the first patients to come through the door.

"I think they'll do very well," said Melody, as she sat down to dinner. "Two, young and handsome doctors should bring a lot of custom."

"Yes, especially from the female kind of a certain age," murmured Olivia.

"Now don't be unkind to Christian," giggled Melody. "I think he's a wonderful doctor and he's probably given up his philandering ways."

"Philandering ways? What's this all about?" asked Guy, shaking out his napkin and placing it across his knee.

Olivia made eyes at Melody. "Well, you started it, my girl. You explain."

Melody cleared her throat and tried to describe Christian's behaviour with his middle-aged amours. By the time she had stumbled through the necessary adjectives and verbs, Guy was shaking with laughter so much, he spilt his soup on the tablecloth.

"I must admit, I would never have thought it of him," he said, dabbing the stain with his napkin.

"But that was last year. He's probably very different now," reflected Melody. She paused before adding, "That's why Celia and I fell out."

Guy frowned. He remembered that his wife and her best friend had had an argument the year before after Melody had attended the funeral of the tenth Baron Sinclair. And he now understood why she had returned to work dispirited and careworn, but she had never actually clarified the reason behind their falling out.

"You had an argument about Doctor Jenner?"

Melody swallowed a lump in her throat and looked towards her aunt. "I…discovered that Celia had…was enamoured of Christian and I felt it was my duty as a friend…to tell her…that Christian wouldn't be…Oh Guy, don't look at me like that!"

He took her hand and kissed it. "Angel, I know you meant well, but Celia would have probably realised that herself when Doctor Jenner failed to show any interest in her."

Melody squirmed with embarrassment. "I know that now. But at the time I didn't want her to get hurt."

The brigadier nodded. "Yes, that's Melody for you. She must protect the vulnerable and fight lost causes."

"Then you must read her book when it comes out in September," said Guy. "What's it called? 'The Silent Voice'?"

Melody lifted her chin defiantly. "No, I changed it."

"You never told me that."

"I only decided yesterday when Sir Jack wanted me to confirm the title for publication."

"So, what's the new title?"

Melody linked her fingers and placed her hands on the tablecloth in front of her and then removed them when Tilly brought in the main course. "It was after Celia had the twins. A boy and a girl. In a way, she had brought the essence of life into the world. Male and female. In the Bible it says that woman is made from man's rib and since my work is about the plight of women, I decided to call it 'Adam's Rib'."

"What a wonderful title," smiled Guy.

Melody looked at him sternly. "Yes, but I've put a note in the front that because woman is made from a bone in man's side it must mean she is meant to walk beside him. If God had wanted us to be subservient, then surely he would have created us from a bone in his foot."

The brigadier chuckled. "There's no arguing with that."

Melody became more thoughtful. "It's a pity the book has already gone for publication. I'd have liked to add a little more to the chapter on 'Learning about Life' and include a section on motherhood."

"What!" exclaimed Olivia. "You can't write about things like that!"

Guy gave an apologetic cough. "She's already written about the ignorance expected of a young girl on her wedding night."

"I didn't realise your book would include those kind of details," said Olivia. "But a young girl is not expected to know things like that."

Melody smiled. "We've had this kind of argument before. Do you remember? In the early days in Hyde

Park Gardens when I asked if you'd have liked a more thorough education."

"Yes, I do remember, my dear. And I also remember telling you that you'll be offending the sensibilities of society."

"With all due respect, Olivia," said Guy. "Melody's female section in the Journal is a great success and her mailbag from her disciples needs two postmen to carry it."

Olivia shook her head. "But you must have your critics?"

"Yes, of course I do," nodded Melody. "But they're mostly from men who feel threatened. And they only feel threatened because they're afraid that education for women will upset the existing state of affairs." She took a sip of her wine.

"So, what you're saying," said Olivia slowly. "Is that women should be informed about the important events in their lives? The moments that are uniquely female?"

"Exactly, Aunt. Men make the rules and these rules are from a man's perspective. But there are things that only we women will experience and childbirth is one of them. An expectant mother shouldn't be left in ignorance. She should be told what is going to happen. I think it will allay her anxieties and prepare her. Why must pregnancy be treated as though it's something to be ashamed of? We are Woman and we should be proud of it."

"Unfortunately, I didn't have a child," said Olivia sadly. "But I understand what you mean and now you've explained it that way, I must agree."

Melody smiled. She had gained another convert that evening.

They had been invited to dine with Celia and Alex. It was the first time the young couple had entertained since moving to London and it would also be the first meeting between Alex and Guy.

"Are you nervous?" asked Melody, as they journeyed to Hyde Park Gardens in the cab.

"Certainly not," he said. "It's about time I met your friends."

The muscles in his jaw tensed and Melody turned her head away to hide her smile.

But when they arrived, their welcome couldn't have been more cordial. Alex shook his hand vigorously and Celia smiled with delight. During dinner, Alex talked enthusiastically about his new surgery and how he and Christian were already receiving a full waiting room of patients after opening only three days.

"Of course, not all the patients can pay in cash," said Alex.

"So, do they bring eggs and chickens like they did at Saint George's?" laughed Melody.

Celia laughed with her. "My dear husband doesn't mind eggs as long as they can be divided by two. A chicken is a little more complicated so we usually invite Christian to dinner then he can share it."

"So, how do you pay your bills?" asked Guy.

"Oh, I still receive the coin of the realm when I visit my private patients."

"One day, Alex will have impressive consulting rooms in Grosvenor Square," said Celia proudly.

"Mmm. Do you mean like Sir Charles Piper?" smiled Melody.

Alex turned his head towards her detecting a note of contempt. "But I thought he treated you very well during your recovery? Don't you like him?"

Melody grimaced. "In a nutshell, no I don't! I think Sir Charles is just a bag of hot air. He's more interested in making money than treating the sick."

"Unfortunately, earning money from one's profession is a necessary evil," sighed Alex. "No one can afford to be completely charitable."

After they had dined they adjourned to the sitting room and the conversation continued over coffee. And then Sally brought the babies down from the nursery. Celia rushed to her and took Georgina in her arms.

"They've started putting on weight. But I'll be glad when a few more months have passed. They're not yet eight weeks old."

Melody rose from her seat and took Henry from Sally and carried him over to the window where she murmured softly to him, pointing out the 'birdies' that were singing in the branches of the trees. Guy watched her. He had never seen his wife holding a baby and the image brought a lump to his throat. It was a sweet, feminine scene and as she tilted her head and smiled at the infant in her arms he couldn't remember seeing such an appealing sight. But then he glanced at Alex and his heart started pounding.

He was watching too, his eyes showing his feelings so plainly. Dear Lord, thought Guy with dismay, he still loves her. Is he thinking she should have been his wife and the baby should be theirs? Guy stared down at the rug. Suddenly all the years behind him began to pile up like a gigantic tidal wave. He had lived a respectable, honourable life, with a marriage and a few love affairs along the way, but he had experienced much and his eyes had seen more than any man's should. If only he were younger, just ten years. What a difference that would have made.

"Would you like a drink, Guy? Brandy or port?" asked Alex.

Guy turned his head and smiled. "Yes, a brandy would be very welcome."

He drank it back in one gulp.

"Did you enjoy yourself tonight, angel?" he asked, as he climbed into bed next to her.

"I had a wonderful time," she smiled. "Did you?"

"It was very pleasant. Celia and Alex are charming."

"I'm so glad they're living in Hyde Park Gardens now. I'll be able to see Celia often and watch the twins grow."

"And see Alex," he murmured.

She waited until he had made himself comfortable. "Does that still trouble you? That Alex and I were once betrothed?"

Guy pulled the pillow up under his head and looked at her. Her eyes seemed darker in the light from the lamp and he could see her anxiety. "Well, he still has feelings for you. I saw that tonight."

"He chose Celia and I chose you. What Alex feels about me is quite irrelevant."

"Let the past stay in the past," he sighed.

"Yes."

Guy bent to kiss her lips. "He's a fine young man and you'd have made a lovely couple."

She snuggled down next to him. "Alex said he knew that I was in love with you, even before I knew it myself."

"He knew?"

Melody nodded. "He told me when I was visiting them in Essex. He said that my expression changed every time I mentioned your name.

Guy couldn't help smiling. "That must have been uncomfortable for him."

"We argued about you the night we broke up."

"Did you?"

"He thought I was having a secret affair with you."

"What on earth gave him that idea?"

Melody didn't answer. A strange thought had suddenly entered her head. Something she hadn't realised but now it seemed so obvious.

"When did you first meet Christian?"

Guy frowned showing his bewilderment at her change in topic. "When you had your accident and he rushed over from the hospital. Why?"

"You hadn't met him before that?"

"Never set eyes on him."

She turned onto her side to face him, spreading her fingers on his chest. "Christian told Alex that he'd seen us come out of the Cavendish Hotel."

"When were we at the Cavendish while you were engaged to Alex?"

"When I was having luncheon alone and you happened by."

Guy tried to remember and then smiled. "Oh yes, of course. The day after you brought me the cheque from Sir Jack. I had an appointment and just glanced into the dining room and there you were."

"Christian must have been passing too and saw us. And when we came out together, he assumed the worst."

"And passed all his assumptions on to your fiancé?" He gave a sigh. "Oh dear, I would call that contemptible."

She nodded. "Even though it was perfectly innocent, Alex misunderstood." She paused for a moment. "But how did Christian know it was you, if you had never met?"

Guy took her hand from his chest and kissed her fingers. "Actually, that's not such a mystery. Editors of newspapers tend to be infamous and we get pointed out on frequent occasions. I've lost count how many times I've been introduced to someone and they've said they know me by repute."

Melody wasn't quite convinced. "I suppose when he saw us together he guessed you were the editor, but it was wrong of him to assume it was a clandestine meeting." She stifled a yawn. "He did apologise to Alex for spreading such malicious gossip so I should forgive him."

Minutes of silence passed as Guy looked up at the ceiling. He pulled her closer and kissed the top of her head. "Angel, you looked so lovely this evening when you were holding the baby. It made me hope...If we had a child, then my life would be complete."

He turned to look at her and smiled. She was asleep.

The church was hushed as the Reverend Wilfred Ansell conducted the christening ceremony, the eleven people standing round the font listening to the melodious words that reverberated off the stone walls and round the nave. Aunt Olivia stood beside the brigadier, Doctor Christian Jenner was next to Sally, the nursery maid, with Georgina in her arms and now and again he would bend his head and smile at the sleeping baby. Alex and Celia stood together with the mother holding baby Henry. And then there was Mrs Carr, dressed in her best Sunday hat. Doctor and Mrs Courtney stayed further back from the rest, as if they didn't want to intrude. Lastly, there was Melody and Guy who had come to stand as godparents to the twins.

Melody looked around the church and her eyes rested on Mrs Courtney. How she had changed. No longer the elegant beauty she once was, she now seemed smaller and frailer. She was watching her son with longing. Melody sighed, remembering the terrible time the previous June when the twins had been born. But she could feel no sympathy for Mrs Courtney; she had lost her family through her own selfish and possessive ways and had only herself to blame.

Melody turned her attention to the service. The reverend had taken Georgina from Sally and poured water over the small head. She didn't stir. Henry protested loudly when it came to his turn and the church echoed to his cries of discomfort. The babies were dressed in beautiful silk christening gowns; Georgina wearing the one Celia had worn at her christening and Henry wearing Alex's. They were both wrapped in soft woollen shawls and on their heads were lace bonnets, removed only for the baptism.

"Don't they look sweet," whispered Melody to Guy.

He put his arm round her and pulled her closer. "Yes, they do," he said.

Melody's thoughts turned to the publication of her book. This was due out in just two weeks' time and she couldn't wait to see all her hard work in print. She wanted it in the bookshops but more than that, she wanted it to be read and appreciated. Guy had warned her that there would be many critics and there was a chance that it wouldn't be well received. But Melody prayed that it would be welcomed and that it would radically change the thinking of society.

And then the day came when Eric was waiting at the door of the Journal when she arrived back that bright September afternoon. "Miss Melody, Sir Jack's here with the first copies of your book." Eric's freckled face glowed with enthusiasm. "Everyone is waiting for you in Mr Wyngate's office."

Melody followed Eric who took the stairs two at a time. He was right, since everyone seemed to be crowded in the editor's room. Marsh was trying to keep order, but he was being ignored. Guy stood with his uncle, smiling proudly as Eric and Melody burst through the door.

"I've brought six copies for you to look at, my dear," said Sir Jack. "Come and see them for yourself."

Everyone parted like the Red Sea, letting Melody make her way to Guy's desk. There was a brown box on the top and sitting snugly within were the first prints. With shaking hands, she lifted one out. It was bound in thin blue leather with 'Adam's Rib' and her name embossed in silver on the front. She flicked through the pages and gasped. It was so strange to see her work in print. Every chapter was numbered and titled, a drawing illustrating the start of each one. She turned to the one entitled 'Shattered Dreams'. Eric's drawing of a young girl standing on a street corner seemed very poignant. She passed it to Eric to see. He grinned from ear to ear at his handiwork.

"It's wonderful," she said and then whispered. "Thank you."

And then the room was filled with tumultuous noise as she was cheered and everyone shook her hand. Marsh had had enough and shooed everyone out and back to their duties.

"So, you're happy with it?" Sir Jack asked Melody.

"I'm more than happy. I just hope people will read it."

"I'm sure they will," said Guy. He picked up three letters. "Sir Jack has had correspondence from the

Continent, Ireland and America wanting copies of your book."

Melody's eyes opened wide. "Goodness me. But it's only just come out here."

"Yes, but booksellers get wind of a good publication very quickly and they're always eager to share in the profits."

Melody nodded. "So, what happens now?"

"I start printing more copies as fast as I can," laughed Sir Jack.

She began to feel a little nauseated. It must be the excitement, she thought. She looked at the watch pinned to her bodice. Five o'clock again. She always felt sick at five o'clock in the afternoon. She had been very busy since coming back to work after their honeymoon, her pace of life quickening with each passing day. She always rushed her mid-day meal and Guy had often told her to slow down or she would make herself ill. But Melody had too much to do and the sickness continued.

CHAPTER TWENTY-EIGHT

Guy clasped his hands behind his back and looked down at his shoes. Melody stared at him, surprise making her speechless. An endless amount of time seemed to elapse before he felt compelled to ask, "Well, what do you think?"

"Live in America?"

"Just for a couple of years and then we'll come back to England."

"Two years?"

"You'll need that long to meet all the pioneering women you've been reading about, plus promoting your book. Sir Jack believes it will be well received over there. And the letter from Miss Anthony proves it."

The letter had arrived three days earlier from Susan Anthony, the American suffragette that Melody had interviewed the day she had gone to Guy's house and proposed to him. Miss Anthony had now returned to America and a copy of Melody's book had finally reached her. The letter was inviting her to do a series of talks in Miss Anthony's native country and Melody had laughed and told Guy that it was a long way to go to talk about a book. But Guy had pondered on it and his suggestion that evening after dinner had stunned her.

"But what will you do while I'm travelling around?" she asked.

"I'm eager to see how the country is coping after the war. And I also want to look into the new newspaper techniques they're using. For example, they're always developing new ways of improving print and there's even talk of putting photographs in newspapers." He grinned. "Instead of being an artist Eric can become a photographer."

"Where will we live?"

"New York City. We can lease a house so we'll always have somewhere to hang our hats." Melody glanced round the cream and terracotta sitting room that she loved so much. Guy noticed and came to sit beside her. "It's only a suggestion, angel. If you want to stay in London then we will."

"It sounds exciting but what about Mrs Carr and Tilly?"

"They can come with us if they wish."

Melody thought this over. New York City sounded wonderful and she caught her breath in excitement. "And the Journal?"

"Sir Jack will be more than happy to take it on. It's only for a few years and he's always said that retirement is much overrated."

Melody studied Guy for a few seconds and then nodded. "Let's do it. Let's make plans now." She threw her arms round her husband's neck.

He hugged her. "Well, we're going to have to go soon," he laughed. "It won't be very enjoyable crossing the Atlantic in winter so we must go by the end of next month."

Melody felt stunned. "At the end of next month?"

"Well, it's September now and I think the end of October should be our deadline. Of course we could wait until spring…"

"No," said Melody, shaking her head. "It gives us a full month to prepare. That's ample time. I want to do it now before something comes along to change my mind."

The next three weeks were a mixture of chaos and sadness. Chaos simply because of the amount of work needed in organising their removal to America, and sadness because of fond farewells from their friends in London.

Soon the house in Hill Street was filled with packing trunks and precious pieces of china, silver and glassware were lovingly stored away for the journey. Dinner invitations from friends arrived regularly and the goodbyes seemed endless, everyone wanting to express their sadness at the departure of Mr and Mrs Wyngate. Melody's excitement increased with each passing day as did Mrs Carr and Tilly's. They too had been shocked at the idea but when told they would be needed they agreed wholeheartedly.

"Well, I never thought I would be leaving England," said Tilly, as she helped Mrs Carr pack yet another trunk. Her eyes sparkled. "But it will be such an adventure. And when we come back I'll have such a lot of stories to tell my brothers and sisters."

Mrs Carr smiled. Tilly had just gone twenty and there was a chance the young woman would never return to England with them. She would meet her future husband in America and settle down there. She gave a sigh. If that happened then so be it. There was nothing she could do about it, but she would miss her.

It was a week before their departure. They were booked on the U.S.S. Alabama bound for America from Southampton. And it seemed everyone was going to wave them off, even Alex and Celia intended to be on the quayside to see the ship leave port.

Melody stood in the street and waited. It was twenty minutes to one o'clock and she knew the surgery closed soon for the rest of the day. She looked up at the men working on the building opposite, re-tiling the roof. I hope they don't fall, she thought, it's a long way down. She made her way along the narrow alley and pushed open the door that led into the small parlour-like waiting room. She was just in time to see a young woman with a small boy disappear into Alex's surgery. Good, thought Melody that means Christian will be the next to call a patient. She sat down and waited. Ten minutes later, Alex's door opened and the young woman appeared with her arm round the boy, his left hand bandaged.

"Keep the dressing on for the next week and try to keep it dry," said Alex. He looked round and saw Melody. "Goodness me. What are doing here? I would have come to your home for a private consultation."

She shook her head. "No, I must take my turn like everyone else." She stood and followed him into the surgery.

"Now what can I do for you," he said, gesturing to the seat by his desk.

"Where's Christian?" she asked, as she sat down.

"Oh, he works at Saint George's on a Saturday, so I hold the fort while he's away."

Melody bit her lip. She had really hoped to see Doctor Jenner. "I think I might be…with child," she said, her face flushing.

It would have been much better if she could have told this to Christian. After all, she and Alex had been engaged and it didn't seem right for him to know her private business.

Alex nodded. "When did you last see your monthly bleed?"

This question seemed strange coming from him. "It was after I visited you at Oaklands. July I think," she answered quietly.

"So, that makes it three months?" She nodded. "Any sickness?"

"Five o'clock every blessed afternoon."

Alex chuckled. "Well, the expression 'morning sickness' must be taken lightly. It can happen any time of the day. Jump up on the couch and I'll make a quick examination." Melody lay down and lifted her skirt. Alex pressed on the lower part of her abdomen, right above her womb. Melody's blushes deepened. Alex took her arm and helped her onto her feet. "You certainly are expecting a child," he said. "And by my estimation that makes you due about April."

"In time for our first wedding anniversary," said Melody with delight.

"How do you feel about this with travelling to America?"

"It will be all right won't it? I mean I'm quite healthy," she said, taking a seat once more.

"You're exceptionally healthy. I'm just wondering what your husband will think about it."

"I'm not going to tell him."

"You're not?"

"Please don't tell him, Alex," she said, watching him.

"I don't think it's my place to tell him although there are many doctors who would. But he needs to know, Melody."

"Oh, I'm going to tell him eventually. But when we're aboard the Alabama or perhaps when we're settled in New York City."

He frowned. "Why do you want to wait?"

"Because he'll start worrying about me and I don't want him cancelling the trip."

"It's up to you when you tell him." His gaze swept over her and he smiled. "Celia tells me you're calling on us this afternoon?"

"I have a gift for the babies, but I won't be staying for long. Aunt Olivia and the brigadier are visiting and

Guy and I are meeting them on the six o'clock train, so I must be home before then."

"Well, don't overdo it and get plenty of rest."

Melody jumped to her feet. "Yes, Doctor." She headed for the door before he could rise from his chair and she was gone before he could say goodbye.

Alex smiled and thought about the woman he might have married. Perhaps everything had turned out for the best. He was very happy with Celia, his devoted wife and wonderful mother to his children. Melody needed a different kind of husband. There was no doubt that Guy Wyngate was the right man for her. But look out America, she'll be like a whirlwind, chuckled Alex, as he locked up for the day.

Melody took her time travelling through the park after visiting Celia. She smiled at the memory of Celia's happy face, now content in her own home with a husband and two beautiful children. And Melody felt happy too, for she couldn't wish for more in life than she had now. As Sultan ambled along, she enjoyed the warm autumn sun on her face and the beauty of the trees. She looked up at the cascade of falling leaves; the browns and oranges of the season filling her with delight. Smiling at the news that Alex had given her, she resolved that she would tell Guy soon, but not yet. She knew him so well and he would be concerned for her health and want to stay in London. And she wanted to go to America.

Eventually she reached Speakers' Corner and to her surprise she saw Christian walking past the park gates, obviously coming from the hospital as he carried his medical bag. She reined in Sultan and called his name.

He stopped and walked across to her. "Good afternoon, Melody," he said, smiling. "You look extremely well."

"I feel very well, thanks to you."

He smiled. "Not all my doing, I assure you." He paused, reflecting for a moment. "I haven't seen much of you since the christening."

"You must come to dinner before we leave. Yes and bring your grandmother with you."

"She's visiting me at the moment."

"How wonderful for you."

"Except she's rather poorly, I'm afraid."

"Oh, I'm so sorry to hear that. What's the matter with her?"

Christian shrugged. "Bronchitis mostly. Mixed with old age."

"Does she have anyone caring for her?"

"I'm her doctor and nurse at present."

Melody gasped. "But you have to work. How does she manage when you're not there?"

"She's used to living alone and she's quite independent. She manages."

Melody felt guilty. Mrs Hunneybell was a lovely woman, a lady of ample proportions, of a strong constitution and used to 'managing'. But she was also in her late sixties and a life of hard work on a farm would debilitate the health of anyone.

"I really ought to visit her if she's ill," said Melody, thinking of the friendly woman who had always busied herself with other people's comfort. "I did think of visiting her at the farm before Guy and I left for America."

"Yes, I heard about your trip to the States. Quite an adventure."

"Tell your grandmother I will come and see her before we sail."

"I think she'd like that, when you have time, that is." He paused for a moment. "Why don't you come now?"

"Now?" Melody looked at her watch.

"I'm on my way home and it's not far."

"I can't, Christian. I'm so sorry, but I really can't."

He smiled. "Not to worry. You can always visit later. It's just that she often speaks of you. It would have been nice to have a cup of tea with her."

"Oh, I don't know. I have to be home for five at the latest. Aunt Olivia and the brigadier are coming to visit and we're meeting their train."

Christian's expression suddenly changed. He blew out a long breath. "I know Gran would really like to see you, but I'll tell her I spoke with you and you're well. You can always visit another time."

The guilt became even stronger. "Well, I could spare fifteen minutes, I suppose," she murmured.

He raised his hand to the brim of his hat and smiled. "No, don't trouble yourself. I must say goodbye and get back to her."

Melody watched him cross the road. "Wait," she called and he turned. "All right, I'll come and see your grandmother. As long as I get home before five."

He walked back to her, grinning with delight. "Gran will be so pleased to see you. It'll cheer her up and go a long way in making her feel better." He glanced at the horse and gig. "Leave that here. Better to walk."

"Leave it?" asked Melody feeling puzzled.

"Well, the alley is too narrow for vehicles and you can't park in the street. We had a bit of a disaster this afternoon. The men working on the building opposite lost a whole load of tiles. The cobbles are covered with them and it's been advised that horses be kept away.

Don't want any tiny bits of slate in their hooves. Sultan will be fine here."

Melody climbed down from the gig.

"Hold your horse for tuppence, miss," said a crisp, clear voice close by.

A young boy about eight years old, his clothes in need of repair and his face and hands in need of soap and water, stood next to the drinking trough.

Melody smiled. "If you look after him well and make sure he has a good drink, I'll give you sixpence when I come back."

The boy's eyes sparkled. "Yes, miss. I'll mind the horse and make sure no one comes near him."

"Good. I won't be long but you'll have to be patient."

"I'm patient, miss. Everyone says that about me."

She patted his cheek and he watched the lady and gentleman walk up the road and disappear round the corner. He led the horse over to the trough and let him drink and then climbed aboard the gig. He snuggled down on the seat. He might as well sleep while he waited.

Christian kept up a constant chatter as they walked along. Melody enjoyed his friendly manner, but felt uneasy. Perhaps she shouldn't have done this. Now that she was with him she wished she had been firmer and told him that she would visit another time.

Melody studied the young man walking next to her. He looked so young and strangely vulnerable and yet he had helped his mother and grandmother run the farm from an infant. He had chased away the crows at five years old, had learned to plough and harvest and look after a small herd of dairy cattle. He knew what it was like to rise with the sun, work all day, and stop working only with the sun setting. And yet from the age of eight he had received an excellent education, attending good schools including Eton. And then gone on to train as a doctor and an amazing one at that. She would always be grateful to him for his care after her accident.

"Here we are," he murmured, as they reached the front door.

The ground floor was taken over by the surgery with it's own private entrance in the alley, but the lodgings were accessed by the main door on the street.

"There doesn't seem to be many tiles here," she said, looking down at the cobbles.

He raised his eyebrows in surprise. "Goodness me, it looks like they've been cleared away already. They've certainly been quick about it."

Seeing Melody wince and place a hand in the small of her back, he smiled kindly. "Come in and have a rest," he said, guiding her through the door.

"I'll need it and a cup of tea," she laughed.

They climbed the stairs to the first floor and then turned at the landing to go further up to the top floor of the house.

Christian opened the door and let her go first into the sitting room. "Let me take your coat and bonnet and then I'll see if Gran's awake."

"Please don't disturb her if she's asleep."

Christian gave a broad grin. "She'll be upset with me if I don't," he said, disappearing into the bedroom.

Melody placed her purse on the table and spent the next few minutes looking at the three portraits on the dresser, all done in a photographer's studio. She recognised a youthful Christian standing behind a seated Mrs Hunneybell and then there was one of an elderly gentleman with large whiskers that she thought must be the late Mr Hunneybell. And finally there was one of a much younger Christian with a beautiful woman Melody took to be his mother. She was so engrossed in the photographs that she was hardly aware of the sudden movement at her back.

Suddenly, Christian's left arm encircled her, trapping her arms. His right hand held a wad of gauze that he pressed hard against her nose and mouth. It hurt and she struggled against him trying to release herself from his iron grip. She kicked out and her legs banged against the dresser scattering the photographs on the floor. He was far too strong. And so was the noxious odour emanating from the gauze. She could hardly breathe and yet breathe she must, the toxic fumes of chloroform making her light-headed until she was falling into darkness that was blacker than night.

CHAPTER TWENTY-NINE

Guy and Olivia came out onto the steps and he looked at his watch.

"She wanted to come to the station with me," he said, frowning.

Olivia nodded. "Well, you know what Melody is like. She's probably met someone and forgotten the time."

"Well, it's nearly seven. Where the blazes can she be."

"Don't worry she'll turn up sooner or later," she said.

Guy sighed and looked at his watch again. "Dinner will be served in half an hour, and she's usually home by now. I'll go and see if she's still at the Journal, although Marsh should have locked up an hour ago."

Olivia suddenly had an idea. "Perhaps she's gone to visit Celia and the twins."

"Yes, that's probably where she is," he nodded, relieved that there might be a tangible reason for her lateness. Guy saw a passing cab and hailed it. He waved as he jumped in. "Don't worry, I'll bring her back."

In ten minutes, he was knocking on the door of number fourteen Hyde Park Gardens. The maid showed him into the sitting room.

Alex jumped to his feet. "Guy? Goodness me, we didn't expect you this evening."

Guy quickly glanced around dismayed to see that Melody wasn't with them. "I'm looking for Melody," he said.

Alex frowned. "Hasn't she arrived home yet? She left nearly two hours ago."

Guy caught his breath. "Two hours ago?"

"Yes, she said the brigadier and Mrs Timme were arriving to spend the final week with you and she was eager to meet them at the station."

"She didn't turn up," said Guy, biting his lip. "I went alone, thinking she would be home by the time we got back, but she hasn't returned yet."

"Was she going anywhere else?" asked Celia.

"I don't think so."

"You know Melody, she can get diverted when she comes across something interesting," she laughed.

"Perhaps she was waylaid by a news story," suggested Alex.

Guy shook his head. "I'd better return to Hill Street. Who knows she might be home by now."

Alex stood. "I'll accompany you home. If your wife hasn't returned then we can both look for her. Let's go out by the kitchen door to the stables and I'll collect the phaeton."

Guy nodded grateful to have some support.

Soon they were aboard the phaeton and trotting through Hyde Park en route to Mayfair. Alex glanced at Guy's tense profile. He couldn't tell Guy that Melody had consulted him that day and he guessed that Guy didn't yet know that he was to become a father.

At Speakers' Corner, Alex pulled up abruptly. "Goodness me, there's Sultan."

Guy jumped down. In moments he was stroking the horse's nose, causing him to neigh.

"Hoi! Keep your hands off that horse, mister."

Guy hadn't noticed the small child curled up asleep on the seat. The neighing horse had disturbed the boy who was annoyed to see a stranger taking an interest in his charges. He wanted that sixpence. The boy scrambled down and flung himself at Guy.

"Steady on, there," cried Guy. He didn't know whether to feel pleased at finding Melody's transport, or cross at the child's outburst.

"Said she'd give me sixpence if I did a good job."

"Who did?"

"The nice lady did."

"Can you tell me where she went?"

"What's it to you?"

Alex came to join them and frowned at the young scamp with dirt smeared across his face. He knew from past experience that a child from the lower classes never gave information free of charge. Guy would have to put his hand in his pocket.

"She's my wife," said Guy. "And this is her horse and gig. I'm looking for her and I'm worried that she might have taken ill."

"Didn't look ill when she went off with that gentleman."

Guy frowned. "What gentleman?"

The boy pressed his lips together and Guy dipped into his pocket and gave him some pennies.

"The gentleman she was talking to. The gentleman with the bag," said the boy, staring at the coppers in his hand.

"Do you know who he was?"

"Nope."

"Which way did they go?"

The boy pointed down the road. "Down there past the church."

Guy thought for a moment. "What kind of bag was he carrying?"

"Big one and black, I think. Couldn't really see."

"Could have been a doctor's bag," ventured Alex.

Guy began to feel desperate and wished the child was a little older. "Can you describe him?"

"You only gave me tuppence, you know!"

Guy resisted the urge to clip the boy's ear and pressed another penny into his hand.

"Tall. About that man's age," said the child, pointing at Alex.

"What colour was his hair?"

"Don't know. He was wearing a hat."

Alex decided to question him. "Do you remember anything about him? Anything at all?"

"Snazzy tie-pin."

"What was it like?"

"I think it was gold. Shiny." He hesitated before saying, "A bit like a flower."

Alex nodded. "That'll be Doctor Jenner. He sometimes wears a tie-pin in the shape of a four-leaf clover."

"Well, if she's with Christian, she can't have come to any harm," said Guy, a feeling of relief sweeping through him.

"But why would she go anywhere with Jenner?"

Guy thought for a moment. "Perhaps she had some questions for him. You know Melody, always doing research on something or other."

"Well, if that's the case, they might have gone to the surgery or to Christian's lodgings," suggested Alex, walking back to the phaeton.

Guy smiled down at the boy. "Would you like to earn another sixpence?"

"Haven't got first one yet," grumbled the child.

Guy groped through his pockets and pressed the silver coin into his dirty palm. "Look after the horse and gig until I come back for it."

"Yes, sir. Thank you." His eyes shone with happiness.

Guy left the boy staring down at the glittering treasure in his hand. He jumped into the phaeton next to Alex who was already in the driver's seat and urging the horse forward. They set off for the building that housed the surgery and lodgings of Doctor Christian Jenner.

Aunt Olivia had fastened her bracelet too tightly. The gold links were digging into her wrist making her cry out in pain. She struggled to tear it from her arm, but now her arm wouldn't move. She opened her eyes to the late afternoon sun, glaring through the window. Blinking hard, she tried to focus on her surroundings, aware that every muscle in her body ached. The smell of chloroform still lingered and made her retch. She had no idea how long she had been unconscious.

She was in the bedroom, but alone. Twisting herself to ease the ache in her back, she realised her arms were above her head, her hands tied at the wrist and secured to the metal frame of the bed on which she was lying. But it was so uncomfortable that the pain tore at her as she pulled on the length of bandage that secured her. She fought to release herself; her flailing feet crumpling the covers into tight ripples.

"Someone help me, please," she called, her mouth drying with terrible thirst.

"There's no use in struggling," said a soft voice. "You'll only hurt yourself." Christian came into the room.

"What have you done? Why have you tied me up?"

"To keep you still."

"Why, for goodness sake?"

"I didn't want you to escape. That's the only way to control a woman like you. Keep her tied up." He laughed. "Perhaps you would have been true to Alex if he'd tied you up."

"Christian, are you playing some sort of prank on me?" She couldn't believe that the doctor, who had been so gentle and considerate after her accident, was now sounding so harsh and cruel.

"No prank, Melody. I'm deadly serious."

"What do you mean, I wasn't true to Alex?"

"I saw the way that man looked at you, Melody. I knew what was going on."

"Who looked at me?"

"Guy Wyngate," said Christian. He said the name as if it was repugnant to him. "He always had his mind set on taking you from Alex."

"Guy was a good friend. My employer," she gasped. "I didn't realise I loved him until Alex and I had broken off our engagement." She struggled with her bonds. "Is that why you've made me a prisoner, because you believe I was unfaithful to Alex?"

Christian gave a laugh that made her blood run cold. "No, not really. Your behaviour is incidental. After all, you turned Alex down and he married foolish, little Celia, who made eyes at me as though I would be interested. I kept telling him to find a rich widow, but out of the frying pan into the fire, I say."

"Then what's this all about," she said, through her teeth.

"Wyngate, of course."

"Guy doesn't mean you any harm. He likes you. Admires you."

"But I don't like him and that makes a difference."

"I don't understand," she said, desperate to escape the discomfort. "Please untie me, my back is so painful."

He lit a lamp on the bureau and then sat on the edge of the mattress, gazing at her slender form lying on the bed. Caressing her neck, he then ran his hand over her breasts and then slowly stroked down to her thigh.

"I always wanted to touch you, even when I was treating you after your accident. Of course, it wouldn't have been ethical then."

She wanted to scream, but instead tried to control her breathing, forcing herself to stay calm. "Christian, please let me go. This will do no good."

"Alex was my friend and he disappointed me. That's the trouble with life, it's full of dreams and disappointments. But Wyngate shattered the most important dream of all."

Melody stopped struggling. "He wouldn't shatter anyone's dream," she said quietly. "He's a kind man and compassionate." She knew that her only hope was to win him round and persuade him to release her.

Christian ignored her. "Isn't fate strange? The way Alex became my friend, and he came to know you. Then you met Wyngate and led me to him."

"Please tell me why you're doing this, Christian."

"He thinks he's a war hero, medal from the queen and all. But he's no hero, he's a murderer."

"Murderer," she whispered. "Who did he murder?"

"My mother and father."

Her mind went numb. "I still don't understand."

He looked down at her, his blue eyes turning angry. "My real name is Menshikov. At least that would have been my name if my mother and father had been allowed to marry. But as you made clear to everyone, I was born a bastard." He waited for a response but Melody decided to remain silent. "Where was I? Oh yes, my father was Count Ivan Menshikov, distant cousin of the Tsar and a member of one of the most powerful and wealthy families in Russia."

"A foreign nobleman fell in love with your mother?" Melody suddenly remembered the conversation she had had with Alex, concerning Christian's lineage.

"Yes." His voice became softer as he remembered his mother. "And little wonder since she was the most beautiful and gentle woman that ever walked this earth. I was the result of that love, but his family spurned her and wouldn't let them marry. Make a decent woman of her, so to speak."

"That was unkind of them," she murmured, trying to keep her voice steady.

"He came to visit me and my mother at the farm, you know."

"You met him?"

"Oh yes, but only once. I thought him a decent chap for all that he was foreign. Spoke impeccable English. He told me that he was trying to persuade his family to accept my mother and he believed he was winning. When they married he would take us back to Russia and I would be his heir. But then the war came and my parents found themselves on opposite sides."

Melody struggled with the binding, but it was too tight. "Your father was a soldier?" If she could keep him talking, perhaps she could buy some time. Guy and the brigadier must be missing her. Surely they would come looking for her. Then she remembered she had left the horse and gig at Speakers' Corner and they would find it. Perhaps the child she had hired would tell them in what direction she had gone and just perhaps, Guy would be able to work out where she was.

"He was an officer. As you know my mother went out to the Crimea."

"To be a Nightingale nurse?"

He gave a derisive laugh. "Not for any altruistic reasons, you understand. She wanted to find my father. But then he was killed and she came home with a broken heart. And as you know, she died a year later."

"What has this to do with Guy? Why do you say he killed them? Surely the war did that."

"My mother died as a consequence of my father's death. And my father died as a result of Wyngate's actions. His so called bravery at the Battle of the River Alma."

With horror, Melody realised what he was saying. "When he threw the grenade at the gun emplacement, killing the soldiers?"

"Now it's becoming clear to you. Yes, one of those soldiers was my father. He was the commanding officer."

"But it was war, Christian. Guy didn't mean to kill them. It just happened."

"It just happened," he mimicked. "Wyngate had no business being there. He was a non-combatant for goodness sake."

"He told me all about it. The faces of those young men have haunted him ever since it happened. Christian, he bitterly regrets what he did." Melody saw a change in his expression and thought she might win him over. "If you talked to him, he would tell you this himself."

He rose to his feet, staring down at her. "It doesn't matter. What's done is done. All the talking in the world won't change anything. And as for the Russian side of my family, they don't want to know me." He reached for a second oil lamp standing nearby, lit it and held it in his hand. The sun was gone and it was dark outside. Melody turned her head to the window. The curtains were not drawn and she could see the moon. "Wyngate cheated me out of my inheritance. If my father had lived, he would have persuaded his family to accept my mother, I'm sure of it. Then I would have been wealthy beyond my wildest dreams."

He was looking at her like a tiger holding a gazelle in its claws.

Terror gripped her. "Christian, please let me go." It was almost a scream and he jerked back in alarm.

"Stop screaming."

Then she realised Mrs Hunneybell was somewhere about. Perhaps she could scream loud enough for her to hear.

"I won't stop screaming, Christian. I'll scream until your grandmother hears me."

He gave a lazy smile. "She's not here."

"What did you say?" She turned her head to look at him.

"Gran's back in Kent, on the farm." He gave a sigh of pleasure. "But I'm off to visit her when I'm finished with you."

"We're all alone?"

"There's no one here but you and me."

"What about the couple on the floor below?"

"Gone to visit their married daughter. No, there's only you and me in this building." Melody let out a scream that faded to a low moan. A look of disgust passed across his face. "I told you to stop screaming. Do you want me to gag you as well."

Melody watched him with dread. He moved slowly, stealthily like a cat, lifting the lamp higher and blinding her with its bright glow. She could hardly see, the discomfort causing her eyes to fill with tears. Her surroundings became blurred, a kaleidoscope of colour and movement.

"But why am I here?"

"Because you're his wife and Wyngate loves you with a passion."

"I don't understand. What's that got to do with it?"

"I had it all worked out, you know. I was going to shoot him. Even brought a shotgun from the farm. I picked my moment carefully. I'd been watching him and I knew what time he locked up the premises in Cork Street. I stood in an alley and waited. But he came out with you and you were in my sights. Had no reason to hurt you *then*."

"Then?"

He gave a low chuckle. "Then came your accident. I was summoned from Saint George's to help a person kicked by a horse. Of course, I didn't know it was you. In fact, I was shocked when I saw it was you. But then I thought of another plan." He stared at her, a slight smile playing on his lips. "It was the look on Wyngate's face as you were lying there." He grinned at the memory. "His utter pain and distress was pitiful to see. And then there were all those months during your recovery. I thought, this is a man who really loves the woman he's to marry."

"What are you planning to do with me?" she whispered.

"If I kill you then I destroy him. He'll live on, but without you. That will be his punishment. To suffer the same agony I have all these years."

Melody finally understood. "Christian, please don't hurt me." She said the next words slowly. "Please, Christian. I'm expecting a child."

He stared down at her in contempt. "Oh really, I'd have thought even you were above that."

She shook her head. "It's true. Really it is. Alex confirmed it this afternoon."

He gave a wry smile. "No, I don't think I'll fall for that old chestnut." Melody was filled with horror. Christian stepped closer, his words coming through his teeth. "They said my father burnt to death. His uniform caught fire when the grenade exploded. He ran around in a ball of flames, screaming in agony."

Melody looked up and saw him holding the lamp for a few seconds before throwing it into the corner. She watched in terror, as the chair caught fire and began to hiss and crack as the bright red and orange flames consumed the wood and fabric. In seconds it seemed to be fully alight and she could feel the heat from it, the shadows dancing eerily round the walls. She struggled with the bindings at her wrists as the flames licked closer and closer. When she looked again, Christian was closing the door behind him.

CHAPTER THIRTY

Guy and Alex travelled at full speed to the surgery. When they reached the three-storey building they pulled up in front of the main entrance in time to see a man coming through the door carrying a doctor's bag and a valise.

Alex was down from the phaeton first. "Jenner, we're looking for Melody. Is she here?"

Christian smiled. "She was here a while ago but she went home."

"She left her horse and gig by the park," said Guy. "And we didn't meet her on the way."

"Probably took a different direction."

Guy watched him and his journalistic instincts began to whirr inside his head. "How long ago did she leave?"

"Oh, a good hour."

Although Christian was still smiling, Guy knew that he was lying. It was at that moment he realised that everything he had ever thought about Doctor Christian Jenner had been false. He had been fooled, deceived by his charm and his skill as a doctor while treating the one person that meant everything to him. The knowledge blurred his vision with anger and he grabbed him by the front of his jacket and pushed him against the wall.

"Where is she?" he said into his face.

"That's for you to find out."

Guy's eyes opened wide in fright. With a yell of rage, his left hand grabbed Christian by the throat. Before Christian could defend himself, Guy had him pinned against the wall; his hand tightening round the slender neck, squeezing the life from him.

Alex rushed to his defence. "Guy, stop! This will do no good."

Guy had known hate before, but never had he wanted to take the life of another man. All his adult life he had been a journalist, striving to bring the news to the people. He had reported on the hatred and cruelty in the world, but not wanted to be part of it. But now he stood, his hands round another man's throat, crushing his windpipe. He wanted Melody safe and he knew that Jenner had knowledge of her whereabouts. He gripped him tighter and then his fist came down on the doctor's mouth with a sickening thud. Christian sprawled sideways and rolled on the ground, crying out in pain, his lip cut and gushing blood.

"If any harm has come to her, then God help me, I'll swing for you yet." Guy looked down at him, his fists clenched.

Alex crouched beside the bleeding man. "Where is she, Christian?"

Doctor Jenner was unperturbed at his beating. He had won and it didn't matter any more. Melody was probably already a blackened corpse. He smiled and pointed upwards. Before they could follow his hand movement, a window blew out showering them with tiny, jagged pieces of glass. In terror, Guy and Alex looked skywards at the top floor, now ablaze.

Once Christian had left her alone, Melody pulled herself up so that her mouth was in direct contact with the binding. Now she could work on it with her teeth, tearing it into shreds. Desperation made her work fast, but the bandage that restrained her was strong and her wrists were already bruised and swollen. The chair was ablaze, the flames spreading across the rug towards her and also in the direction of the window and curtains. It was becoming unbearably hot and she choked on the smoke, its acrid smell filling her nostrils, making her eyes stream. It stung her throat, and mouth open, she tried to draw in desperate gasps of fresh air.

She managed to loosen herself enough to wriggle one hand free. Now she worked with fingers and teeth on the remaining shreds that had twisted into a thin cord that bit cruelly into her wrist cutting off her blood. Her hand became blue and she lost feeling in it. She kept stopping to take in much needed air, but there was only smoke to breathe. Still working with her teeth she watched, with growing horror, the flames creeping towards her. She tried to pull herself to the far side of the bed, her feet hanging over the edge, wrapping her dress round her as the flames crept closer. Her mind was numb with fear but the will to keep fighting still persisted. Until the fire destroyed her she would fight for her life.

The flames caught hold of the bed and the covers ignited. The cotton and wool blazed into a small wall of fire, slowly creeping towards her gown. Her wide skirt was going to kill her, she was sure of that. No matter how hard she tried to pull the muslin material away from the inferno, it seemed to have a mind of its own and insisted on billowing out towards the flames. And then the material caught and with her free hand she grabbed the pillow and beat out the fire. It wouldn't be long now, just a matter of minutes before she would be a human torch. The thought of burning to death filled her with terror and she let out a harrowing scream.

Guy ran for the main entrance and pushed it open, Alex a step behind him. They took the stairs two at a time to the first floor.

"Make sure they're out," said Guy, pointing to the rooms on that floor.

Alex banged on the door. "I don't think anyone's at home," he cried, following in Guy's footsteps.

Guy called Melody's name as he ran, but there was no answer. They reached the door leading to Christian's lodgings and Guy tried the handle. It was locked.

"We'll have to break it down," he shouted.

They both heaved against the wood and almost fell into the room. A piercing scream from the bedroom and the smoke coming from under the door stopped them momentarily, before they were kicking it down.

Guy was first through the door, with Alex following him. The sudden draught of fresh air fed the flames and made them roar. For a few seconds they were blasted back by the heat but putting up their hands to protect their eyes, they hurtled into the room, jumping over a patch of blazing carpet. Guy saw Melody, one hand tied to the metal frame of the bed, coughing and choking, her face blackened by the smoke, her long auburn tresses clinging to her face and hanging down her back in thick, matted strands.

"I can't get loose," she cried, tears flooding down her cheeks and causing dirty streaks.

Guy delved into his pocket and pulled out a small knife, skilfully flicking the blade from the handle. At the same time, Alex grabbed a jug of water standing near the washstand and threw it over the flames licking at her gown. Guy cut the remaining pieces of bandage and pulled her to her feet. Melody clung onto him, her eyes stinging with the smoke. He guided her to the bedroom door, through the sitting room and out onto the landing and then it was down two flights of stairs and into the street, the cool evening breeze fanning their faces.

They collapsed onto the cobbles and sank down, still clinging to one another.

Guy glanced at Alex. "You shouldn't have come," he wheezed. "You have a wife and family to think of."

Alex shook his head. "No, it needed both of us."

Guy smiled in gratitude and offered his hand.

There seemed to be people everywhere. Not only neighbours coming out to take a look at the burning building, but the fire engine had arrived and buckets of water were being carried upstairs to quench the flames. Guy held his wife, kissing the top of her head, as he watched the flames reaching upwards. He looked around and realised that Doctor Jenner was nowhere to be seen.

Melody was wrapped in a blanket and helped to her feet. An elderly lady brought them some ale and they drank it back, trying to dampen down the smoke that burnt their throat and lungs. A police constable came across to them and Guy felt he had no choice but to tell him the full story. The constable raised his eyebrows at the details of abduction and attempted murder as well as the crime of arson. There was no doubt that Doctor Jenner had to be caught.

Olivia and the brigadier were more than relieved to see them when they arrived home and Tilly immediately brought hot water so that they could wash the sooty grime from their hands and faces. Melody was starting to recover, although her lungs hurt and her throat was still very sore. Her cough was relentless.

Alex insisted on examining her before he left and Guy was turned out of the room.

"I want you to tell him now," he whispered.

"But I told you I prefer to wait."

"No, Melody. You've had a shock and you might be in great danger of losing this child. So tell your husband tonight."

Olivia pricked up her ears. "Did I hear the word *child* mentioned?"

Melody turned to her aunt. "Yes, Aunt. But Guy doesn't know yet."

"When do you plan telling him?"

"In time. I've something else to tell him first."

Guy was allowed into the room and Melody told him why Christian had imprisoned her. He listened with mounting alarm, the implications of an action that had haunted him for so many years. At the end of her story, her eyelids began to droop with weariness and Olivia tucked the blanket round her. She was left to sleep.

Outside the night breeze tasted sweet. Even the smells from the city had a special magic about them. Alex and Guy shook hands.

"Thanks for everything," said Guy.

Alex jumped aboard the phaeton and snapped the reins. The horse lurched forward. "I'd like to say it was a pleasure, but it wasn't," he laughed.

Guy watched him as he trotted down the street.

He stood at the door for some time looking up at the moon. It was a new moon and now and again it became obscured by the gathering clouds. But when it broke through it illuminated the buildings and filled the street with bright, silvery rays. The breeze felt moist as if heralding the onset of rain.

Guy looked down the street and saw a very tired Sultan coming towards him. The gig pulled up in front of him, the brigadier in the driver's seat.

"I discovered it where you said, by Speakers' Corner. Had to pay sixpence to the boy," he smiled.

In the sitting room the story was discussed once more.

"We've got to be thankful Melody wasn't hurt," said the brigadier. He blew out a relieved breath at how it might have turned out.

Guy nodded sadly. "The police will be searching for Jenner so I suppose we'll discover where he's gone eventually. I feel sorry for his poor grandmother. She's as much a victim as Melody."

A short while later, Guy went upstairs. Melody was sitting on the edge of the mattress.

"How are you, angel?"

"My throat and lungs hurt, but I'm well," she rasped. "I want to get up."

"Are you sure?"

"Yes, I want to go downstairs."

Guy helped her. "Very well, if you think you can manage it."

"I know I can." She gave him a smile. "Exercise is good for an expectant mother."

Guy nodded and put his arms round her, guiding her towards the door. Melody waited for her news to sink in. They were halfway across the room when he stopped walking.

"Expectant mother?" he said quietly.

The rest of the evening was spent sitting next to each other as Mrs Carr and Tilly bustled in and out. Melody's throat and chest were still very sore and she often went into coughing fits that made her squeal with pain. Mrs Carr prepared a composite of eucalyptus leaves and menthol oil, suffusing them in boiled water and soon Melody was under a towel and breathing in the soothing vapour.

Guy slept next to her that night, holding her in his arms.

Alex called the following day to see her again. This second examination brought a certain amount of concern, since it was obvious that Melody's lungs had suffered with the smoke and heat from the fire. Placing his stethoscope in his bag, he felt he had to speak plainly, knowing that Melody wouldn't want it any other way. Her breathing would be affected for the rest of her life, he told them in a hushed voice, a life probably shortened by her experience.

"I'm going to write a letter, Melody. A letter I want you to take to New York City with you. There's an eminent doctor there who specialises in respiratory problems. He can help you."

Guy frowned. "Is there no one in London?"

"Yes, but if you're going to America, then I suggest..."

"Then we'll not go!" Guy took her hand. "We'll stay in England until you're better. It's a long voyage and these talks you're planning will be very tiring."

"No, Guy," said Melody, her eyes pleading. "I want to continue with our plans. We must go to America. I'll do what talks I can and then I'll rest before the baby comes. Mrs Carr and Tilly will be there to help."

Alex couldn't stop grinning. "A sea voyage will help your condition, there's no doubt about that. The salt air will help clear your lungs somewhat."

Guy wasn't so sure, but seeing Melody's eager face, he knew he had no choice. But one thing he did know for certain and that was his wife would never again enjoy the robust health she had known before she had met him. And deep down, he knew it was his fault.

Mrs Hunneybell took the news of her grandson's attempt on Melody's life very hard, her eyes filling with tears.

"I knew no good would come of my Grace falling for a Russian, especially a nobleman at that," she said, sniffing into her handkerchief. "Better stick to one of your own kind."

They had visited Mrs Hunneybell three days before they were due to sail. Sitting in her comfortable kitchen, Melody held her hand and assured her that all was well and despite her dreadful experience, she bore Christian no ill will.

Mrs Hunneybell smiled. "You've got a good heart, my dear." She gestured to the dresser. "A letter came for Christian only yesterday. I think it's from Russia, but I didn't open it. I think I should now. Will you fetch it?" Guy opened the drawer and found it. He passed it to Mrs Hunneybell, but she shook her head. "No, you read it to me."

He opened the envelope and Melody and the grandmother listened in surprise. It was from the present Count Menshikov, younger brother of Christian's father. It seemed there had been a change of feeling in the family and they wished to meet their English relative at last.

"It was all for nothing," said Guy. "It need never have happened."

Mrs Hunneybell put her hands to her face. "Oh, and now he's gone. What's to become of him? My poor, poor grandson."

News from Christian arrived the day before their departure to Southampton. Believing he was a fugitive from the law for the crime of arson, abduction and murder, he had fled to France and then Portugal. His letter to his grandmother had been sent as he was boarding a ship bound for Australia.

"Do you think the law will catch up with him?" asked Melody.

"Well, there's no better place to hide than in a country so vast," said Guy.

"I suppose he'll find a remote place and continue being a doctor."

"He still abducted you, angel. And he intended ending your life. That means a long spell in prison if he's caught."

Melody felt desperately sorry for the elderly lady now left on her own. "I hope Mrs Hunneybell will be all right."

"Your aunt and father are going to visit her regularly. They'll make sure she comes to no harm."

"But Christian must be told that I'm alive."

"We'll leave that to his grandmother, but at the moment I'm heartily relieved he's on the far side of the world."

EPILOGUE

Everyone came aboard the U.S.S. Alabama to see them off. The weather had stayed kind for the start of their sea voyage, the sun pleasantly warm considering it was the end of October. The crossing would take about two weeks and the sturdy steam-sailing ship, over four hundred feet long and sixty feet wide, had four steel boilers to drive her engines at the speed of ten knots. She was carrying five hundred passengers and four of them plus their family and friends had already inspected the luxurious cabins and first class music lounge containing a minstrels' gallery, plush seating and potted palms. The dining room was just as opulent. Mrs Carr and Tilly were looking forward to a few weeks of absolute pampering and not having to lift a finger to prepare their meals.

But now everyone was on deck.

"All ashore who's going ashore," called a voice near the gangway and people started to stream off the ship.

Melody and Guy were hugged and kissed and they watched as those they loved made their way onto the quayside.

"I'm going to miss everyone so much," said Melody, trying to hold back her tears.

"I'm sure you will," said Guy. "But we'll not be away forever." He smiled at the sight of Mrs Carr reprimanding Tilly for leaning over the rail and shouting and waving 'like a fishwife'. "And when we come home we'll have a child to bring back with us."

Melody gave a giggle. "We're away for two years. We'll probably have more than one."

Guy sucked in a breath. "Yes, well let's take it one step at a time shall we? I'm still getting used to the idea of being a father again."

Melody reached up and kissed his cheek and he responded by pulling her close and pressing his lips on hers. And then they turned their attention to those standing on the quayside. Eric waved frantically, tossing his hat in the air. Alex raised his hand and Celia and Sally held up the babies for a last glimpse. Aunt Olivia and the brigadier were shouting 'good luck', Olivia's white handkerchief fluttering in the gentle breeze. Sir Jack waved his hat, his bald head gleaming in the bright sun. Marsh, Holbrook and Henri were also waving their hats, their cries of 'goodbye' and 'bon voyage' lost in the many other shouts of farewell. And last of all were Tilly's large family who had come to see her on her way.

Melody smiled to herself. Everything was going to be different from now on. A new life and a new experience. She leaned against Guy and his grip tightened round her waist.

The first mate shouted orders and the gangway was removed. Then the thick ropes were untied from the capstan and hauled aboard. They started moving slowly as the steam tugboats prepared to pull them out to sea; the waving and shouting becoming more frantic from the quayside.

Melody felt the trickle of tears down her cheeks and Guy handed her his handkerchief.

"Goodbye everyone," she whispered. "Goodbye England."

Guy smiled and comforted her. "Aunt Olivia and the brigadier are coming across in time for the baby, so you'll see them again in less than six months."

She nodded. "I know and I wouldn't change this for anything. I've always thought it would be wonderful to travel and see something of the world."

She had come a long way since her teaching days at Miss Lawson's Academy at the tender age of seventeen. Sometimes the path had been rocky and she had stumbled along, but then there were other times that had been wonderful and filled with magical moments that she would always remember.

The figures on the quayside were becoming smaller and their voices no longer carried. England was retreating too. In their luggage they carried the letter for the doctor in New York City. Melody knew that her health was delicate and her lungs were damaged, but while she was with the man she loved, she knew that all would be well.

She slipped her arm round her husband and they turned from the rail to look up at the two tall funnels already belching black smoke. Another journey was beginning and a new life beckoned. She watched Mrs Carr and Tilly laughing and pointing at the white foaming wave breaking against the side of the ship. Melody leaned her head against Guy's shoulder and her heart soared with the seagulls in the sparkling blue sky. And she was filled with hope.

* * * * * * *

ALSO BY JULIA BELL

If Birds Fly Low
Broken Blossoms
To Guide Her Home
When Lucy Ceased to Be
A Pearl Comb for a Lady
Nyssa's Promise
Songbird: (The Songbird Story – Book One)
A Tangle of Echoes: (The Songbird Story – Book Two)
Deceit of Angels

These novels are available as ebooks on Amazon, but are currently in the process of being published in paperback

IF BIRDS FLY LOW

Since her mother's death, Charlotte Scott has been reared by her Aunt Faith. But her childhood has been plagued by strange knockings on her bedroom door in the dead of night. A summons she never answers since she fears what might be waiting for her behind the door. Meeting Noel Chandler, a tutor at the university in Cambridge causes tension, since Charlotte thinks him prejudiced against women. Noel is actually Squire Chandler and lives at Martlesham Manor a Tudor house in Suffolk.
It is while visiting Martlesham Manor with her cousin, Adele, that Charlotte learns the story of Prudence Chandler who, in the seventeenth century, was denounced as a witch by her husband and mother-in-law and consequently hanged.
Charlotte becomes absorbed with the story of Prudence and realises there are many mysteries at the Manor. Who is the woman who moves silently around the house at night? Why is there a terrible feeling of dread that permeates the old building? And why do the birds fly low since there is always a threat of rain hanging over the Manor?
As their love grows, Charlotte and Noel start to uncover the truth of his ancestral home. But the truth will involve Charlotte more intimately than she could possibly imagine.

BROKEN BLOSSOMS

At the age of fifteen, Katherine Widcombe, the niece of a baronet, is found missing from her bed whilst visiting her maternal aunt in Bristol. She is returned to her aunt and uncle's home, Widcombe Hall, blindfolded and with the weight of a terrible secret on her young shoulders. Six years later, she is invited to spend Christmas with her cousin, Philippa and her new husband Conrad, Earl of Croston. She is horrified when Conrad confesses his love for her. Dismayed by the awful truth of her past, Katherine returns to the Hall and decides to accept the marriage proposal of Sir Herbert Fox, a man thirty years her senior.

But marriage doesn't bring her the peace she craves and in fact, she discovers that her husband has secrets of his own and this will bring terrible consequences for Katherine.

These consequences will mean a perilous journey and privations that a woman of Katherine's wealth and rank would never be expected to endure and will draw on all her strength and courage to overcome.

TO GUIDE HER HOME

In the late nineteenth century Lydia Prescott has no ambition to settle down to marriage until she has travelled and seen the world. But her life and emotions are shaken up when she meets Doctor Russell Brooks. Unknown to Lydia, Russ is actually an electronics engineer and living in 1998. They are linked by Lydia's home, Prescott Grange on the outskirts of Worcester. In Russ's time, this has been converted into stylish apartments and he has discovered a winding staircase that leads him into the Victorian era.

Russ finds he's attracted to the beautiful fair-haired young woman; a woman very different from those he knows in the twentieth century. But is their love possible when it spans over one hundred years? Russ endeavours to turn himself into a nineteenth century gentleman hoping to win Lydia's heart by playing to her rules. A rival in the person of Doctor Aiden Kinkard spoils his endeavours since Kinkard is determined that Lydia will become his wife.

Russ hopes that one day he will persuade Lydia to live with him in his time, but this has terrible consequences for Lydia and will put her life in danger. As Russ learns more about Doctor Kinkard and begins to question the man's motives and identity, he comes to realise he has met pure evil.

WHEN LUCY CEASED TO BE

Having lost her mother the previous year, twelve-year-old Lucy Paget tries to make a contented life with her father on their farm in Ilkley, Yorkshire. But her father, Sid, would rather spend his time and money in the public house. One day in a fit of pique, Sid sets her up on a chair and tries to sell her to the men in the public house. There are no buyers until a certain gentleman shows an interest and decides to take up the offer. Edwin Beaumont has plans for poor Lucy and for the next eight years, she is trapped in a life of secrets and deceit as she adopts the guise of Edwin's daughter. Meeting her 'cousin' Theo Keeton brings some consolation and over time, his friend Matthew Raynor wins her heart. But Edwin's deception will not only lead to heartbreak, but also Lucy has to face the truth that Matthew might not be the man she thought he was when he is suspected of murder.

A PEARL COMB FOR A LADY

This is a romance through time.
A pearl comb weaves its way through the centuries, falling into the hands of three very remarkable but determined women. Their stories encompass courage, betrayal, survival and romance, as they find the path that will lead them to true love.

Christabel is feisty with an overactive imagination. Aged 18 and living during the Battle of Waterloo, she's in love with a soldier who only wants to use her to advance his military career.
Victoria, living in the mid-nineteenth century is sweet-natured but haunted by the loss of her child.
Finally there's Jenny, a 21st Century career woman who's unable to sacrifice her pride and forgive the man she loves.

NYSSA'S PROMISE

Since childhood Nyssa Wheeler has lived with her stepsister Gwen in a small house in Fulham, London. But Nyssa possesses the ability of a psychic empath and can read people's emotions through touch. This 'gift' has enabled her to pursue the work of a private investigator.

In the year 1904, she decides to take the position of companion to the Dowager Lady Kirby, living at Kirby House near Bodmin in Cornwall. Here she meets the dowager's two sons, Sir Howel, the sixth baronet and Captain Daveth Kirby, newly home from fighting the Boers in South Africa.

Although seeking a quieter life, Nyssa is drawn into the mystery of the disappearance of Lady Marie Kirby, Sir Howel's new wife. Her investigation involves her in the legend of the Beast of Bodmin Moor, a creature that supposedly prowls the moor. As the deaths mount up, Nyssa and Daveth must find the murderer before Nyssa, herself, becomes the next victim.

SONGBIRD
THE SONGBIRD STORY – BOOK ONE

In March 2019 Songbird: (The Songbird Story - Book One) won a Chill Book Premier Readers' Award.

In 2016 Songbird was featured in Baer Book Press as the best opening line in a historical romance.

Isabelle Asquith has only one ambition in life and that is to become an opera singer. To do this she must attend The Royal Academy of Music in London and become classically trained. Isabelle is a widow and has a young son to support and the fees for the academy are beyond her means as a music teacher. Her only recourse is to apply for the annual scholarship.

In the summer of 1885 after losing the scholarship for a second time and eager to earn more money, she decides to answer an advertisement. This simple act and the meeting of a mysterious man called 'Karl' will change her life forever. In the coming years, Isabelle is destined to discover not only her true potential, but also the lengths she is willing to go to realise her ambition.

A TANGLE OF ECHOES
THE SONGBIRD STORY – BOOK TWO

Venice Asquith is the granddaughter of both an earl and a viscount, but this has not prevented her from wanting to train as a doctor. In the London of the 1920's, women physicians are not completely accepted by the medical establishment and Venice has an uphill struggle to realise her ambition.

Meeting the mysterious Tristan Cavell throws her into turmoil. She is not only physically attracted to him, but also intrigued by the secrets he seems to keep. Tristan comes from the poverty of the East End of London and is a veteran of the Great War. He has done well for himself and owns a lucrative hotel and nightclub. But he also owns a casino, an activity that is on the fringes of the law. He believes Venice is out of his league and that her family would never accept him.

However, Venice disagrees and she decides that she must either become his wife or his mistress. Throwing caution to the wind, this decision is made on the toss of the dice and it's a decision she soon comes to regret. When Venice becomes involved in a tragic incident concerning Tristan's business partner Larry Johnson and Larry's girlfriend Martha, she discovers another side to Tristan's nature; a side that alarms her. Although Tristan only wants to protect her, she finds his behaviour controlling and suffocating.

Venice is unaware that her grandmother's secret is waiting in the wings to bring terrifying consequences. She and Tristan will have to face these consequences together and this will test their love for each other. The tangle of echoes from the past will change their lives even though the events occurred many years before they were born.

A Special Note from the Author

This story is the sequel to my novel **Songbird**, but I firmly believe that you don't need to read **Songbird** to enjoy **A Tangle of Echoes**. In **Songbird**, I told the story of Isabelle Asquith, but in **A Tangle of Echoes**, it is Venice's story (Isabelle's granddaughter) that takes centre stage.

If you've already read **Songbird** then I know you'll enjoy **A Tangle of Echoes**, but if you haven't then perhaps you'll feel intrigued enough to give Isabelle's story a try and discover how her secret came about all those years ago.

DECEIT OF ANGELS

For nineteen years, Anna Stevens perseveres with a faithless husband in a marriage that destroys her plans to go to university and follow a career. When Anna escapes to Bristol to work for Jason Harrington, the attractive and wealthy owner of Harrington Rhodes Shipping Agents, she has finally made the decision to leave her husband and make a new life for herself.

But Anna has told Jason that she is a widow and when she and Jason fall in love, Anna finds herself trapped in her lies. When her estranged husband finds her, Anna must pay a devastating price for her deceit - a price that would have lasting consequences for her and the man she loves.

A LETTER FROM THE AUTHOR

Dear Reader,

Thank you so much for choosing to read **The Wild Poppy**. I love writing but having my books read makes them come alive. Until they are read, the characters are only in my imagination and they need to live and be enjoyed. So, I hope you enjoy reading all my novels and you're able to spare a little time in telling me about it.

You can do this via my website.

Julia Bell
JuliaBellRomanticFiction.co.uk

Printed in Great Britain
by Amazon